Hope dances :

Cynthia Neale

The Irish Milliner

CYNTHIA G. NEALE

The Irish Milliner by Cynthia Neale

Copyright © 2017 Cynthia Neale

This is a work of historical fiction. While based upon historical events, any similarity to any person, circumstance or event is purely coincidental and related to the efforts of the author to portray the characters in historically accurate representations.

Cover design by Christine Horner

Interior design by Jacqueline Cook

ISBN: 978-1-61179-380-2 (Paperback)
ISBN: 978-1-61179-381-9 (e-book)

10 9 8 7 6 5 4 3 2 1

BISAC Subject Headings:
FIC014000 FICTION / Historical
FIC027050 FICTION / Romance / Historical / General

Address all correspondence to:
Fireship Press, LLC
P.O. Box 68412
Tucson, AZ 85737

Or visit our website at:
www.fireshippress.com

Praise for *The Irish Milliner*

"Cynthia Neale's beautifully written well-researched novel is a gift for our times. To witness the immigrant experience at a tumultuous period in our history through the eyes of *The Irish Milliner* and Norah McCabe softens the heart, expands the mind, and drives home once again Burke's quote, 'Those who don't know history are doomed to repeat it.'" ~**Joanna Rush, actor, playwright, author of** *Asking For It*

"It's a pleasure to take up the story again of warm-hearted Norah battling against the odds in this fascinating account of a pivotal time in American history." ~**Kristen Gleeson, author of** *In Praise of Bees, The Celtic Knot Series,* **and** *Anahareo, A Wilderness Spirit*

"The Irish Milliner is a finely-crafted novel and powerful story of a woman caught in the social and political backwash of a rapidly-changing country that will shape her and her family's lives forever. Norah McCabe is an unforgettable Irish-American woman who is spirited and imbued with a remarkable sense of independence and self-will, of steely courage and a burning desire for justice and human rights for all—black or white, slave or freeman. Above all, it is her unshakable and buoyant spirit that shines through these pages. It is a story that stays with you long after you put the book down." ~**PJ Curtis,** *A Nightingale Falling*, **now an Irish feature film**

"Cynthia Neale's passion for a bygone era races across the pages of *The Irish Milliner* with literary grace, poignancy and perfection—she captivates the reader! We are instantly engaged with Norah McCabe, a more than three-dimensional character with surprising grit and the ability to survive, and ultimately thrive, in the face of ever-present turmoil and the uncertainties of 19th century New York." ~**Lucinda Marcoux,** *King of the Forest*

Dedication

To my love, TIM, which is also an acronym for *The Irish Milliner*

> *Let me not to the marriage of true minds*
> *Admit impediments. Love is not love*
> *Which alters when it alteration finds,*
> *Or bends with the remover to remove:*
> *O no! It is an ever-fixed mark*
> *That looks on tempests and is never shaken;*
> *It is the star to every wandering bark,*
> *Whose worth's unknown, although his height be taken.*
> *Love's not Time's fool, though rosy lips and cheeks*
> *Within his bending sickle's compass come:*
> *Love alters not with his brief hours and weeks,*
> *But bears it out even to the edge of doom.*
> *If this be error and upon me proved,*
> *I never writ, nor no man ever loved.*
> > *~Sonnet 116, William Shakespeare*

The Irish Milliner

CYNTHIA NEALE

FIRESHIP
PRESS

Chapter One

'Tis the look of the dogged Irish in his face, and not just the hardened sadness as is wont to be on most men. His face is etched with noble sorrow that softens the eyes.

Norah glances at the tall, gangly visitor standing in the doorway of the Sunday school class at the Five Points House of Industry. She has been trying to teach a Bible lesson to a roomful of restless Irish and Italian orphans. Her daughter, Katie, sits at her feet and points at the stranger and hiccups. Norah picks her up and places her on her hip, waiting for the visitor to speak. She thinks this man has probably come to give a donation, but surely he looks like he needs one himself.

"Stand children and be still. We have a visitor."

The thirty-eight children, from four to fourteen years of age, make a racket getting out of their chairs. They have been to the bathing room before breakfast and although scrubbed, they are disheveled and malnourished. Some of the children were taken off the streets just a few days ago, and there is only so much the mission can do. At least they have shoes, as worn out as they are, proper food, and they're being taught some skills, Norah thinks, as she scans the room. *I've a mother's heart and don't I know that there's no class to teach them about love.*

Mr. Washburn, director of the mission, stands in the doorway with Mr. Lincoln.

"This is Mr. Abraham Lincoln come to visit us here in New York. This gentleman might become our next president."

The children glance nervously at Norah and then at Mr. Lincoln. Norah watches Mr. Lincoln closely as he looks around the room. He says nothing for a few minutes and his eyes look sleepy and his mouth, although resolute, reveals tenderness in the corners. Norah ponders the man.

I think he must kiss the cheeks of his children, if he has any; he's no bigwig, but a poor looking one for the likes of becoming a president. How far he's come, then! It's hope for the lot of us.

"Go ahead, then, Mr. Lincoln, give the children here a word or two and someday they'll say they met the president of the United States," Mr. Washburn said.

"And you, Ma'am, must be the teacher of these fine children," Mr. Lincoln says, looking at Norah. She gives a slight curtsy and smiles, adjusting Katie on her hip. The child is nearly three now and is too heavy to carry around.

"Yes, sir, Norah McCabe is one of our most dedicated teachers. She's also a fine milliner and occasionally instructs some of our young women in this skill."

"Well, well, now. I've just bought myself a new hat, a stovepipe, as you can see, from the gentleman Knox's store." Mr. Lincoln holds his hat in his hands. "Maybe you could have made me one of these for a lesser price."

"Oh no, Mr. Lincoln, I haven't yet tried my hand on hats for men, only the ladies' hats, but maybe Mr. Knox will be selling my hats in his store someday." Norah thinks Mr. Lincoln's speech is odd. It comes way too slowly with something invisible hanging onto each word that the listener is supposed to fathom.

A loud thud interrupts their conversation and all look to see that a little boy has fallen into a faint onto the floor. Mr. Washburn and Mr. Lincoln rush to him and Norah sets Katie down. Katie cries and clings to Norah's skirts.

"Get the boy some water!" she commands an older student who runs out and comes back in with a tin cup. Mr. Lincoln picks Katie up and she cries even harder. The boy who has fainted was found sleeping on the doorstep in the morning and he is hardly fit for standing very long.

"Take Anthony to his room," Norah instructs the student and takes Katie from Mr. Lincoln's arms. Katie stops crying and Norah and Mr. Lincoln peer at one another. Are there tears in his eyes or is it her imagination? She is used to the filth and sorrow in this neighborhood, but maybe he is not.

"Tell us a story, Mr. Linkin!" a boy of seven cries out.

"Please do, sir, please give us a yarn!"

Many of the children are roused for some excitement and begin cheering Mr. Lincoln on.

He raises his hands in the air and the children quiet.

"Sit down now, and take the weight off your feet and I'll tell you my story."

The children scramble for their seats and the room hushes with expectancy. Katie sits on Norah's lap with her thumb in her mouth looking up at the strange man.

"I had been poor, maybe even poorer than all of you. I remember when my toes stuck out through my broken shoes in winter, when my arms were out at the elbows, when I shivered with the cold. When it seemed impossible to go on at times. We had a dirt floor in the log cabin we lived in and my father asked me to say a blessing for a pot of roasted potatoes, the only food we had to eat. I couldn't pray and said to my father, 'Pa, I recall these potatoes a mighty poor blessing.' But I vowed to myself and to God I would do my best and I began to see the sun rising and setting in its beauty, enough to thank God for. And I was always first at school and always my head was in the books. I couldn't get enough of reading in those days because I had to split logs and walk to the mill. But I never stopped trying to learn. And you here in this school and home have arrived at a stopping place for a spell in your young lives. But it's an important stop because you're saved from the streets and from hunger, and so you must try hard to learn and make better lives for yourselves."

A small child sighs loudly and puts his head onto his arms. A few other children do the same and there's whimpering in the room. Norah, with Katie, goes to each child, "Be still now, all will be grand."

Norah looks up to see Mr. Lincoln dabbing at his eyes with a handkerchief.

"Not a fine applause you got there, Mr. Lincoln. I'm sorry the children are lacking."

"Oh, no, Mr. Washburn. These children are feeling my words and this indeed is fine applause!"

And then each child stands up from his or her desk and with meager claps, they thank the towering man with kind eyes who looks like he could have walked out of one of their fairy tale stories and into their lives.

"Do go on, Mr. Linkin, do go on," a boy cries out.

At this pleading, all the little hands clap harder.

"That is all, children. Please sit down. Mr. Lincoln has places to be going to now," Mr. Washburn says.

The children obey and reluctantly sit back down. Norah smiles and nods to Mr. Lincoln and then he dons his top hat and, as he walks out the door, it catches on the top frame and falls to the floor. The children giggle and one boy rushes to retrieve it for him. A hush falls over the room after he leaves, as if the sun has set and twilight has brought peace and thanksgiving for the day.

"I do think we've had our Bible lesson for the day," Norah says.

The next evening, Norah stands uncomfortably jammed into the second row in the Great Hall of the Cooper Institute staring at Mr. Abraham Lincoln who is sitting on stage with other important men. She is being jostled and eyed with suspicion by all sorts of slick newspapermen. There are high and low reporters--from the Sun, the Tribune, the Evening Post, the New York Daily, and from the scourge of dailies printed in this groveling and beguiling city. Yes, she thinks, New York's publicity engine has been primed just like Harrigan told her it would be. The ambitious, ogling newspapermen from Printing House Square have turned out to hear the lanky, bedraggled senator from Illinois speak. Norah wonders if Mr. Lincoln can see her and if he'd remember her. She is intrigued with the face of the man, even from where she is standing.

He's clearly not an Irishman, but the pained look on his face reminds me of Ireland's great liberator, Daniel O'Connell, but if this fellow is to be the fine liberator of slaves, as Harrigan keeps telling me, 'tis the luck then he's not from the ole country.

"These two rows are for the papers, Miss, for the newspapermen. The hoop skirts and bonnets are not to be taking up room here," a pimply-faced man no older than Norah yells at her from the first row.

The men in the two rows turn to stare at her. She smiles politely and nods to them and carefully removes her hat that is a striped straw bonnet covered with amber silk ribbons and colorful flowers. She had meticulously designed the bonnet for that rare wealthy patron who never came to pick it up. Money had been lost but now it is her favorite hat. She has walked in the rain and worries it might have been damaged.

"Gentlemen, I've removed my bonnet and I'm not wearing any stays. I'm a newspaperwoman myself, from the *Irish-American*, reporting on Mr. Lincoln's address."

There is a sudden blast of a horn and Horace Greeley, editor of the Tribune, announces that Mr. Abraham Lincoln will be giving his speech shortly. Norah stares at all the men seated on the stage with Mr. Lincoln towering amongst them with his top hat perched on his head. *He looks more like an act come from Barnum's.* She quickly sits down, determining not to be pushed out for lack of room and for being the only woman in the front rows. She immediately thinks of the lines of the poem that the ghastly, but intriguing, poet, Walt Whitman, wrote:

> *City of the World! (for all races are here,*
> *All the lands of the earth make contributions here)*
>
> *And my contribution is as important as your own, then, you*

11

conniving newsmen! These are Norah's thoughts as she removes a pad of paper and writing utensil from her purse. She keeps her eyes cast down, trying to keep from trembling. She hasn't seen but a few women in the room, demure looking women clutching the arms of their husbands. She is alone amongst so many barking men. Suddenly, guffaws and stifled laughter reverberate throughout the room. *I will not tolerate their antagonism*, she thinks, as she lifts her head to tell them off only to see that Abraham Lincoln has stood up and is standing before them all, his clothes rumpled and him looking like a right scarecrow on a stick perched high in a garden. Bemused, Norah watches him remove his hat and hold it upright in one hand while stroking his long hair back with claw-like fingers. He smiles meekly at the audience and pulls out of the deep bin of his top hat the crumpled pages of his speech. There are more ripples of laughter and then the immense crowd grows quiet.

When craggy-faced Mr. Lincoln begins speaking in his wrinkled ill-fitting suit, Norah feels pity for the man. She had liked this empathetic Mr. Lincoln when he visited the House of Industry, but it's different here amongst so many highbrows. He is a sorry looking sight, this man who told the children he had pulled himself up by his bootstraps and taught himself the learning needed to be successful in the world. Surely he will falter, embarrass himself, and she will have risked her reputation coming to hear him speak. She is aware that her neighbors care little for Mr. Lincoln and there has already been an onslaught of criticism for her friendship with Miss Elizabeth Jennings, a Negro woman. Pebbles, not rocks, thank Almighty God, had been thrown at her back a few times, once when she was with little Katie and another time when she was with Elizabeth. When a boy pelted her with the pebbles one day, she had clutched Katie to her bosom, hiding her under her wrap.

"Take yer kinchin and move outta here, mab!" he had yelled, pelting her with stones and insults.

And there was another time when stones were flung at Elizabeth and Norah. Norah had hunched her shoulders and walked fast, but not Elizabeth who turned toward her attackers and yelled,

"For every stone you throw, you'll be cursed with bad luck!"
And then Elizabeth picked up the stones and put them in her pocket.
After they hurried away, Norah asked her why she had saved the
stones.

"For when I pray, I'll place each one before my God, so's not to
become a bitter woman."

Norah hadn't picked up the stones flung at her, but the stones and
words that struck her back implanted something akin to bitterness,
and now when she walks the streets, she feels their heaviness. No
need to be thinking about these things, she thinks, and returns to the
present and the excitement she feels as a newspaperwoman. Fierce
determination and pride well up within her. *Lay aside the anger,*
she reminds herself, *for it will pollute the river of colors flowing
through you.* This is what dear Elizabeth had said to her last week
after former customers from Five Points visited Norah who came to
tell her they'd not be doing any further business with the likes of her.
Her best customers are from Five Points, her own people, by God,
Irish women in need of sprucing up their ragged wardrobes with
fancy hats they can afford. These women, like herself, pour over
Godey's Ladies' Book and Frank Leslie's Magazine and dream of
buying an expensive hat. Five Point women bring in old things they
call hats that smell like mold and Norah cleans them up and turns
them into lovely hats they can afford. And now these women are
calling her a Black Republican and telling her to keep her friendship
with Elizabeth Jennings hidden, at least. She hasn't been selling hats
and Harrigan at the *Irish-American* doesn't pay her a pocket full of
rocks for her newspaper writing. What will she do? How will she
feed her little Katie and pay the rent on the apartment she and her
friend, Nellie, have together?

Norah has drifted away from Mr. Lincoln's speech again. She
sits up straight and forces herself to listen, to really listen, for she
needs to have something to give to Harrigan for the paper.

*"Neither let us be slandered from our duty by false accusations
against us, nor frightened from it by menaces of destruction to the
Government nor of dungeons to ourselves. Let us have faith that*

right makes might, and in that faith, let us, to the end, dare to do our duty as we understand it."

She thinks his words are quite eloquent and certainly this duty is to stand against slavery. Norah quickly scribbles down his words and some thoughts about his speech. One thing is clear to her about this speaker. He is a feeling man as well as a thinking man, and in this regard he is very much like Daniel O'Connell.

And with these last elegant sentences rolling out from Mr. Lincoln, whose face is lit up and transformed, there is a thunderous standing ovation. Everyone in the building jumps to their feet and yells and cheers. The men surrounding Norah throw up their hats in the air, catching them with glee and merriment. She wants to throw her bonnet in the air, too, but then thinks better of it; so she puts her fingers in her mouth and makes a sheer whistle so loud that the men in front of her turn around and the man next to her says, "Where in the name of God did ye learn how to do that?" He laughs and pats her on the back just like she is one of the boys.

Chapter Two

After Lincoln's rousing speech, Norah hurries to the office and stays until morning writing the article and assisting James Harrigan with the next issue of the *Irish-American*. When they finish their work, they sit together on the circular sofa sipping tea and nibbling on mince pies bought from the bakery next door. Norah misses her Katie Marion who always climbs into her bed early in the morning before the sun is up, pushing a beam through a crack in the wall. Sure, icy wind shoves through the hole in the winter, but the sunbeam is their hope. Cuddling with her daughter and breathing in her baby fresh scent dispels all gloomy thoughts about their future. Nellie volunteered to take Katie to the Ladies' Home Mission Society where she teaches while Norah worked on the article with Harrigan. Katie oftentimes stays at the House of Industry when Norah works on a deadline for her hats, but Norah worries that the older children will fling the filth of the city on her Katie, like a dirty, wet dog shaking itself on everyone nearby. She admonishes herself for her superior thoughts, for these children still have a measure of innocence trailing them, even if they are already grizzled since coming from the warm wombs of their mothers. Norah has watched the babies of the poor born healthy with the stars of heaven in their eyes giving their parents the wherewithal to fight for survival, but then just one slap of evil brings despair. Those stars are out of their reach now, the parents claim, but her friend Nellie believes in the power of divine love. Norah would like to be as optimistic as Nellie about these ragamuffins, but one thing she is certain of, and that is children had to be the salvation of this city. And she will make sure her Katie never casts her eyes downward into hopelessness.

Harrigan stands up from the sofa and straightens his clothes.

"He's got it now. I know it, Norah. This Abraham Lincoln is in. Seward won't win the nomination. It'll be Lincoln, alright. The man's famous now. Did you see the papers? Was he really that dignified, Norah? He's no dresser, is he? Ha! Maybe I can become his personal assistant and help the poor bugger look halfway decent! They're saying that his speech was brilliant and who can argue with the founding fathers? He doesn't want slavery to spread, but he's moderate, not radical like Seward."

Harrigan goes to his desk and picks up the freshly printed newspaper.

"Your article is fine and rather good. You've got the pulse on the matter. Lincoln's being moderate, but he's being wise about slavery. It can't happen all at once. We need to convince the hardheaded Irish to see that the man's on our side. That he's one of us."

"You won't be selling many papers in Five Points, Harrigan. The Irish aren't for him, but he does remind me of Daniel O'Connell in some ways."

"The Irish think the abolitionists should focus on the six million white slaves in Ireland and not the slaves in the south. And then your O'Connell fellow caused a big stir years ago when he put his two cents into the slavery issue."

"What did he say?"

Harrigan fumbles around in his files and pulls out an old newspaper.

"Here it is. I found it!" He sits on the corner of the desk and crosses his legs.

The black spot of slavery rests upon your star spangled banner, and no matter what glory you may acquire beneath it, the hideous, damning stain of Slavery remains upon you; and a just Providence will sooner or later, avenge itself for your crime.

Norah is excited, "I'll copy those words and read them to Elizabeth Jennings. She thinks most Irishmen are against her people!"

"We're not all cut out of the same cloth, are we now, Norah. Look at our Bishop Hughes. He's not against the south owning slaves, but he's for keeping those rebel states clinging to the rest of us. Mr. Lincoln wants the same."

Norah puts her head back on the sofa and closes her eyes while Harrigan tidies up the office. She still thinks about poor Margaret Fuller buried in the sea with her baby and husband. She had been a woman with a brain afire with knowledge and life, and Norah wants the same. She keeps Margaret Fuller's, *Woman in the Nineteenth Century*, by her bedside and the pages are dog-eared and worn. But there's so much she can't comprehend about the woman's writing no matter how she tries! When Norah had been distraught with grief after the shipwreck and losing her husband, Murray, she had found Margaret Fuller's powerful words: *Though many have suffered shipwreck, still beat noble hearts.* These words had given her solace. And when she learned that Margaret Fuller had written these words before her own death at sea, she felt the woman's spirit was with her. To be sure, Norah is no real partaker of women's rights. The likes of Margaret Fuller and even the feminist Lucy Stone she once heard speak, are cut from the same cloth and are educated women, a different class altogether. But now it's Elizabeth Jennings who has been filling her head with the reforming escapades of such Negro women like Sojourner Truth and Harriet Tubman. These are the women who fascinate her! No matter Irish women's skin is as pale as buttermilk, the Negro woman and the Irish woman have much in common. Hate and poverty visit all shades of skin, she thinks.

"No worries about Bishop Hughes caring about our opinions. He's got bigger fish to fry," Harrigan said, interrupting her thoughts. "We're little fish in a big pond. We can afford a couple of issues going against the tide. We don't have Tammany loving us, anyway,

Norah. I don't think they even know we exist."

"This is the only issue I'm working on now, Harrigan. I've got bigger fish to fry myself, in case you haven't noticed. A millinery business, remember? As poorly as it's been doing lately, it's my livelihood so you'd best be paying me so I can buy my materials."

Norah stares at Harrigan's striped blue cravat as it moves up and down over his large Adam's apple. He's an incorrigible dandy and maybe a homosexual for all she knows. But she doesn't want to know, not really, if he visits men's lodging houses. He loves his togs and dresses elaborately each day, although mud and garbage often spatter onto his trousers. Three years ago, she had been ready to tie the knot, become hammered for life with this man, her dearest friend other than Nellie and, of course, Sean. Sean! *God be praised! I forgot he's meeting me at the eatery joint for an early lunch.*

Norah stands up, smooths out her skirts, and looks into the large beveled glass mirror Harrigan has prominently displayed in his office. She is certain he stands before this mirror many times during the day. Back when she worked for him full time, he had accused her of wasting time staring at herself and she couldn't deny it. She and Harrigan are two peas in a pod when it comes to fashion and vanity. She looks over at him as he brushes the crumbs off his ruffled shirt and vest. His dark brown hair is brushed forward into a cowlick and his whiskers are clipped close, but he still wears the horrid Dundrearys, the hanging sideburns that look like two mice crawling up the sides of his face. In spite of this popular style she hates, he is winsome and a sort of a swell, appearing to be rich and fashionable. In reality, he has a modest income, but his style is lavish. Harrigan stays up all night and still manages to look fabulous! She, on the other hand, is a mess after a night of no sleep, but there is little time to worry about how she looks. Certainly Margaret Fuller would not have done so! She looks in the closet for her corset she had taken off earlier. She rarely wears one these days, but she had wanted her waist to appear especially slim in the burnt umber silk Zouave ensemble she wore at last night's lecture. She finds the corset, but decides against wearing it and hides it behind some boxes. She puts on the matching jacket that covers up her wrinkled white blouse. Both pieces of her outfit are richly trimmed with a dark blue embroidered pattern she had sewn herself when she owned *A Bee In Your Bonnet* used clothing store a few years ago. Now *A Bee In Your Bonnet* is her hat label and she is pleased to create new designs and not have to restore and embellish used gowns worn by rich women. She had always felt that the clothing, as gorgeous as it was, possessed some of the spirits of the women who had once worn them. She had to engage in some sort of exorcism and fill the bodices with lavender to make them new again, but the gowns she wears now have become her very own and carry no trace of any other women's perfume or personality. Her feelings about being as serious as Margaret Fuller wane as she sizes herself up in the mirror. She indeed likes her fashion!

"Can we go for lunch, Norah? How about the Astor? Oh, do say yes, my dear, for it's been forever since we dined in style together, hasn't it?"

Norah sits back down on the sofa with Harrigan and shakes her head no while putting on her Victorian spats that are peach with exquisite cream-colored lace. Harrigan quickly falls on his knees before her and grabs her right leg.

"Allow me, dear Norah!" he exclaims and then begins the tedious work of lacing up one boot and then the other. Norah laughs, basking in Harrigan's pampering. Their relationship is easeful and pleasant after the long strain of discomfort they had caused one another three years before when they nearly married.

Norah thinks back to those painful times, all in a flash. She often does. She had survived the shipwreck that carried Irish rebels and all the money the Irish leader, John Mitchel, had raised in New York to fight the British, but her husband, Murray, had drowned at sea. Soon after, she had learned she was pregnant with Katie and lived a year in grave mourning. She sold her used clothing store and fell numbly into the arms of Harrigan, but only briefly. And then her childhood friend, Sean, returned to New York as if he had risen from the dead, eager to become a part of Norah's life. She sighs and looks at Harrigan patiently tying her laces. He seems to take things in stride, but she doesn't. She hasn't had time to meet herself coming and going, *but perhaps it is the way I wish it to be.*

Norah reaches for her bonnet as Harrigan finishes lacing her fancy boots. He looks up at her with admiration.

"My lovely Norah with the luxurious, unruly hair who should never cover her head although she's a milliner…please be cautious on these mean streets of New York."

"Sean's waiting for me! He'll be fussing if I'm late!" She rises from the couch.

Harrigan stands and straightens his cravat, looking in the mirror.

"Sean, another young man to take you way from me…"

"No, not so, Harrigan…I'll see you in a week for tea and newspaper talk."

She laughs at Harrigan. He flirts without any intentions. Norah wraps her cloak around her shoulders and hurries out the door to meet Sean, merry and lighthearted. This city might not be so bad, at that, she thinks. Meeting Mr. Lincoln is a sign that her life isn't just going to be about squeezing a few coppers out of Five Points women who purchase her hats. A pittance for her creations! She'll be selling her hats to better customers soon. She is sure of it! And isn't she adored by two men, not one man, but two, even if one is a dandy and one a laborer. She loves them both, she does. And if that wasn't enough, didn't she also have her friends, Nellie, Miss Elizabeth Jennings, and most of all Katie, her own babe, always reminding her of Murray's love.

Norah makes her way through the bustling wintry streets, stepping over refuse and avoiding contact with the wild dogs roaming the streets. A boy carrying a basket keeps pace with her and the delicious scent of fresh baked bread wafts in the air.

"Come along, then, keep up with me and I'll give you a coin for a roll."

"Taking these to Jack's Eatery, Miss. Not for sellin' on the street."

"It's where I'm going, lad, so ye can accompany me there."

She increases her stride and the boy has difficulty keeping up with her. Eventually, he trips on her skirts and falls onto the street, his basket toppling. Two rolls are stepped on by people scurrying to their destinations and Norah retrieves the rest spilled out in front of her.

"Nothing wrong with these, lad. Just clean them off a bit and they'll be good as new!" she says, wiping them off on her skirts and putting them back into the basket. The boy gets on his feet and stares at her curiously.

"And ye wouldn't mind having them with your tea, then?" the boy asks, incredulous that the spiffed up hen in fancy rags would eat rolls that have fallen onto the street.

Norah faces the boy and pulls the basket from his arm.

"How much money will the Eatery give you for these?"

"Five shillings a roll, Miss, but now two are ruined, and the rest..."

"Never you mind!"

Norah pulls a handkerchief from her purse and wraps the rolls in it and places them in her bag. She drops a handful of coins in the basket.

"Give the bakery the money and tell them that the Eatery wants more rolls."

The boy counts the coins in the basket, gives Norah a toothless smile, and takes off running. Norah continues down the street thinking how pleased Nellie and Katie will be to have rolls for breakfast tomorrow. And, by God, she won't have to be making soda bread in the early morning, either.

Just before Norah arrives at Jack's Eatery, the wind whips up and blows her bonnet off. She hadn't tied the ribbon properly and now her most expensive hat is floating down the street as if it has a life of its own. She lifts her skirts, clutches her bag, and chases after the bonnet. It nearly comes down on the dirty street, but the wind lifts it into the air. Norah gets close to reaching for it, but the wind rises it up as if teasing, and the illusive bonnet is swept up into the sky, finally coming down and hitting the face of a boy hawking fried chick peas in newspaper cones. He grabs the bonnet with his greasy hands and Norah yells at him to put it down.

"Take yer damn bonnet!" he says and tosses it at her. She catches it and glances at the cones holding the chickpeas that are all lined up on the vendor's wagon.

She reaches for a cone and shakes out the chickpeas.

"Hey! You have to pay for them peas, Miss!" the boy yells.

Norah takes a shilling out of her purse, hands it to the boy, and stands against a building. She unrolls the newspaper and there she is on the front page of the Sun! Her fingers are in her mouth as she whistles in glee at the end of Lincoln's speech. Her cheeks are puffed out and there are men's hats in the air in front of her. The artist has sketched her standing amongst rows of men looking like she's one of Barnum's circus people.

Sean is suddenly at her side, thrusting his arm confidently around her, "Norah McCabe! I've been waiting for you for an hour. Let's get us some grub. I've got to be back on site or I'll get me arse fired."

He glances at the newspaper and doubles over in laughter.

"If it isn't Norah McCabe, the grand milliner of Five Points, all dressed up at a Republican meeting like a bigwig, but carrying on like one of the boys."

Norah makes a face at Sean and marches off in the direction of the eatery with him following. When he catches up with her, she puts her arm in his and they walk into the eatery and sit down at the counter. She is cold, but Sean's arm is warm and his body next to hers immediately calms her. In his presence, Norah becomes keenly aware of her femininity and sensuality. When she is with Sean, she doesn't worry about being as knowledgeable as Margaret Fuller or being the capable newspaperwoman. It is the nearest sensation she experiences that is similar to her time with Murray, and it eerily comes through Sean, a man so unlike her deceased husband. He is her childhood friend, her first innocent love, who had disappeared from her life for years. When he told her he had worked on ships that traveled the seas for commerce and slave trading, he wept. *It was evil that chained not just those dark-skinned ones, but me, too. When I saw evil had me in chains, I knew those men were free in a way I wasn't. All I could do was leave. I couldn't free them, but I could free me.* Thinking of this makes her heart ache for him and she clasps his hand.

"Now what did I do to deserve such attention?" he responds, smiling at her, careful not to show his teeth that embarrasses him in front of Norah. He read in one of Norah's fancy magazines that honey mixed with pure pulverized charcoal was an excellent way to clean teeth and make them white. And so he is at it morning and night to make his teeth and himself presentable to Norah McCabe.

The boy with new rolls arrives a few minutes later, winks at Norah, and hands her one of the rolls, laying down a few shillings in front of the cook behind the counter.

"For the fancy lady, sir."

Chapter Three

Norah, Nellie, and Katie live above a storefront on Chatham and Pearl in the Fourth Ward. It's a lively, bustling intersection with many old storehouses, junk shops, and second-hand stores. Boisterous saloons, stables, as well as groceries that sell decaying and unwholesome meat and wilted vegetables line the cobbled streets that are in shoddy condition. Just as it is in the Sixth Ward, there are overcrowded and disease-ridden tenements with narrow alleys emitting the sour odors of sewage and refuse that house miserable, unfortunate families.

The *Tenant-House Rot* is what Norah heard a sanitary inspector say to their landlord who owns the dry goods store below them. She had walked into the store to give Mr. Barker the $20.00 month's rent when she heard this proclamation. *There are miserable abodes where decay, pestilence and crime are the fungi of this city! I am pleased to see you care more than most, sir!* The inspector stated this to Mr. Barker, who nodded his head and smiled with pride. Just the month before, Nellie had asked Norah to accompany her on a visit to one of the families living in a building on Mulberry Street. The mission that employed Nellie wanted her to bring food to a mother and her children. When Nellie and Norah opened the door to the apartment after climbing the dark, tottering stairs, there sat the mother, a wrinkled creature, rocking an infant with pallid and lifeless features. Green mold spotted the walls and the damp air was laden with effluvia. Later, Nellie told her that the woman was only thirty years old! *How could these people live like this?* Norah and her family had lived in the darkest of tenements in the grip of extreme poverty when they first came to America, but they had never lost their spirit and quest for cleanliness. Norah told Nellie that she never wanted to go into another tenement building like that one as long as she lived.

Although the Fourth Ward courts a raucous dalliance with its indiscriminate neighborhood of the Sixth Ward, Norah McCabe conceives of the Sixth Ward as being in another world altogether that has nothing to do with her new life living above a storefront in the Fourth Ward. Right well does she recall hearing people say more than once, "No one respectable ever came from Five Points!" Sure, most of her patrons walk over from Five Points, but they walk right out of their dark apartments to *A Bee in Your Bonnet* on Chatham Street. And isn't she able to help them in their abject lives to afford a fine hat and become respectable! Norah believes that each woman who purchases one of her hats can experience a turning point and can seek out the finer things of life. Surely, she has done so and will continue to do so. And if she hadn't dared to step away from her sorrow and plight, she might have never met Miss Nellie Gorman at the New Labor Employment Bureau or gone with her to the Seventh Annual Women's Rights Convention. Although she and Nellie differ on many aspects of religion and politics, they share the same feelings about people, especially women and children, having opportunities for love, success, and even some tantalizing adventure (not that she's had any of late). Who else will invite a colored woman into her home for tea and scones, but someone as open-hearted and open-minded as Nellie Gorman! Nellie adores the dark-skinned Elizabeth Jennings as much as Norah does. And it was Nellie who introduced her to the Irish girl, Kathleen Hartnett, an experienced milliner, who now has her own fine shop in Boston. Kathleen (known as Kitty to her Irish friends and family) is as bold as they come, for a woman, and especially for a woman born in the old country. Norah and Nellie gathered with Kathleen and a few women many evenings in their apartment to learn from her the art of millinery. Norah also received a firsthand lesson about women going into trade being perceived as vulgar and disrespectable.

"*They* say…and who are *they*, I want to know, but I'm apt to believe *they* are the men of industry, who say it is not genteel or fashionable for young ladies to work. *They* should marry, *they* say. The hell with *they, I* say!" Kitty had proclaimed.

"Honest industry, or vulgarity, as *they* say, is preferable to starving…or marrying, for that matter!" one of the girls chimed in. They all laughed.

"Here! Here!" Nellie said, holding up a shot glass of whiskey. The others held up their glasses. They were celebrating after meeting together for months to learn from the successful and fashionable Miss Hartnett.

"I've always been obliged to work or else starve. 'Tis a hard-faced necessity to work when it's considered a disgrace to do so," Kitty said.

And although creating hats isn't Nellie's cup of tea, she helped Norah set up a corner in their living room for her *Bee In Your Bonnet* millinery business. In the beginning, Norah worked in housekeeping at the Stewart Mansion just to secure enough earnings to purchase the materials required to make five or six hats. It was a good year scrubbing floors and writing a few articles for Mr. James Harrigan at the *Irish American* so she could save enough money to start her business. The jobbers she bought her materials from refused to give her credit at first, but then they saw how timely she was in paying her bills. And now she is able to purchase enough stock to make fifteen hats, including wire bonnet frames and rough bodies.

Norah hasn't told her Mam and Da who live in upstate New York about her millinery business. There is the occasional visit with Katie to the small farm they have outside of Rochester. Norah desires to share her dreams with her father like she did as a young girl, but is determined to be independent and self-reliant even if it means not being genteel, according to Miss Hartnett. But genteel she does not want to be if it means feigning weakness. Dignified, yes, and self-sufficient, and able to care for her daughter and herself. And she just might be able to make the world, her New York City world, a more beautiful place! How she misses Da's companionship, but for now it has to be so. And it is regrettable that her family has resumed their country ways since moving out of the city. Where is the plenty? Where is the lessening of hardscrabble work? Norah feels estranged each time she visits them and this pains her. After a few days with her family, her insides feel as if they have been whipped up into a giant windstorm and her sanity is leaving her. She can't fight what is natural for her and this means staying in New York City to make her life with her daughter. It is in this exhilarating, complex, and starry-eyed city that she will give Katie a good life.

Norah desires to attract a fashionable clientele by creating original aesthetic millinery, although she hasn't been able to afford the latest Paris trimmings that are popular. She has found exquisite French trimmings on old hats in used clothing stores and talked the owners into giving her a good bargain for them. Her clients from Five Points, however, are starting to dwindle since it was rumored that Negro women patronize *A Bee In Your Bonnet*. One Negro woman! Miss Elizabeth Jennings!

"The girleen is catering to the likes of the coloured ones now; most likely her hats are of a poorer quality than what she's been makin'," an old Irish woman told Mr. Barker one day at his store.

Mr. Barker had only laughed, "Balderdash! I don't care beans whether a Yidisher, a Celestial, or a Negro woman comes to purchase Norah McCabe's hats. As long as she can sell her hats, she can pay me the rent."

Norah and Nellie like the fair and kindly Mr. Barker and feel a bit of fatherly protection from him. He even put a sign in his front window advertising Norah's business. It reads, *A Bee In Your Bonnet, Fine Millinery by Norah McCabe*, with an arrow pointing to the stairs her clients can use rather than having to go through his store. It is also important to her clientele that she be endorsed by Mr. Barker, a respected store owner, as there are a few fancy ladybirds who pose as milliners whom Norah has heard tell of. She was humiliated when a copper came knocking on her door one day because he saw her business sign in Mr. Barker's store window and thought it was a front for stargazers! To imagine respectable Mr. Barker as a whore's minder! He tried to assure her,

"I thought you had thick skin, my dear. Of course you must know that the respectability of any woman entering the public, commercial world is open to criticism."

It was after this incident and low sales that Norah decided to seek out department store proprietors to hire her to set up a millinery department. Most of the stores primarily sold men's hats and clothing, but a few stores sold the latest fashionable bonnets, albeit quite dear in price. Society women patronized small, respectable millinery shops to have their hats sized and made to order. Most women, even Five Points women, no matter their lowly station in life, desire a special hat. And Norah McCabe was making it possible for them and not charging the astronomical prices the established shops charged. The department stores were becoming popular and Norah feels certain that having a milliner set up in a corner of a store would soon become quite in the vogue.

Nellie isn't sure it's a good idea, "I'm afraid they'll not be too eager to help a woman set up a shop in their fancy stores, Norah. They're mostly after assisting their brothers, uncles, and the men climbing off the boat who come from their own counties in Ireland. They'd prefer to have the women stay in the homes minding the children and running the households."

"But there are women who have little shops…what about our successful Kathleen Hartnett?" Norah said.

"Kathleen? She's a rarity. She's a spitfire. And she's lucky."

"I have spitfire, too, and I'm more than able to create gorgeous hats for the aristocratic ladies. There's a French milliner in Paris teaching women! I read about it in Godey's Ladies Book, Nellie. Please don't be discouraging me! How am I going to pay the rent and feed my Katie Marion if I don't do this? I don't want to be only sellin' me hats to the *Cailleach* in Five Points!"

Nellie laughs, "Old woman…old biddy?"

"You're learning the Irish, Nellie!"

"Not so much, for you're doing away with the brogue and words, except when you're good and angry, like right now."

"I'll never be giving up me Irish, Nell, but I can talk as high falutin' as any big bug here in New York!"

"You're the real deal, Norah McCabe, and far be it that I should be trying to dissuade your spirit and determination! I'm just trying to look at all sides of this. You'll find a way…we'll find a way. I'm your dearest friend and believe in you!"

Later in the day, Mr. Barker tried to dissuade Norah from setting up her hat business elsewhere.

"No need…there's no need for you to try and hawk your hats in the grandiose Ladies' Mile, my dear," Mr. Barker told Norah when she was preparing to leave the apartment with three of her best hats in a bag.

"Chatham Square is a favorite destination for all kinds of buyers and if you would like to set up a table under my awning…"

"Thank you for your gracious offer, Mr. Barker, but you see…." (She didn't want to offend the modest store owner).

"I don't see, Norah McCabe. I do see that you have notions your hats are of superior quality and can be sold at Bloomingdale's or Lord & Taylor's, but please let me give you some advice…"

Norah set down her bag and sighed. She cocked her head to the side and smiled at Mr. Barker before she spoke.

"You're a successful dry goods store owner, Mr. Barker, and unlike most store owners in this ward, you have integrity. But, without giving you offense, I must remind you that Chatham Square is a bazaar and many struggling laborers come here to shop. They don't really come here to shop for hats, but for necessities…"

"Let me interrupt you yet again, Miss McCabe or Mrs. Murray, or whatever it is you go by…you need to stick it out here and eventually most of your Irish customers will be back. There's no other milliner as fine as you in these wards and the Irish women like their hats.

They'll get over your friendship with that Negro woman…you just wait…that's what I say, anyway."

"Thank you for your sage advice, Mr. Barker, but I'm not planning on closing up my shop here in Chatham Square. I'm just broadening my horizons."

"Yes, that's what I'm about, as sure as a cat has whiskers, Mr. Barker. I'm *broadening* my horizons on Broadway!"

Mr. Barker threw up his hands and walked back into his store, shaking his head. He liked this Norah McCabe and after hearing about the shipwreck she'd lived through, he thought even more highly of her, but she was one to put on airs at times. *She'd have to learn the hard way,* he was afraid.

It's an early, warm April day when Norah jaunts off to the Ladies Mile in search of a department store that will hire her to set up a millinery department. Springtime is usually very busy for milliners, but Norah only has a couple of orders. They are for simple lightweight summer straw bonnets that won't bring in a lot of money. She strides confidently down the streets of New York wearing one of her loveliest straw hats embroidered with tiny violets and ribbons. This hat is the first straw hat she has created and her fingers were sore for a long time after.

When Norah reaches Tiffany & Co. on Broadway, she slows her steps to gaze at the elegant six-story showstopper with enormous windows and decorative bronze rosettes on the mouldings. The street is lined with ornate black carriages with decorative scrollwork of gold. Norah watches footmen open the doors of the carriages and assist ladies dressed in elaborate silk and satin gowns and beribboned bonnets to the red carpet that flows down the steps from the magnificent front door of Tiffany & Co.

The atmosphere palpitates with the lure of wealth and success. Norah thinks she sees gold flecks falling from trees lining the avenue, but it is only the sun shining on a few leaves in the breeze. Sweat beads on her forehead and she feels conspicuous in her French blue silk taffeta dress. It has a short-sleeved bodice with an open neck trimmed in pleated ribbon and cream bobbin lace. The cashmere shawl she is wearing over the gown is merely for show and to cover her arms, for short-sleeved gowns are for evening, not the day, and yet she cannot endure the long sleeves of an afternoon dress on such a warm day.

The voluminous, unlined trained skirt with large pleats has a raised hemline of four inches. Some of the women turn to stare at her. Is her hemline too short? Her French silk ivory parasol is tattered and when she glances at her feet, her blue satin high shoes have come untied and are covered in dirt after her long walk. The ladies' bonnets are covered in satin ribbons and exquisite silk flowers and appear very different from her bonnet. Their hats are elaborate with flowers and long ribbons hanging down past their shoulders. Norah feels out of place and awkward.

"High-falutin' codfish aristocracy!" she whispers under her breath.

The ladies jut their peacock necks out to try and hear what she is saying. She smiles, adjusts her hat, lifts her chin, and walks down the street as if she never intended to climb the regal steps into Tiffany & Co. She has to admit that perhaps her hats aren't fancy enough for this store. What was she thinking, anyway! She walks further and comes to Lord & Taylor on Broadway at Grand Street and encounters a few more ladies dressed up to the nines. Again, she feels underdressed and walks right on by, heading to Bloomingdale's. When she arrives, there are purple, claret, green, cobalt blue, and black carriages lined up in front of the bright department store. It is an utter delight to experience the swooshing and the swirling of crinoline, parasols, and skirts. Norah smells lavender, Bergamot, lily of the valley, and rose. The air is thick with these scents, as if heaven itself has sent down a rainfall of perfume. She inhales deeply and wants to sit right down on the steps just to take it all in.

Norah slowly makes her way through the crowd of women who look like confectionery treats. A dark-skinned man dressed in a blue uniform with brass buttons and white gloves opens the door for her. When she walks in, others follow, trying to elbow her out of the way, chattering like morning birds and exclaiming over everything they eye as they walk through the store.

"The Ladies' Notions Department is up the stairs and to the right, Madam," Norah hears a store employee direct a female shopper. She follows behind the large woman who is wearing flounces of petticoats looking like a powder puff. Norah giggles. Hosiery, shawls, and jewelry line the shelves. Norah scans the department looking for hats. Of course there wouldn't be any hats! Women want custom-designed hats made especially to their own original taste. Each hat has to be unique, but not so different from other hats that a woman feels out of her class. She is hopeful that when the Bloomingdale owners see her special designed hats, they will surely wish for her to set up in this department. *There might be a place for me here*, she says to herself, as she moves excitedly to and fro around the department.

"I'd like to speak to one of the proprietors of this store, if you please," Norah says to the female clerk standing behind the counter where necklaces and earrings glittered under glass. She has also noticed a copper standing in the doorway who has been eyeing her since she came into the department.

The clerk lifts her chin haughtily, "That's impossible, Miss. Both Bloomingdale gentlemen are only available by appointment..."

"Norah McCabe! If it isn't Miss Norah McCabe!" interrupts the copper. Norah turns to see that it is Officer Leary...Officer O'Leary. She hasn't set eyes on him since her return from the shipwreck. He had been the one to bring the good news to her parents that she was still alive, and for this she is grateful, but there is a pang of anguish to see him now. He, too, has suffered great heartache in his life. He and Norah's most precious friend, Mary, had been in love and planning marriage. And then Mary had died from an abortion procedure. Norah's heart not only suffered the loss of her husband, but the loss of the best friend she had known since arriving from Ireland as a child.

"Isn't this store grand?" Officer Leary comments, all the while moving from one foot to another. He is clearly nervous in her presence.

"Tis! How long have you worked here? I thought you were in the carting business and had an entire fleet!" Norah says.

Leary looks away for a moment and then at Norah. She can see sorrow etched into the creases beneath his eyes.

"Too long, I'm afraid. I gave up my fleet after Mary died. And since the change in the police department and Mayor Wood losing his grip on the Metros, I've been back with a club at my side. But I don't mind," he said, shaking his head and looking away again, "No, I don't mind. It's this security work here I like, watching the panorama of the riches of the world parade before me."

"A fine palace of a place to work, I'm sure. Better than the streets and all the shenanigans that go on."

"Oh, there can be trouble here, too… Norah, are you here to shop?" His eyes widen. She knows what he is thinking. *No young woman from Five Points would be shopping at Bloomingdale's!*

"No, I'm not shopping today. I'm doing a little business is all… no, not shopping today."

"And might I be asking…"

Norah pulls out one of her hats and shows it to Leary.

"I'm a milliner, O'Leary! My *Bee in Your Bonnet* is the label on the hats I design and make myself!"

"Oh…yer doing grand then!"

"Well, at the moment, I'm not doing so grand."

The women milling around in the department have stopped looking at items and are clearly eavesdropping.

She moves closer to Officer Leary to speak more privately. She detects a strong citrus scent on him. He is clean shaven and handsome if you like a ginger-haired muscular man with lots of freckles and small eyes. Her Sean is of the same coloring, but he's tall and wiry with eyes as lovely as bachelor button flowers. And Sean holds a spell over her that this one could never do.

"I'm not selling very many hats these days, for you see…well…I'm not in the Sixth Ward now and some of my customers don't shop on Chatham Square where I'm living at the moment and where my shop is. But I'm hoping to sell my hats in bigger stores…like this one."

"Have you tried the Knox store? This Knox lad is from the ole country and he's the biggest toad in the puddle."

"He's from Ireland, is he? Sure, everyone knows about his store. His name is plastered on every window of his building, as if he's afraid of no-one finding it! I was going to stop there today, too…but the saints be praised, I didn't know he hailed from Ireland!" Norah whispers.

The store clerk interrupts their conversation, "Excuse me, there's a disturbance downstairs. I think you should be attending to it, if you don't mind," she said to Leary, coming out quickly from behind the counter. Leary tips his hat to Norah and hurries downstairs. The ladies browsing in the department follow after him, eager to learn what is happening.

Norah turns to the clerk and sighs, wondering if she should ask her about employment, but the clerk screws up her overly powdered face as she looks at Norah.

"Are you not as curious as the others?" she asks, indicating she wants Norah to leave.

Norah leaves the store and stands on the street. Shiny lacquered carriages are lined up and Leary stands with his arms folded watching the drama of the well-heeled society women coming and going.

"Is there any rambunctious activity going on, O'Leary?" Norah asks.

"None, a'tall! And why is it that you insist on putting an 'O' in front of my name, Mrs. Murray?"

"You should be proud of your Irish heritage, Officer O'Leary!"

"Are you? I don't see or hear much of the ole country in you!"

"Nor do I detect much of it in you!"

They both laugh.

"I think I was affronted in the ladies' notions department, Officer. Can you take the puffed up snoot to the station now and book her for rudeness?"

"Oh, that woman is always sending me on wild goose chases. She doesn't want me hanging around her department, I guess." Leary moves about nervously and then says, "I'm off duty in a few minutes. Let's go to the grocery-groggery for a whiskey or two and I'll escort you to your man's store."

"I'm not much of an imbiber these days, O'Leary, but I'll have a good strong cuppa."

Later, at the grocery, Leary tells Norah the story of Mr. Knox who came from Donegal when he was merely thirteen, just like Norah who came from Ireland at that age. And although he didn't have to hide out in a dresser alone on a ship like she had, he and his ten-year-old sister had encountered a vicious storm that threw them off course. They ended up in Delaware and walked a hundred and twenty miles to New York City where their parents and eight siblings lived.

"He's a fine example of someone from Ireland making good. I'd think you'd do well to speak with him about your hat idea. It's known he helps the Irish. I hear he's a member of the Friendly Sons of St. Patrick's and makes strong contributions to charity. He has a few houses, too, and I've seen a couple of them myself. His top hats are the finest hats in the city."

"Abraham Lincoln himself was wearing one that this man, Knox, had made just for him. I saw Mr. Lincoln twice wearing that hat. But ladies' hats are another matter, altogether."

"If anyone could convince our man, Knox, to give you a position…it'd be you, Norah." Leary gives Norah a squeeze around the shoulders and kisses the top of her head. She's surprised, but warmed by his affection. They have both been through a lifetime of suffering.

Chapter Four

Knox Great Hat and Cap at 212 Broadway is impressive, but not as imposing and ornate as Bloomingdale's. There is only one carriage parked outside the building and a few well-heeled women have climbed out without the help of a footman. Norah follows them up the steps as they quickly walk through the corridor doors and disappear. A colored man wearing a red suit with brass buttons and a cap with a gold rope entwining it smiles at Norah and asks if he can help her.

"I've a mind to turn right around and go home after the day I've had! Is this the Knox Hat Company?" She's embarrassed; for it's obvious she is at the Knox store, being that the name, Knox, is everywhere.

"I'm a milliner…you know…a hat maker. I design hats. I draw them on paper the butcher gives me and then I purchase my bodies and materials from jobbers. I have good credit now…unlike in the beginning when no one knew if I was to be trusted…"

"Yes'm…I surely know what a milliner is being that I work here."

Norah takes in a deep breath and lets it out slowly, unable to say another word.

"Knox sells them popular beaver hats, Miss…some top hats is his fancy, but he's not much for the ladies' hats…" the doorman said.

"I know…I saw with my own eyes Mr. Lincoln's hat that Mr. Knox made personally for him and I was thinking he might like to expand his business. I brought my specially designed hats to show Mr. Knox."

Norah pulls a hat from the bag and the other two hats tumble onto the floor.

The doorman picks them up and holds them out to her at the same time a young man with a mass of curly light brown hair and a pleasant face comes through the door.

"Harold, my good fella…are you helping a damsel in distress?"

"Yes, Mr. Knox, I'm trying to help this young lady…"

Norah turns to the young man, thrusting a hat in his face, "Oh, tis you, then, Mr. Charles Knox! I would have thought you'd be much older with all your success!"

The young man takes the hat and lifts it up to view with keen interest. A number of businessmen come through the doors and greet him before going into the store.

"These are lovely hats, Miss…"

"McCabe. Norah McCabe."

"Pleased to meet you Norah McCabe. Miss?"

"Miss, sir…no, I'm actually Mrs. Murray, but…"

The young man and Harold laugh. Norah is embarrassed and takes the hat from the young man and prepares to leave.

"I'm sorry to offend you, Mrs. Murray…Miss Norah McCabe, but…"

"I *am* Norah McCabe, but I was married for a very brief time and sometimes I forget who I am!"

Harold stifles his laughter, but the young man continues to laugh. And then Norah, who has been so wound up with all her cuppas and eagerness, laughs, as well. The three of them stand in the corridor laughing until a very distinguished man with close cropped grey hair comes hurrying towards them.

"And what is the meaning of this ruckus…Harold! Edward! The noise is being carried throughout the building!" Everyone stops laughing and Norah stares at the older man with puzzlement. He has a prominent full mouth that is set in the conviction that he knows right from wrong at every turn in life.

"My apologies, sir, but the young lady would like to meet you," Harold says.

The tall, handsome gentleman approaches Norah and slightly bows his head to her in greeting.

"I'm Mr. Charles Knox. May I help you? Do you need directions or are you here to purchase clothing for your husband?"

Norah looks at the younger man for a moment. It is obvious that he doesn't carry the same serious countenance. His eyes sparkle with devious good fun. She turns to the other man and smiles.

"Oh, you must be the real Mr. Knox, then."

The younger man turns to the older man, "Miss Norah McCabe is obviously unable to make up her fashion conscious mind and carries many hats with her…just in case she changes her mind and wishes to wear another…or another," he said, taking the hats from Norah and showing them to his father.

Norah takes the hats from him, "That's not true. Don't listen to this comical fellow who is a bit rude, if I might say, pretending to be you all the while I stand here in earnest!"

Norah places the hats in her bag and turns to Charles Knox, "Good day to you, sir. Another time, then."

Harold opens the door for her, "Good day, Miss," and as she starts out the door, the young man jumps in front of her.

"Oh, please, Miss McCabe Murray, don't leave. My father, the real Mr. Knox, certainly will speak to you about the business you came here for."

And so it is that Charles and his son, Edward, escort Norah McCabe Murray to the office of Charles Knox, owner of The Knox Great Hat & Cap to discuss her business proposal. And later, the scintillating Mr. Edward Knox takes Norah out for a cuppa at the same business Leary has taken her for a cuppa. She nearly has a whiskey, but thinks it best she refrains because her mind is in such a state of excitement. She had become so disheartened over the response she received from Mr. Charles Knox about her hat venture that she had dissolved into a pool of tears while sitting on the plush mahogany chair looking at two portraits of the Charles Knox family. Edward had pointed out his father's family who had been born in Ireland, twelve in entirety! The second portrait was of the father, his wife, and two small children, one being Edward when he was merely five years of age. And next to the portrait was a painting of Ramelton, Donegal, a village in Ireland, where they had hailed from. Charles Knox had listened to her with rapt attention and then responded slowly and with much kindness. Norah thought Mr. Knox was quite fatherly and had immediately warmed to him, but her heart had been so set on creating hats in his department store that she was unable to control her emotions when he told her it would be a poor business venture, indeed. He explained that it wasn't a good business decision at the moment because most women, his wife included, purchased their hats from reputable small shops that carried the best materials that came from Paris. His company could not afford to invest in this kind of individualized business. However, his beaver and top hats were similar in style and cost of production was not as varied as it would be in creating other hats. Perhaps in the future, he told Norah, perhaps in the future as the company prospered. Prospered? *How prosperous could one man from the ole country become*, Norah thought, as she looked around his office. And in the meantime, might he let her know if his wife ever needed some domestic help at their home? As tender and sincere as old Mr. Knox was (who had indeed lost his Irish accent), she had been crestfallen that he did not see her hats as artistic creations unlike anyone else's designs. No one could tell whether she had used ribbons from Paris or not! She had been so disappointed by this interchange, but when she saw the village in Donegal ablaze in the sun in the painting and not in the rain she had known so well, it made her think of Cork and her village. Homesickness for Ireland, and even for her Da and Mam came over her! Memories came so quickly that she couldn't contain her emotions. It was as if a mask had been removed from her face and she was sitting as a wizened woman with lines around her eyes like dried up streambeds. She knew this auld one was familiar, but she had ignored her quite well until now. She remembered feeling that the Cailleach had come to dwell within her when she had climbed into the dresser to come to America, but at the time she assumed the woman had come to remind her of when she indeed would become old, a time she couldn't even fathom. And then this day in a plush office, all of these reminders brought about a barrage of tears that surprised and embarrassed not only her, but the two Knox men, as well. It wasn't merely a few tears sprung from her eyes that any young woman would experience from disappointment that could be assuaged by a handkerchief and comforting words. No, it was the auld one, the Cailleach from Ireland, who had torn off her mask and she could no longer hold the tears back. For Norah McCabe Murray hadn't really wept all that much after returning from the shipwreck when she lost her husband and nearly drowned herself. It was loud sobbing, and because she saw in the eyes of the old Mr. Knox that he knew her kind of sorrow, but saw in the eyes of Edward that he did not, she would carry shame for this outburst. But it was Edward Knox, not the old Mr. Knox, who knew how to respond to her grief. He gently took her hand and helped her from the sofa, gave her his handkerchief, and cooed to her that everything would work out. He picked up her bag of hats, placed the hat she had been wearing and had taken off, back on her head, and said to his father,

"We'll go for refreshment, Father. I'll return in due time to help out at the store."

Charles Knox smiled weakly, hurried from behind his desk, and gave Norah a tender pat on her back as he said farewell to her. Norah noticed that his knobby, long-fingered hands were shaking when he opened the door for her to leave.

At the end of the day, Norah returned to Chatham Square with her bag of hats. On each street she walked towards home, she had changed hats and tried to display a different countenance, although she knew well that she could never really be anyone but Norah McCabe, not even Norah McCabe Murray, for she hadn't been her long enough to have acquired a married countenance. How had Mr. Charles Knox and others from the ole country become successful? How had they hid their ignorant ways of Ireland? How had they come from nothing to have just about everything wonderful that an American city had to offer? Walking usually cleared her head, but by the time she arrived home, nothing was clear to her except that she did not have sufficient income for her and Katie to live, she could not sell her exquisite and painstakingly made hats for a price worthy of her labor, and her heart had not stopped beating at an elevated and musical pace since Mr. Edward Knox placed a very warm and lingering kiss on her cheek when he said goodbye. She walked into the apartment and little Katie rushed into her arms. Nellie looked at her and said, "Something's astir, Norah...I see it in the flush on your face. I'll make us some supper and we'll talk all about it after Miss Katie is in bed."

Norah smiled at her friend, sat down on the couch with Katie, and listened to her chatter on about all her friends she played with at the Ladies' Home Mission.

"By the way, your Sean left a note on the door for you." Nellie handed Norah the note.

May I have the pleasure of escorting my gal to Pete's this Saturday evening? the note read.

Norah sighed, put her head back on the couch, and her heart stilled to a regular beat. "Yes, Sean, I'll be pleased," she said quietly. Later, Norah tells Nellie all about her day, not leaving out a detail except she didn't tell her about the warm kiss Edward Knox had left on her cheek.

"We'll manage, Norah. Please don't worry. We'll not be out on the streets."

Easy for Nellie, Norah thinks, for she has never known hunger and poverty. When Norah falls asleep, she dreams of Ireland and the bodies thumping in wagons behind the cart they road in on their way to Cobh Harbor to leave for America. In the dream, she falls out of the cart and the wagon with the dead and their grass-stained mouths run over her. She is spared by the crush of wagon wheels and after it has passed, she stands up and runs to find the cart her family was on, but they are nowhere in sight. She wakes drenched in sweat, her heart pounding.

Chapter Five

"I don't hold it against you, Norah, just because one of your own people tried to throw me off the streetcar."

"How did you know he was Irish?"

"I told him I was a respectable person, born and raised in New York and had every right to be on that streetcar. I told him I didn't know where he was born, but that he was a good for nothing impudent fellow for insulting my friend and me on our way to church."

"You're a brave one, Elizabeth! What did he say to that?"

"I'm from Ireland," he said, and then he tried to haul me off the car. I told him my father was no poor African man and he'd be in trouble if he hurt us."

"But he did, didn't he?"

"He pushed us off, alright, but we took him to court, my father and I did. We took this incidence to Mr. Horace Greeley and to Frederick Douglas."

"Oh, Elizabeth, we're not all the same, we Irish. You have to understand that we've fought our own battles…and we haven't even won! And then we come here to a new country and we're hated… hated as much as you all are!"

"But your people have white skin and you'll never be treated as badly as we are."

"Because of what you did...because of you, Miss Elizabeth Jennings, a true revolutionary, all the streetcar lines in this city are open to African-Americans."

"But some of them signs are still up saying, "No Negro Persons Allowed."

"And some of the newspapers in this city say, "No Irish Need Apply!"

Norah sighs and offers Elizabeth more tea. She has asked her to come and visit the apartment, determined to keep their friendship.

"Have you heard about old man Wilkins, your Negro fellow down at the docks, and his new wife, Mary Hennessey? She's as white as buttermilk and no-one minds them."

"It's not that typical, Norah."

"It's a known fact there are Irish women married to African men living here in Five Points. And don't the African and Irish people mostly get along fine compared to the rest of the city!"

"New York is mighty tense over the South threatening to secede if Mr. Lincoln becomes president and takes their slaves away. And you and I both know the Irish fear we'll be taking their jobs."

"Not every Irish person hates the African, Elizabeth! And look at our Mr. Horace Greeley and others. Why, I've danced at Pete Williams Dance Hall owned by an African man and we all mingle our feet in fine tapping and stepping. And those feet are black and white feet! Irish feet and African feet!"

Elizabeth takes a sip of tea, and after setting the cup back in the saucer, she stands up and tries to do a jig. Norah stands up with her, takes her hand, and demonstrates. The two women laugh as Norah hums a tune and teaches her friend how to dance.

"Mammy! Me, too! I want to dance with Miss Elizabeth, too!"

Katie Marion comes out of the bedroom after her nap and rushes to hold Elizabeth's hand to dance with her. Her reddish brown curls bounce and her green eyes are full of joy. She's an easy going, as well as a serious, child. After a few minutes, they all sit down and have more tea. Katie climbs up on Elizabeth's lap and snuggles against her. Katie Marion isn't shy about loving the right people,

Norah thinks. She only sits on the laps of those she trusts. Norah looks at the two sitting together; well aware of the contrast that is so singular and beautiful, and wishes she could sketch the two of them.

"And so now…ye'll be accompanying me and my gentleman friend, Sean, to the dance hall this evening!" Norah said to Elizabeth.

"Me? I can't dance! As you can see, my feet have no rhythm!"

"Let me tell you something, Miss Elizabeth Jennings! As a child I danced in Ireland, but I thought I'd never dance again after coming here. And then it was at Pete Williams' place when I was just thirteen that I found my dancing feet again. It means so much to me to dance, to not ever give up dancing, and it would mean the world to me if you go dancing with me!"

"My father will have a stroke if I go to a saloon or one of those grog houses. It's not fit for a Sunday school teacher! There's revelry of all sorts that goes on in those watering holes. Why do you think they're called free-and-easy?"

Katie hums a tune and plays with Elizabeth's coarse hair.

"Think of this child, Norah! You don't want her growing up and going into those places of debauchery."

"Oh, not so, Elizabeth! Mostly 'tis grand! Of course, there's some impropriety that takes place in the back rooms, I've heard, but I haven't seen it myself. Some women drape their bodies clothed in garish, low-bodice dresses over their partners. The ribaldry of the B'hoys and G'hals is sometimes unsettling, I do admit. Sometimes I ask Sean if we're like a G'hal and B'hoy, but we're not. Sean pays the ten cents cover charge and when I hear the music, I come alive! I'd never be leaving my Katie an evening to go to a dangerous place."

"Never been to a dance, 'cept at a bonfire with some fiddling. What's it like, the music and all, Norah?"

"There's fiddlers and a tambourine man who play music that shakes first in my rib cage and then it goes right down through my legs to my feet. And then I dance for hours, it seems. Sometimes I forget Sean is my partner, for I'm passed around to other partners from time to time, but never do I feel mauled or mishandled."

"It sounds both thrillin' and frightening at the same time," Elizabeth said.

"I don't know, Elizabeth! It's the music and the dancing is all. I forget all my troubles, my past, and even my present when I dance. I feel ecstatic and lifted out of my own skin sometimes. Out of my own Irish skin, my woman skin…and time seems to stop."

Norah gets up from the couch and looks out the window into the street. *Dirty, noisy, and everyone scrambling for something all the time…desperate people…so ugly…*

"I'm sorry, Norah. I'm not meaning to offend you…maybe I'd like to be going with you, after all, even if I'm a Christian woman. I need to see us and your people doing something good together. And maybe I'd like to climb out of my own black skin, my woman skin, too."

"We'll go to Uncle Pete's then! A fine saloon for your people and mine. I know you'll like it well enough."

Elizabeth smiles weakly and Norah tries to ignore her comment about her being a Christian, as if she isn't one herself.

In the evening, Sean escorts Elizabeth and Norah out of the apartment and down the steps to go to Pete's. He likes Elizabeth, but worries they might cause a scene walking through the city together.

"You let Auntie Nell read you a story before you go to bed and don't ye be giving her any trouble now," Norah said, kissing Katie on both cheeks again and again as they stand on the street. Katie is clinging to Norah's skirts while holding Nellie's hand.

Mr. Barker is standing under the awning of his store looking quite cross.

"I'd be careful, young folks, if I were you. Things getting heated up a bit since Mr. Lincoln was nominated. Those Southern fellas have been comin' north to stir up trouble."

Sean looks back at Mr. Barker and grimaces. He doesn't need this do-gooder questioning him about keeping the women safe.

"We're going to a dance hall. We're not going to a low-life dive where's there only rubber tubes to drink from, Mr. Barker," he says.

Norah shivers and brings her shawl close around her neck and looks up into the sky between the buildings. There are no stars dancing in the sky this night. She loves the sky and sometimes climbs out onto the roof of Sean's tenement building where he lives with a few men he works on the docks with just to look at the stars. This is where she feels most close to God and is transported to a place within herself that connects with the vastness of the world. If the moon is merely a smiling crescent, the bright stars wink wildly at her and she imagines each one assuring her that all will be well. But there are times when the moon is full and the stars recede into the background to let the moon have its sway over all. As much as Norah loves the moon's full, magical shine, it sometimes brings forth more wildness in the streets and in those around her. And now as they walk down the street, she looks up again and there is the moon, full and demanding. She shudders again and Sean puts his arm around her shoulders.

At the dance hall, Sean leaves Norah and Elizabeth to go out for a smoke and some fresh air. The friends watch the dancers cavorting, bowing, and flinging one another to and fro in their dance. The musicians are playing a Negro folk song, 'Cooney in de Holler' and the room is thick with moist, perfumed air. The place is well lit, the floors are nicely sanded, and there are well-dressed people all around them.

"I never seen so many different kinds of people dancing away together!"

"I said you'd feel at home here. There's no place like it!" Norah whispers loudly in Elizabeth's ear.

"Are you going to get up and dance?" Elizabeth asks.

"I should wait for Sean. Him and his cigar smoking! I hate it!" Norah looks towards the door for Sean, but doesn't see him.

Elizabeth and Norah watch the dancers until Norah can hardly hold still. When a young man asks Norah to dance, she hesitates and looks at Elizabeth who smiles and tells her to get on the dance floor so Norah can show her how it's done. Other than with Sean, it's the first time Norah has ever been asked to dance. The invitation is accompanied with a deep bow from the waist and then Norah takes the fellow's hand and lines up to dance.

The two lines of dancers face one another, male and female, all mixed races. The music starts out slowly with a jig. As the dancers progress, the fiddlers and other musicians play faster and pick up the pace with reels and soon every part of the dancers' bodies are in motion. The fiddlers compel the dancers to quicken the tempo further and soon all the figures are forgotten and every dancer is stamping, hollering, and jumping about. Norah glistens with sweat and her curly hair loosens from a full bandeaux fastened by a pearl comb and hangs down her back. Her partner's hair has a top wave that is well-greased and he sports a handlebar moustache. Elizabeth is keenly watching and can see in the light of the hoop chandelier blazing with candles that Norah's partner's large, dark eyes are wild with excitement. She doesn't quite know what to think, except that she is a church-going abolitionist's daughter visiting a dance hall! She stands up from the table to get a better view and although she likes the music, she's unsure about liking the unrestrained and riotous behavior of the dancers.

Suddenly, a shirt-sleeved and barefoot African dancer leaps in front of her. He is dripping with sweat and his shirt is open at the chest that reveals thick, coarse hairs. Elizabeth is startled and backs up, but he grabs her hand and tries to pull her onto the floor, his feet still moving. She resists and swats at him. He lets go of her hand and moves away, dancing furiously across the room. Elizabeth is ready to go home! She is surprised by the alteration in Norah's appearance, for she has only ever seen Norah exhibiting modesty and perfect decorum, although oftentimes Norah's speech can be colorful. In fact, they both know how to express themselves quite well together. But Elizabeth has never seen her friend with her hair down. As entranced as she is by her beauty and spontaneity, she fears Norah and the dancers are turning into howling, possessed dervishes who will soon collapse into a depraved heap upon the floor. She rushes to Norah and touches her arm to get her attention. Norah continues dancing and pays no heed, but when Elizabeth touches her again, this time with a pinch, Norah turns towards her friend. Her eyes open wide and she looks at Elizabeth, as if remembering where she is for the first time. She walks with Elizabeth to the table and sits down. Elizabeth goes for some water and brings Norah back a glass, but when she returns Norah's dancing partner is sitting opposite her and reaches across the table for Norah's hands.

"You can be looking for another dance partner now," Elizabeth said loudly in the man's ear.

He stands up quickly and faces Elizabeth, "And you can go to the devil, darky!"

Norah stands and shoves the man in the chest, "You'd best be shut pan and get your no-account arse away from both of us!"

The man slowly backs into the crowd of dancers and disappears. Norah finds her bandeaux and comb that has lost its pearl when it was kicked into a corner by the dancers. She tries to arrange her hair the best she can, but a few frizzy curls hang about her face. She quickly ties her gipsy hood around her head even though she is still hot from the dancing. Elizabeth does the same and both girls arrange their shawls around their shoulders and prepare to leave.

"We can't leave without Sean!" Norah said to Elizabeth as her friend put her arm through Norah's.

"I'd say we walk right outdoors, find ourselves a decent buggy we can afford, and get safely home."

"Wait for me outside, Elizabeth. I'm going to look for Sean."

Norah walks down a hallway past the bar. It's difficult to see in the darkened hallway, but she hears singing and as her eyes adjust to the dimness, she sees men and women embracing and talking. There are a few chairs lined up and women sit on men's laps sharing cigars with them, laughing loudly. Norah sees a man place something in the low bodice of a woman who is wearing a short, full skirt and sporting corkscrew curls that are long and comical looking. The woman wears not one, but two combs, as well as a bright red ribbon. Her lips are red and shine out in the darkness. She smiles widely at Norah and then the woman nearly falls to the floor as the man whose lap she is on jumps up.

"Sean!" Norah turns and runs down the hall to the front door. She finds Elizabeth standing on the sidewalk and when Elizabeth looks at Norah's face, she clutches Norah's arm and the women quickly walk down the street away from Pete William's.

"I just want to go home!" Norah's charming hood comes untied and hangs about her neck, her hair again falling out of the comb.

"Norah! Wait!"

Sean catches up with them and reaches for Norah's arm. The two friends slow down, but Norah still holds onto Elizabeth. And then she turns to Sean and yells at him.

"You're a right bastard!"

He says nothing in response and they stare at one another. Norah is surprised that Sean, who has worked hard at making himself a gentleman after they had been lost to one another since childhood, has resorted to this lowly life. Sean, whom she trusted with her dreams and intimacies!

"I hate you for this, Sean O'Connolly!"

Elizabeth places her arm around Norah's shoulder. Sean, who stands on the street with his hair disheveled, his shirt half-out of his trousers, and his waistcoat unbuttoned, has nothing to say in return. If he defends himself, it will lower himself in her eyes even further, as well as in his own. He turns away from the woman he loves more than his own life. And now for the second time in his life, he lets Norah McCabe go, but as he walks down the street elbowing anyone who gets in his way, he purposes in his heart that he will do whatever it takes to get her back.

Chapter Six

It's a pleasant Sunday afternoon in May, and Nellie, Norah, and Katie hold hands and stroll on the Ramble in Central Park. Creeping vines, violets, and lily of the valley carpet the dusty paths and grassy hillsides. Flowering dogwood, apple, and cherry trees bedeck the grounds with white and pink flowers. Delicate blossoms float on a light breeze and fall upon their bonnets, adding a further touch of adornment. Fancy carriages and gigs pitch past leaving a cloud of dust and there are a myriad of people out for a walk. Nellie is humming a tune, but stops and leads Norah and Katie to the side of the pedestrian path. Still clutching Katie and Norah's hands, she merrily recites from Robert Brownings' Pippa's Song:

> The year's at the spring
> And day's at the morn:
> Morning's at seven;
> The hillside's dew-pearled;
> The lark's on the wing;
> The snail's on the thorn:
> God's in His heaven—
> All's right with the world!

Just the day before, Nellie had to convince Norah to go on a picnic in Central Park. Norah had insisted that the park was unsafe for them to visit.

"It's still not finished and there's too much dirt and broken stones and rude workmen…the likes of them are probably Irish and live in Five Points!" Of late, Norah had been prone to fits of moodiness so unlike the spirited optimism she usually displayed.

"It's safe as can be! There are all these military-looking policemen who line up at the entranceway and around the park who watch your every move," Nellie had replied.

"And they don't allow anyone to sit on the grass. Harrigan said that he and his friends went on a carriage ride through the park and then stopped by a bridge for a picnic, but they were told they couldn't sit on the grass, so they ate in their carriage," Norah answered.

"Then we'll sit on one of the bridges and dangle our feet over the water and have our picnic."

"Go to park, Mama. Go to park!" Katie had cried and Norah reluctantly gave in. For days, she was anxious over Sean and the state of her millinery business. She had only sold six hats in the past four months. Her meager income at the House of Industry and the sales from the hats had not been sufficient to pay her half of the rent. She no longer had a savings and gave what money she had to Nellie, who never made her feel indebted and uncomfortable with her plight. But Norah was ill at ease over the lack of work and money. She hadn't been working at the newspaper, of late, and didn't want Harrigan to know her plight. She also hid her situation from her family and was determined not to tell her sister, Meg, because she would scold her for being foolish, as Meg had done a month ago when she visited Norah.

"Most hat-making dreamy, cow-eyed young girls go out of business in a few months or a year. What makes you think you would be any different, Norah?" Meg had said. And now Norah feared Meg's portentous warning was coming true. Soon Meg would visit with her children and Norah would have to be very cautious not to let her know how dismal her hat-making venture had become. And then she received a long letter from Mam relaying she couldn't abide so much time going by without seeing her grandbabies and Meg and Norah must come for a visit or she was coming to New York City herself. Norah didn't want to travel with Meg and her brood all the way to Rochester and so she wrote back a letter saying she was too busy, but would plan a visit in July. *For the 4th, Mam! Katie and I'll come for the 4th! Does Rochester have fireworks for the 4th of July?* she wrote, trying to sound cheerful. She would have to go in July now and she only hoped she would have the money to travel. Da surely would send the money, but Norah didn't want to depend on her father for help. Mam and Da were just getting on their feet with farming and she didn't want to burden them after all they had lived through over the years.

Norah's thoughts returned to the present when Katie exclaimed, "Sing, Auntie Nell! Sing!" Nellie has been happily humming songs since their arrival in the park and little Katie has been trying to sing along with her.

"I don't know the tune to the words of the poet, pet," Nellie answered.

People throng the pathway and Norah peers into the myriad of different faces. There are bigwigs, merchants' wives, and the gentlemen and ladies of society. These are the privileged ones whom have their own carriages or can afford to hire a carriage. She thinks about the laborers who work for low wages to make this park beautiful. They've all gone from the park on a Sunday, these poor ones who probably walk ten miles to dig in the dirt to create fine gardens and bridges for the wealthy visitors.

"Look, Nell," she whispers, pointing with her chin in the direction of a few street hawker types, including the oyster sellers and red-cheeked apple vendor women clutching tightly to their disheveled porky men who wear yellowed woven cotton work shirts underneath tattered wool vests.

"They're wearing such funny hats. No top hats for those men!" She says.

"They're sporting the bowler hat or Derby, whatever you want to call them."

"They're so poor looking compared to the bigwigs, Nell. I feel for their plights so." She turns to Nellie, unable to control her emotions.

"God may be in his heaven, but it's not alright in the world!"

Norah scoops Katie up and walks through the crowd until she spies a bench unoccupied. As she hurries to it, pebbles fall into her embroidered canvas pumps and stick between the high black lacing.

"Damn!" Norah says, trying to kick her shoes free of them.

"Damn!" Katie said, "Damn…damn…damn."

"No, Katie, don't say that word."

"Damn Mama!"

Norah limps to the bench, hot tears in her eyes. Katie's right. Norah is a damn mother and if she was a good mother, she would be working in a shop and getting a regular paycheck or she would have moved to Rochester to live with her family so Katie could have a better life. What was she supposed to do! She will have to work as a domestic, scrubbing on hands and knees for a meager wage with the man of the house trying to get a feel or even more. God have mercy, she'll mop floors for Katie. She'll do just about anything for her daughter. But she won't subject herself to a man who'd be grabbing her behind. These dire thoughts prompt her to think of Sean. Did she think he never frequented the stargazers at The Jolly Jar or at any of the free-and-easys? If he can get his thrill at Pete Williams, surely he must be a regular at one of the bagnios. Just that morning, Norah read the headline on the front page of the Herald: *Bishop Simmons Declares New York has 20,000 Whores!*

Norah sits on the bench and holds Katie who is squirming to be free to play in the grass. The child points to the flowers that are flourishing in small circular gardens. The sash on her pink and white calico dress has come undone and the end is in her mouth. Her bonnet has come untied and Norah places Katie on the ground in front of her to re-tie the bonnet and sash, but Katie darts away onto the grass. She picks marigolds and the poppies swaying in the breeze, exclaiming joy as she pulls each one out of the ground. In a flash, a gray uniformed policeman makes his way through the crowd to Katie. He picks her up and carries her across the lawn, swatting the flowers out of her hand and reprimanding her for picking them.

Norah jumps up to retrieve Katie from the policeman. She trips on one of the laces in her shoes and a smelly oyster vender with a handlebar moustache catches her before she falls to the ground. She pushes away from him and rushes after the policeman. She falls again, this time hitting her head on a stone. She tries to get up, but is dizzy, and closes her eyes. And then she hears the voices from long ago Ireland as if they are right in Central Park.

"Ocras! Ocras! It's a wailing cry of hunger and despair. And before her stands bony, withered, and ghost-like beings, their faces and arms covered in soft fur. Norah forces her eyes open to come back to the present and then there are strong arms that help her up and walk her back to the bench. She is given water and a cold cloth for her head. A small lump is forming on her forehead, but she is relieved to see that the policeman is holding Katie's hand and smiling at her. It was the oyster vendor who had helped her and he stands before her now holding out a box of fried oysters. Nellie takes the oysters, thanking him for his help and gives him some coins. He walks away and the policeman says,

"I know your youngster doesn't understand, but there's no picking flowers here in the park, Miss."

"You needn't be so harsh with a child," Norah responds and the policeman grunts something, pats Katie on the head and walks away.

Nellie sits down next to Norah and lifts Katie to set her on her lap. Katie is stuffing oysters in her mouth, as she hums a tune. And then she pulls out a fistful of violets and marigolds she had put in her dress pocket.

Norah and Nellie laugh and hide the flowers.

"Do you want to go home now, Norah. You took quite a fall." She peers at Norah's head.

"I think it isn't serious. Just a small lump, but maybe we should go. You've not been yourself since the ordeal with Sean."

Norah looks dreamily across the park. It was too startling to have been thrust back into the past so easily and then returning to a happy picnic in the park.

"I remembered the past, Nell...Ireland..." but then Norah doesn't say anything further, for suddenly someone sits down next to her. She turns to see that it is Mr. Edward Knox! The apertures between the past and the present at once close and the dark visitors from Ireland fade as Norah relaxes in the warmth of the day and the surprising presence of this handsome gentleman dressed in a blue and white gingham cotton frock, white waist coat, and pantaloons.

"And how many hats do you have with you today, Miss Norah McCabe Murray?" Edward asks, picking up Norah's bonnet that is lying on the grass next to her feet.

"Oh no, some of the flowers from my hat are gone!" she exclaims, taking the hat from Edward and looking at it closely. It is a leghorn bonnet, one of three hats she designed last winter in anticipation of spring customers. None of the bonnets sold and she has worn this one to the park today. The lilac silk ribbon that wraps around the crown and comes down to tie under the chin complements the lilacs and the large dahlia that decorates the inside of the front rim. And now some of the expensive artificial lilac flowers she bought from her jobber, Patrick Corbett, have disappeared. *Maybe they're strewn amongst the flowers in the grass and I'll never find them*, she thinks, but then looks at Edward and decides they aren't that important, after all.

"Shall I look for them?" Edward asks.

Norah puts on her bonnet and ties the ribbon tightly underneath her chin.

"Katie and I'll look for the flowers," Nellie said, standing up with Katie.

Norah stands and reaches for Katie, "I can't bear to have her away from me after what just happened with that horrid policeman!"

Nellie places Katie in Norah's arms, "He was quite stern, but there was no harm done."

"I thought he was quite rough with her and then I saw..."

"What did you see, Norah?" Edward asked.

Norah couldn't speak about the hungry ones, especially to

Edward. Nellie and Edward, or anyone not ever having been to Ireland, would never fathom the ghosts that paraded before her at times.

"I guess it's my overly protective ways!" she said.

"Did you see something I didn't see, Norah?"

"No, no, nothing, really…it's just that I was worried about Katie."

"I promise to hold Katie's hand and never let her out of my sight," Nellie said.

Norah reluctantly puts Katie in Nellie's arms, "Go with Auntie Nell, Katie, and look for Mammy's pretty hat flowers."

Norah trusts Nellie to care for her daughter because Nellie had cared for an infant placed at her doorstep not too long ago. Eventually, the baby was taken away by the mother and Nellie has missed her ever since. Nellie is a natural at motherhood, Norah thinks, even more so than herself. Nellie and Katie skip down the path and step off the edge to peer into the grass looking for Norah's flowers. There are signs scattered across the park instructing park goers how to conduct themselves properly in the park, including staying off the grass.

"Would you like to walk a little? A stroll, we'll call it, rather than a ramble," Edward asked.

"Most people visit the park with a companion or two. Have you no-one to ramble with, Mr. Knox?"

Edward laughs, "My mother, father, and the rest of the Knox family are rambling in perfect style in their carriage throughout this park as we speak. I begged them to let me out so I could exercise my legs and my right to some freedom from my little brothers and sisters."

Edward's face at once alters from amusement to seriousness.

"I apologize. You perhaps aren't free to stroll with me. You have Katie?" Edward asks nervously, hoping Katie was only Norah's charge for the day.

Since meeting Norah, Edward has been unable to stop thinking of this charming and spirited Irish woman. It is more than her image, which is not unattractive, in the least. Norah McCabe does not have the countenance of the pampered aristocratic women he has seen at the balls on Fifth Avenue. Light freckles sprinkle across her nose and a look of defiance crosses her face that is anything but demure. No, he thinks, she is not a typical beauty. Her looks aside his interest is peaked when Norah speaks and her face lights up and radiates a liveliness and eagerness for life. He has not seen this in the women around him. There is a hint of a brogue, but a slight one, and he isn't offended by it and by the ignorance it might imply. Even his dear sister, whom he is close to, does not exhibit the spark and enthusiasm that Norah possesses. Norah was refreshingly candid and openhearted when he met her, although when she burst into tears it had made him uncomfortable. But it also had tugged at his heartstrings for the country of his father's birth. His father's repetitious words to Edward and his sister have been, "I came to this country with one shirt and an Irish shilling." These words have been unconsciously inscribed on his heart and he recognizes his father in Norah. It makes him feel love for his father. He looks at her closely and wonders what her age is. He has to admit that he is smitten and doesn't care if he might just be a greenhorn and buffaloed by this interesting woman.

"Katie *is* my daughter, Mr. Knox. Do you remember me telling you I had been married briefly and my husband died? It's a long and sorrowful story that I don't wish to recollect to you right now. It's a lovely afternoon in spite of policemen and too many rules, so let's stroll, then, as you suggest."

Norah takes Edward's arm and they walk down the pedestrian path and away from the road the carriages are thronging on. When they meet up with Nellie and Katie, Nellie smiles broadly at Norah.

"You two go on a walk this perfect spring day. I'm thoroughly enjoying Katie. We'll meet you back at the bench in an hour's time. Katie and I'll look for your flowers and have our picnic on the bench."

Nellie is pleased that Edward Knox is keenly interested in her friend. She recognizes the name of this fellow! Who doesn't know the father of this son whom it has been said, *Charles Knox is reliable, responsible, and a gentleman.* And although she'd never admit it to Norah, Nellie is relieved that Sean is now out of the picture. She thought him too unreliable and not good enough for her dear friend.

Norah turns to Edward, "I'm ready to ramble on the Ramble, Mr. Knox."

"Call me Edward and I'll call you Norah," Edward says, poking his face around her bonnet. He's relieved she isn't married, but he has a few reservations. Who is this woman surging into his life like the spring flowers that are burgeoning in the park? Just a month ago, the park had been barren of any color and likewise, he felt his life had been colorless and gripped by winter's gloom. But her pleasing face erases any doubt for the present time and he is devoid of any care in the world, intoxicated by spring and Norah McCabe.

Chapter Seven

Edward and Norah walk down Broadway and Edward recites poetry above the din of the city, "The comet that came unannounced out of the north, flaring in heaven, and the strange huge meteor procession, dazzling and clear, shooting over our heads…"

Edward committed to memory a few of the poet's words because he had been impressed that Norah memorized some of Walt Whitman's poetry when she was younger. Edward likes Walt Whitman, though he is not so famous and a controversial figure. The poet has been accumulating friends and attention as a regular visitor to Pfaff's Saloon, a dim and dusky tavern Edward likes to visit. He told Norah that Pfaff's is a gathering place for certain young, cultured journalists and artists who called themselves Bohemians.

"There are rebels, writers, and artists who flaunt convention, and my family has no idea I visit there! My father cannot comprehend the allure of anti-establishment ideas I possess, Norah. And they never even know when I leave home on an evening to go to Pfaff's."

"I'm intrigued by the Bohemians and excited about new ideas and the fervor for Lincoln. I want to share all of this with you, Norah, for you possess a keen mind," he said to her a few weeks ago.

Unlike Edward, Norah has a certain disdain for Walt Whitman who has written disparagingly about Irish Catholics. She tried to explain to him at the time that she wanted nothing to do with politics or any movement.

"I once was a rebel, but I want nothing to do with any revolt. I will not become involved in anything controversial. I believe in women's rights and for the Elizabeth Jennings of the world to have as much freedom as any white woman, but...what can I possibly do about it all!" she had said with exasperation. This discussion had taken place in August when Norah and Edward were sitting in Central Park. Norah had been irritable and disconsolate.

"Other than doing a little writing for Harrigan's old newspaper about these matters, and being a friend to a woman of color in spite of what Five Points biddies say, I have to uphold the laws of the land. I'm a mother and I won't jeopardize Katie's life for any cause, no matter how important!"

Edward had taken Norah's hands in his, mesmerized by how long her fingers were, and how fragile they seemed.

"Abolitionism is radical and it has wild claims, but slavery can't continue for our country to remain a union and prosper. And as far as women's rights, the women aren't as pretty as you, my dear, but don't you want Katie to grow up and be able to vote and have equality with any man or woman? You might have to fight for your daughter to have a good life, Norah."

Norah had pulled her hands from Edward's.

"Please don't tell me how to live my life!"

Edward sat quietly for a long time before speaking to Norah again that day. She, too, had remained still and pensive. He understood her fury had more to do with her past than his ideals or anything he had said. But soon all was forgotten and the two lovers were holding hands and walking through the park.

Norah laughs at Edward's recitation of Walt Whitman's poem and presses close to him. He guides her down the sidewalk while they watch the parade of stomping, marching men in the street that are bellowing out Stephen Douglas' name. Norah watches the men, along with a scattering of women, carry torchlights and the glowing orbs with flowing tails loom over a multitude of heads. At odd moments, she thinks of these lights resembling the string of fireballs that had grazed over New York in July and inspired Walt Whitman to write, *Year of Meteors,* that Edward likes to recite. She had read that the rare occurrence of the majestic sweep of falling stars had a possible foretelling of the future for many.

It is now October and the brittle, frost-filled air pulls the breath from the young lovers' lungs. Their breaths mingle and hover before them and form warm shapes, perhaps heart-like, which wrap around their heads. They are dizzy from this love. Norah has been out of breath since meeting Edward Knox in Central Park in May. Edward, likewise, is full of romance for the singular Norah McCabe. He, however, has disappointed his family, his mother mostly, and ended an early courtship with a daughter of a high-society family. The young, glamorous debutante has aspirations of becoming a concert singer and her voice is rapturous as birdsong, albeit Edward is reminded of the nuptial calling of some birds for mates each time she sings for him and his family. Florence is a darling petite woman and her voice and person are as colorful as a bluebird. He was not against courting her in the beginning. As self-possessed and optimistic as Edward is, and as much as his familial obligations regulate his life, there is an untamed, wild boy-spirit that was boxed up and put away long ago. Florence certainly stirred his social ambitions and had given him happy entertainment, but it is Norah who has extracted that forgotten, hidden boy entombed somewhere in his maturing manhood. When Edward confided to his father that he wanted to end the courtship with Florence because he was in love with the alluring Norah McCabe, he felt he had reached behind his own wings and unclipped them. It felt liberating, but as soon as he professed the truth of his love and looked upon his father's pained face, a countenance etched with the story of deprivation and struggle, he was riddled with guilt.

"I care about the people who live in the Sixth Ward," his father said with his head down. I care about the poor. But I've labored hard so my children will not have to suffer want the way I did as a lad. Norah McCabe is an admirable young woman. She is talented and passionate, but…Edward, you're young… can't you see that she is different from you? She has no connections, education, and where are her people? You were born in this country and she was born in Ireland. It will take time for her to overcome…Edward, please listen to me. I don't wish to be harsh…"

Edward had wanted to interrupt him and defend his love, but he kept quiet and didn't respond. Although he knew all along what his father thought about his relationship with Norah McCabe, to have him air these words about the woman he adored made Edward feel the strength of those words. It was true. His father was pragmatic and a realist, not an unkind and cruel man.

As usual, the evening city streets teem with people and since Norah's flashback of Ireland in Central Park in May, she is uneasy and discomfited in crowds. The two lovers walk by bagpipe players in kilts and one of them lifts his kilt and winks at Norah. There is a dark-skinned organ grinder with his monkey who grabs at her skirts when she walks by. She clings tightly to Edward's arm and tries to breathe in and out slowly, a calming method she has long ago learned.

"I'm all for Mr. Abraham Lincoln! I met the man and he's America's man of the hour, Edward. Call me a Black Republican! I don't give a darn for the boot-lickers at Tammany! They're a bunch of rat-faced, pimping, swindlers!" Norah proclaims, halting a moment to stomp her foot. Edward and Norah laugh loudly.

Edward walks more quickly and pulls Norah through the mass of people on the sidewalk who are shouting back at the marchers. They reach a side street and because there are few people, they walk down it. After a few feet, Edward turns left onto an alley that is empty of anyone. A few stray cats wander through.

"Why are we here?" Norah asks, curious but trusting Edward to take her anywhere, even into a dark alleyway.

Edward gently pushes Norah against a building and leans into her. He is excited and wonders if she can feel his arousal through all of her petticoats and cloak. He takes off his gloves and stuffs them in his waistcoat pocket. And then he cups Norah's face and lightly touches his lips to hers, light as a feather. Ever so delicately, the tip of his tongue touches just inside her lips. Norah shudders and with her eyes closed, relaxes into this tantalizing experience. It is only the second time Edward has kissed her and although a ghostly trembling of past memories with Murray flooded through her the first time, it fled soon after. And when she thinks of Sean and his ardent and hurried desire for her, she is glad it is Edward she is with. Yes, she had been eager for Sean's roughened hands that knew years of living on the seas to be all over her. It had helped to be with Sean so she could forget Murray. But what was this she was undergoing with Edward that shook out fears and sorrows all in one embrace?

Edward steps away and places his hands on Norah's shoulders.

"You ought not to swear so, Norah! It makes me want to kiss you all the more!"

Edward and Norah. Two syllables each, their names are sonorous when spoken together. In early November, the two young lovers visit Pfaff's and although Norah is nonchalant and unimpressed meeting Ada Clare, a feminist writer, as well as playwrights and journalists, she secretly takes pride in the novel experience. She is relieved that Walt Whitman is not present and she and Edward spend a few hours drinking and cavorting with the patrons in the dark cave-like setting. Norah, eager to find common ground, asks Ada Clare if she has ever met Margaret Fuller. Ms. Clare is surprised that Norah McCabe claims to have read Fuller's *Woman in the 19th-Century*. By the end of the evening, Ms. Clare concludes that this interesting woman has indeed shaken off much of her bog-trotting ways, but perhaps the young woman is remiss and too eager to be clothed in the ways of enlightened, educated Protestant women.

"And what did you think of the book, Miss McCabe?" Ms. Clare asks her.

Norah blushes and fidgets with her shawl that is probably too fancy for this dark, basement tavern. She doesn't quite understand what these people are about or what sort of apparel is appropriate to wear. Mostly she has come to Pfaff's with Edward in order to please him, although curiosity has also been the reason.

"I'll be honest and say that there's much I don't understand about her book, but I've found that Margaret Fuller's words echo some of my feelings."

"Really?" Ms. Clare is intrigued. "Tell me more!"

Norah glances over at Edward who is in an earnest conversation with a journalist. He is wearing one of his father's beaver hats and hasn't taken it off inside the saloon. He looks silly wearing it, she thinks, and wishes he'd take it off and come over and rescue her from this intensely, prying woman!

"Though many have suffered shipwreck, still beat noble hearts."

As if Edward hears her thoughts, he rushes to her side and greets Miss Clare.

"You must be Ada Clare!" he says, "I'm Edward Knox."

"Oh, I see…" Ms. Clare said, staring at Edward's beaver hat.

Edward reaches up to remove his hat.

"Pleased to meet you, Mr. Knox…and I do hope you're not a mad hatter!" Ada Clare said, laughing. She does not extend her ungloved hand to Edward. Norah is uneasy wearing her gloves and folds her hands behind her back.

"I'll leave being a mad hatter to my father, Charles Knox."

Ada Clare laughs again and turns to Norah, "I'm sorry to interrupt you, my dear. Now what were you saying about Margaret Fuller's writings?"

Norah hoped this woman had forgotten about her question. She has read and re-read the book, but only certain phrases make real sense to her, and she is certainly not going to talk about shipwrecks!

"You're right, Norah, Margaret died in a tragic shipwreck with her husband and child…and some of her writing was lost, too. There was no one like her! She was a prominent intellectual and a Transcendentalist. She also worked for *The Dial*…oh, I'm going on. I'm sure you know these things already. Please…do tell me what you think of her book."

Edward is surprised that Norah knows of Margaret Fuller. He

had only learned of her through the terrible news of the shipwreck off Fire Island. He smiles radiantly at Norah, this woman who is full of surprises.

Norah pulls off her gloves and places them in her bag. She doesn't know what to say. She doesn't quite know what a Transcendentalist is, not really, except that a group of writers, men of letters, poets, all Protestant and well educated, believe in God being in everything, nature and people. Their words, like Margaret Fuller's, sound romantic and Norah likes the idea of rising above the muck and mire of life. But she wonders if they have much experience with muck and mire like most people she knows. She peers at Edward and sees in his countenance that he believes she knows what she is talking about! A flush of embarrassment in her deception creeps up her neck into her face. She has kept the harrowing details of her life from him and she wants no pity from Edward Knox, but only his love, simple as that.

"What woman needs is not as a woman to act or rule, but as a nature to grow...as a soul to live freely and unimpeded..."

Margaret Fuller's words just come to her and flow right out of her mouth! She is relieved and now wishes to leave this stuffy, elitist underworld of Pfaff's, even if Edward believes it's a freethinking place for all people to speak their minds in equality.

Ada Clare claps her hands, "I agree, Miss McCabe! And I hope that you continue to live freely and grow fully into your own dreams!"

"And you, as well!" Norah said smiling warmly. She turns to Edward, "I'm feeling a little tired. Can we go now?"

Edward and Norah say their goodbyes and leave Pfaff's Saloon to walk out into the night air that is crisp and still. They walk closely, clasping hands as Edward leads her down one street and then another, and eventually they stand alone on a secluded, dark street. He faces Norah and wraps his arms tightly around her. She hasn't paid any heed to where they were walking because her mind is engrossed in the evening's conversation with Ada Clare. Perhaps if she studied more, but there is no time for books. Her hats aren't selling, she can't pay her rent, and Sean has decided to visit her a few times to ask for her forgiveness. And this evening, Edward has asked her why she never allows him to call at her apartment. How can she! The streets in her neighborhood sometimes pile up with two feet of garbage! She always meets Edward elsewhere for their rendezvous.

Norah's mind reels back to the present with Edward's arms around her. She removes herself from him and looks into his trusting, sweet face and realizes he knows very little about her life. He is quite a few years younger than her years, but they never speak of their age difference. In some respects, Edward is more mature than she, except in love. And in this, she knows she has the upper hand.

"I want to marry you, Norah McCabe! And I want to be a father to little Katie," Edward says. His eyes are full of the future and possess no dark aspect in them. Norah steps away from him and looks up to the sky to peer at the formation of the stars. She can see them clearly and isn't it well worth it to see the hope of stars! There is a bigger world beyond New York and Five Points, and a world bigger than herself. And then she kisses Edward again and again.

Just the week before, Norah had stopped by the grocer's in Chatham Square to glance through Godey's Lady's Magazine, but they had all been sold. Instead, she saw a newspaper called Scientific American and as she flipped through the pages, she saw drawings and pictures of stars, including the Pleiades star cluster. They were bright blue stars that swarmed together like jewels. They sparkled and cast a spell on her. The newspaper had printed a painting of them glittering like fireflies.

Norah pulls away from kissing Edward and looks up into the sky again, "Do you see them? The stars are dancing women! They're free and liberated from all the encumbrances on this earth. Maybe Margaret Fuller is one of them."

"I love you, Norah McCabe! And if you marry me, I'll not encumber you, except with my love."

Norah eases into Edward's arms again. He is clad in the best wool and clothing money can buy, for he is the son of Charles Knox who owns a department store and a few houses. If she marries Edward, she and Katie will be liberated from dangling over the edge of the cliff of poverty. And surely now, she loves him as much as she loves the stars in the sky.

"A springtime wedding, Edward! Can we have a May wedding in Central Park?"

"Can I possibly wait half a year to call you my own?"

Norah says with solemnity, "I will never be owned by any man or anyone, Edward Knox, but I do wish to marry you."

Chapter Eight

Norah returns home after agreeing to marry Edward and watches Katie Marion sleep. She leans in close to Katie's face and inhales the baby scent that reminds her of innocence and the persistence of life. The child's features poignantly resemble Murray's. Katie will never know her father unless she keeps him alive for her. She worries Murray is slipping from her memory each time she is with Edward and is carefree and happy. She gives Katie a light kiss on her forehead, thinking just how different it is with Edward than how it had been with Murray. How tempting to marry someone like Edward Knox.

A restless few days ensue with lingering uncertainties before Norah decides to follow her heart with her hat dreams. Each time she walks the streets she notices women, from the rag picker to the shop owner, more animated and pronounced in their countenances and strides. What these women are experiencing she doesn't know and she feels it in herself, too. Could change come so rapidly that no one can explain or define it? Once, Norah watered a plant and watched it grow taller as if it was reaching up and giving thanks. What water is this that is giving nurture and confidence in the midst of such uncertain times? This new spirit cannot be entirely from the thunderous speeches of the feminists that are becoming more vociferous in New York. For her, it issues from the turning of the soil of her heart, preparing it for some kind of planting. She envisions a fresh style and elegance in each hat she crafts and thinks of the women she watches on the streets who might wear them. She enjoys the deftness of touch her fingers have when manipulating fabric into hats. There is creative play and a myriad of colorful designs become possible. All of this has certainly been a surprise. With few sales and less money to purchase materials from jobbers, she is welcoming more originality in the design of her hats. Feverishly working on new hats in the corner of her apartment while Katie sleeps in the evenings, Norah slips into a shadow self that has been following her for years. She is sketching wild designs of pompous looking hats as well as small, delicate ones with a single artificial flower. She has drawers full of drawings and whether they ever became hats, she doesn't know. It is the freedom to think, experiment, and create that she has come to love more than following the latest fashion and trying to imitate it. Perhaps this newness has something to do with Mr. Edward Knox, but it is more than that. Yes, this young, gracious, and interesting man from an established business family in New York has given her a warm acceptance of herself, but it is also the paucity and scarcity of the times, her times, and these times when whispers of liberation have come to women. She is making hats that please her. And in spite of the guards at Central Park forbidding the picking of any flower, including wild flowers, Norah has secretly picked a few wild ones to dry. She adds color and dips them in paraffin before attaching them to her hats.

But after this long and wonderful time of frenetic joy, she quietly tucks her hats away because she has to make a real living. It is the maddening month of March. Abraham Lincoln has been inaugurated and the country is breaking in half, but not in equal parts. Norah reads the newspapers and is perplexed. This monster of slavery has its own interpretation of freedom in regard to states' rights and is now demanding that freedom be cut in two pieces. It is taking its share and sulking off, its freedom one-sided, lop-sided;

this, a freedom of ignorance, many are thinking in the north.

And so it is that Norah is a lucky one to have secured a job, although it isn't taking custom orders for making hats. Edward introduced her to the two Devlin brothers at their department store and through his recommendation they hired her as a cutter. She is working long hours and doesn't see Katie until late in the evenings. And her income isn't all that grand. On the other hand, she and Katie have been saved from sinking into poverty, for a few southern states have seceded and the city is suffering with people out of work and living on the streets. The hoop skirts and all sorts of goods have piled up in New York factories because the south is no longer buying them and is not paying its debts!

Norah told Harrigan that the Devlin owners are Irish men who have made good just as Charles Knox has made good. Harrigan is one for keeping a list of the Irish making good in America and publishing it in his newspaper. Norah likes the look of the Devlin store, which is a five-story, late Italianate temple-like building whose interesting weathered stone surfaces ranks of finely proportioned rounded windows. When Edward took her to see where she was going to work, she was impressed.

"They cater to gentlemen and boys alike, Norah. There's ready-made clothing, a custom department, and a furnishing department. Many of my shirts, underwear, collars, cuffs, umbrellas, and neckwear have been bought from this store."

It is the custom department where Norah has been hired to work in and she is grateful, but would like to ask the Devlin brothers if they have any plans to make women's clothing.

"The thought of cutting out patterns for your underwear seems somehow absurd, Edward," she said, laughing. Edward didn't laugh. He was taking it all quite seriously and so should she.

Norah cuts and measures all day long, until her fingers are red and sore, and her neck hurts from bending over. When she designs her hats in her apartment, she does much of the work with the hat bodies at eye level. At Devlins' store, she has to sit at a low table and is instructed not to get up until it is time for lunch and then to go home. If she needs to use the privy, permission from the manager must be received!

Now when Norah walks through the streets and reads the newspapers, the flurry of optimism she felt amongst her sex is hidden, just like her hats packed in boxes. There is great anxiety that is almost palpable over the southern states defiantly having left the allegiance of their union to build a flimsy new confederacy.

"They want to inhabit their old ways, slave-mongering ways, and they hate change!" Norah states to Edward. He, too, rants about the times they are living in.

"How can the millions of dollars in debt the southern states owe be paid back to their northern creditors? And to my father! Did you know that in January, a few prominent businessmen, including my father, insisted that James Buchanan force, if necessary, Fort Sumter at Charleston, Fort Pickens at Pensacola, and other federal posts in the South to stay in the union. It's a disaster!"

"But Abraham Lincoln is now the president..."

"Is the president a hypocrite, Norah?" Edward interrupts.

"He's anti-slavery, supposedly, but he's said that his purpose is not to interfere with the institution of slavery."

After this conversation with Edward, Norah felt dark in mood and spirit. It was bad enough she had to cut out men's underwear and shirts, but now America is falling apart and her Mr. Abraham Lincoln she believed in is not acting the hero she considers he should be acting

Just before Lincoln's election, Elizabeth sat in Norah's and Nellie's apartment worrying over the outcome. She was holding Katie on her lap when she blurted out, "Did you read *The Daily News* today? Fernando Wood's brother, Benjamin, said that if Republicans won, we'd be finding Negroes amongst us thicker than blackberries!" Katie had shouted, "Blackberries, Mama!" And Elizabeth had looked down at her and replied, "Yes, Miss Katie, that is not such a terrible thing, is it, to be a blackberry." And Katie had laughed and called Elizabeth a blackberry. Norah and Nellie were quiet and said nothing for a few moments and then Norah told Katie not to call Miss Beth (as she always called her) a blackberry for that was a fruit you picked in summer to eat.

"There'll be war and it won't be about slavery, not really, because most abolitionist northerners don't want no African sitting down in restaurants with them and making the same money they make. Northerners have high and mighty principles, alright, but when push comes to shove, they'd rather shove us Africans right back down south or even back to Africa."

"No, Beth, I don't think Mr. Lincoln is this way."

"Where have you been, girl? Even kindly Mr. Lincoln proposed a movement to send us to Haiti. Some of the lily-white abolitionists are saying our chains should come off and we should be free, but we all know they want us to be free somewhere else!"

"Edward says it's all about keeping the Union together and if secession lasts, Mr. Lincoln will lose the support of financial backers and then the Republican Party will be undermined. I don't understand it all, but it's about politics first and foremost."

Katie squirms on Elizabeth's lap, feeling her agitation. She scrambles down to the floor and runs around the room reciting, "I want blackberries...blackberry pie, Mama!"

Norah is nervous, not knowing how to answer her friend or continue the conversation. And she wishes she could make a pie to make everything better. But there's no sugar in the house and she doesn't know how to bake a pie, anyway. Maybe she'd like to learn, she thinks, her mind longing to go where there is quiet and something simple as pie.

"If the bonds of slavery really are broken, the African will still be broken and it will take a long time to heal. I understand these things, Norah, in a way you can never understand."

Norah sighs and gets up to pour them both more tea. She thinks that no matter how many conversations she has with Elizabeth about how the Irish people lived with the British lording over them like they were slaves, Elizabeth states it's not the same. It has started to create a gulf in their friendship and Norah is weary of trying to persuade her friend she understands. Perhaps she just doesn't and can't, but who can understand anyone else's suffering, anyway? She has had to ignore the insults she receives from her neighbors about her relationship with Elizabeth, too. She doesn't want to step on Elizabeth's feelings over North and South, black and white, Republican and Democrat, and all that comes in between. She just wants to be her friend.

A few weeks later, Norah is walking to work whispering aloud to herself, "I am suffocated and lost when I have not the bright feeling of progression." She quietly repeats Margaret Fuller's words as she walks. Speaking the words aloud gives her resolve until fresh vigor rises within her like the first buds of springtime that spread over the branches of trees in a mad rush to get on with growing. Soon she arrives at the store and walks down into the basement to sign in with the other employees. She looks down at her skirts and wishes she had worn something else. Her clothes are drab and worn out and she feels ugly. A week after Norah started working at the store, her manager had taken her to her office to reprimand her about her fancy clothing being inappropriate and that it made the other girls uncomfortable.

"But this is a department store, Miss Johnson..."

"I don't expect back talk or insolence from my employees, Miss McCabe!"

Fine and dandy, you clucking hen, I'll be wearing my woolens then, but I'll be walking in wearing my own fine hats that I just might forget to take off, Norah had said under her breath after leaving the manager's office.

Norah is still stinging from Miss Johnson's words and the way the girls in the department treat her, but wearing one of her designed hats helps alleviate her discomfort. She reaches up to adjust the hat she has worn to work today and smiles to herself.

"Norah McCabe! From the Sixth Ward! Did ye forget to get dressed this morn?" Nancy O'Reilly said to her as she passed by, jostling her and knocking her hat off, "But ain't you the lady with the fancy hat!"

Norah picks up her hat from the floor and puts it back on. The taunts each day are worsening. She walks away, but Molly, another fine specimen from the ranks of Five Points tenements brushes against her, "Did ye wash your face this morning, Norah? It looks to be getting darker by the day!"

Other women from Norah's old neighborhood who work at Devlin's have come into the basement. They giggle and stare at her. Norah has heard their loud whispers about her at the lunch table.

"The high and mighty Norah McCabe is a milliner with big notions and has now moved away from us because she's so grand. And she's been seen coursing around the streets of New York arm and arm with a Negress."

When Norah told Nellie what she had heard, Nellie tried to console her.

"What really irritates them isn't so much that you've bettered yourself, for I've heard they were sympathetic for your plight when you suffered heartache after the shipwreck. They think highly of you for raising Katie alone, Norah, but they're just jealous."

"Why would they be so? We're all working our fingers off at that store together!" Norah had responded.

"Oh, Norah, they're watching you closely each evening after your shift is over. They're right there on the street when your young, dashing Mr. Edward Knox, the son of the illustrious Charles Knox, comes to meet you. You must know that it is the dream and envy of nearly every single girl — Irish, German, English, or a lowly native, to clutch the arm in romance with a fine gentleman coming from the upper classes. With Mr. Charles Knox's success, who remembers that he had walked from Delaware to New York City after arriving on a ship from Ireland?"

Norah realized it was true what Nellie said.

"But they all should be happy and hopeful from such success by someone like old Mr. Knox! These mean Irish girls need to know that Irish boys, like Charles Knox and the Devlin brothers, lived hardscrabble lives and worked like mules, but they shuffled off their bog trotting ways to became successful men. These men, Nellie, now flow in the same stream of commerce as Elisha, Daniel, and John Brooks of Brooks Brothers. These girls should try to do the same and not resent me for trying to do the same!"

"Go piss up a tree!" Norah shouts at Molly, shoving her out of her way. Molly and a few other girls circle Norah and prevent her from going up stairs to work. Molly pulls Norah's hat from her head and throws it to another girl.

"Anyone want a hat? Catch!" the girl yells. Norah's hat is tossed back and forth from girl to girl. This goes on for what seems to Norah to be forever, but it is only a few minutes. And then the hat falls to the floor and one girl and then another stomp on it. All the while, Norah is held back by Nancy O'Reilly who is as big and muscular as any man who works on the docks. When Norah finally frees herself from Nancy's grip, the girls leave her alone and walk upstairs to work, laughing and carrying on, their words of derision echoing in Norah's head. After they have all left her, Norah looks at her ornate trimmed bonnet lying on the floor. It is crushed and many of the artificial flowers have fallen off and are scattered on the floor. They are dear, Parisian flowers she had bought from Patrick Corbett. She had haggled over the price, but in the end, she had to pay an exorbitant amount of money for them. Now they are strewn across the floor as if a flower girl in joy had dropped them there during a wedding ceremony. Norah quickly picks up her bonnet and notices that the plaid ribbon ties and tulle ruching have been torn and soiled, too. Filth from Five Points streets that has adhered to the heels of the boots of the employees at Devlin's had ground itself into her hat! Norah picks up the colorful and expensive artificial flowers from the floor, crying as she does. She doesn't realize that the manager has come into the room.

"Miss McCabe, this dissension and carrying on is uncalled for. It's an honor to work at this prominent establishment, especially when many people in this city are out of work. But since your arrival, you've incited the other girls to envy you because of your high-minded ways. My dear girl, why is it that you are wont to taunt them each day, first with your clothing and now your hats? Don't you know many of them wear threadbare skirts? I forbid you to wear your hats from now on!"

With this last dictate, the manager leaves the room and click-clacks up the stairs in her finely laced fancy boots. "The nerve!" Norah says aloud. Miss Johnson wears more fashionable skirts, shawls, and boots than any of the other female employees at Devlin's! Norah finishes picking up the pieces of her hat and sits down on the floor, pulling her skirts around her. She has to put the pieces of her thoughts back together in her mind just like she has to put this poor hat back together. She can clean the hat, sew it up differently, and recreate an entirely new one in spite of the damage. "Miss Johnson is wrong! "I don't think I'm better than the other girls!"

Norah fumes and ponders her plight. She can't fool herself or anyone for she is still in Five Points even if she is living in Chatham Square. She remembers well coming from Ireland and the ragged clothing she wore for years until she learned to sew, barter for cloth, and open her used clothing store. As she calms down and can think clearly, she knows what she has to do. She has to devise an entirely new way to make a living for herself right now, even if it isn't selling her hats and working in a department store. She stands up, grabs her shawl from the hook, and climbs the stairs. It is time to pay a visit to Mr. James Harrigan to see about working for him full time and for more than just a pittance. But first she has to give her notice to Miss Johnson and then she must hurry home to put on one of her prettiest gowns. She can't be visiting the fancy-man dandy, himself, Mr. Harrigan, dressed in her old woolens.

Chapter Nine

"The saints be praised! It's lovely Norah come to visit her old friend!" Harrigan exclaims when Norah walks into his office. It is late in the day and his employees have already gone home. He is sipping tea with his feet up on his desk while reading an edition of the Tribune.

"Don't get up, James," Norah says as he puts the paper down and untangles his legs, preparing to greet her. Norah doesn't want him all over her with more mushiness than she can withstand. And then his awful cologne will cling to her when she meets Edward later. As Harrigan comes towards her, she thinks of Edward. He won't even care about another man's cologne, and she also thinks how odd it is that he isn't jealous of Sean. When she told Edward about Sean's visits, he was only curious as to what sort of fellow he is. And Edward always laughs over Norah's descriptions and stories about Harrigan, the best dressed newspaperman about town. So it is that Norah feels she could have many men in her life and Mr. Edward Knox would only smile and want to be friends with them all.

"No, no, Harrigan. Sit down...sit back down. I've just come to have a chat. You look too comfortable to get up. I can sit here and we can blow kisses at one another."

Harrigan relaxes back into his chair with his feet back up on his desk and Norah sits down in the large leather chair opposite him and boldly puts her feet on his desk. She is wearing her favorite Victorian spats. They laugh and Norah is hopeful that everything is going to be fine for her and Katie.

"I'm lonely, Norah. I have no real friends, but you, and you've left me out of your life for much too long."

"You're lying, Harrigan. You have friends and go on picnics and out to dinner with them."

Harrigan looks down at his cravat, fumbling with it nervously. He hasn't said much about these friends to Norah. He insinuated they are similar to some of the young men who meet at Pfaff's and discuss homosexuality. He told her they are sort of a secret society because many of them have laudable jobs in the city and don't want their liberal views known. Harrigan had confided in her that he had begun to socialize with them in the last year. Norah was pleased for him to have new friends, for she had been his only friend for many years.

"Well, Norah, I don't see them much anymore." He sighs and fusses with his tie.

"I don't make a good fit in any social setting, it seems." He smiles weakly at Norah, but then sits up at his desk and looks intently at her.

"But enough of this talk about me. I am lonely, but I'm also very content. My newspaper has more readers than ever before and I'm not so afraid to write articles that are controversial, thanks to you, dear Norah. And now here you are looking rapturous! I can only hope you've come to tell me you want to work for me again!"

Norah is pleasantly surprised.

"I'll be honest. My hats aren't selling. Not a single one for months now. Edward found me a job..."

"Yes, Edward Knox. You did say you were stepping out with the chap. But what of poor Sean working on the docks? And how is it I'm to have two of your suitors to contend with now?"

"Let me finish! Edward found me a job as a cutter at Devlin's, but I just quit today because the other women...well, never mind why, but I had to quit. I haven't told Edward yet, nor Nellie, and I'm not so proud, Harrigan, to ask you for help. No, not a hand-out, as I need to make my own way, but I fear Katie and I will have to move in with Mam and Da if I don't find a way to make a living. I need a position where I don't have to sell my soul or have my clothing criticized and my hats torn off my head…"

Norah didn't expect to be so emotional, but tears come and she wipes them away with the back of her hand.

Harrigan stands and gently pulls Norah up and hugs her. His scent will be all over her now, she thinks, but she is touched by his tenderness. She quietly sheds a few tears against his shoulder and it feels good. He gives her his handkerchief, she sits back down, and he leaves her to make them cups of tea.

"Are you still working at the House of Industry?" he asks, when he returns.

"Not really. Katie stays there during the day until Nellie picks her up. On weekends, I help with housekeeping and teach Sunday school. It's an arrangement I have with them."

"Probably not ideal for Katie to be amongst the children just come from the streets, but the institution has become respectful. In fact, I'd like you to write an article about the House of Industry. Of course, that's it! What do you say?"

Harrigan claps his hands and smiles broadly, his handsome eyes cheerful.

"Well, we would need to discuss hours, pay…"

"Can you come each day around eight o'clock? And then you can leave here around two so you have time to retrieve Katie and spend important time with her. On Wednesdays, you will have to stay late because the paper, as you know, goes to the printer on Thursday morning, but you can bring Katie here to play. She'll grow up getting to know how a first rate newspaper is run and might go into the business someday herself."

"Honestly, James, I don't think working so few hours will suit me…at least not until all this war talk is over and we're selling to the south again and my hats are selling…and things aren't so confusing and chaotic with Mr. Lincoln."

"Norah! Stop, my dear! These times are trying, but Mr. Lincoln is going to take our country to a new place. It's temporary, all of this. Not that I'm not worried about the unemployed men living on the streets, but I do believe it will change. And we have to have our news to get the message of change out there, don't we? We have to print those stories you always told me I should print. Stories that are worthy and stories about our new president! I might even change the name so we can become more inclusive and not always worrying about Bishop Hughes, Tammany Hall, and pleasing our people."

Harrigan is animated and talking so fast and excitedly that he knocks over his teacup. He and Norah clean up the spilled tea and save his papers from being ruined. They laugh again, but Norah doesn't quite know how to tell him that she needs more hours and more pay just to survive.

"And now we must discuss your pay, Norah, so sit down, please," Harrigan says, as if reading her thoughts.

"Will $8.00 a week suit you?"

Norah can't believe her ears. How can Harrigan afford to give her this much? Maybe his paper is doing much better now that there is so much news that is controversial and frightening. There are so many newspapers all over the city and the *Irish-American* is no *Tribune, Sun,* or *Herald.*

"I know what you're thinking. No worries. I've been very careful with my savings over the years and it's now time to invest in this newspaper. And I want to invest in you! I'll give small raises to my other two employees, but you'll be my assistant."

Norah doesn't want his pity and charity and his pay offer just doesn't seem proportionate to the few hours she'll be working.

"It's not charity, my dear. Not at all." He knows her well. "You've already had newspaper experience and you're a smart one. You're certainly deserving of a good income."

Norah leaves Harrigan's office feeling more optimistic than she has felt in quite some time. Harrigan and she have both changed and grown through many obstacles and personal problems. To think that now Harrigan is willing to change the name of his father's newspaper, for there had been a time when he had been adamant about not changing a jot or tittle of his precious paper. When she left, he agreed she should start in two days and they will begin by discussing a name change and then she will write an article about the House of Industry. Yes, the times are rapidly changing in many ways! Norah went on an errand and walked home, humming the tune, *St. Patrick's Day in the Morning*. People smiled at her and she smiled back. She became so engrossed in this new turn of events that she completely forgot she was supposed to meet Edward in front of the department store after work. And then she became so busy helping Nellie with dinner, it still hadn't occurred to her.

Norah has a spark of new energy as she cleans the apartment and hauls up water for their baths. In the evening after dinner, Katie is asleep and Nellie and Norah are sitting together in the living room that has a small kitchenette attached to it. In the corner of the room Norah sits at a table and her nimble fingers are attaching organdy flowers and lace to a hat body she purchased months ago. It is the popular oval spoon bonnet that many women have been wearing since spring. After meeting with Harrigan, she became so optimistic that she went to Patrick Corbett to purchase some trimmings for the hat. She is certain she will be out interviewing all sorts of people for the newspaper and wants to wear at least one hat that is the latest style. The saints be praised, Norah thinks, their newspaper is going to become as popular as the *Post* or *Tribune*, maybe even the *Sun*! Nellie is working on a lesson for the next school day and in spite of the boisterous street noise outside their front window, it is peaceful inside. Norah hums a ditty as she works, but suddenly jumps up from her chair, dropping her hat and tools.

"I forgot all about Edward! He was to meet me outside of Devlin's after work!"

"Does he know our address? Have you never invited him here?" Nellie asks.

"No, I haven't. He's asked to call for me here, but I've always met him elsewhere. And then he usually sends me home in a carriage."

"Are you ashamed of where we live? There are worse places, Norah. But I know how you feel. Mother and Father live in Albany and I have my mail delivered to the school, so they don't know my address. I don't want them to worry. But really, is it so bad with Mr. Barker watching out for us?"

Norah sits down and thinks a minute. It isn't shame over where she lives that has kept her from inviting Edward here. Edward knows she lives in Chatham Square. She doesn't know, really, why she wants to keep Edward away from her life in Chatham Square. Sean has been a frequent visitor, but Sean is of her world, her Irish world, and Edward, although Irish, is not. Edward is different and has lived extravagantly, although he doesn't put on airs. He's just young, a free thinker, jovial, and he loves her and everyone. He's almost too good to be true, she thinks. *That's it, then! He's too good to be true and I need to keep him at a distance just to be sure of him.*

"Edward is like that rare sweet after dinner, Nellie. I adore him, but I want to keep this friendship away from my everyday life. Does that make sense?"

"No, it doesn't. He's asked you to marry him and you tell him yes and then no, but he says he will wait. And then Sean comes back with his tail between his legs begging for forgiveness and you tell him he'll have to earn it. It's clear to me that you have too many suitors and I have none at all!"

Nellie laughs, shuffles her papers together, and turns down the kerosene lamp she is reading by. Norah looks over at Nellie and is happy for her friendship with her. Nell isn't jealous of her, for it isn't in her nature to be so. But Norah sometimes feels foolish like a silly schoolgirl when she is with Nellie. Nellie has never had anyone but a school chum who has shown her any romantic interest. Norah thinks Nell is very attractive with her light brown curls and slate-blue eyes, but she's a trite too reserved and although expansive in her philosophy of life, she dresses and acts conservatively. She states she'd never go to Pete Williams to dance with Norah and she rather fill her time with teaching and volunteering. Norah gets up to look out the window, feeling chagrin over the preoccupation with herself, for she should be helping those less fortunate and not going out with Edward all the time. She notices a few people huddled together in ragged clothing under the street lamp. There are so many poor people and the times are getting worse. Maybe she should alter her dresses for everyday wear for some of the women she sees on the street wearing the same dirty dresses. She turns to Nellie to talk to her about this, but there is a knock on the door.

"Nellie? Norah? It's Mr. Barker here. You've a visitor who came knocking on my office window downstairs. Are you gals decent? Can we come in?"

Norah opens the door and there stands Edward, his silk top hat crooked on his handsome head standing with Mr. Barker who looks worried and ready to scold.

"Forgive me, Norah, but you weren't at Devlin's today and when I asked the other girls where you were, they laughed. And then I walked up and down the street for nearly an hour, but saw it was a lost cause and gave up and went home. I had dinner with my family and then told them I had to go out. I knew you lived in this neighborhood, but I wasn't certain exactly where and so I've been knocking on people's doors and nearly got my head blown off by an angry drunk across the street!"

"Come in. I'm so sorry. So much has happened and I forgot all about meeting you. I've left Devlin's and won't be working there…"

"Were you sacked? How will you be able to pay your rent? You haven't been selling those hats of yours, either!" Mr. Barker says as he steps into the living room and Norah wishes he'd just leave.

"No…no, I wasn't sacked and I have another job, Mr. Barker. Please don't worry. I can pay the rent. Edward is a friend of mine. Did he tell you his last name? Knox. His father owns the Knox store. And he helped me find my job and we're good friends…"

Mr. Barker's face changes from distress to all smiles. "Yes, yes, of course. You don't say! A fine store, indeed! I have a beaver hat from your father's store that I wear all the time."

Mr. Barker turns to leave, "I must go. The Missus is going to be concerned. Now I know you're in good hands. But don't be keeping her up too late now, young man!" he says to Edward, winking and smiling, before closing the door behind him.

Nellie goes into the kitchen and prepares tea for everyone. She invites Edward to sit down and pours him a cup of tea in a delicate fine-bone china cup. But before he sits down, there is another knock at the door and when Norah opens it, there stands Mr. Barker again, and this time Sean is with him, grinning from ear to ear.

"Ye are a popular one, Norah McCabe, but you should be telling your gentlemen friends not to come calling so late in the evening from here on out!"

Chapter Ten

And so it is that the two young men who adore Norah with all their human fallibilities meet for the first time. They are very dissimilar men in regards to class, education, and temperament. Sean left school when he was twelve and Edward is years younger and doing studies at St. John's College. They have every reason to be at each other's throats in regards to the woman they think they can lay their lives down for. But rather than a competitive, territorial spirit emerging between them, they bond immediately. Norah and Nellie sit quietly while the men enthusiastically converse over tea, soda bread, and jam. It seems they hardly notice Nellie and Norah sitting at the table.

At one point, Nellie looks at Norah and raises an eyebrow in wonder. Surely, both men know that the other is in pursuit of her. Why Nellie has not caught their eye in romantic interest is a wonder, for she has much to praise, but Sean and Edward were smitten by Norah McCabe before they ever met Nellie. It can only ever be that they will care for Nellie merely as a friend of Norah's. Norah smiles back at Nellie with the assurance that she understands what is happening between the two men. She has forgiven Sean for his indecent discrepancy at Pete's, but has kept his ardor at bay because the course of passion, like a powerful river, has changed and it is now carving out another direction in her life. She hasn't spoken to Sean about her romance with Edward, but she has alluded to their friendship. She will always love Sean as much as she loves a member of her own family. She couldn't bear to not have him in her life. But it has become more important for her to follow this compelling route that includes creating new tributaries for Edward's affections. Nellie has chastised her for stringing Sean along, but it just isn't so. She has explained to Nell that her love for Sean has developed into a place that is serene and deep, and there is no reason to journey any further with it.

Norah listens to the two men she cherishes and it occurs to her what has formed their immediate attachment. Her Da once told her that Irish hearts are knit together in Celtic knots and that ancient circles and patterns form their rib bones. Surgeons, he said, could see these same Celtic designs when opening Irish chests on the operating table. She had laughed at Da's exaggerated storytelling, but now she understands what he means. Irish people, no matter how diverse or what continent they live on, must have hearts fused together because of the same blood that dwells within their veins.

"Father says this panic is worse than in '57," Edward states, "the merchants, department stores, including our store, have merchandise piling up because the southern states have gone crazy. They're not paying their debts! Lincoln is trying his damnedest to keep the union together."

"The storeowners should be selling their goods at half price to the poor ones on the streets who've lost their jobs," Sean responds.

"First they're trying to get nearly full price by putting ads in the papers," Edward says.

"There's people looking for shelter in the police stations and going to the poor houses. I can't walk into my building but there's entire families sleeping on the stoops. The landlord comes in the night to shoo them away. One night, the fellows and I brought in a mother and her two wee ones. We gave them some bread and they stayed a couple of nights before finding shelter. They're mighty fine people, but the man of the house lost his job in the shipbuilding."

Norah sees that Sean is worried when he tells Edward this.

"We've had more people coming for meals and seeking shelter at the mission," Nellie interjects, "and we've had fewer donations. People are living in deplorable conditions, but that isn't new. It's just worse now."

"These are some of the issues I'll be writing about at my new job," Norah says, at once feeling self-conscious.

Edward and Sean turn to Norah and ask, "Where?"

"Harrigan's paper again, but this time I'm his assistant and he's paying me a weekly wage. My hours will be until 2:00 so I can have time with Katie."

"That man's right strange, Norah. I'd not be trusting him again," Sean says.

"You don't understand him. And I'd say you're jealous."

"Nothing there to be worried about, being that he's a bit of a Nancy boy."

"Harrigan? Really? Norah, how interesting," Edward says, looking at Norah in wonder and interest. This woman is always surprising him.

"Harrigan is intelligent, warm-hearted, and one of my best friends, so I'd appreciate you all being kind,"

"You almost married the man!" Sean said. "Begorrah, I don't understand how you almost tied the knot with a Nancy-boy and you've said no to me."

Edward stands up from the table, his cheerful countenance disappearing. He knows who Harrigan is and he knows that this Sean is a friend and was once a suitor, but listening to Sean just now makes him uncomfortable. He likes the rough acting fellow, but is Norah considering tying the knot with him? What does Norah intend to do with all of them, anyway, he wonders. And could there be others?

"I have an early morning class and then I'm helping Father with inventory. I should be going."

Sean stands up and shakes Edward's hand vigorously, "It's a pleasure meeting a fine gentleman as yourself, Edward. I hope we meet up again."

Sean faces Norah, "Let's bring the lad with us to Pete's to show him some dancing!"

Norah walks with Edward to the door and Sean sits back down. He realizes his mistake in bringing up Pete's. He wonders if Norah will ever dance with him again. He engages in a conversation with Nellie as Edward and Norah stand by the door talking in whispers.

"I didn't realize there are so many interested in marrying you. And you've been married already, and maybe you've been married more than once?" Edward asks in a low voice.

"There's much you don't know about my life and if you can't accept me as I am, you'd best not come around." She looks away from Edward's pleading face before turning back to him.

"I can't hide who I am, Edward. If you don't like what you've heard this evening, ye should spend more time with your family's high falutin' friends and forget about me."

"Oh, Norah," Edward moans as he leans into her and presses his lips to her neck.

Norah looks over at Nellie and Sean who are engrossed in an animated conversation. She is relieved that they aren't paying any attention to her and Edward.

"I don't care, not really, how many have loved you and even love you now. I know Sean does, too, for I see it in his eyes," Edward quietly tells her, "but I want to be the one you marry."

When Norah is with Edward, she doesn't think about the hard things in her life, or that she was once a poor child from Ireland. She is merely overflowing with the sweetness and sighs of young love. Everything and everyone, but her Katie, seem to fade into the background, including Sean. But when she glances at this young warrior from her childhood sitting at the table with Nellie, this young love fades.

"Can you love me without wanting to marry me? Can you love me without knowing whether tomorrow we'll be together?" Norah whispers back. The closeness to Edward arouses her and she desires to kiss him and hold him.

"I can. I will, but I need to touch your hair, kiss your neck…"

Norah pulls away. She desires him so fervently! Sean's chair scrapes the floor as he gets up and Norah backs away from Edward. Sean walks over to the two of them.

"Tis more romance than a dime store novel goin' on here. I felt the heat across the room. I like this lad, Norah," Sean said looking at Edward, "but I'm not going to compete with him. You'll have to be making a decision. It's either him or me."

Sean turns to Nellie and says goodbye and then he nods to Edward. He gives Norah a peck on the cheek and leaves, slamming the door hard behind him.

Edward's face is grim.

"I'm sorry, Norah. I won't compete either. Please give me your answer this Sunday when we meet in the park."

Edward says goodbye to Nellie, gives Norah a peck on the cheek, and leaves, but he doesn't slam the door. If Norah can make a decision based on who slams the door and who doesn't, it'd be easy. She would choose Edward, for she has had enough doors slammed on her and wants no more. But it isn't that easy, and after forgiving Sean for his sexual indiscretion, she wants him always to be in her life. She wants Edward in the immediate present and she wants him more passionately than she had realized. But Edward is in the present and she wants his love now. As Nellie clears the table while commenting about Norah's love life, she playfully scolds her friend, but Nellie's voice dims in the background. Norah only hears her own thoughts. She will marry Edward come May. And as for Sean, she believes he will never leave her, but what she doesn't dare think of is whether Edward would leave her if she said yes to Sean.

Chapter Eleven

April brought more than showers and wedding plans for Norah. On April 12th, South Carolina forces fire on Federal Fort Sumter and President Lincoln declares it an act of insurrection. He immediately calls for 75,000 volunteers to sign up for three months and Edward Knox heeds the call. In spite of his family's objection and Norah's pleading and tears, he enlists in the 8th New York Volunteers. He fears his handsome baby face might not get him accepted into service and draws a moustache above his lip and opens up his own recruiting office. Norah is incredulous that he feels more passion for righting the wrong of the south than staying with her in New York. He really is too young to enlist his services to bear arms against an insurrection, but his height and determination get him in.

"When this ludicrous rebellion is nipped in the bud...and it will be soon, we'll be married," Edward whispers to Norah before marching off with his regiment amidst the cheers and fanfare in a parade that Bishop Hughes arranged. The lovers had spent most of the previous night on the sofa in Norah's apartment murmuring words of affection and caressing one another with a passion that was new to them. Their ardor had been quietly contained in the months of their stepping out together, but at the brink of possible loss, it had cascaded through them as a snowmelt in spring.

"Even if Katie and Nellie weren't sleeping in the other rooms, I wouldn't devour you as I'd like," Edward says. But then he kisses Norah's neck, his lips moving further down to her décolletage and the enticing outline between her breasts. Animal-like instincts are overriding his intention to wait and be the gentleman with Norah McCabe. He feels her arousal in her breaths that are full of longing. Edward kisses her breasts and begins to pull away her bodice until Norah pushes him away, moaning. They sit up on the couch and straighten their clothing; fearful they had gone too far or would go too far. Norah remembers the sublime ecstasy in lovemaking and she doesn't want to stop. She places her hand on his thigh and caresses him, closing her eyes and waiting for him to continue. Edward isn't that experienced with women and he wants to wait for their marriage night, but then he thinks it might be ridiculous to wait. Norah wouldn't be his virgin to create new memories with, anyway. This thought dims his arousal and makes him uneasy.

"You've been married. I haven't. I'll be a poor reminder. I won't be your only…"

Norah presses her fingers to his lips and tells him to be still. Edward sighs and kisses her fingers, but then moves away from her and stands up from the sofa. Norah lays back on the sofa and closes her eyes until she brings her breathing back to normal. She can hear Edward fussing with his clothing. She sits up on the sofa.

"I won't compare you to my husband."

"How about Sean? How do I compare to him?"

"What might you be asking me?"

"I know very little about your life with your husband, but I know you and Sean…"

"Sean and I have never been together like you think. And you, Edward, have you visited a prostitute, like most men?" Norah reaches for her shawl and wraps it around her shoulders, waiting for him to answer, but he is silent.

"I'm trying to tell you I love you and this love can't be compared to my husband's or what I have felt for Sean."

"Or feel for Sean?"

Norah stands up and gives Edward a light kiss.

"You're going to war and what if I never see you again? I couldn't live with myself without honesty. I love you and will marry you after the war is over. If you can't trust me, how will you be at peace and have a strong presence of mind going off to fight?"

Norah makes Edward a cup of tea and they resume their whispers of love but without touch. Edward's doubts about Norah retreat to the back of his mind. He leaves around 3:00 a.m. and has to be ready to march at 7:00 a.m. After he is gone and Norah locks the door behind him, she feels as if a door has closed within her, as well. The feelings she once had with her husband, Murray, she had never intended to have again. She wept quietly until there were no more tears and then slept until early morning.

New York voices clamor with cries of patriotism and slogans such as, "You are either for your country or against your country!" Horace Greeley, editor of the Tribune, condemns slaveholders in the south, stating they are violent, ignorant, and degraded citizens of the country. Abolitionist leaning people, vociferous in the belief that slavery stifles the soul of the country, nevertheless fear that liberating the South's hordes of uncivilized Africans could also be untimely and dangerous.

"Lincoln isn't advocating freeing the slaves," Harrigan says to Norah one day at the office, "the insurrection of southern states is his immediate concern."

Harrigan discusses the politics of the times with Norah over many cups of tea. She soon gathers enough information from him and from reading the papers to form her own opinions. She laughs when she read that the charismatic and enigmatic Fernando Wood thought New York ought to secede like some of the southern states and become its own country. She learns that old Whigs had scrambled to join the Republicans because they didn't want the country divided and believed that the lawless south needed to be disciplined and brought back to order. They didn't mention abolishing slavery, however. Harrigan said that these men were strong for government and order and against anarchy and lawlessness. Slavery is not the issue for them and many others, unfortunately, he tells Norah. Elizabeth Jennings understands this well. And Harrigan despises the conservatives, for they agree President Lincoln shouldn't allow slavery to spread into the west, but declare that he shouldn't take away the property rights of plantation owners, either.

"The poor buggers with their plantations just might lose their rights, Norah!"

"I suppose it's only right that this new president try to keep the country together, one nation under God," Norah responds, smirking.

"It's all about commerce and greed. The businessmen who send goods south, the big newspapers with large subscriptions in the south (obviously not our paper), the brokers of railroads, and the ship owners who haul cotton care only about money. Oh, and of course, there are the bankers who accept slave property as collateral for loans! These men all roar the loudest and want conciliatory efforts to be made at all costs over these turn of events."

"I didn't know about the bankers accepting slaves as collateral," Norah says, becoming gloomier by the minute.

Harrigan is on a roll and she sits back to listen.

"New York City has always been the alluring and tempestuous grand dame of the nation; a dizzying array of novelty, poverty, and affluence, and now it has become a storm center with all these spiraling winds of change. And you never know what they will say next in the papers. The slick city's policy makers and newsmakers only halt for a moment and either change direction or increase their velocity."

"And look what's happened," Norah said, "New York is now the established headquarters for the Army's Department!"

Harrigan and Norah continue to discuss and print news during this whirlpool of change. On April 23rd, there were six regiments dispatched with ceremony and pomp and by the end of 1861, sixty-six regiments were sent out to the killing fields from New York.

In addition to all the talk of war, Five Points is more difficult to live in for Norah. She feels it pulsating even more with its predictable downbeat of last-gasp survival and desperation. Harrigan makes sure she gets safely home each evening, for Tammany thugs are more active thronging the streets piled high with decaying vegetables and filth promising jobs for votes and loyalty. And there are fewer jobs and less food in the year after the firing on Ft. Sumter and the start of the war. Norah watches the pestilential tenement dwellers become more destitute than ever. To her annoyance, the rest of New York, and especially the do-gooder Nativists, storm against Five Points in newspaper articles with vituperative editorials. Their consensus is that Five Points is nothing more than a den of thieves, murderers, and prostitutes.

"Listen to this, James," Norah said one day, reading from the Sun,

"The despicable character of the Five Point population is intensified by the numerous Irish women who are spitting out mixed-race babies faster than one can say Jack Robinson."

"Last week, to rouse up tempers even further, a high and mighty Senator was quoted in the Sun newspaper saying that the abolitionists are enforcing the unnatural system of amalgamation, and that this is inordinate and immoral mingling of blacks and whites!" Harrigan responded.

Norah's head feels pummeled with the rapid-fire opinions sprouting up from every corner of New York in regards to the south, war, and slavery. She reads every newspaper she can get her hands on so she can write news-worthy and intelligent articles for Harrigan's newspaper, newly dubbed, *The Rousing Clarion.* Harrigan has been true to his ideals and is not paying heed to the noisy Democrats or radical Republicans. He attempts to bring light to both sides of the issues and Norah is trying to bring light on the issues in between, for that is where she is. This daunting and busy time helps her to not think of Edward day and night, as she is wont to do. As fervor grows over the changing times, Norah also works on new hats that pile up in the corner of the apartment. One day when Harrigan and Norah are taking a break, Norah airs some of her thoughts.

"In some ways, Five Points is more free-thinking than the rest of this city. I don't think most Irish hate the African, but they're worried liberated slaves might take away their lowly jobs. None of the Irish lads I know want to fight for the slave's freedom when Ireland's freedom is still needed. Oh, by the way, did you go to the meeting with that Irish fellow, Michael Corcoran?"

"Yes, I did! You should have come with me! He's the commander of the 69th. He spoke to the Fenian Brotherhood and said that the Irish must avoid the war because their purpose is to liberate Ireland and not die in a war between the fanatical native-born secessionists and abolitionists who hate them. He warned them that the best Irish fighting men will be killed before they can serve old Ireland and liberate her."

Norah is quiet, thinking back to how she once believed in fighting for Ireland's freedom. She drinks her tea and goes to her desk. Harrigan does the same and neither of them speaks about these matters again for some time.

One morning, Norah walks through Five Points on the way to the newspaper office and notices poverty-stricken families huddled in doorways. She spies a bedraggled mother and her suckling baby leaning against a door on the top step of an old tenement building. Norah lapses into the past and a vision of Famine Ireland returns to her. She slowly walks up the steps while shielding her eyes from the bright morning sun. In a dizzying moment, she slumps down next to the mother and her nursing baby on the steps of an old building with broken windows that sits on the corner of Mulberry and Cross Streets. It's a warm day and with the sun beating down on her head, the choice to wear a bonnet rather than a straw hat has allowed no air to circulate around her head. Her mind is throbbing and full of war news, Edward's letters, and worry over Katie being safe at the House of Industry. Of late, the mission has been running out of food and beggars were attacking some of the workers. She wonders why she has climbed the steps to this woman and she stands up to go back to the mission to retrieve Katie and bring her to work with her. But she turns and looks at the woman.

"Ocras! Ocras!" screams through her head, the Irish word for hunger.

"What did you say?" she asks, getting close to the woman.

"Hungry. I'm hungry. I need to eat to feed my baby, Miss," the woman replies.

"Where is it that you live? Your husband, is he at work?" Norah asks.

The baby squirms and cries, for there is little milk coming from the mother's breast. The woman's arms shake as she gently moves the baby to her other breast, trying to cover herself as best she can with her dirty, ragged shawl. The shawl is discolored and a faint pattern reveals that it has been colorful at one time.

"We moved to this rat-infested place where there were as many prostitutes as vermin crawling through it. My husband...my Howard..." The woman puts her head down and Norah watches the baby wince as a few tears splash on his tiny, pale puckered face.

She looks up at Norah and takes in a deep breath. The baby loses its hold on her nipple, but roots frantically to find it again.

"He was a ship-builder, but lost his job and now he's gone off to build a railroad. I haven't heard a word from him for months and we've run out of money. This building with its groggery and poor rooms to let out was shut down two weeks ago and the families were forced out. There's no-one living in the place but the beggars come to sleep here at night."

"Do you have family in the city?" The woman has the face of an Irish mother, maybe even her own mother.

"I canna' have them see me so. I ran away to marry my husband and haven't I made my own bed to sleep in?" She laughs nervously, "But the irony of it all, Miss, is that I have no bed at all to sleep in."

"If you're able, come with me to my office and I'll see that you and your baby have food and a place to sleep. This is a country with fine people and there's still hope for the lot of us. I've a saying that comes from my own land, a sorrowful land, but still a land of beauty; *The luck that is not on us today may be on us tomorrow.* "I think sometimes there is a God who gives us a long pause of

96

hardship before we get back our breath and can dance to life again."

The woman looks at Norah with tears trickling down her face, "Where does such kindness come from? And how is it you would have enough to feed us?"

"It's easy to halve the potato where there's love," Norah said as she reaches for the baby so the woman can stand. Her Mam's voice is coming through her!

The woman is a reminder of the mother of her childhood friend in Ireland who had been with hunger. She is every woman she had seen on the roads in Ireland begging for bread. And this woman and her baby also become her and her own Katie. For a brief time, there is no separation between the past and the present and no difference between her and this woman.

In the days to come, Norah settles this woman into a room at the House of Industry in exchange for her work as a seamstress. Maryanne, the bedraggled and hungry woman Norah found on the stoop of a tenement building, grows strong in body and spirit again and her fingers tirelessly turn old clothes into new. And as the war escalates and regiments increase, Norah goes to battle on the streets of New York. She, Nellie, and Elizabeth walk through the streets gathering women and children left penniless through neglect or the death of their husbands and find shelter for them. And then Elizabeth marries her childhood sweetheart, Charles, and they are soon expecting a baby, but Elizabeth still keeps up her charity work. Letters from Edward arrive sporadically, but each one is precious to Norah and she reads them over again and again each night before going to bed.

Sean is visiting Norah, of late, ranting and raving over the talk of war. He hates slavery, but he loves his new country and to see it being torn in half is tearing him in half. Norah sometimes needs his strong arms to help her on the streets with the women and children, and he needs a listening ear so he can sort through his feelings about secession and defending the union. One day he sits with Norah on her sofa talking about the war.

"Ye are sidin' with the bigots, Norah. The rich in this city support the Republican Party. We Irish do not. And the rich buggers see us as rebellious and ignorant monkeys. You and Nellie can be against slavery. I am, too, after what I'd seen working on the ships. It's a terrible situation, a peculiar institution altogether, slavery is, but it's a fixed truth in this country. This whole country has to decide against it, not just half of it. No bishops are standing with them abolitionists and ye know how you're stirring up the maggots in Five Points to be throwing stones at you and Katie every time you and Elizabeth Jennings go parading around together. They don't want one of their own defending the Negro when they don't feel anyone is defending them!"

Norah folds her hands in her lap with resolution and tells Sean her feelings about slavery and war. The two friends never seem to agree.

On an evening in May, Sean is going to accompany Norah and Katie to the House of Industry for the mission's tenth anniversary celebration. Norah implores Sean to spiff himself up and not wear the tattered old clothing he wears working on the docks. His hours on the docks have been shortened and his pay lessened and he can't afford buying the fancy man's clothes that her dandy friend, Harrigan, wears. But because he loves and admires this high-spirited, opinionated, and his queen of a woman, he spends a good deal of his paycheck buying a matching suit with a light blue silk and cotton waistcoat and dark blue checkered pants, a new shirt, and a pea jacket. He sports his old bowler hat that is dusty and worn and although Norah will find fault with it, he hates the top hats. This ole hat gives him a jaunty, cocky look he likes. His ginger curls stick out all around the hat and he refuses to tame his hair with the perfumed macassar oil men like Harrigan use. Even Edward reeked of the stuff when he last saw him marching off to war. Yes, his Norah is all cow-eyed and crazy over Edward, but Sean is certain it is only infatuation with the boy. And he suspects she is still punishing him for his stupid stunt with the prostitute at Pete's. If only Norah could understand that no matter what woman he is caressing, it is Norah he is thinking of.

When Sean shows up at Norah's door to take her to the celebration, she gives him a once over and berates his hat, his sailor's pea jacket, and his worn-out brogans. He takes the cigar out of his mouth, crushes it on the outside of the building, smiles, and gives her his arm and reaches for Katie's hand. Some things just aren't up for debate and change, and when Norah looks into his sea-worn blue eyes crinkled up with laughter, she shuts her mouth about his odd apparel. No matter the stares of her neighbors that she is used to, she is proud to have him by her side. She talks loudly as they walk through Five Points.

"The abolitionists aren't all bigots! Nellie, Elizabeth, and I are siding for what's right, not with the abolitionists. It's true that I can't tolerate some of those pampered pusses that hate Ireland and our faith. They're not all the same. It isn't clear as you think. Black and white and north and south! What are you going to do yourself, Sean? Michael Corcoran rallied the 69th and even got blessed by Bishop Hughes at St. Patrick's. They've already marched off, as did my Edward. He's with the 8th New York Militia," Norah said.

"I know the regiment he joined. I saw him, alright," Sean responds, clutching her arm more tightly.

"You were there saying your goodbyes, but then scurried off so fast afterwards, I had no one to dry my tears, Sean," Norah said, and is quiet before she speaks again.

"And will you also be going off to fight?" Her heart quickens in fear he will say he is going. She couldn't tolerate having both Edward and Sean going off to fight the south.

Sean takes in a deep breath before he exhales his answer, "I'm all for preserving the Union, but I'm no fool, Norah. This country can't be held together by force. If it looks like it can, maybe I'll go, but for now, I'm here protecting you and Katie."

Chapter Twelve

There is increasing angst amongst the Catholic community against Mr. Lewis Pease whom they believe is hell-bent on cramming Protestant lies and aversions down Catholic orphans' throats at his mission, The House of Industry. Indignant Catholics parade out in front of the mission on Sunday mornings to persuade children to go to their Sunday schools rather than be corrupted by Pease's Protestant Sunday school. Norah and a few of the Catholic women who volunteer or work at the mission determine it is more important that children have food and clothing even if they are learning Jesus has been taken off the cross and put in their hearts. And Mr. Pease has been more tolerant than any other Protestant charitable mission in the city and has developed a reputation for gentle persuasion to simple faith, be it Protestant or Catholic. He jokes that *appeasement is my aim and it is even part of my name.* He proudly claims that Catholics as well as Protestants are permitted to teach and preach the great principles of their common Christianity in his institution. Norah has been given a Sunday school class of Catholic children to teach, but she was made to understand that particular dogmas have to be abstained from being taught. Everyone can go to Jesus on their own, without any intervention of a priest or the saints. People know, however, it is really the Protestant faith that Pease and the Protestants believe will reign in orphan souls by the time they leave his mission. At least it is Jesus all the same, Norah thinks. She is ambiguous about religion, undecided, and she loves a God that is both magnanimous and puzzling. She holds at arm's length her mother's Catholicism. It is of Ireland and she will always be of Ireland, but she has no need for the incessant prayers and rosaries, or going to Mass.

Not far from the House of Industry is Bishop Hughes' Church of the Transfiguration, which began conducting mass meetings to bring in errant Catholics, but Norah has no interest and this, too, is a detriment to her in the eyes of her neighbors. Not only is Norah McCabe an ebony loving Black Republican, but she is also a wayward Catholic. Once when Norah picked up Katie from the nursery, Katie loudly sang a hymn she had learned,

> What a friend we have in *Jeshush,*
> All our sins and *grease* to bear!
> What a *privige* to carry
> Everything to God in prayer!

At first Norah laughed at her daughter's pronunciation of some of the words, for clearly she was too young to fathom the meaning of the hymn. She was pleased that her daughter felt loved and cared for by Jesus, but when they left Sunday school late that day and Katie was singing for all to hear, a nun from the Church of the Transfiguration had approached them and admonished them for not singing in their own church.

But on this warm May evening with her arm in Sean's and little Katie holding his hand, they are dressed in lavish clothing to celebrate the House of Industry's ten-year operation. And none of these differences matter to Norah. Since the war began, the usual elaborate attention Norah gives to her apparel is not as important. There is little time in the mornings to devote to corset and lace, but also she wishes to help the young women on the streets and not worry over her attire. In the evenings, she rips apart old, elegant dresses to give to Maryanne to fashion into reasonable clothing for the women she meets on street corners lingering and begging in their ragged, dirty day dresses. She brings them to the mission promising not just a good meal, but a hat or dress to wear.

But tonight is different and Norah looks ravishing in her royal blue ribbed moiré silk gown with a collarless neckline and paisley cashmere shawl. She is wearing blue satin shoes she found in a used shop. She has donned one of her favorite headdresses, made with wired blue tulle with handmade French knot accents. It is trimmed in black Chantilly lace, lined in rich blue tulle with a bobbin lace accent at the back. Katie looks very pretty herself, wearing a blue silk taffeta dress with velvet ribbon and rhinestones.

They arrive at the House of Industry's celebration at Irving Hall and see a few Catholic protesters standing with signs. One sign reads, "Don't Enslave our Irish Children!" Norah hurries up the steps with Katie, pulling Sean with her. Once inside, she breathes a sigh of relief. *This mission is doing more good in this city in spite of being Protestant!* She looks around at the large audience and all the children who are milling about dressed in brand new frocks. There are over three hundred children, in about equal proportions to boys and girls, and they beam in joy as they prepare to entertain with song and dance performances for the guest benefactors and officers of the institution.

"There's my sweet violet girl!" Elizabeth Jennings exclaims, walking up to Katie who is hiding behind Norah's skirts. Katie isn't usually shy, but never has she seen so many children all in one large room. But as soon as she sees Elizabeth Jennings, whom she adores, she rushes to her and hugs her waist.

"I'm surprised you came after all, Beth!" Norah said, planting a kiss on Elizabeth's cheek. "Did you bring your father? Or even Frederick Douglass?"

Elizabeth laughs, "No, I'm afraid not. There's a meeting at the Tabernacle. I've got to get over there myself because Rev. Beecher is speaking. My father expects me to attend, but I told him I was coming here first."

Sean is clearly uncomfortable, and after greeting Elizabeth he leaves the women and walks around the room to see if he knows anyone. There are more women in the hall than men and he is certainly getting stares for his odd get-up he's wearing.

"Can I go with Miss Beth to the Tabernacle?" Katie asks her mother, pulling on her skirts. "Can I, Mam? Please Mam?"

"Miss Kate, don't you want to sing with the others from our Sunday School class?" Norah asks.

"I want to be with Miss Beth!"

Of late, it is Elizabeth and Nellie whom Katie is spending more time with than with Norah. Her friends take turns picking Katie up at the nursery to take her home a few times during the week when Norah has late nights at the newspaper office. And when she and Nellie work with the women on the streets, Katie stays with Elizabeth at her home.

"You spend a lot of time with Miss Beth, already. Why don't you stay close to your Mam this evening," Norah said.

Katie looks disappointed and Norah gives in, "Right then, Miss Katie. You and Miss Beth can walk around and look at all the decorations and get some refreshments. I'm going to talk to a few people and then I'll meet you back here."

Elizabeth looks at Norah quizzically, "Are you sure it's a good idea? They all might think I'm the child's nanny and ask me to serve them their refreshments," Elizabeth said in jest.

Norah looks around the room and sees very few adult Negroes, although there are a few colored children. She has asked Elizabeth to come to the House of Industry's anniversary celebration to meet Mr. Pease. Elizabeth is always busy with her church and teaching children at the Broadway Tabernacle, but Norah thinks that maybe Elizabeth might get some work teaching at the mission, too. Elizabeth didn't think it'd go over well to apply for work at a predominantly white institution, but Norah told her that Mr. Pease and the officers of his fine institution would probably like Protestant Elizabeth more than her Irish Popish self!

"Go on and parade about in this high moralizing mission, Elizabeth. They need to learn to live what they preach!"

Norah winks at her friend and gives Katie a kiss. Katie pulls on Elizabeth's arm and they leave Norah standing by herself, but soon Sean is back at her side and when he puts his arm around her waist, Mr. Pease suddenly appears and grimaces at her.

"I hope your children are prepared to sing tonight, Miss McCabe. Shouldn't you be gathering them into the classroom for a little practice?"

"They're ready as they'll ever be. Mr. Pease, I'd like to introduce you to my friend, Mr. Sean O'Connolly. I've known Sean since I was a child first come over from Ireland."

"Grand to meet you, Mr. Pease. Ye have a fine establishment in this city," Sean said as he shakes Mr. Pease's hand.

"Pleasure to meet you, Mr. O'Connolly. If ever you think of donating any time in carpentry or building renovation, we'd be glad to have you," Mr. Pease replies.

"Certainly, sir," Sean said nervously. He removed his hat when they first arrived, but his wild, curly hair is all a mess. Mr. Pease stares at his hair, his eyes moving to the right and to the left, as they talk.

A horn suddenly blares and everyone looks across the room at the stage to the well-dressed superintendent, Benjamin Barlow, who is trying to get everyone's attention to begin the evening's performances.

"Ladies and gentlemen, may I have your attention, please."

People hurry to find seats and Mr. Pease excuses himself and goes quickly up to the stage to sit with his directors and benefactors. Norah looks around the room for Elizabeth and Katie, but she doesn't see them anywhere.

"Find seats in the back and save enough for all of us. I'm going to walk around the room to find Elizabeth and Katie," Norah said to Sean.

She scans the crowd nervously as she circles the hall and back. She thinks she sees them sitting in the front row, but as she starts towards them, one of Pease's employees tells her to find her seat as the program is beginning. Norah gives him a menacing look and considers ignoring him, but then she'd best not cause undue attention to herself. *As long as they're together in the front row, I guess it's fine,* Norah thinks, but is disappointed not to have her sweet Katie proudly sitting next to her. As the program begins with the dull reading of the annual report, Norah repeatedly stretches her neck to look over the heads of the crowd to the front of the room. *Is that Katie and Elizabeth?* She can't be certain. If only Elizabeth would turn her head, surely she'd know, but the woman is ramrod stiff and never moves a muscle.

"We are proud to report that 1,633 persons have received partial or entire support from this charity during the past year. 285,215 meals have been distributed and 864 children have been enrolled on the school register. The number of children lodging at the House now is 87 and the number admitted during the year was 720. And I'm pleased to report that a large portion of the admitted children have been provided with comfortable homes in different parts of our country. And although, of late, there has been considerable apprehension expressed by our Catholic neighbors over the removal of children from the Sixth Ward to board trains to go to new homes in other parts of our country, might I ask you, ladies and gentlemen: should a five year old girl living in squalor without proper food and clothing being beaten by her drunken mother whose father has left for good not be given a proper chance in life?"

The audience cheers and claps, but Norah is growing increasingly uncomfortable sitting in the back so far from Katie. She doesn't particularly like the superintendent who is speaking. He snubs her when she's at the mission. Norah is well aware of the growing controversy over children being removed from their homes, such sorry homes as they are, in Five Points. She strongly feels that everything possible should be done to help the poor drunken mother to better herself before taking her children from her and sending them across the country. Just two days before, a mother had dropped her two-year-old boy off at the mission pleading with Mr. Pease to place her son in a good home. But that didn't give the Industry the right to assume every child in a dirty, poor home should be sent packing to another state. Norah's heart accelerates just thinking about this matter and not having her daughter next to her. Harrigan has asked her to write an article about the plight of children in Five Points being sent to so-called better homes, but because of her work at the mission, she has been putting it off.

The long-winded Mr. Barlow finally finishes giving his annual report and Norah hears the sighs of relief come from the audience surrounding her. She quickly stands up to look for Katie, for she has to meet her Sunday school class students in the room to the right of the stage. They have been instructed to meet her there before going on stage to perform.

"And where are ye goin', love?" Sean asks.

"To find Katie and meet with my students. We're to perform soon."

"Want me to go with you?"

"You can stay put until after the program."

Sean rubs his bristly, whiskered chin, "Would ye mind, Norah, if I might step out for a smoke and a walk around the corner. I'll be back to escort you all home."

"I do mind! If you're that attached to the fags, I'm sorely disappointed in you. Go get yourself some more tea and cakes instead and then just sit back and enjoy the show!"

Sean cringes under Norah's command. Why couldn't the girleen see he is about the only man in the audience and that he has already gone the extra mile to put on his fancy clothes and escort them to this dull event!

Norah walks around the hall looking for Elizabeth and Katie, but never finds them. She goes into the rooms in the back and even outside to stand on the top step to look for them. The horn blows to indicate the intermission is over and it is announced that the performances will begin. As everyone hurries to their seats, Norah frantically scans each row of seats as she walks up the aisles. Her heart is pounding so loudly; she doesn't hear Sean come up beside her.

"Where's Katie? I saw you going around the room like a nervous hen looking for them."

"I don't know where they are! Help me find them!" Norah rushes to the room next to the stage and Sean follows.

"We're supposed to meet here," Norah said, hurrying to open the door of the room they're scheduled to meet in. Her students stand before her all sparkling clean and merry.

"Miss, oh Miss, are we to practice now before we go on stage?" a boy asks, pulling on her skirts. Norah ignores him, as her eyes look at each child to see if one is her own Katie. Katie isn't in the room!

"Sean, stay with the children. Katie's not here!"

Norah leaves and runs directly into Mr. Pease and his wife.

"My Katie's disappeared! I can't find her!" Norah says.

Mrs. Pease puts her hand on Norah's shoulder, "Calm down, Miss McCabe. She was here just a moment ago with your colored friend. That one can't be difficult to find, really."

"Go with Norah to look for her, Ann, and I'll tell the first class we're delaying the program for a few minutes or so," Mr. Pease said. He really is a caring soul, at that, Norah thinks.

Mrs. Pease and Norah search the entire premises in the next few minutes, but they never find Elizabeth and Katie. The program has to go on and Mrs. Pease has found one of the policemen acting as security for the event and she tells him Norah's plight. She quickly gives Norah a hug and then goes to Mr. Pease to help him with the continuation of the evening's programs.

"Put a report in, my dear, and go into the Negro part of the neighborhood to look for your child. I'm sure your friend took her there, for some reason, only God knows why."

Norah is surprised to see that the security officer is Officer Leary. She hasn't seen him since they went for tea after meeting at the department store. Maybe it's a good sign, she thinks, for there are plenty of policemen in Five Points and here he is standing before her. He greets her solemnly and assures her he can help.

"Let's look for Katie on the streets!" Norah rushes out of the building and down the steps. A young boy breathlessly runs up to Leary who has come out of the building.

"I seen something not right, officer. Right here, it was. I seen them pull the colored lady and her baby onto a wagon, rough-like. They was all fancy dressed and the colored woman was screaming for help."

"Where did they go?" Leary and Norah asked at once.

The boy points down the street and Leary runs to a carriage parked in front of the hall. He tells the driver it's an emergency. The driver is waiting for passengers attending the House of Industry celebration, but he quickly accommodates Norah and Leary and they are soon heading in the direction the boy indicated. Adrenalin shoots through Norah like lightening and she reaches out and strikes the driver on the back with her purse.

"Hurry! You're driving the beasts too slow!"

Leary takes hold of Norah's hands and holds them down on her lap.

"There's a mess of people in the streets, Norah. He can't go any faster."

Norah's eyes are peeled for a wagon with her daughter and friend in it.

"We should have brought the boy to help us," she said.

"You look straight ahead and I'll look down side streets and around," Leary said.

The usual jingles fill the early evening air, as the hawkers of food never give up until the late night drunks topple their stands and run off with their food and sometimes even their earnings.

"My clams I want to sell today, the best clams from Rock-Away!"

Norah shivers beneath her shawl, her fancy dress now full of wrinkles and folded in a big bunch on her lap. She wants to tear her clothes off, tear her hair out, and lie down, and weep for her daughter. Her heart is torn in half and all she can hear in the night air is Katie calling for her and *Rock-Away* makes her think of rock-a-bye baby. When she finds Katie, she will never let her go. She will never leave her with Elizabeth Jennings or Nellie or let her stay at the House of Industry again. Her daughter will stay by her side until she can stand and fight on her own, like she herself has learned to do. But if something happens to Katie…sparks of light fill her vision and she can't see. She is crying and the gaslights flash ominously before her, these silver balls that prevent her from seeing down the street.

"Stop! I hear her. I hear Katie calling me!"

The driver pulls his horses over to the side and Leary and Norah climb out of the wagon. Norah runs in the direction of the voice she thinks she hears, holding Leary's hand so she can remain upright, for her vision is skewed, but her sense of hearing has become keen.

"This way! Can you hear Katie?"

Officer Leary can't hear a child crying, for all he can hear are muffled voices coming from the docks, as well as the many clip-clops of the horses pulling carriages.

Norah breathes in a sob and smells the briny sea, tasting her own salty tears as she runs for Katie with the realization that the sea is once again trying to take from her, to seize what she loves most in her life.

Chapter Thirteen

Norah and Leary run to East River Wharf in time to save Katie Marion and Elizabeth Jennings from being abducted by slave-catchers who claim they are using their legal right to enforce the Fugitive Slave Law. Fear over losing her daughter is unlike any fear Norah has ever experienced. No emotion is as fierce. Norah screams and kicks the massively built man who is pulling Katie onto a ship. Another man has Elizabeth by the arm. Katie and Elizabeth are crying and yelling when Norah and Leary arrive. The commotion brings police officers to the scene and eventually a Federal Marshal arrives and although the men shove false affidavits in his face, the Marshal obtains the truth that Elizabeth Jennings is not an escaped slave from Georgia and Katie is not her mulatto daughter. Elizabeth only looks like a runaway slave who has an enormous price on her head. This incident shakes Norah to the core and she considers moving to upstate New York to be with her family so she can keep Katie safe.

But Norah loves the city and has been attending meetings at the First Colored Congregational Church with Elizabeth. Katie goes, too, for Norah won't let her out of her sight, except when Nellie takes care of her at their apartment. Sean hates going to these radical meetings, but Norah is taking such a strong stand against slavery that he fears for Norah and Katie's safety. And soon after the abduction incident, Harrigan asks Norah if she would write an article about the slave trade for the *Rousing Clarion*. It is a wise suggestion, for Norah can channel her fear and anger into the writing of the article. She reads it aloud to Harrigan after doing one last edit.

> *Slave trading has been a capital offense since 1820, but it is now 1861 and only one slave trading ship captain has been hung for it. One hundred slave ships have been launched from New York since 1858 and our government has turned a blind eye to this epidemic. There are prominent businessmen in this city who have invested in slaving voyages that have enabled the slave trade to prosper. A ship that costs $13,000 to make fit for slaving brings in $225,000 after the human cargo is delivered. This blood money is placed in bank accounts of some of the wealthiest merchants in our fine city. But now the Lincoln administration has taken office and changes are rapidly being made to clean up slave-trading crimes. Shame on New York for being the chief port in the world for the slave trade!*

Harrigan prints Norah's article and the ensuing days are filled with war news and confusion. It's a time of great insecurity for all and hungry mouths are crying out for help. The landscape is different in gray tones, not green, and Fifth Avenue still stands in all its glory just like the big houses in Ireland had stood during the Famine. Norah allows the recollections of her past to be transformed through compassionate work. She can no longer be uninvolved regarding the slavery issue. When there is a meeting Elizabeth is planning on attending that is for helping fugitive slaves hide from bounty hunters, Norah and Katie go also. And Norah is making hats for the women escaping to Canada for their freedom. Often wearing homespun, ragged clothing, these runaway slave women without proper hats and gloves will be noticed by the bounty hunters. The stack of hats in the corner of the apartment is beginning to dwindle because Norah is giving them to these women, as well as to the women who come to the House of Industry without a proper hat. It is a financial loss for her to give away her hats, but the spiritual gain means more to her.

Leary and Sean became good friends after Leary helped Norah find Elizabeth and Katie on the evening of the anniversary celebration of the House of Industry. Leary is also becoming a regular visitor at Nellie and Norah's apartment and Nellie and Leary have been drinking many cups of tea together. The day Leary shows up with his officer's hat in his hand and a bouquet of violets in the other, it is Nellie, not Norah, who answers the door.

"I picked the wee violets along the streets before they were trampled on. They're all a droop, but here you go. Ye can put them in a cup of water," Leary says, thrusting the wilted flowers at Nellie.

"Norah isn't here. She and Katie are visiting a church in Brooklyn with her friend, Elizabeth. Norah and Elizabeth are trying to raise money in the church to help purchase the freedom of slaves."

"Is that so?" Leary is astounded at this news and peers off to the right while he stands on the steps. Norah seems to be always getting herself into some kind of trouble, he thinks that day, but at least it isn't going off with a rebel to fight the British this time.

"You must be O'Leary!" Nellie exclaims, "Norah's told me about you!"

Nellie blushes and looks down. She had no idea that this Irish fellow would be so attractive. Nellie knows that this O'Leary had once loved Mary, Norah's best friend, who had died a terrible death from an abortion.

"I'm Leary now, Miss, but it's no matter. Norah's always telling me I need to be proud of the O, but don't we live in times when names beginning with that letter can keep us from going forward."

"From what Norah has told me, you'd be going forward whether or not you left off your O in your name, Mr. Leary," Nellie says, smiling and very much liking this friend of Norah's. At least he, too, isn't in love with her friend!

"Ye can tell Norah I stopped by to see how they're doing…she and Katie…"

"Please come in. Norah would chastise me for not inviting you in for a cup of tea. After all you've done for her! I feel as if I know you already. Mr. Barker downstairs, I'm sure, saw you come to the door. He's our landlord, owns the store, you see, but he watches out for us, and is also a bit nosey… I'm rambling!"

Nellie laughs and moves from the doorway to let Leary inside. He enters her apartment and her life all in one springtime day. And throughout the heady month of May when the violets and forget-me-nots are blooming alongside dirty streets, Leary visits Nellie at Chatham and Pearl with bouquets and tea. Often, Norah and Sean and Nellie and Leary go for walks to Taylor's Ice Cream Parlor, discussing war news and the freedom of slaves. And now there are two strong men to help the women with carrying buckets of water up to their apartment for their clothes washing once a week.

"Are you a Catholic girl, Norah McCabe?" asks Elizabeth's father, Thomas L. Jennings. They are having cake and tea after one of the services at the Plymouth Church of the Pilgrims in Brooklyn where Henry Ward Beecher preached.

"I am. I'm a Catholic, but I don't attend Mass, Mr. Jennings," Norah replies. She clutches her hands together, worrying she has given the wrong answer. Katie is teasing her to run and play with the other children in the church, but Norah won't let go of her hand.

"Let the child have some fun, Miss McCabe," Mr. Jennings says.

Elizabeth sidles up to her just in time and takes Katie's hand.

"Don't you be worrying now, Norah. We won't be going out on the stoop for some fresh air this time and even if we did, those slave-catchers know better than to come sniffing around this church. Mr. Beecher is known in this city and it would be to their demise if they came around."

Katie and Elizabeth wander off to a Sunday school room and Norah doesn't know what to say to Mr. Jennings. He's a successful tailor and well respected in the Negro community, as well as with abolitionists. They really have nothing in common, only their relationship with Elizabeth and their mindset that slavery should be abolished.

"With all due respect to your Catholic faith, Miss McCabe... for I'm a man with an open mind...your Bishop Hughes is another matter, altogether. Do you know that he claims that slavery is evil, but...and I tell you that when anyone says *but* after they've made a statement, the *but* usually erases that statement. *But*, the good bishop declares, slavery is not an absolute and unmitigated evil because it has brought Africans to Christianity. And so here I stand, although I was not born into slavery, my family was. And thus, dear child, your bishop also says that he feels slavery has improved the condition of the African because of this!"

"I don't agree with everything Bishop Hughes says. I respect him as bishop...he's done a good deal for the Irish in this city that wouldn't have been done. But on this that he says about slavery, I don't agree. Or I wouldn't be here now, would I? No, he's not my *good* bishop, Mr. Jennings. But, and as what you say about the word *but...but* he still is my bishop, I suppose"

"Come here, girl, and give me a big hug!"

To Norah's surprise, Mr. Jennings' strong arms reach around her neck and bring her to his shoulder. Norah feels tenderness and affection coming from her friend's father. And grief must have been waiting in her, for her eyes fill with tears as he hugs her. She thinks of her Da and how much she misses him, although hugs around the neck have never been a common thing between them. After Mr. Jennings releases her, she finds a handkerchief in her purse and dabs at her eyes.

"There, there now, Norah. These are difficult times, God have mercy on all of us. I know you've had enough sorrows in your young life and should have no more. Elizabeth has told me all about it and if all your Irish tears flowed out, they might turn the Hudson green."

With this acknowledgement of her past, Norah's tears flow even more. Mr. Jennings pats her back, saying, "There, there, the Lord our God is merciful. Yes, He is."

"Mam!" Katie comes rushing to Norah and hides in her skirts. "Why are you crying, Mam?" she asks.

"I'm alright, pet. No worries. Mr. Jennings is being very kind is all and they're good tears."

When Norah and Katie leave the church that afternoon, Norah feels as if her insides have been rinsed, like some kind of bathing. Maybe likened to what Elizabeth's church called a water baptism down at the river each summer. But it wasn't the preaching tonight that did it, although Mr. Beecher was spellbinding in fulminating against slavery and going on about how much God loves us unconditionally. She didn't know really, but only that for the first time since her Da held her after Murray had died and she nearly lost her mind, she was given permission to weep and have pity on her past. And maybe it was God Himself giving her this through Mr. Jennings.

The Rousing Clarion of Five Points is fast becoming a newspaper to be respected, for there are more substantial articles about social issues than information about who sold the best and cheapest lamp oil, the opening of a new Irish pub and dry goods store, and who married whom. Norah reads all of Mr. Beecher's articles in *The Independent*, which combines social and religious messages in the newspaper. The abolitionist preacher is a columnist for the newspaper and signs his articles with an asterisk. Harrigan said this made Henry Ward Beecher a star reporter. He also told Norah that one of the priests from The Church of the Transformation came to speak to him about whether his paper was to stand for Irish-Catholics, for Catholics in general, or for the Protestants and Republicans, as well as the very Nativists who try to trip up faithful Catholic immigrants at every turn.

"Why are you not emulating *The New York Freeman's Journal*, our strong Catholic newspaper, he asked Harrigan, "You're going against the very blood of your people, as well as all the work Bishop Hughes has done in this city."

"History will tell, Father Murphy. Only history will tell. But no worries, for we will continue to print the news of the good Catholics in our community."

After this visit, Harrigan had intended to write an article to appease his Irish-Catholic readers, for the *Freeman's Journal* was really Bishop Hughes' organ for his views. Instead, he flames the fire of dissent:

> *It has been said most recently that the Irish-Catholic Democrats don't believe slavery is a blessing and under the right circumstances, they would like to see it abolished. However, they don't believe it is the right of politicians to interfere with moral issues and slavery should only be considered abolished if the majority of all classes of people oppose it. These are lofty opinions touted by our friends at The New York Freeman's Journal, but might I suggest that politicians are involved in moral issues all the time! None of us wish to see our country torn asunder and the rights of men and women undermined or taken from them, but as Horace Greeley stated succinctly in his Tribune article, "In order to line our pockets, must we utterly stifle our souls?*

It may have been coincidental, for there are always gangs hanging around the streets where *The Rousing Clarion* has its office, but bottles thrown through the windows the day after the priest's visit don't make it seem so.

Norah, Elizabeth, Nellie, and Katie attend a lecture by the abolitionist, William Lloyd Garrison, one Sunday at the Plymouth Church of the Pilgrims. Norah is surprised to see Walt Whitman in the audience, as well as Sojourner Truth, whom she learned about through Elizabeth Jennings. Sean accompanies them, at his insistence for keeping them all safe. This time, Norah persuades him to wear more somber clothing.

"I'm no Quaker...and I'm no Protestant do-gooder either, but for you, darlin', I'll wear black. After all, these are hard times we're living in and even if you won't go stepping out with me to Pete's Place no more, I'll be a true gentleman and escort you and your lady friends to these meetings. But speaking of gentlemen, how is it that your Mr. Harrigan doesn't come 'round to these important meetings?"

"He's busy at the paper and works late. He expects me to go and get the news at the meetings. One of us goes out for the news and the other puts it all together. But he always goes around Five Points to get news."

The truth is that Harrigan is uncomfortable attending a Protestant church and as liberal minded as he has become over the years, he is unable to overcome the feeling of bringing curses down on him if he sets foot in one. As well, he said he'd feel more conspicuous in his fancy attire in a Protestant church. It's not that he didn't feel out of place in the Catholic Church, but there is no expectation of hand shaking and socializing afterwards. He can go to Mass and then sneak out a side door easy enough.

After the lecture by William Lloyd Garrison, Elizabeth whispers to Norah that she would like to take her to the basement of the church to meet the slaves who have escaped from Georgia and are en route to Canada.

"Plymouth Church of the Pilgrims is also called the Grand Central Depot," Elizabeth says. "It's the hub of the Underground Railroad. The collection plates that are passed are to raise money for fleeing slaves."

"I want you to meet some women you're giving your specially designed hats to. They're grateful. And they're strong and brave. Braver than I was to take the trolley company to court. They remind me of you, Norah, because of the story you told me about how hungry you were in Ireland. And how cruel the British were to all of you…and how you came over on a ship and almost died. Just like an underground railroad in some ways."

Norah is uncomfortable. Although Elizabeth is whispering, Sean and Katie are listening. She and Sean don't talk about Ireland any longer and she has never told Katie about what happened in Ireland.

"Maybe another time…"

"There might not be another time…"

"Mam, I want to go see them," Katie said.

"How do you know if there might be bounty hunters right here in this church, Beth? They might be posing as abolitionists. And they could see us disappear to the basement and follow us."

"We know every person here right now, but if you're disinclined to meet the women who'd love to see the pretty Irish woman who made them their hats, then I can't be persuading you."

"Let's go home, Norah," Sean interjects, "I've seen enough slaves on ships."

Norah touches her heart with her right hand and presses while she thinks about whether she should meet the women. If she meets them, will she want to do more than what she is doing already to help? Or is it that if she meets them, it will be another reminder of oppression and how her countrymen are still in bondage in Ireland?

"I'll go with you to the basement," Norah states quietly.

Chapter Fourteen

Norah had never been in a Protestant church as large as the Plymouth Church and was surprised by its simple beauty. It was inviting to Norah with its circular seating and plush red cushions. She looked up into the balcony and it was full. Elizabeth had said that it was full every Sunday because people from Manhattan are curious to come and listen to the powerful, charismatic Rev. Henry Ward Beecher boldly preach against slavery. Just Sunday last, Norah saw a mock slave auction held to reveal the horrific realities of human beings being auctioned off for kitchen work or field work; their arms pinched, their hair pulled, and their mouths forced open to check their teeth. Even their eyes were forced wide open with their necks gripped as if they were animals in surrender. It was so authentic that Katie and the other children cried. Sunday school teachers came to usher the children out of the sanctuary and into Sunday School rooms, but Norah wouldn't let Katie leave and held her tightly on her lap, whispering that it wasn't real and that it was a story being acted out and no one was really being hurt, but Katie kept asking why. Finally, Norah and Katie left the sanctuary to wait until the mock trial and service was over. Elizabeth and her husband, Charles, accompanied Katie and Norah home where Nellie had prepared a ham dinner with all the fixings. Norah will never forget that day! As they walked home to Chatham and Pearl, a few children threw stones and yelled obscenities at Elizabeth and Charles, but they both kept on talking and laughing as if it wasn't happening. Norah had picked up Katie, who was heavy, and carried her in her arms the rest of the way. The sun had shone radiantly through their windows that day when they had a feast, almost as if it was a last supper, a holy unspoken last supper, with Leary, Sean, Norah, Katie, Nellie, Elizabeth and Charles.

Norah is standing in this church waiting for Elizabeth to lead them to the basement while she thinks back to that companionable dinner together. The last few months have been difficult in learning about the harsh and traumatic realities of slavery. But they have been laced with the idealism of the Underground Railroad and freedom. And now here she is nervously waiting to meet real slaves in the basement of the Plymouth Church. She said yes to Elizabeth to meet the women who will wear her hats to freedom.

Norah follows Elizabeth through the hallway to the back of the church and down steep steps into the basement. Norah walks down the stairs and a rush of cold air strikes her. She pulls her shawl tight around her shoulders and tries to keep from trembling. *The hold of the ship felt this cold and hopeless,* she thinks, but she tries not to think of the past but of the dreams these slaves possess to be delivered from their bondage.

When they reach the basement with Harold, a church employee, following them, Elizabeth lights a lantern because it is very dark when they enter a large room. In the center of the room is an enormous coal furnace full of apertures and pipes. Next to the furnace is a huge pile of coal and two shovels. And next to the pile of coal, there is neatly stacked chopped wood that runs the length of an entire wall and up to the ceiling. Elizabeth releases Norah's hand and she and Harold quickly remove blocks of wood from a place in the pile. Then Norah sees an opening and Elizabeth motions for Norah to enter. It is just large enough for a person of average height to climb through. After Norah and Elizabeth climb through, Elizabeth tells

Harold to return for them in half an hour. Harold doesn't say a word, but nods, and then Norah sees that he is quickly putting the wood back in place over the opening. A feeling of suffocation comes over her, but she takes a deep breath and follows Elizabeth. Ahead of them is a tunnel-like passageway.

"There's no air here, Beth. I smell smoke. I can't breathe!"

Elizabeth grabs her hand, "There's air, Norah, but it's a different kind of air. It's air that has angels flying through it, and you're one of them right now. There's some smoke from an old stove the runaways are cooking on. The stove pipe hooks up to the chimney the church uses so nothing looks suspicious."

Norah and Elizabeth walk down the passageway and Norah hears voices faintly singing. Eventually, Elizabeth leads them to the right and after removing a large stone placed in the wall, they climb through. When Norah walks in after Elizabeth, her sense is that she has entered a holy place. It reminds her of the holy wells in Ireland that her mother brought her to as a child. Most of the wells had rendered her silent in the midst of an unspoken and unseen presence. But here are three women and two men huddled together around an old cook stove. They stop singing, stand up, and turn sharply to see who has come into the room, their instincts alert to danger. When they see Elizabeth and Norah, they smile and continue singing, motioning for the girls to join them. Elizabeth leads Norah into their circle where there are tree stumps to sit on and Norah sits down and looks around at the faces of the runaways. Never has she been the only white person amongst all colored people. She feels humbled and recognizes that she is face to face with a suffering of a different kind than her own. It is fresh and raw, this sorrow, whereas her own has been wrapped up and put away within her Irish dresser and her soul. Here Norah sits and looks upon the most dignified of faces, uplifted to the heavens as if they didn't see the ceilings that kept them from peering into the sky. The two men have many scars that resemble meandering sentences etched onto their faces. Their stories will always be read on these men. When they open their eyes, they are large and pool with glistening tears. One man smiles while he sings, but the other man isn't singing and stands resolutely looking up, his eyes closed, and his arms folded. He is angry, Norah thinks, and for good reason.

Follow the drinking gourd! Following the drinking gourd. For the old man is awaiting for to carry you to freedom if you follow the drinking gourd...

Their voices harmonize and the runaways sway to the music as they sing. There is clapping, foot tapping, and at the end, a lot of humming and to Norah's ears what sounds like deep moaning that is musical. Norah is mesmerized and wishes she could join in as Elizabeth stands and sings with them. She closes her eyes and taps her foot to the music. And then when this song ends, everyone is silent with their eyes closed and then they begin singing again.

Wade in the Water...wade in the water...wade in the water, children.

God's going to trouble the water...God's going to trouble the water...

Norah stands, taps, and sways to the music, feeling her body move freely to the mysterious sounds that are strange, but comforting. These people sing as if they have learned how to drink from their own souls, for there has been no other place to drink from. *How simplistic and real,* thinks Norah, and her thoughts reel back to when she sat by the hearth in their cottage in Ireland. Da played the fiddle and then everyone would be silent until a neighbor sang *sean-nós* in the Irish language, their voice the only instrument. It was always a voice of storytelling that gave embellishment and meaning to their lives in this peculiar way of singing. It had made them feel they were living as kings and queens in spite of their hardships and toils. She hadn't realized how much she missed this musical way of life. She wonders at how her music has changed for it to come swirling together in vibrant shapes, tones, and taps at places like Pete's Dance Hall! This Negro music is sung from the fields of hard toil and her own Irish music sung *sean-nós* from the potato fields of hard toil. They are mixing together at Pete's in a new manner that is gutsy and jubilant.

The singing stops and the five runaways look to Elizabeth and ask her when they are going to leave.

"One more train is all. They've been told they're receiving a shipment of five large kegs of dark ale. Tonight, you'll be led out in some fine clothes and there'll be directions to the train. And then three quilts will be drying on the line. Pay attention to the middle quilt. It will tell you where to go next to meet a wagon that'll be taking you to Lake Ontario. Your stockholder is Frederick Douglass himself. He's a generous man; his own freedom was purchased close to $750.00."

While Elizabeth gives them directions, the men walk around the room nervously. The angry man punches an old hat repeatedly and the other keeps looking over at Norah, giving her a weak smile that is more like a grimace. Norah is confused because she has no idea what Elizabeth is telling them and why they'd need a stockholder. They all sit down on the tree stumps and are quiet for a few moments, and then one woman starts humming the last song.

"It's codes, Norah. Everything is a secret and let me tell you, it's these perfect secrets that lead our people to their freedom. It's all in train language and whoever contributes money to help someone get free is called a stockholder. My brothers and sisters here still have a long ways to go to get their freedom."

The other two women begin singing and everyone joins in:
Get on board, little children; get on board, little children. There's room for many more.

"Yes'm, there's room for many more, like my own two babies left in Georgia," a woman says and cries out, "Oh Lord have mercy on my children!" She puts her head in her hands and weeps, her tears flowing through them onto her lap.

Norah goes to the woman and puts her arm around her shoulders, thinking of her own Katie walking the unsafe streets above with Sean. What if...she wants to hurry and get back to her life, for she feels like she has fallen into another world. There is only so much she can do to help and hasn't she done enough by giving away her prized bonnets?

The woman stops crying and rocks back and forth humming. Norah leaves the woman and walks near the door. Elizabeth looks over at her and nods, as if to say they will leave soon.

"Norah here, her face lit up like a lantern amongst our dark ones, is the milliner, and she has been my dear friend for a long time. She made your bonnets so you look like you're dressed in style and no slave-catcher finds you in rags to send you back to your soul-drivers."

The woman who had been crying stands up and goes to Norah and takes hold of her hands.

"The Lord bless you, child, for your good heart!" she said.

She reaches into her skirts and pulls out a small bag and places it in Norah's hands.

"For you, Miss...I see there's angels around you 'cause you been through your own sorrowing. Those beings tole me to give you my lucky charm. Passing it on to keep the luck and blessing so we's moving forward to the freedom land."

Norah looks at the small bag made out of calico cloth and wonders what to do.

"What's your name?" she asks.

"Sarah..."

"Never mind tellin' your name, woman! We's not to give out our names to nobody, especially a white girl we know nothin' about!" the angry looking man shouts.

The woman ignores the man and smiles at Norah while she opens the bag and lets the contents spill into her hands.

Norah sees a few strands of horsehair, bones of a wee animal, and a skin of a snake that makes her squeamish. There is also a small block of wood that Sarah picks up and carefully pulls apart to reveal a four-leaf clover pressed into one side of the wood.

"Double the luck if I pass this on," Sarah said, "And luck is what we've had escaping to freedom, but more luck the good Lord needs to be giving us so we get to Canada all in one piece."

Norah ponders this small symbol of faith, hope, and luck that has been given to her. She wonders if she still believes in fairies.

Sarah puts the other piece of wood on the clover.

"It stays together fine 'cause my husband, Joshua, God have mercy on his soul, made it to last forever."

Sarah turns from Norah and puts her head down. Norah can see that she is crying quietly. The others look away and Norah hears a lot of sighing going on in the room. Elizabeth walks to the doorway to peer out, for she has been keeping watch to make sure no one has followed them. And then Sarah turns back to Norah and speaks to her in a whisper.

"Master Jenkins, he hated my Joshua with a fury and found any reason to whip him, but my husband is strong and powerful. He's a smart one, too, but Master beat him too many times and he run off. I know he's got his freedom and we'll be meeting in Canada. But some folks says he was found and hung, but I know in my heart these be only rumors and he's alive and waiting for me."

Sarah takes the other charms still in Norah's hands and puts them back in the bag. And then she holds up the block of wood and continues her story.

"Before he run off, the Master beat him like never before. He fell to the ground and stared at the grass as the whip came down again and again. Later when I was cleaning up his wounds and loving this good man of mine, he tole me what he saw in the grass all the while he was being whipped. It was this four-leaf clover God Himself put before him to give him hope. And then he went out late in the night and under the light of the moon, he found it and preserved it in this box. I give it to you cause I'm nearly home now and you need it more."

Norah is silent and fearful of taking such a powerful charm from this woman. She has never intended to become this entwined with the Negro just because she is friends with Elizabeth Jennings. She wants to leave. She can't get enough air in her lungs and her heart is pacing in her chest like a frightened animal. She doesn't know how to tell Sarah she can't accept this lucky box. Sarah needs it more than she does and Norah doesn't believe in any luck that can double. The woman's own beaten husband made it for her. Why would she give it to her, she wonders. She wants to get back to Katie and Sean and go home for a strong cup of tea.

"Where are the hats that Norah made?" Elizabeth asks, interrupting the interchange between Sarah and Norah.

Sarah rushes to the corner of the room and pulls the bonnets out of a burlap bag. When the women put them on their heads, Norah sees the women transformed into free, dignified women in the candlelight. They smile at her and then she carefully places the four-leaf clover charm inside her bodice and near her heart.

Chapter Fifteen

Norah sits with her feet up on her desk reading an old issue of the *Sun*. She is trying to understand the escalation of the war so she can write an article.

On July 4, 1861, President Lincoln, in a speech to Congress, stated the war is "...a People's contest...a struggle for maintaining in the world, that form, and substance of government, whose leading object is, to elevate the condition of men..." And then Congress authorized a call for 500,000 men to go to Washington.

"How can war elevate the condition of men when they are dying?" Norah says aloud. She has been in the habit of talking to herself. "It's elevating them alright, straight to heaven or hell!"

She folds the newspaper and throws it in the wastebasket, thinking of her Edward and the war.

Edward's letters heretofore had alleviated her worry with claims that he and the soldiers were doing nothing but marching endlessly back and forth in training. He had written that there had only been skirmishes that didn't amount to much. He had even joked about a couple of rebels who raised a white flag and then hollered over at the enemy for some decent coffee. She had been placated and believed he was going to be fine, especially since his volunteer term was soon going to be over.

She sighs and remembers his sweet kisses and their longing before he left. Three long months is all, he had said, and he would be home and they would plan a wedding!

"Darling Edward, have you altered as much as I have?" she says aloud.

Norah is certain Edward will be surprised to see that her clothing is less extravagant and that she has become somber and pensive. The letter she received a week ago said that his militia would be returning soon and he was eager to hold her in his arms and see little Katie. He has frequently asked about Sean and she has been honest with him about his visits. She had written Edward that Sean was accompanying her to the meetings she attends. He wrote back that he was thankful for Sean's care while he was away and he would take him out for a few pints when he returned. Norah is pleased Edward isn't jealous. Norah stands up and looks out the window, wondering how it will be to see Edward again. Harrigan left a few minutes before to go to the corner eatery to buy them food, for they are going to be working late. An hour passes and Norah wonders where he is. She walks to the door to open it and look for him and then Harrigan comes rushing in.

"I'm here, Norah!" Harrigan drops the food onto her desk. He moans and slumps into her chair, shaking his head.

"What's wrong? What's happened?" Norah asks, knowing there is more war news he has heard and it isn't good.

"The boys won't be returning soon and if they do, they'll be going right back out for more fighting."

"Edward's militia is due home the end of this month. What's happened?"

"The first major defeat has happened, that's what's happened! The battle took place at Bull Run." Harrigan pulls a newspaper out of one of the bags on the desk. He opens it and reads to Norah.

"The Union troops retreated and fell back to Washington with 2,700 casualties. The Confederates lost 2,000 men, but they had been victorious. President Lincoln and everyone now know that this is really war and it will be a long one."

Norah moves to the window, but she can't see the street below. Hot tears temporarily blind her.

"I'll be back. I'm going to Knox's store," she said, taking her purse from her desk and rushing out the door.

Charles Knox isn't surprised by Norah's visit and he immediately welcomes her into his office after the secretary came to tell him she was downstairs waiting to speak with him.

"Yes, my dear, I have heard about Edward. Please sit down." He is standing by the painting of his family hanging on the wall.

Norah sits at the edge of the sofa clutching her trembling hands. Although it is a humid summer day, she shivers and a heavy cloak of despair wraps around her shoulders.

"I received a telegram that there were over 2,000 casualties, but Edward, thank God, was spared…"

Norah jumps up to hug Mr. Knox, immense relief flooding her. She's embarrassed and he is, too, and she sits back down on the sofa and waits for him to continue.

"Apparently, the Union army commander in Washington, Brigadier McDowell, started campaigning before the men's 90-day enlistments expired. They weren't adequately trained and this, it is believed, led to the overwhelming Confederate victory. The Confederates lost men and our Union troops retreated with loss and then fell back to Washington."

"Thank God it's over then!" Norah exclaims, "When does Edward come home?"

"Norah, I'm afraid our hope to have a quick end to this war has dissipated in the light of such a terrible defeat.

Charles Knox sits down, fumbles with papers on his desk, and says nothing. Norah thinks he's overcome with feelings for his son. *Or might he be dismissing her?* She and Edward had agreed not to tell his father and family of their wedding plans for the present time. Edward told her that he proclaimed his love for her to his father. Norah looks at Mr. Knox and thinks she might tell him now that they were going to be married. Edward said that his father had given him sage advice about love and told him he was too young for serious involvement. But when Norah had pestered him further, Edward admitted his father said that Edward had much better prospects for marriage.

Looking over at Edward's silent father and remembering the day Edward told her this makes her angry. She had known right away who the better prospects were. Better prospect, that is. Florence. The sweet little singer his family had introduced him to. When Edward had seen how hurt Norah was by his father's words, he assured her of his undying love and Norah had believed him and wasn't worried. But now as she sits before his father she thought she once liked, she has some doubt. *And silly me,* Norah thinks, *just because Mr. Knox came from Ireland as I have, doesn't mean he has a soft place for me in his heart. False confidence I had,* she thinks now, watching Charles Knox stare at the papers on his desk.

Norah gets up from the sofa and walks to Mr. Knox's desk.

"I know you don't approve of me... for many reasons. I'm from Five Points and I'm older than Edward. There's still a slight brogue to my speech that reminds you of where I came from. Where you came from. It would be hypocritical of you to disapprove of me for coming from Ireland and I don't think you're that kind of a man, but sometimes we don't live out our ideals, do we, Mr. Knox? You're a kind man...honest and hard working. I admire you, but you are no better than me. I am as hard working as you are, Mr. Knox, and I love your son."

Mr. Knox immediately gets up from his desk and puts his arm around Norah's shoulders.

"We are both grateful and must give thanks to God for Edward's safety. And we must pray for the families who have suffered great loss. Please, Norah, be safe on the way home," he said to her. *Now he is dismissing me.*

They walk to the door and he smiles. Worry lay heavy over his forehead and in his eyes. "Do you need me to get you a carriage, Norah?"

"No, sir, I have to return to work and it isn't far from here."

She doesn't know if he knows where she works, or if he even cares to know. Norah walks out of his department store that day and understands that although they are both from Ireland, there really is very little they share in common, except for loving Edward. *An ocean is crossed and then there's a hell of a lot of blood letting for some, like Mr. Knox. He's gone and got himself all new American blood!*

Edward came home with his regiment, but only for a brief reprieve. During this time, Norah learns that Edward is quite the storyteller. They are sitting in the midst of his family in Edward's opulent parlor on East Eighty-Third Street. She is most uncomfortable sitting with his beloved sister, mother, father, and other siblings sipping cordials and tea after they have eaten a five-course dinner. *A fish out of water*, she'd heard people say at times, and right now she feels as if she is flapping around on the beach gasping for breath. She attempts to interject comments, hold her teacup properly, and *fit in. How does a person like herself fit in*, she wonders. She need not worry about adding sparkle to the conversation, for Edward himself is all aglow as he relates his war experiences.

"We were all green, like the shoots come up in springtime, easily trampled, yet strong. Soldiers were running so fast that the money they had received as wages the day before fell right out of their pockets!" Edward says.

"Money to convince them to stay and fight when they were no ways ready!" his father interjects. Norah's notices that Edward's mother looks down at her teacup for the longest time, as if she is trying to find a message in it. His siblings fidget, but his oldest sister, Margaret, sits in rapt attention. So does Norah.

"Everyone's talking about you, Edward. You're just one of the swells of Piccadilly!" Margaret proclaims.

The family laughs and it is clear that Edward is basking in all this attention. *And rightly so*, thinks Norah, *for he is so brave to volunteer for his country.* His family listens with interest as Edward recounts the battle with humor and lightheartedness, as if he has only been an observer and not a partaker of this serious life and death experience. Not only is Norah sitting amongst the wealthy Knox clan for the first time, she is also detecting a curious side of

Edward she has not known. He likes the limelight! But more than that, he has been fearless and courageous in the face of battle. She is proud of him, but wonders how he can be this nonchalant about the dangers of war and loss of life.

"The poor lads ran so fast that by the time they reached Washington, they weren't only shoeless, but penniless as well. All that money they accepted fell out of their pockets!"

Everyone but Norah and Edward's mother laugh.

"Some of the men ran so fast that their toe nails were missing when they finally found themselves out of the sounds and smells of the conflict!"

It turned out to be an odd day altogether, Norah remembers later when she is in bed with Katie trying to sleep. Edward's family had huddled around him with adoration, hanging on to every word he spoke. It had made Edward all the more the storyteller, as if it was a glorious thing, this war. His mother had said she was glad it was over and now he could get back to school and help his father out at the store. Edward had looked over at Norah and winked to remind her that there would also be a wedding. For a brief moment, she had relaxed into this knowledge that soon she'd become Mrs. Edward M. Knox and Katie and she would be a part of this big, successful family. And she could bring her own family into this one and it would be even larger and grand because their roots had grown from the same soil in Ireland. But then why didn't Edward announce it right then and there to his family? She felt belittled, somehow, and when he escorted her home she wanted to tell him so, but then he enthusiastically started on about re-enlisting and responding to Lincoln's cry for more soldiers. He was returning to the war and there would be no wedding plans.

The Irish 69th Regiment of New York State Militia led by Colonel Michael Corcoran had secured Annapolis, an important connection between the seacoast and Washington. They had arrived in the capital in May and set up camp on the grounds of the Catholic college, Georgetown. Abraham Lincoln visited them and praised them for coming to the government's rescue just a few weeks after the war broke out. The 69th had built Fort Corcoran in Arlington Heights. There had been other regiments employed in constructing forts and trenches around the capital, as well as repairing bridges and railroad lines damaged by Confederate sympathizers. But right away the 69th earned a reputation for arduous, heavy labor, for they were mostly bricklayers and skilled carpenters who had worked on crews and gangs in New York. After Fort Corcoran was built, a priest offered a Mass in June to baptize the cannons of the fort, but he was removed from his post for his sacrilege. Nevertheless, the celebration of the fort was for a momentous feat, for it was large enough to contain three regiments and the Irish boys had certainly received the praise of Lincoln and the men in Washington. The Irish lads were getting due attention and were not to be reckoned with! Although defeat hung over the Union Army after Bull Run and the brave Colonel Corcoran was taken to a Confederate prison, along with over a thousand Union soldiers, no one now could deny the loyalty of the fighting Irish.

The young and impressionable Private Edward M. Knox who had been coddled and cherished by his loving and affluent business family understood all of this. He had never even had a rowdy or a bunch of punishers thrust a cudgel or stick in his face. The Irish Brigade appealed to Edward, for he was wise enough to know who to align himself with so as to bring about victory not just for his country, but for himself and his family name.

Norah thinks otherwise about the glory of the Irish soldiers and had confided in Sean after Edward told her he was joining the Irish Brigade. Sean had agreed with Norah that the Irish soldiers were foolish to think they were that important and honored.

"No matter how much the U.S. government values the dedication and bravery of the Irish soldiers, Norah, the Irish born are still rebellious and dirty Irish in their eyes. It will take a long time to be free in a country that shouts freedom at every turn of the corner."

And as much as Sean respects and likes Edward, he tells Norah that he sees clearly that the young stud is a greenhorn in matters of mankind's illusions about liberty and justice.

"And furthermore, the lad has not been born in Ireland or Germany. You can polish up the brass, but the rust will still come through. All shine until trouble arrives."

Norah replies that Edward had already been in a battle and he had shone right through it.

Norah pleads with Edward not to re-enlist and, although she is beginning to believe that maybe the abomination of slavery can be abolished by an all-out full-scale war, she does not want Edward or Sean to be sacrificed for this cause. Edward makes his case clearly to her about the war.

"You can't cut off half a man and expect him to live!" he says.

"The South is trying to do this and the Union won't survive. And if slavery can be halted to the west, it might wither and die on the vine in the South. It's a worthy cause. There's no other way, Norah!"

When Norah, Edward, Sean, Leary, and Nellie were together at the apartment discussing the war, Sean made his feelings known and he and Edward nearly came to fisticuffs over the issue. Norah knows Sean well enough to know that there is no way in hell Edward could make him feel less of a man because he wasn't signing up. Norah can clearly see that Edward had been insinuating this. But she knows that if there is one thing Sean is sure of, it is his manliness.

In the end, Norah gives up begging Edward not to go and prepares her heart for loss. It is the only way she can possibly survive the days ahead. But before Edward leaves with all the pomp and circumstance presented to the marching units as they depart New York, she gives the newly made 2nd Lt. in the Battery of Artillery of the Irish Brigade, Edward M. Knox, the little box with the four leaf clover. It is a magic thing, she is sure of it, for she had heard that the five large kegs of dark ale had safely arrived in Canada. She wishes she knew if Joshua was there waiting for Sarah, but she never found out. So she sends Edward off with the little box with the four-leaf clover, and she and Katie wave little paper American flags along the street as the units parade proudly into the war.

Chapter Sixteen

In the absence of Colonel Michael Corcoran who is now being held in a Confederate prison, Thomas Francis Meagher becomes the new commander of the 69th. The man's patriotism has taken a turn, Norah thinks, when she reads the news in the papers. He claims that any Irish veteran can "take his stand proudly by the side of the native-born, and will not fear to look him straight and sternly in the face, and tell him that he has been equal to him in his allegiance to the Constitution." Norah is dumbfounded, for Meagher was the former leader of the Young Ireland of the 1840s, the Irish revolutionary group that her husband, Murray, had been a member of. It ultimately had claimed her husband's life and nearly her own! And now her beloved Edward is following this revolutionary lawyer who had once escaped from a Tasmania prison into the dangers of war. And then she reads the news that John Mitchel, the former Irish patriot whom she had traveled with on the fated ship, has joined the Confederacy. *These men have warring hearts and care not so much for ideals, but for their own glory!* Disbelief and anxiety consume her when she says goodbye to Edward once more. And it startles her that she has never told him about her life with these clandestine leaders of the Young Ireland movement. It is too late now, for he is gone, she thinks sadly day after day. And as practical as Norah has become, the mythical meanings of her past and Irish superstition are as intricate as a Celtic knot design. Is there some kind of curse upon her life that forbids her love?

There is no time to ponder her misgivings for not telling her history to Edward, nor can she give way to the fear that some Irish curse has followed her to America. There is much to do and activity gives her some relief from her conflicting feelings. She keeps up with the news from Washington for *The Rousing Clarion*, teaches Sunday school, and continues her efforts to provide hats for the runaway slaves. And along with the Irish women in Five Points, Norah sews flags and banners for the troops. She is especially pleased to sit with a committee of women headed up by Maria Daly, the wife of the prominent judge, Charles P. Daly, and emblaze an Irish harp in the center of a green flag made by Tiffany & Company for the 69th Irish Brigade. Charles P. Daly, another Irishman made good like Mr. Knox and many others, is a Democrat, dislikes Lincoln and his administration but supports the war effort. Norah can't help sharing her good news with the women about her engagement to Edward M. Knox, a soldier from a good family serving in the revered brigade.

"I never saw anything posted in the papers or the *Rousing Clarion*. Haven't you publicly announced this prestigious news, Norah?" a wife of a prominent member of *The Friendly Sons of St. Patrick's* asks.

Norah is vexed.

"No, it hasn't been announced and I didn't realize my marriage plans would have to be published!"

And now because she has blurted out they are going to marry after the war, she fears Edward's parents will hear and she will bring embarrassment to herself and Edward. *Will his father be ashamed of hearing this news through a member of a sewing circle? But why should it be so?*

Norah shakes off her anxiety while sewing gold onto green, an apt symbol, and chatters on about her work at the *Rousing Clarion*. None of the women are interested and don't engage in conversation about the articles she has written for the *Clarion*. Well, what can I expect of them? The *Clarion* is quite a liberal newspaper, at that, and these women are of the old traditional and conservative ways, she thinks, disappointedly.

The city bustles with frenetic activity in response to the war effort. Many Irishmen join the *Irish Rifles*, a militia that was formed in the 1850s in hopes of liberating Ireland. There is a high rate of unemployment amongst Irishmen and thus they sign up for the money, but also think it will ultimately culminate in victory for ole' Ireland. It is believed that after the war, Irishmen will have gained valuable training and America certainly will come to the warriors' aid to help free Ireland. Signing up for this civil war is also for personal honor, for they can't sit by after being cajoled into believing that they owe America for welcoming them into their country. It doesn't matter that it is a reluctant welcome, at that, even a hostile one. But the Irish come from Ireland have already learned to be thankful for the crumbs that fall from the table.

The Friendly Sons of St. Patrick's contribute $1,500.00 to help equip and sustain the 69th. Daniel Devlin of Devlin & Company provide uniforms free of charge and Brooks Brothers and A.T. Stewart soon have army and navy contracts for making uniforms, although they scrimp on materials and there is talk of shoddy work. Charles Knox is also contributing to the war effort through provision of hats and Norah volunteers to help with packing and shipping. Letters from Edward arrive on writing paper and envelopes with pro-Union sentiments. He uses shamrock envelopes that read, 'Here's to Ireland's SHAMROCK, may its pure unsullied green, as a bond of love and UNION 'midst the Irish ever be seen. And may it help to bind the love by the exile Irish shown, to the land which gave them liberty, shelter and a home.'

"Why does Edward feel the need to be aligned with this Irish sentiment when he was born right here in America?" Norah asks Harrigan one day.

"These indeed are perplexing times, Norah dear. Be glad for his patriotism to both his country and Ireland."

Some of the women in Five Points who once snubbed her over her friendship with Elizabeth Jennings are now sidling up to her with heartfelt sentiments for her Edward's service in the 69th. These Irish women are proud to have the son of the prominent Charles Knox serving in the Irish 69th Brigade. *He is a true Irish lad, he is, this Edward M. Knox!* As Norah sews with these ladies in a circle of new friendship, sometimes she tries to insert her thoughts about abolishing slavery. Indeed, their sympathies surprise her at times, for they aren't so far from the memory of the domination of British landlords. They are certainly of a different sort than Maria Daly's do-gooders and she is much more comfortable with them.

Eventually, the Union is broke and the banks respond and loan the government money. And after this, the Union nears bankruptcy and Congress authorizes the treasury to print money. In February 1862 they begin issuing "greenbacks." Although this is the first uniform currency for the nation, the banks continue to print an abundance of notes. And then Congress reorganizes the entire banking system and the federal government charters the national bank. The Republican administration institutes taxes on manufactured products and businesses in order to raise money to pay the interest on its bonds and greenbacks. The government is forced to rely heavily on New York financial houses to sell bonds and negotiate loans. Money becomes abundant and facilitates the war boom and bondholders, bankers, manufacturers, and the wealthy all become beneficiaries of this prosperity.

Norah can hardly understand the feeding frenzy this Congress has created for the rich to get richer, all in the name of freedom to preserve the Union and liberate the slaves. And what of A.T. Stewart's new store that rises into the heavens with five stories and a great rotunda. Stewart himself compares the graceful arches in the Venetian manner to "puffs of white clouds." Customers can purchase outfits for balls, silks, men's outfits, linens, and just about anything one can imagine. Many of the women in the women's rights movement must think women's rights are coming to fruition because women are now entering the sales force for the first time.

"But it's really the men who are climbing ladders of success, such as A.T Stewart, another Irishman who has made good," Norah says to Harrigan one afternoon.

"And I heard he received a huge inheritance as a lad," she continues with angst.

"Don't forget that although he received a big inheritance as a lad, he also sent over shiploads of goods to Ireland during the famine and even brought back a ship full of immigrants."

Norah didn't want to argue with Harrigan that it was mostly Protestants he helped and so she kept quiet. But how is one to know just how sincere A.T. Stewart is while he's making a financial killing from this horrid war? The man now has the largest retail store in the world and is using the latest technology with steam engines that heats all the floors with water that is pumped to the laundry and powers up sewing machines. Norah is skeptical, but likewise mesmerized. She wants to be a part of this Irishman's luck and so she is soon hired to work on a sewing machine in the carpet-manufacturing department. But she quits after a week of ten-hour days that make her feel like a cog in a wheel. And there had been no time for Katie or helping Harrigan with the *Clarion*.

Harrigan suggests the *Rousing Clarion* speak truthfully and forthrightly about the suffering of the soldiers, the widows, and orphans while the bigwigs splurge and binge on shopping and food, including Mary Todd Lincoln herself! And in order to write a worthy article, James Harrigan wants to go for dinner at the most elegant Delmonico's restaurant to ogle the new millionaires decked out in their fineries.

"No!" Norah responds.

"Why not?" Harrigan asks.

Norah slumps down on the couch in the office. She doesn't want to be amongst the uppity classes with their newly minted money and stinking arrogance. But there is a side of her that doesn't want to be a mere spectator and sure now, she can dress the part.

"I don't have the proper clothes...and I can't afford them!"

"I know better, my dear. Miss Norah McCabe, who loves her apparels, would not have given away all of her hard-earned wardrobe to the poor. And dinner is on me."

Harrigan sits down on the sofa next to her and takes her hand, "On second thought, I shall not be profligate like the rest of the bastards in this newspaper industry. Just because I'm selling more papers, I won't be spending it all at Delmonico's! Let's go for a late lunch and then linger long enough to see the bedecked patricians and be bedazzled!"

In the end, Norah agrees to go. Although she is not that energetic, for the war efforts and her worries over Edward have drained her, she is radiant amongst the pampered poodles. And when Norah looks at the women in their fineries and extravagant clothing purchases, they look similar in dress and style, as if they have come off A.T. Stewart's militaristic production line.

Norah wears a French blue taffeta gown with wide grey stripes and a lovely tulle & lace head-dress, wired black tulle with handmade French knot accents that is trimmed in black Chantilly lace and lined in rich blue tulle with bobbin lace accent at the back. She wears high-button boots made of gingham wool with a twill lining that matches her gown and hat. When she stands before Nellie and Katie as she waits for Harrigan to arrive to take her to Delmonico's, Nellie says she looks scrumptious and Harrigan might propose marriage. Norah makes a face at Nellie and Katie jumps up and down with glee for she cherishes Mr. James Harrigan. Certainly Norah's gown is fabulous, a dress leftover from her shop and although not an evening dress, it is proper enough for a late lunch at the famous Delmonico's on Fifth Avenue and Fourteenth Street, the most sumptuous of the Delmonico restaurants. Harrigan, as usual, is dressed impeccably, sporting a cravat knot worn with a beige Grafton collar, a silk vest, and an olive-colored derby to match.

"My dear Norah, you are ravishing!" Harrigan said, picking up Katie and bouncing her around before they leave for Delmonico's, the first real luxury restaurant in New York.

Women accompanied by male escorts are allowed into the Astor

Hotel Restaurant and Delmonico restaurant, for the times are rapidly changing. There are so many newly-minted men of fortune, who gives a care if a woman dripping in pearls and diamonds is on the arm of a new millionaire who recently signed yet another prosperous deal with a manufacturer?

Norah is not dripping in pearls, nor did she own any jewelry of worth and thus decides not to wear any. Harrigan is quite astute about Norah McCabe, thus when he comes to pick her up in a shiny equipage, he also brings her a pair of earrings.

"These are French, my dear. They're the Swan's Shadow. And they're opal diamond earrings for you not only to wear today, but for you to keep and wear whenever we partake of haute cuisine."

"I can't accept such exquisite earrings! I'm not your paramour, your wife, nor a relative..."

Harrigan puts his white-gloved finger to Norah's lips, "Shhh, no objections. I've known you through tragedy and triumph and you've given me much joy, as well as headaches. I've changed for the better because of you. And for this and our first Delmonico experience, it's my gift to you."

Norah says not another word and, with a blush, she puts on the earrings.

Delmonico's is one block west of Union Square and houses a café and restaurant in a converted mansion. Damask draperies frame the tall windows, and as they pull up to the building and the restaurant, it appears to Norah as a sanctum of decorum for gentility.

"Let's go somewhere else!" Norah whispers as they approach the restaurant with large, imposing columns and heavy wooden doors. Harrigan says nothing and merely presses the small of her back with a firm hand and escorts her inside. They are eyed curiously as they are led through the restaurant to a table in a far corner of the large room. Norah keeps her head up and her eyes on the host's back as they walk to their table. She doesn't hear the rustling of crinoline or detect the fragrances of wealthy women, but then again the smells of roast meat dominate the room. She thinks it is eerily quiet, for there is no tinkling of silver or loud conversations. Certainly not like

Pete's Dance Hall! When she is seated and presented with a menu enclosed in a leather folder, she becomes nervous because she will have to use more than two utensils and order from a menu that has fare she knows nothing about. Although comfortable with Harrigan, she doesn't believe he'll know how to conduct himself in an eatery such as this one that is full of the moneyed elite of the country. They both open up the folder and Norah fingers the menu that is printed in gold. To her chagrin, the only word she recognizes on the page is Menu! She looks across the table at Harrigan, but he is holding the menu in front of his face and she can't catch his eye. She sets the menu down and looks around the room.

There is a high gilded ceiling, as well as marble portals, shining chandeliers, over-sized paintings on the walls, and mahogany wood accents everywhere. Their table is laid with a crisp white linen tablecloth. An oriental vase with a large pink peony sits in the middle of their table. Norah brings the vase to her nose, closes her eyes, and inhales. The fragrance is intoxicating and calms her nerves. She relaxes back in her chair and exhales a little too loudly. She is not going to be intimidated and will figure out what to order even if she has to pretend and point to something on the menu.

"Is something wrong?" asks the impeccably dressed waiter who comes to the table. Norah detects a German accent from this waiter who possesses a very stiff and serious demeanor. She resists doing something atrocious, like knocking over her water glass.

"Everything's perfect!" Norah smiles up at him, fingering a curl that has fallen out of her chignon.

"We have an extensive wine cellar, Sir," the waiter said, smiling at Harrigan, who has been so absorbed in trying to read the menu that he's startled when addressed. He flips the menu into the air and the prim waiter catches it as if it is a common happenstance. Harrigan cocks his head and grins at Norah.

"My dear, shall I ask for the wine list or would you like something else? Perhaps a matutinal cocktail…absinthe…sherry-and-bitters? How about an Evening Pony? Oh no, it's not quite evening, is it? Maybe a mint julep then? Even a foaming champagne cocktail?"

The waiter stands erect and doesn't reveal impatience or irritation.

Norah giggles and holds her napkin to her mouth.

"A foaming champagne cocktail sounds superb, my dear Harrigan!" she answers.

"A champagne that bubbles over with enthusiasm and delight, please, just as the lady does herself," Harrigan said to the waiter, "And a bourbon on the rocks for me!"

The waiter nods and leaves. Harrigan and Norah stifle nervous laughter.

"Look discreetly…three tables to your right and you will see the dapper Mayor Oakey Hall with his green frock coat with pure gold coins for buttons. And I do believe an Astor or Vanderbilt is with him."

Norah looks over and sees men decked out in velvet coats and gold chains. She wouldn't know an Astor from a Vanderbilt, or even the mayor. She is more interested in the exotic looking plates of food going by her, carried effortlessly by one waiter. The aroma is tantalizing and rich and she knows immediately that this is what she wants to order, whatever it might be.

"What's on the plates the waiter is carrying?" she whispers to Harrigan.

Harrigan stands up and looks over the shoulder of the waiter and then tiptoes back to the table. There are diners at the other tables who stare at them. She blushes and looks down at the menu.

"Plump partridges…" Harrigan sniffs the air noticeably and diners continue to stare.

"I detect an exquisite ingredient, one that is not all that familiar… hmmm…" he says, closing his eyes in concentration.

"Never mind, Harrigan…whatever it is, I want it. Now we've just got to figure out which one it is on this menu!" Norah says, staring at the menu.

"Truffles! Truffles!" Harrigan says way too loudly. "That's it, partridges stuffed with truffles!"

Their waiter serves their drinks and after setting them down, he leans down to Harrigan and whispers, "The management has asked that you refrain from any further outbursts, Sir."

"Absolutely!" Harrigan says so loudly that the waiter jumps back and presses a finger to his lips as he backs away.

Norah points to an item on the menu and shows Harrigan, "I think it's this: *Bécasses bardées.* Do you know how to pronounce it?"

"Well, my dear, it might be best to order the Canvas-back duck, for we are assured of what that is…and I can pronounce it."

"Do you see anything that might be the partridge?" Norah asks, sipping her champagne.

"He speaks English, this waiter, Norah…begads, he's only a waiter and not the king or the Mayor himself! We can tell him we want the partridge!"

"I want to order it from the menu," Norah said.

"Then take a chance. I know some French and I don't see the partridge anywhere, but you're right, perhaps this is right…I'll order for you."

They put their menus down, take sips of their drinks, and the waiter is back at their table. He turns to Harrigan for the order and waits.

"The lady will have the *Bécasses bardées,*" he says, pronouncing it without any hesitation. And I shall have the canvas-back duck, thank you."

The waiter repeats the order and his pronunciation of *Bécasses bardées* sounds quite different than Harrigan's.

When the waiter places the *Bécasses bardées* plate in front of Norah, she is surprised it does not look like what Harrigan said were partridges. Whatever she has been served smells delicious, but she wants to know what it is she is eating. Although not a picky eater, she is not used to anything that veers too far from a stew, potatoes, and root vegetables. Harrigan's duck at least looks like real food.

"Is there anything else, Sir?"

Harrigan looks at Norah and she makes a face at him. She is irritated that the waiter won't address her.

"Excuse me, but please tell me what this is on my plate."

"*Bécasses bardées*, Madame, as your escort ordered for you."

"Yes, I know, but tell me in English what it is, please."

"Encased woodcock, Madame, an extraordinary dish prepared by our renowned French chef, Charles Ranhofer."

"Sort of like a wee chicken, Harrigan" she says, after the waiter leaves them to their dinner.

The champagne relaxes Norah into the delights of eating this exotic meal and she and Harrigan utter exclamations of glee while eating, which prompts the attention of the diners again. Norah licks her fingers, glances around the room and laughs. When they finish and the waiter brings them their *Napolitaine* for dessert, a young man comes to their table and introduces himself as Mr. Timothy O'Sullivan who says he reads *The Rousing Clarion* with great interest.

"I'd be obliged if you took a seat at our table while we finish our sumptuous dessert, Mr. O'Sullivan," Harrigan said.

"Waiter!" Harrigan calls a little too loudly, "a drink for this young man."

Introductions are made and conversation ensues about the weather and the delicious fare at Delmonico's. After Norah and Harrigan finish with their dessert, Mr. O'Sullivan places his arms on the table, clasps his hands, and leans in to indicate he wishes to speak solemnly.

"I like your paper, Mr. Harrigan. It's balanced and doesn't mince words about Lincoln's anti-constitutional measures and the anti-war movement. However, I note strong abolitionist overtones, of late. Whether going to war for this is reasonable, moral, or otherwise, I don't know. But you do get a man thinking with your paper..."

"And I'm sure the paper gets women thinking," he said, smiling and nodding to Norah.

"I'm pleased you think so. Our sales are high and we're working day and night. For much of the thinking part of the paper, Mr. O'Sullivan, I have to recognize my assistant here, Norah McCabe. She's a free-thinking woman, she is...a feminist of sorts, but not all out, mind you and she—"

"Please, Harrigan, you're making me feel embarrassed. You shouldn't be drinking so much of the bourbon!"

Mr. O'Sullivan and Harrigan laugh and Mr. O'Sullivan leans in again to speak quietly.

"I'm a photographer and I've just returned from Mathew Brady's office in Washington. I've been an assistant, as you, Norah, and I've also worked with another photographer, Mr. Alexander Gardner. We've been on the battle fields and it's not a pretty picture we've been taking."

Timothy O'Sullivan puts his head down a moment and Norah thinks about men's ability to endure having to kill and seeing those killed. But then she remembers that she has seen the dead in Ireland, those killed slowly by the British with starvation. *Women see, too.* She imagines Edward and it pains her to think of his gentle hands that caressed her face holding a gun. Her mind has stored up photos of the dead strewn across fields in Ireland who hadn't been gunned down or blown up with cannonballs in a war. These pictures are always available to her.

"You have pictures of the war? They'll tell the story for generations after we're gone. But do you know how to destroy the photos the mind takes and stores? And do ye think that they are passed down to our children's children? If so, they wouldn't be clear, would they? The photos of the mind," Norah's thoughts tumble out.

No one speaks for a few moments and the waiter returns to ask if they need anything else. Harrigan hands him a wad of money. New greenbacks, Norah thinks.

"Yes, Miss McCabe, I suppose there are two types of photography, but it's up to us to destroy the pictures in the mind as best as we can, for they'll destroy us if there are too many, for then there will be no room for pictures of goodness. But the photos of this war will endure. I feel the importance of these photos that will help keep a nation from destroying itself again."

There is further awkward silence as the murmur of polite conversation amidst opulence and plenty rubs up against the horrors of war, like an adoring cat against the boots of a cruel master.

Timothy O'Sullivan explains that he and Alexander Gardner are leaving Mathew Brady's office and setting out on their own to photograph the Union army. He tells Harrigan that he can send some sketches for the *Rousing Clarion*, if he desires. He said he isn't much of an artist, but he'll try.

"Harper's doing a good job with the illustrations of this war, why not *The Rousing Clarion*?" Harrigan said, animated and excited.

"The photographs have to be engraved on wooden plates in order to be printed in publications. It's an arduous process and takes time and so the newspapers rely on the artist for sketches. I wouldn't be too good at writing up a story about the drawings. My photos would have to tell their own story. Course now, I can give name and place."

"If I was a brave one, I'd be going to write up the stories for your photos, Mr. O'Sullivan," Norah said.

"I need you here, Norah, and although I've been hearing about women going to the battlefields, mostly they're going to nurse the injured."

Norah's courage had once prompted her to join a rebel movement to fight for Ireland's freedom, but that courage had been gilded with zealous love. And since that adornment had been washed away, her courage had crumbled. She has none, except for Katie's life. Her mission is to create some sort of lasting beauty with her hats and to help the runaways. She is no brave soldier for story or otherwise. It is Edward who is fearless and gallant, as well as the runaway slaves whom she admires.

Mr. Timothy O'Sullivan, Harrigan, and Norah promise to stay in touch and yes, indeed, Harrigan said he'd be proud to print his sketches of the war and they'll do their best to write something up to go with them.

Chapter Seventeen

As the bloody conflicts continue and the death count increases, Five Points' residents are ambivalent over the purpose of the war. But when they learn about Gen. Ulysses S. Grant being unprepared when Confederate troops conducted a surprise attack at Shiloh on the Tennessee River, they're convinced the war is in vain. After a horrid struggle, 13,000 Union soldiers and 10,000 Confederate soldiers are killed or wounded. Three of the soldiers are from the old tenement building Norah and her family had lived in. After Norah read the news in the papers in the morning and walked by the building, she heard the families of the soldiers weeping loudly. It sounded like utter hopelessness.

Later, she arrives at *The Rousing Clarion* and agrees with Harrigan to write an article about the battle. While she writes, the war is unreal in some ways to her. She has been to see Charles Knox in the morning to ask him about Edward. Edward hadn't been in this battle, but she imagined all the sweethearts, sons, and husbands who had been. Will Edward die in the next battle?

A few days later, Harrigan said it isn't just Five Points angry over the war, but according to the newspapers, the entire city seems to be so.

"Every man, woman, and child seems is protesting against this war. They're saying that it is for the rich to get richer and the poor to get killed. And don't we know there are a lot of poor Irishmen getting killed!"

Tucked away in Norah's journal, as well as in her worried heart, are Edward's letters. He writes of the defeat at Fredericksburg under Gen. Ambrose Burnside with the loss of 12,653 men. He doesn't say how he got through it and she wonders how he survived.

A few times a week after work, Norah rushes to St. Brigid's to light a candle for Edward. Da told Norah a few years ago that St. Brigid's had been built by Famine immigrants. What a sorrow, she thinks. She also read that the Reverend Mooney had been forced to return to this church after he had been with the 69th regiment. In his zeal, the priest had blessed a cannon and got in trouble with the canon of the church. She is glad for this pastor's presence in the church, for he is obviously motivated by love more than the laws of his church. Does she believe, she asks herself time and again? She doesn't know, but she is shaken by this war and her love for Edward. And when Edward wrote matter-of-factly about Burnside's Mud March and how he had come forth unscathed from a bog looking like his ancestors in Ireland, she was not amused by his story. *Is he merely trying to assure her of his safety or is he too light-hearted about the war?*

Abraham Lincoln issues the final Emancipation Proclamation on January 1, 1863. Norah and her friends attend an Emancipation Jubilee at Cooper Union and celebrate further at her and Nellie's apartment. As they near the apartment, Norah shouts, "Just think, everyone! The slaves in territories held by Confederates are free!" Nellie and Norah splurge and make a pot roast with all the fixings. Sean, however, is nervous and keeps telling Norah that she should keep quiet about her feelings over the slaves being freed in the south.

"Sit on the fence, Norah. Five Points people can't afford to be for or against, so ye should keep still and not be shouting the news in the streets! They don't have a newspaper job like you and fancy clothes and all. They're scared of losing their jobs to the free

Negroes coming up from the south. I have nothing against the Negro and tis so that slavery is unnatural, but this war is about Americans fighting Americans and it's all wrong."

"I won't sit on any fence, Sean!" Everyone is quiet and the celebratory spirit wanes. They have already had their excitement nearly doused after leaving Cooper Union to walk to the apartment. Someone had yelled, "Dirty Niggers and Black Republicans make good bed partners!" Norah had turned around to fight back with words of her own, but Elizabeth and Graham told her to ignore the remarks. Sean grabbed her arm and pulled her away. Norah thought of the sewing circle the night before when a few women had made snide remarks about Lincoln and then stared at her. She had said nothing, but after she went home, she had been spitting mad as a March hare and ready to fight for freedom…for the runaways…for justice and for what is right. The rumble of anger was coming from deep within her, as if stored there for all wrongdoings.

After dinner, they enjoy a raspberry pie Nellie has made. Sean is fidgeting in his chair and keeps looking out the window. He stands and retrieves a newspaper out of his coat pocket and everyone watches him as he sits back down and opens up the paper.

"This Irish judge, McCunn, is complaining fairly strongly that we're expending millions of dollars in a war against slavery. Now listen to what he says here…and I apologize before I read to you, Beth, and to you, Charles…." Sean said, glancing nervously at Elizabeth and Charles Graham.

"According to this Catholic paper, McCunn says, ' "He has seen the Negro at the mouth of the Congo River, and the Slavery of the South was a paradise in comparison The Negro was a prince in the South compared to his situation at home.' "

The noise of the clatter of teacups being placed in their saucers is the only sound in the room. Norah's chair scrapes across the floor when she pushes back from the table and stands up.

"Holy Mary Mother of God, what has gotten into you bringing this nonsense to a table full of our friends. These feelings are not our sentiments, but I'm wondering if they're your own? Why else would you feel the need to read this to us now?"

"Are you worried freed slaves will come and offer to take your job for less pay than you receive? Are you worried about this, Sean?" Elizabeth asks.

"Maybe you would feel degraded to a level with us, then," Charles said.

Sean doesn't answer, but takes a slurp of tea and then stares into his cup. Nellie gets up to clear the table and Leary gets up to help her. Norah sits back down and they drink more tea, saying nothing for what seems to be a long time.

Sean finally gets up and puts on his coat and stuffs the newspaper into his pocket. He looks over at Charles Graham.

"I've seen the backs of slaves whipped so much they resembled raw meat. I want nothing to do with furthering slavery. But I want nothing to do with war. I saw enough fighting as a boy in Ireland. I'm worried, alright, but not about a Negro taking me job. I'm worried here for this woman and child I love more than my own life. You've got her all fired up to work for freedom of the slaves down south and she's putting herself in danger. And what about you, Charles? Why you especially...just hanging around Norah can get you killed! Just last week, a Negro was accused of assaulting an Irishwoman and then he was lynched. I won't describe what they did to the poor bugger!"

Norah sets her teacup carefully onto the saucer and gets up to go to Sean, but he walks out and slams the door. It's the second time he has slammed the door in her face and this is a sign to Norah. She has had enough of his volatile and unpredictable ways. But more than that, she must let the door shut between them, for this love he has for her and Katie is like a storm that can only bring damage to her and Edward.

Everyone says very little after Sean leaves and soon Charles and Elizabeth leave and Leary follows them out.

"You know that freedom doesn't spring forth like flowers in springtime. Declaring it is like planting the bulbs in autumn and there'll be a long winter of struggle before it emerges," Norah says to Nellie after everyone leaves.

That evening, Nellie holds Katie Marion and rocks her to sleep as Norah works frenetically in the corner of the living room sewing artificial lily of the valley and tiny rosebuds on a felt hat. Soon, Nellie carries Katie to bed and returns to sit next to Norah as she works.

"It's true, Norah...what Sean said tonight. President Lincoln's proclamation has brought to the surface hatred for the Negro that's been seething for a long time. It's everywhere in this city, but when you parade about with Elizabeth in Five Points now, you can expect to have a brick thrown at your head. You have to consider Katie in all of this. What would she do without you if something...?"

Norah puts the hat down on the table and says to Nellie, "I haven't survived so many horrid things in my life to die on the streets of Five Points, Nell! I'll continue to make my hats for the runaways, but I promise to be careful."

"There are those who believe that Lincoln is going too far by detaining and arresting men who are standing strong against this war. Some believe he's far too radical and violating the rights of the people. And in Five Points, crazy Fernando Wood has denounced Lincoln and says that emancipation substitutes niggerism for nationality."

"Nell! Enough! Not everyone in Five Points believes this!"

"I'm against slavery, too, Norah, but I'm a realist and will do anything to protect you and Katie. Nellie gets up and kisses Norah on the cheek, "I'm going to bed now," and leaves Norah alone.

Norah continues to sew late into the night, her nimble fingers moving rapidly to create elegance to dissipate the dark storm hovering in her mind.

The ominous cloud of racial and political pressure that has brooded over New York for two years explodes in the spring of 1863 when Congress institutes a draft to supplement the dwindling voluntary enrollments. There is a conscription clause that allows a draftee to find a substitute or pay $300.00 in lieu of going off to war.

"Fine and dandy that the rich son-of-a-bitches can pay the greenbacks, but the poor asses can't pay a dime!" Leary said to Norah and Nellie one day when he stopped in for tea.

Norah thinks how ironic it is that Edward would have been able to pay the fee to get out of going to war, but Sean probably cannot or wouldn't pay it, anyway. She hasn't seen Sean since he left the day he read the newspaper aloud to them. He showed up at her door the next day, as she knew he would. She had left a letter attached to the door telling him she will always hold him dear in her heart, but that it is best if he doesn't visit her and Katie for the time being. *Maybe after this sorrowful war is entirely over, Sean, and then we can get back to taking meals together again,* she wrote, *for I hope to always have you in my life.* But she didn't write that after the war was over and she and Edward were married that then they could all be friends. She wanted to write this, but held back from telling him so because she knew it would hurt him. And now hearing the news about the draft that Lincoln and Congress has issued, she immediately thinks of Sean and fears for his life. She wants to race out the door to go to him and beg him to pay the conscription fee or go back to Ireland, but she doesn't.

Later, after Norah learned federal officials began choosing the first draftees, Norah got on her knees before the window facing the street and looked upon a sliver of a moon shining between two buildings and prayed for Sean. He had left his cap, his old, worn out hat she had brow beaten him over when he wore it to the House of Industry celebration. That night, she took it bed with her and fell asleep inhaling the lingering scent of his ginger hair.

Sean saw the same sliver of a moon frowning over New York as he lay on the roof of his tenement building. Not only is the summer heating up, so is the war, and so is the anger of Irish-Americans who don't have the means to pay the money to get out of being drafted. He doesn't want to fight in this war, but he also doesn't want to let go of his hard-earned money to get out of fighting. He is saving it for a house someday, a house befitting his Irish queen and her babe, and who knows, maybe a boy or two they might have together. Shipbuilding has increased and he has been in demand as a joiner and caulker, or for any other work he is able for when they ask. And because he is versatile in skill and has a keen mind and muscular build, as well as an easy-going disposition, he is asked to fill all sorts of positions in the ship building business. But then his union decides to strike and in some ways, he's glad for it because food costs have risen, coal prices are up, but wages have hardly increased and unions all around the city are striking. And sure as there's fire in hell, Sean thinks, the Negroes everyone feared would come take their jobs, are offering themselves up to work for a mere pittance. But it isn't only those poor people who need work like anyone else, he says to a friend, it's the god damn English and other Europeans coming to work in New York and around the country.

In August, Sean learns that his Irish brothers threaten to burn the Watson & Lorill and other factories unless hundreds of Negro women and children don't quit their jobs and leave the plants. He thinks it's a mercy the police arrive in time before a battlefield was created right in New York City. *Isn't there enough blood running over the fields of his new country that should be flowing with milk and honey? Is there no place on earth where peace flows like the River Liffey in springtime that he remembers as a boy?*

Sean has ground his sweat into the docks of New York over the years, polishing his patriotism and endearment to his new country. There's no way he will ever return to ole Ireland, unless it's on a pleasure trip with Norah McCabe and Katie, and that isn't going to happen soon. He is a New York City man now, an American willingly taken captive by the lure of freedom to map out his own pathway of dreams. And dream he did! Not only having Norah in his life, but owning a ship one day he'd be captain of. It'd be one of those majestic passenger liners that come soaring into the harbor of New York like a royal queen. He has been hired on occasion to bathe these ships after their long journeys and they are elegant and powerful, exacting respect. He has imagined the boats humming tunes of love in his ears as he worked. The Smythe and Cunard

Lines are the most luxurious he's ever seen and if he can someday buy an old lady in the line and fix her up right, he'll be the happiest immigrant in America. He dreams of salt spray, gleaming decks, and big silver fish twirling up from the ocean before the helm he'll stand at. In his mind, he never sees puking immigrants limping off these ocean liners in rags, nor does he remember his own passage on a cattle ship when his brother and neighbors died and he nearly starved to death himself. That was in the past and Sean O'Connolly is in the present shooting into the future, but not with a gun. No, warring is not for him, no matter what the cause.

Sean is sitting with some of his neighbors at the *Come to Roost Pub* in Five Points after working all day at the docks.

"Even under old mother England, it might fair better for us than going to war for a country that might perish from the earth in the end," his friend, Thomas complains.

"I can't get all hell-fired up about dying for a country that wants to spit us back to Ireland!" another said.

"It looks like the survival of this nation that is supposed to be indivisible is plummeting all to hell. The South is defeating the Union and now they want poor arses like us to sacrifice our lives in a last ditch effort. I ain't going, I tell you. I don't give a rat's ass if they hang me!" Sean proclaims, slamming his fist down on the bar. He will not return to Ireland like his friends talk about. Surely, America, as divided as it is, is a big country to hide yourself in and he'll high tail it out and come back when the war is over.

"Lee defeated the Union Army at Chancellorsville and is headed to Pennsylvania. Our Army is pathetic and disorganized and the Irish boys are dropping like flies," Thomas said, "I ain't going, I tell you. I ain't!" With that statement, he calls for a round of drinks for his friends.

"That's my man, Thomas!" Sean said, deciding he'll get himself right wallpapered before he makes any real decisions about the draft.

Chapter Eighteen

"Richard Daly, Thomas Herd, Patrick O'Hallaran!" a provost marshal shouts into the crowd. The draft office is in a four-story building at Forty-Sixth Street and Third Avenue in the Ninth District that is populated mainly by poor Irish immigrants.

"A rich man's war!" someone yells.

Sean had read the *Daily News* that morning anticipating the drawing of the first draft on the morning of July 11th.

There is a lurking mischief in the atmosphere that surrounds this unwelcome stranger.

"Piss on the government!" he says later to Thomas whom he's been doing a lot of drinking with. "The Union isn't winning the war and thousands are dying on battlefields. Now they're coming after us!"

They're standing in the draft office with a few draft protestors who are singing a song called *We are Coming Father Abraham:*

> *We're coming Father Abraham*
> *three hundred thousand more,*
> *We leave our homes and firesides*
> *with bleeding hearts and sore,*
> *Since poverty has been our crime, we bow to thy decree,*
> *We are the poor who have no wealth to purchase liberty.*

Sean, his friend, Thomas, along with a few others, had been drinking in the *Come Home to Roost Pub* for most of the night. They join in the singing and then grow quiet when names are called. When Thomas, a member of the Black Joke Fire Company, is called, there's a hollering all around the room. He steps forward and waits and a somber spirit cloaks everyone in the room. The men have assumed the firemen are exempt from any federal draft just as they have been from previous state drafts. No one has really taken this draft thing seriously, not Sean, and especially not the Black Joke Fire Company.

A church-like hush falls over the room as slips of paper rolled tight with the names of men are placed in a cylindrical drum and rotated before drawing.

"Wheel of misfortune!" Sean yells and men cheer, but he is told to keep quiet. And then his name is called along with a string of others. He nods to his buddies and immediately walks out into a day full of sunshine. The air and light, as well as the seduction of whiskey, fill him with hope. He walks down the street, whistling and devising a clear plan in his head, for he has no intention of being drafted or paying the conscription fee. Mr. Lincoln can't force him or others to fight in this war amongst brothers. It's un-American and he hasn't come all the way across the sea from a god-forsaken country to fight in his new country. He is confident that there will be plenty more men who think like him and together they'll show this Mr. Lincoln a thing or two! Sean disappears from the Ninth District and stays in his apartment until he is certain of his plans.

At the end of the drawing, one-half of the 2,500-man quota for the Ninth District have been drafted, and overall, it had been peaceful in spite of the angry protests and singing. But come Monday, when the lottery starts up again, the rage seething within the bowels of men who have been denied a decent paycheck and living conditions, erupts with venom that poisons the city forever in the annals of history.

It begins when the firemen decide to take action. These men are more than able to extinguish a fire started by a careless person in a rickety, old tenement building and they have no doubt they'll douse this fire of drafting free men started by a careless government. And because they are comfortable with fire and live and breathe fire, it is only natural to use fire to fight fire. They charge the office, destroy the lottery wheel, and set fire to the building. Thus begins a citywide riot over the next week with crowds of maddened working-class whites, immigrant and native-born, torching draft offices and destroying pro-Lincoln newspaper offices. Luxurious mansions are attacked by mobs, Horace Greeley's New York Tribune office is razed, and Negroes are targeted with beatings and burned out of their homes. Three hundred orphans escape out the back door before rioters burn the Colored-Orphan Asylum as they shout, "Burn the niggers!"

James Harrigan didn't know what hit him when he went down and all he could think of was that his Regency cravat knot with his Grafton collar was choking the hell out of him. He also thought that it was the most difficult to tie of all his cravats and it would now be ruined. He had been walking to work when a mass of rabid red-faced men and women carrying brick bats and clubs descended upon him when he turned the corner. He heard yelling and screaming before walking right into their midst.

"Get the three hundred dollar son-of-a-bitch!" he heard before he was clubbed and fell to the ground. He felt someone quickly pull his gold watch and chain from the buttonhole of his vest and then he was kicked in the back. While he worried over his cravat and watch, it occurred to him that Norah would be on her way to work to meet him at the office. He had to find her and save her from this demon-possessed mob, for he didn't want her to undergo another violent catastrophe in her life. He struggled to his knees, but was knocked over and hit in the head again. This time, he became unconscious as blood trickled from his mouth onto the street.

Norah felt the rumblings of a riot surrounding Five Points, but nothing had happened of much significance except drunken bands of young men shouting out curses and breaking a few lights the night before. She has a lot on her mind and is eager to talk to Harrigan about the draft article they're working on. An errand boy for the mission Nellie works for comes by in the early morning to tell Nellie not to come to work.

"The mission is boarding up their windows because some of the colored children have been threatened, Miss. Best to stay home until it all blows over."

"I'll stay here with Katie, but are you sure you should go to work today?" Nellie asks Norah.

"I'll be fine. I've nothing to do with the draft. It's the provost marshals and officials who should be watching their backs. I'm going to finish this one article and I'll come home straight away."

Norah leaves and hurries down streets, ignoring distant sounds of a city breaking its own heart. By the time she is close to the newspaper office, she is sweating and nervous. Gangs of men and groups of women and children are swarming the streets like angry hornets whose nest has been disturbed. She has been pushed and shoved as she walked, but no one has singled her out for injury. She has to get to the office, but now that she sees the city has turned on itself and is choking on violence, she wonders if she should turn around and go home. *Will Mr. Barker be downstairs in his store? Can he protect Nellie and Katie?* She is confused as to what to do, and when she turns the corner and her mind registers what her eyes see, it's clear to her that it is Elizabeth and Graham who are in grave danger.

Norah stares at the quivering body of a black man dangling from a rope that is tied to a vigorous and graceful maple tree in full bloom. The unsettling dissonance of rampage is all around her, but she sees only the one man whose beautiful dark-skinned face looks up to the tree as if to ask for help. In slow motion steps, she moves towards him, but before she can reach him, a man she recognizes from her neighborhood…*is it Tommy O'Halloran who has to work night and day to feed his old mother and siblings*…takes a torch and lights the body of the man. And then she watches, as this maple tree can stand it no longer and shakes its limb until the man is flung to the ground in a blaze of fire. As Norah turns to flee the horror, there is another Negro man a few feet from her who is being beaten and thrown to the ground. Men and women are throwing rocks at his head and kicking him in the face. He lies on the merciless earth squirming and crying out to God, his arms trying to cover his head. She turns again to run from this carnage and comes face to face with Maggie, her tormentor at Devlin's Department store from months before.

"Still wearing yer fancy hats?" she says and then spits into Norah's face.

"I've heard ye are a right nigger lover!" she yells, pulling off Norah's bonnet.

With strength mustered from within her, Norah raises her right arm and punches Maggie hard in the face. The girleen is soon on her back cursing and Norah steps on her hand with her good strong boot and picks up her bonnet. She quickly leaves and pushes her way through the mob, but not in the direction of her apartment where Nellie and Katie are.

"We ain't fightin' alongside a nigger!"

"End this nigger war!"

"If Abe arms niggers, we're going south!"

Norah listens to these cries of hate all around her and is emboldened and furious as she elbows her way through the crowds to get to the boardinghouses where mostly Negroes live. There Elizabeth and Graham will be at a meeting and she has to help them. *Do I really think because I'm white and Irish, these Irish gangs will not hurt me? Are they all Irish, these monsters?*

Norah has been writing about them, her people. She's scribbled frantically about their desperation and pent-up wrath. She hasn't been able to put an article together yet, and now she's face to face with the rage that is unleashed against a people they believe will destroy their opportunity in a new land. As she runs down the streets, she feels crazed and fears violence has come issuing from her in the same manner she has just witnessed. It felt good to punch and kick someone who is full of hate and jealousy. She shoves and yells as she hurries, but no-one pays her any mind. By the time she reaches the house on Thompson Street where she had once visited with Elizabeth, her outrage is as potent as is the mob's on the streets.

Norah climbs the steps and pounds on the door, but when it opens there stands a woman she doesn't recognize who is holding a pot of steaming water.

"Get the hell out!" the woman screams and then another woman from behind her yells.

"It's Norah McCabe!" The woman pulls Norah inside and slams the door shut, bolting it.

"Where's Beth and Graham?" Norah asks, looking frantically around the room. This is where they had once sat in a circle, a prayer circle, her and Elizabeth. They had talked about teaching in the churches, abolitionism, and freedom; all the while Norah sewed little darling flowers on hats for the Underground Railroad women. She hadn't been the only white woman in the room that day. There had been Janie McNamara who sat with them because she was married to a Negro and had moved into the neighborhood. Janie wore scars from the rocks thrown at her since marrying her black man.

"Most of us, honey, are staying at home if we knows what's good for us. Elizabeth and Graham are back home on Broome Street tending to their sick boy. He's been having convulsions."

The two women leave her and go into the kitchen. Norah's courage and anger collapse and she sits down on an old chair with stuffing coming out of it. Her body trembles and tears roll down her face. The horror of what she has seen is sinking in. She gets up from the chair and tries to put the stuffing back into the hole it has fallen from. Then she walks to the kitchen and sees five black women at the stove hovering over large pots. One of them looks at her standing in the doorway.

"We's brewing a mix of water, soap, and ashes for them coming for us."

Another woman turns from stirring a pot on the stove, "King of Pain we brewing, honey."

"What will you do with the pots?" Norah asks, already knowing what they are about.

"We'll fling hot water on 'em and scald dar very hearts out," the woman who had answered the door says to her, and Norah sees distrust in her eyes.

"Oh yes, honey, we're ready. We been practicing at another house already."

Chapter Nineteen

Sean went home to sleep off his hangover and woke to find his beloved city roiling in tumult and fury. Heretofore, he had ignored the city's relentless grudges and contempt against immigrants and Negroes. He saw the rays of the sun shining through the drafty walls of tenement buildings and spied the full moon smiling down on New York and had refused to be dissuaded that life wasn't good. God was always waiting for everyone to look up and be warmed by hope and Sean believed anything was possible. It just took time, hard work, and love is all. It had been as simple as that for Sean until he woke up and smelled smoke and knew the devil had been let loose in New York.

His first thought is to protect Norah and Katie, so he heads over to her apartment with his switchblade knife tucked into his belt. He has never used it, except to threaten to use it a few times when he had been in danger. But he won't hesitate to use it this day. He quickly walks through swarms of angry protesters and comes to Chatham Street where a mob has descended upon a saloon, old Mr. Crook's place who hires Negroes. He sees the god damn rioters pulling out the Negro waiters employed there. As he makes his way to defend one of the waiters, Captain Jourdan and his police force arrive and a severe fight gets underway. Sean has to get to Norah and quickly leaves the scene.

He reaches her building and climbs the stairs to the apartment and pounds on the door, but fears he's too late. He breaks a window and climbs through, but no one is there. He checks Norah's bedroom and spies his old, crumpled hat peeking out from underneath a pillow on her bed. He chuckles to himself and hurries out the door. *The crazy girleen loves me hat and 'tis a good sign she loves me, too!*

When Sean leaves and walks down the street, someone throws a brick that misses his head, but there are so many people, he can't see who it is. He hears someone yell, "Yer woman is a god damn nigger lover!" He rushes into the crowd to find the person, but it's useless. *Where are Norah, Nellie, and Katie? Did they go to Elizabeth and Graham's?* He goes back to be certain they aren't somewhere in Barker's store. They might not have heard him upstairs breaking the window. As he walks, another rock whizzes by his head. He ducks and makes his way to the store and rattles the door handle, but it's locked and dark inside. Barker must have left with his family and maybe he took the girls with him, he hopes. He runs down the alley to the back and rumbles around garbage cans and clothes drying on lines.

"We're here! Sean, we're down in the cellar!" Sean runs down the steps and Nellie and Katie are standing in the doorway.

"I looked out the tiny window and saw your ginger hair glowing in the sun! I'm so glad you're here!" Nellie says as she holds Katie to her side. Katie reaches up to Sean and he picks her up and hugs her.

"Mam's not here! I want my Mam!" Katie cries. She's only seven years old, but the child has an uncanny sense about adult behavior. She knows when they are not telling her the truth.

"Where is she?" Sean asks Nellie.

"She went to work for a few hours at the office and hasn't returned."

"Can you stay in the basement until I find her? I've seen the police out fighting the mobs. It should calm down soon."

"Don't leave us! Mam is coming!" Katie cries out and Nellie

takes her from Sean. Before he leaves, Sean kisses Katie and promises to be back.

He hurries in the direction of the newspaper office and is elbowed hard in his ribs a few times, but keeps on moving, his legs feeling rock heavy with the weight of distress. The faces of the mob remind him of the frenzied tales of Irish yore and how the hero, Cuchulain, turns into a raging monster when he goes into battle. As a young boy, he had been frightened by the stories of this hero who became horrendously altered when he fought from his chariot anyone who got in his way, knowing neither friend nor foe.

Sean walks a few feet and looks down the street through the rabble of vexed rioters resembling wild animals. And then he sees his queen coming towards him. She isn't wearing her bonnet and the sun glimmers off her hair that has fallen to her shoulders and curls around her face causing her to appear as the child he had first met. He pushes people aside to keep his eyes on Norah. Her pale moon face, awash with light flecks of amber he knows so well, is almost before him. As he nears her, he notices that her top lip is pulled down and covered by her bottom lip. Sometimes when he tried to kiss her, she'd do this same thing and he'd have to cajole her to relax. He desires to kiss her now and keeps his eyes looking into her green eyes that glower in the crowd. And then they simultaneously call out one another's names and hurry to embrace. They cling to one another a few moments and Norah pulls away and asks about Katie and Nellie.

"They're safe. They're safe in the basement."

He clasps her hand and leads her through the crowd towards the apartment, but when they're walking down the alley, a rock streams through the air and strikes Norah in the back so hard that she falls forward onto the ground.

"Nigger lover!"

Sean pulls his knife from his belt and rushes back into the crowd and Norah stands up with her forehead and nose skinned and bleeding. She stumbles through the alley to the back of the building and yells for Katie. Nellie comes rushing up the steps and helps

Norah into the basement. After Sean returns, his eye is swelling from someone having struck him.

"I knifed the son-of-a-bitch!" he says.

Katie sees the knife Sean is holding and screams. Blood covers the blade and Sean wipes it on his leg, remorse washing over him.

"The lad ain't dead, wee one. He was going to kill me and I got him in the arm is all."

Norah doesn't want to ask if this is true. She doesn't want to know what happened. All she knows is that the entire city has opened up and dropped into hell and demon-possessed savages throng the streets. *Are she and Sean becoming like them?* She thinks of Da and Mam in the country where there are lush green fields and most of all, serenity with no crazed mobs calling her a nigger lover. She has to get Katie out of this city to be sheltered and protected with her Da and Mam. Her sister, Meg, and her children are already there for the summer months. Katie will have her cousins and a real home there. Yes, she thinks, she will have to flee this city that has become an abusive lover.

The Secretary of War orders all the New York regiments to return to New York City to restore order. Troops numbering up to 4,000 arrive in New York immediately after fighting in the Battle of Gettysburg, the deadliest battle in the war thus far. Thereafter, confrontation occurs between soldiers and rioters near Gramercy Park on July 16th. And after this outrage against the city and themselves, most of the returning soldiers go to their favorite taverns before being called back to the fields of war. The Irish soldiers, wondering what the hell they are doing fighting a losing battle, go to fellow Irishman John McSorley's place on Seventh Street in the Bowery.

When Norah hears the murmurings from her neighbors that soldiers of the 69th regiment are eating a special dinner prepared by McSorley himself at his tavern, she leaves Katie with Nellie and, with her heart drumming in her ears, runs to McSorley's ale house. When she arrives, she knows the drill all right, but it doesn't matter to her now. She feels strongly that Edward is inside, for he had frequented there a few times.

Norah stands on the street trying to screw up her courage to go inside. A few ruffians jostle her as they walk by her on the street, as if a woman shouldn't even be on the street in front of the tavern, let alone inside. She thinks back to when Lincoln spoke at Cooper Union. All the newspapermen went across to McSorley's place because it was rumored that Lincoln himself was going there to have a drink after his speech. Norah had begged to go along, and although her shrill man-like whistle had impressed the newspaper boys, they would not consent, nor would McSorley himself do so, they told her. "The great man himself, McSorley, said, and we all agree, that drinking cannot be done in tranquility in the presence of women," the pimply-faced reporter had said to her. They all laughed then and there were more pats on her back. *Oh well*, she thinks now, *to hell with their sentiments. If my Edward is in there, I must properly toast him.*

Notice. No Back Room in Here for Ladies is the sign that meets her gaze when she walks up to the big black doors. *I'll just rush in before their drunken stupor eyes and then Edward will see me before I get thrown out.* Norah takes a deep breath and pulls open the doors and sprints inside the dark tavern. The thick sawdust on the floor was made for men's heavy boots and not the delicate Victorian spats Norah is wearing. As she slips to the floor and onto her backside, she inhales the sour scent of ale mixed with onions and smoke from corncobs. The atmosphere is thick with smoke and she can't make out any of the men's faces, but one. She supposes it is McSorley himself who leans over peering into her face looking like he wears the head of a big ole' onion that he smells of.

"Madam, I'm sorry, but we don't serve ladies."

He helps her to her feet, hands her a small pewter mug of ale, and ushers her out the doors as the men in the tavern shriek and cheer.

Before McSorley slams the black doors behind her, he says, "When ye finish my ale that is only brewed for the male species, ye can leave the cup to the side of the door. And ye'll do well to never set foot in my tavern again!"

Norah drinks the ale in a couple of swigs and places the cup near the door. So her Edward Knox is not at *The Old House at Home* of McSorley's. Surely, he would have seen her if he was and he'd be next to her side right now. Where is this lover who thought it best to care for his city than for her? She shakes the sawdust off of her skirt, straightens her bonnet, and walks towards home. Feeling a few moments of disgrace, she smiles and chuckles to herself. *Tis glory itself that I, Norah McCabe, walked boldly inside McSorley's tavern and lived to tell the tale!*

Sean, not prone to discouragement, felt as if the world had gone mad. 50,000 soldiers from both sides were dead and strewn across the luxurious summer fields of a state he had never visited in his new country. And now the New York soldiers coming from that bloody conflict had come home to another battle to fight, not to tea and a wife or a mother's comfort. He is determined to leave before he's arrested for draft evasion, for some of his friends in Five Points have already been jailed.

First, he makes sure that Norah, Katie, and Nellie are safe back in their apartment and that Mr. Barker and his family will watch over the girls. He doesn't tell Norah he is leaving, but gives a letter to Nellie and makes her promise not to give it to Norah until a week has passed. He packs his things and is soon on a train traveling somewhere to the west. Later, someone on the train announces that the draft has been suspended in New York for the time being, but he doesn't turn around. *Until this war is over, the god damn government men will be after every poor Irish bugger left in New York to send off to the killing fields to be rid of us all for good.* He can no longer play down the hateful remarks he has heard about the good for nothing Irish. His buddies always laughed at his optimism, but he has changed just in twenty-four hours.

"You think ye have a fightin' chance of being one of their kind on Wall Street?" his friend, Thomas would ask him, chuckling and patting him on the back.

"Ye'll do it for all of us then, Sean lad, sure ye will…"

But after he shoved a knife into someone, not even knowing where or how bad the injury, the stars in his eyes clouded over and his confidence waned. Hundreds of fires in his city had been set and there were one hundred and twenty known dead, many of them his Irish brothers. And over 150,000 Irish brothers had joined the Union Army with loyalty, patriotism, and courage, but for what? Some weren't yet citizens and were not sympathetic to the cause of freeing the slave. *Do they think they'd be accepted and their new country will honor them now for their service?* He's riding the rails with the acrid taste of bitterness, but when he sees the sun set out his window throw its rays his way, flickering hope rises within him. Sure now, he thinks, this war will end, life will be better for all, and I'll have Norah by my side.

Harrigan was taken to a hospital and suffered a small concussion and many bruises, but he was back at the *Rousing Clarion* in a week's time writing furiously about the riots. He is trying to bring understanding of what the *Irish-American* newspaper called, "a saturnalia of pillage and violence." He desires to write to counter the humiliation and blow to the reputation of the Irish community after the riots. George Templeton Strong, the acerbic diarist who writes despairingly of the Irish, stated, 'Stalwart young vixens and withered old hags were swarming everywhere, all cursing the bloody draft and egging on their men to mischief."

Harrigan does not condone the violence, but he wants the rage to be understood. He also writes about the priests on battlefields who march amongst the Irish green and Union blue, but now in retrospect, he said they, in their black robes, resemble angels of death. *Too many Irishmen dying for America!* This is the title of the article, but *The Catholic Freeman's Journal* did not like it, nor do they like his tone in all his articles. But then he writes glowingly about Bishop Hughes opening the Catholic Protectory for Homeless orphans after the Catholic Orphanage in Brooklyn was destroyed by fire. And the *Freeman's Journal* is pleased with this article.

"How ironic it is, he said to Norah, "that in January, a Grand

Requiem Mass had been held at St. Patrick's Cathedral for all those who died in Irish units. It was thought that so many deaths were an atrocity then, but now after Gettysburg, what kind of Mass should be held?"

Harrigan asks Norah to write about Meagher who had resigned his command of the Irish Brigade and had criticized the government for being willing to sacrifice the "heroes of the Green." Norah titled her article, *Know This! The Irish Soldiers Rally On!*

Norah wrote, *Meagher appealed to Lincoln for rest and recruitment that never came, thus the numbers of soldiers in the Brigade diminished. Meagher resigned, but these men rallied on and were brave Irish men who continued to fight at Gettysburg in a battalion of six companies under the command of Colonel Patrick Kelly. And then more Irish boys joined the fight after Corcoran was released in August of 1862 and organized his own legion of the New York Irish Brigade. The Irish rallied to war, but most of the Emerald green soldiers lay slain on the misty green fields of battle. And to add to the tragedy of the loss of Irish young men in America, another famine strikes Ireland as severe as in the 1840s. Irish families in New York waiting for their boys to come from battle take the little they have in their pockets and send it home to Ireland.*

The people of New York, and perhaps the entire nation, are unable to lift their heads to see beyond their troubles and note that the sun, moon, and stars are still shining on all of them equally. The bedrock of heartache has twisted and knotted in the men and women who once pulled rotting potatoes from the earth. And then their hate struck like lightning. The city has thundered and now limps despairingly into the future. The stampede of rage has created dust that hasn't settled back down in New York.

To Norah, New York will never again be the same city with its struggles and shining possibilities. She walks through the streets and the dust spirals up from the earth through paths of sunlight that expose particles of crimson, not gold. And she has just learned that in Gettysburg, there are fields colored with crimson and bodies still unburied. And doesn't she know that what is worse than a body not washed and lamented over for burial, is the body not found, as if it not mattered to anyone, not even to God.

Edward M. Knox never returned from Gettysburg with his regiment to help restore tentative calm to New York. If it wasn't for Katie, Norah told Harrigan one day, she'd be on a train to go look for him. Time passes in slow motion as she visits Charles Knox each day to learn if he has heard anything. She takes Katie with her everywhere she goes, refusing even Nellie to watch her. And then one evening after a long day working at the office with Harrigan, whose long, delicate fingers shake since his attack, Nellie hands her the letter from Sean.

Wee one, I haven't given up on this country yet, nor have I given up on you, but darlin,' I won't be fighting in a war between brothers. Our Negro brothers need a place at this freedom table, too, but killing one another for it or for the money that war puts in rich men's pockets is wrong. It's more complex than I gather in me simple head, but I know before God it's wrong for me to fight. Before I left, I went to Mass at that abolitionist church you like so well and heard the priest say what Jesus himself said, "Those who take up the sword will die by the sword." How simply true, Norah, and it's happening to our own from Ireland. Our Irish brothers in the South are fighting our Irish brothers in the North. Didn't we all come here to escape to freedom with dreams rattling around in our pockets instead of the coins? Please don't think of me as a coward, for I'd lay down my life for you and Katie any day, and under the right circumstances, I'd lay down my life for this country. Light a candle for me, Norah, and I'll be breathing your name, along with our Lord's, each night I lay down to sleep.

So now there are two candles to light each day when she and Katie stop at St. Brigid's Church after they leave *The Rousing Clarion*. Norah's heartache courses through her body and beats so loudly in her head that she is often oblivious to the noise around her. Katie chatters and Norah doesn't hear her. Norah sometimes places her hand on her chest and imagines the two upper chambers of her heart receiving the sorrow that flows through her. One for Edward and one for Sean! She carries this mourning inside the private rooms of her heart and whispers it into prayers at St. Brigid's. Rev. Thomas Mooney, pastor of St. Brigid's greets Norah and Katie with empathy and concern in his eyes each time they visit.

"Deep within the black hole of tragedy, there is light and love. We are not alone, Mrs. Murray. No, 'tis the final fate of even the most reprehensible person to fall into the just and forgiving hands of our God. And there he or she will stand to receive grace or to cast it away. No final verdict remains, no matter how bleak the terrain of war."

Norah basks in the reprieve of Father Mooney's warm acceptance and perhaps God Himself, but it is St. Brigid whose presence gives her strength. This saint she has grown to love, Mary of the Gaels, has been with her throughout her childhood. She had nearly forgotten her in America, but found her again in this church, Brigid's namesake. Norah adores this saint who had been a daughter of a pagan and a Christian. She lived only for Christ, for the poor, and gave away everything she owned. She performed miracles and started a monastery, but mostly Brigid was her own woman and this is what Norah loves best about her.

One day when Norah and Katie walk to St. Brigid's as the setting sun and the darkening evening mingle in an alluring dance over New York, Norah feels strength circulating through the chambers of her heart, rinsing her sorrows with a certain peace. After she enters St. Brigid's and they sit down in a pew to pray, she pulls out a prayer card from the rack. No-one is in the church, except Father Mooney, who is watching from behind the curtains of the sacristy. Norah and Katie whisper the prayer together:

> *Brigid, You were a woman of peace.*
> *You brought harmony where there was conflict.*
> *You brought light to the darkness.*
> *You brought hope to the downcast.*
> *May the mantle of your peace cover those who are*

troubled and anxious.
And may peace be firmly rooted in our hearts
    and in our world.
Inspire us to act justly and to reverence all
    God has made.
Brigid, you were a voice for the wounded
    and the weary.
Strengthen what is weak within us.
Calm us into a quietness that heals and listens.
May we grow each day into greater wholeness
    in mind, body, and spirit.
Amen.

After work the following day, Norah, Katie, and Nellie visit Charles and Elizabeth Graham who were kept safe during the riots in their home on Broome Street. However, while the city had catapulted into paroxysms of hate and violence, Elizabeth and Charles watched helplessly as their young son, Thomas, convulsed and collapsed into death. Disease is always taking away too many children in the city, Norah thinks, and worries over Katie being next. To Elizabeth, full of inconsolable grief, God has turned his back not only on the city she loves, but her son. Norah, the day after visiting St. Brigid's and finding some relief for her heartache, baked two oatmeal loaves in the shape of a cross. As much as Norah didn't like to bake, it was a holy act in response to her unexpected peace. It is also a remembrance of when her mother baked the bread for the Feast of Imbolc and St. Brigid. She gives a loaf to Charles and Elizabeth, her tears flowing down her cheeks onto Katie's head who stands hugging Norah's skirts. Outside on the street after saying goodbye to Elizabeth and Charles, Norah, her face streaked with tears and her eyes wide with determination, says to Nellie,

"Katie and I'll be traveling tomorrow to stay with my family. I don't know when I'll be returning and because I don't want to leave you burdened with paying all the rent, I'm giving you this. She hands Nellie a purse that contains enough money for three month's rent.

Harrigan gave her an advance and she withdrew more money out of the Emigrant Savings Bank for her trip. What she didn't tell Nellie, Katie, or her parents when she wrote to them, was that in a little over a week's time, she was meeting Mr. Timothy O'Sullivan, the photographer she had met at Delmonico's. She was going to travel to Gettysburg. Harrigan had been against this because he needed her all in one piece in New York at the office, but she had argued with him with much passion.

"There are rivers of blood there, Harrigan, and no more to spill out from guns, cannons, and swords now, is there? It isn't the end of this war, but it's a turning point. Don't ye want me to sketch what I see before it's too late? And I can write about it and dispatch everything to you for the paper."

Harrigan relents after her persuasive speech. She will be a sketch artist and write for *The Rousing Clarion* describing what happened at Gettysburg. It is important, he said, because everyone in New York is in a state of shock after this battle. But Harrigan and Norah say nothing to one another about the real reason she is going to Gettysburg.

Chapter Twenty

Norah steps down from the carriage with Katie and stands before a white clapboard farmhouse situated in a verdant field on a hill. A few trees and flowers adorn both sides of the house. The lowering sun creates layers of blue-lavender and coral that cast over the house and field. It reminds Norah of the landscape that cradled her girlhood. The earth is green and fecund as in Ireland, but here the McCabes have a home they can never have imagined having in the land they remember with sorrow.

"We're home, Katie Marion," Norah said, placing a hatbox containing two cherished hats, in Katie's hand to carry. She leaves her large trunk sitting on the grass and carries two more hatboxes up the path to the door that opens with cheers and greetings. Norah has never seen such wide and open smiles on the faces of her Mam and Da. She enters and inhales the scent of freshly felled trees that have been laid for the foundation of a new life. There is a wooden floor, not an earthen one, but it feels enduring because the strong earth is below them. Here is home away from home, Norah thinks, as the mayhem of New York City disappears from her mind as quickly as the early morning dew in the blaze of a summer sunrise.

The McCabes purchased the land in Corning, New York soon after Da came home from his employment on the Leavenworth,

Pawnee and Western Railroad he had worked on since 1857. He laughs when he says that for every railway story he has, there is a deep crease in his face. He said he quit when his back was killing him and younger men vied for his position.

"I'd had enough, Norah, and I want to work the land, no matter how old and battered I am. And when I started farming here, learning from neighbors what to plant and when to plant, my back pain disappeared!"

Mam said their life was much better than it was in Five Points and Rochester.

"I saw him walk with a bit of a stoop when he first came home. But now the only stoop I see is where I sit in the back of our house, waiting for him to come in from a field." She laughs and pats Norah's shoulder with affection.

Meg and her children are happily settled into the farmhouse for the summer and the tension between Meg and Norah dissipates in this new ambiance of certainty and goodness. For one week that spreads out into memorable timelessness, Norah secrets away her love and worries for Edward and Sean and places them into the bottom chambers of her heart. It's different here, she thinks, for the war hasn't spilled over its hatefulness here. There aren't signs of its sinister ways, as in New York City, although many young men from Corning have gone to war and many died at Gettysburg. And the members of this community solemnly go about their work as if it is a prayer for their sons to come home. Mam is involved with the ladies of Corning who hold linting bees in their homes. She tells Norah there is little cotton to be bought and industrious women scrape their linen tablecloths into fuzzy lint for compresses for the hospitals.

"It's the Almighty's blessing to see the young people gather blackberries and the same linting bee mothers turn them into blackberry cordial for the army hospitals."

Norah wants to make sure to take some of the cordial with her to Gettysburg. She also learns the Underground Railroad passes through Corning and she plans on meeting the leader of the movement here. Indeed, Corning is just what the doctor ordered for Norah and although she needs to be away from war weariness before venturing to Gettysburg, she accompanies some Corning residents to hear a lecture by a visiting abolitionist. She learns there are many abolitionists in Corning and that the stage version of *Uncle Tom's Cabin* has been produced in their little theater.

The McCabes have a few milking cows, pigs, and they grow corn, buckwheat, and potatoes. Mam has a kitchen garden she is proud of and right away she showed Norah all the rose bushes Da planted for her. Norah and Katie giggle over the snorts and grunts of the few pigs they help feed, but Norah doesn't tell Katie they once had Mr. James, a pig who slept with her and her sisters in Ireland. How different life is now! The farm also has a rooster and a few hens and Katie begs to have one as a pet because Norah did tell her daughter about the favorite pet of her childhood.

"Miss Maggie Hen is her name, just like your pet in Ireland, Mammy!" Katie exclaims one morning, pointing at a strutting hen in the barnyard when they're feeding the chickens. The renewing bonds of familial love return and Norah relaxes into a slower rhythm that is more natural, an easeful cadence reminiscent of her childhood before the Famine.

On the evening before Norah's departure to New York City to meet Timothy O'Sullivan, the McCabes host an evening of music and dance.

"A hooley! Lively, Irish music and dance, we'll be having!" exclaims Da. Mam worries the neighbors might think their hooley too uncivilized, but Da assures her that this is country living now and it's best not to be too refined. "And look at all the Irish living in Corning, my love!"

"We'd be more likely snubbed for persnickety airs, so 'tis best to be playing the airs for them." Mam laughs heartily, something she is doing more of these days.

In the evening, Da plays his fiddle and there are a few musicians who come with fiddles, guitars, accordions, the spoons, and even a hammer dulcimer. The neighbors bring platters of food and jugs of whiskey. There are dishes made from the game they have hunted and the chickens they've raised on their farms. There are corn fritters and cornbread from the corn they've grown, along with pies from the berries they picked in their fields and apples from their orchards. Just that morning, Norah, Mam, Katie, and Meg's girls went berry picking behind their house. They brought back black raspberries and made two berry cobblers. It's been a long time since Norah thought about where the food she ate has come from.

At the hooley, a caller who has a knack for remembering dance figures intrigues Norah. Hezekiah Bailey is one of those *hail-fellow-well-met* types and he welcomed the McCabes when they first moved to Corning. As soon as the musicians begin playing jigs and reels, Norah's feet can't hold still. She springs up and dances alone in the kitchen. After, everyone claps and praises her sprightly dancing. Hezekiah calls the dances and asks Norah to be his partner. Some of the dances she doesn't know, but she quickly learns to dance the schottische and minuet because Hezekiah is an easy partner to dance with. He is a tall, lanky, lad who is partially deaf and wasn't drafted into the war due to this handicap. He is light on his feet and it is said that although he can't hear a thing without a cone held to his ear, when it comes to music, he hears every note.

At teatime, Mam whispers to her, "He's a fine lad, Norah, and runs the family farm since his folks died. Just because he's deaf now, he's not dumb. He'd make a fine husband and you and I'd be neighbors."

Norah leans in close to Mam and says, "Well, you never know." She and Mam laugh. Norah can't imagine being the wife of Hezekiah Bailey who has very large ears that don't work.

"His dancing skills just might win me heart, Mam," she whispers and they laugh some more.

At the end of this enchanted evening, she can picture herself living this kind of good life, far from the uproar and pace of a city. Everyone is friendly and although many of the farmers have boys gone off to fight, no one speaks of it this evening. Da said that when he goes into town, the war is all everyone talks about because there are over three hundred boys from the Corning area who went to fight for the Union. And some of them died in Gettysburg.

Late in the evening after people have gone home and to bed, Norah and Da sit together in the kitchen. It is as it has always been between them, as they sip tea late into the night. There is the same open and warm relationship. And now Norah waits for his blessing and wisdom to come through his storytelling conversation. But this time, the blessing doesn't come, although she feels affection. Rather, Da is candid in his feelings about her going to Gettysburg.

"Thanks be to God I'm too old to go to war, Norah, and if I wasn't, I'd be running from the provost marshal as fast as the Copperheads. Plenty of them Peace Dems hiding in the woods in this part of the country and here's me own daughter going off to war."

"I'm going to one battlefield, Da, and the battle has already been fought and now the tide of this war has turned against the South. The Union is stronger because the Confederacy has split in two. We'll have victory and the public needs to know about this battle in a way they didn't need to know about the others. There are many make-shift hospitals, I've heard, and all of this needs to be recorded."

Norah takes in a deep breath and places her violet patterned teacup in the saucer. As she lets her breath out slowly, she is shaky and at once unsure of her plans, but she continues the conversation.

"Only the wounded can tell us the real story, Da, and that's what I aim to do for our paper, *The Rousing Clarion*. You do read the copies I send you?"

"Aye, Norah, I've been proud of your writing and meticulous thinking. Your Mam goes to the sewing circles at her church and her tongue wags continuously about you like the trembling leaves of the aspen."

"Is the gossip good? In my favor, I hope."

"Aye, 'tis.."

Da takes a puff from his pipe, a habit he has picked up since moving to his new home. Norah smiles watching him and thinks that the pipe and the upholstered, wraparound chair he sits in makes him quite the country gentleman.

Norah stares into the cup for a few moments and then raises it to her father for him to look inside.

"Look, Da, there's a heart in the bottom of my cup!"

And sure enough, bits of tea leaves have sunk to the bottom and are in the form of a heart. Da knows his daughter will take this as a sign that her decision to go to the bloody fields of Gettysburg is right. He stares into the cup, trying to come up with the words to discourage her from going. But he sadly knows it'll be useless, for Norah is a stubborn one, at that, as he remembers her going off with rebels to fight for Ireland's freedom. No one could have stopped her.

"And the dead, Norah, will they be speaking to you in Gettysburg?"

"As the dead always do, Da, for don't we know that even a sea can't separate us from the dead in Ireland. Sometimes, more than I wish, I remember being in the wagon on our way to the ship. We passed by the dead ones alongside the road. And do you remember the wagons traveling by us? They carried the long since dead, their flesh picked clean by the ravens. I'll forever hear the rattling of their bones."

Da bows his head a moment and is silent, the memories returning to him.

"Then why should ye go for more sorrow to inscribe on your mind and heart? How could ye possibly have room for more? I've heard that thousands have left for Canada and 200,000 Union conscripts never showed up at the enrolling offices. I read the papers, Norah! And not far from here, there are rampages against the pro-Lincoln newspapers and the African churches. Soldiers come to enforce the draft and even the women throw bricks at them. Forcing men to fight shouldn't be. There are men being imprisoned without a trial and without the protection of their own government. Look what happened in your city of New York, A Chara, and to think you were there with so much violence! Our new country is becoming a battlefield as bloody as ole Ireland!"

"But there's real hope for the Negro to be free."

"At what price, Norah? So Mr. Lincoln frees the slaves, but they don't know where to go and how to live and they'll be killed by those who hate them. Our people sacrificed too much to sacrifice again and even if the Negro had skin the color of our own, it wouldn't matter, for their color we've never minded. Didn't the fight drain out of our Irish men on their own potato fields? Sure now, the Irish in the brigade are all puffed up about being true Americans and winning glory and honor. They're doing it without the right kind of fight in them. They don't care for the Negro and they don't care about this war, but they need some glory and don't we know they need the money that the army's giving them! And God have mercy, many of them have died and will die!"

"I hate the war, Da, but if a disease of the body attacks that body it's a part of, it's got to be cut out so the whole body doesn't die. And that's just a simple part of the entire mess, I suppose."

"Too simple, Norah. And what about Katie? Isn't it your part to protect your daughter and be here, alive and whole, to care for her?"

"Da, how many times have I explained that I'm only going to where a battle already happened."

"But that O'Sullivan fellow will be going on to whatever battles break out now. He's a bloodhound for the pictures of the dead! And General Meade didn't end the war once and for all and capture Lee after Gettysburg, did he? There'll be skirmishes and battles exploding all around you!"

Da pounded his fist on the table and stood up from his chair, snuffing out his pipe.

"I've already lost one daughter and I don't want to lose you, A Chara!"

Norah sits for a long time at the kitchen table after Da went to bed. She stares at the imprint of Da's lap left on his chair and becomes melancholy. This is the chair that no-one is allowed to sit in, but him, and she momentarily thinks about sleeping in it for the night to try and gather his warmth and the blessing he hasn't bestowed upon her.

Norah sighs and thinks about this chair that has come to be in her family's new home. It's an expensive Sleepy Hollow armchair that he keeps next to the kitchen stove. Norah recognizes the kind of chair it is. It is one usually found in well-to-do homes. Da told her he purchased it after the house was built and he didn't care if it wasn't supposed to be in the kitchen according to the etiquette of the times. It is his and he's proud of it.

Norah washes out her teacup and walks into the parlor. The parlor is bereft of furniture, except for a simple, straight-backed rocker and the old Victorian sofa Norah had found full of mice nests that had been cast off on a New York City street corner. She had bribed a wagon driver with some of her mother's soda bread and a dress from her shop for his wife if he'd carry the sofa home for her. She had worked hard at re-upholstering the wreck and then slept on it until she moved in with Nellie.

The parlor has a fireplace, reminding her of her childhood hearth. She adds more wood from the stack next to it and lies down on the sofa. She soon sleeps and dreams of the fields of Ireland strewn with the famine starved, their mouths stained green and opened wide like hungry birds. They had sought their mother earth for some sustenance and had found none. And then the dream eerily changes to a field of blue and gray clad bodies with eyes opened wide beseeching the heavens. Their opened mouths are stained with crimson that flows out of them and onto the earth, changing the grass from green to red. She wakes up weeping just before the sun rises. She gets on her knees before the hearth and prays to St. Brigit for the mantle of peace.

Later that day, Norah surprises Mam with a straw bonnet adorned with red silk ribbons and tiny rosebuds designed just for her. Mam laughs excitedly and puts it on, but then takes it off and says she has no need for such a fancy thing, being that she's a farmwoman again.

"You have a church to go to now, Mam, and ye should wear it there and tell all the ladies I can make them each a hat…but the price will be high now because I'm a real milliner with a business in New York City."

Mam puts the hat back on and twirls around like a young girl, laughing easily. Had her Mam laughed in Ireland, Norah wonders? Ireland seems so long ago and yet so near. She remembers that her mother had taken the few teacups, lace, and memories of their cottage in Ireland and hid them away. Da always speaks fondly of Ireland, but when he does, Mam scolds him. Norah remembers the two of them going on about it when they all lived in Five Points.

"Tis wrong to be longing for the ole country when God and the Holy Mother have brought us here and given us new blessings greater than we ever had in Ireland."

"Tis wrong to forget the land that gave us life. Tis wrong to forget the famine ghosts who'll always rise up in our memories."

Mam had turned away then and made a noise that sounded like something between a whimper and a growl. Certainly her mother had scoured her memories of Ireland as severely as she scours her new home. Daily, the woman does penance on her knees, scrubbing away all she doesn't want from her past so as to belong in her home and life now.

Mam stops laughing and prancing about in her hat and looks at Norah with severity.

"I don't want ye to go to where there's danger, Norah. Your Da and I have already lived through enough of your shenanigans and it will be killing us now when we're this old."

They all stand next to the carriage that is going to take Norah to the train station in Corning and tears run down Mam's face. Katie becomes frightened.

"You said you were going to work for Mr. Harrigan's paper. Is it dangerous, Mam?" Katie lifts her arms to Norah and although she is too heavy to pick up, Norah does so. Katie buries her face in her mother's neck.

"No, Mam, don't go then. Stay here with the family!"

"I'll be home soon, pet, and you'll be crying when we have to leave to go back to the city. Ye must enjoy your grandfather and grandmother now, as well as your cousins and Miss Maggie Hen and the days will fly by and I'll be back. I'll send you a letter and it will be your first one to ever receive."

Da takes Katie from Norah and kisses Norah, "A Chara, never have I loved you as much as I do now," and Norah remembers when he said this before he placed her in the dresser to be hauled on board the ship to America. She was only thirteen years old. Norah hopes her journey now won't be as harrowing and tragic as the one that brought her to America.

Chapter Twenty-One

Norah's trip on the New York Central Railway to New York City is more rigorous and uncomfortable than her earlier travel from New York to her family's home. She is already homesick for Katie and although she has obtained a copy of Charles Dickens' *Tale of Two Cities*, she is unable to concentrate. A pervasive unease over potential derailment and the terrible racket that comes from the cars rolling over the tracks puts her in a bad mood. The soot and ash from the locomotive's smokestack comes floating into the cars and onto the passengers. Norah is irritated that her clothing is becoming dirty. She is wearing a simple blue Bolero jacket and a blue and gray checkered skirt, but without a hoop. She removes her straw spoon bonnet with blue ribbons and places it in her hatbox. This bonnet is suitable for her travels, but she doesn't want it soiled so soon. She wears a decorative hair net with French knots and has two more headdresses to wear while traveling.

Timothy O'Sullivan advised her to pack light, but she didn't really know how to do so. She packed a medium-sized trunk with homespun dresses and her blue and green plaid silk gown, just in case there is an opportunity to wear it. Under clothing, drawers and a cotton wrapper she'll sleep in are also in her trunk. How long will they be traveling, she wonders? She is disappointed she hasn't taken a train by herself to Gettysburg. But women didn't travel alone and she gave in to Harrigan and Nellie's pleadings to go with O'Sullivan. He can teach her about photography and wants to enlist her help. He, Gardner, and another photographer were already at Gettysburg a few days after the battle. They took photographs and went to his office in Washington, and now they're selling the photos in New York City. Timothy said he'd meet her right off the train in Vanderbilt Square and they will head out to Gettysburg in his horse-drawn buggy. It isn't a pleasure trip, for certain, and wishes now she hadn't packed her silk gown.

Norah glances at her skirts and is amused, for she hadn't considered any meaning in wearing a blue and gray-checkered pattern. She wonders if anyone will construe it to be symbolic. She peers around the car, but everyone is either talking or looking out the window. No one pays her any mind. She touches her headdress and wishes she had brought more of her bonnets, for she doesn't like these hair nets that tuck away her curls and resemble fishing nets. Mam gave her two homespun cotton dresses she had made long ago and never wore. One was a blue and peach checkered dress and the other was a brown and blue-checkered dress. Norah is wearing her high-buttoned blue gingham cloth and leather boots. They are very comfortable, as well as modestly elegant. In her trunk is another pair of high-buttoned black leather boots that are more practical. She has left most of her gowns and hats in Chatham Square with Nellie. She is planning on continuing her millinery business in the city after she returns from Gettysburg. These thoughts about her clothing and business help her to not think about the uncomfortable train ride and what is ahead in Gettysburg.

Norah tries to read again, but puts the book down on the empty seat next to her. The train is rocking and loud and she is becoming more nervous as it chugs down the tracks. Train travel didn't bother her before, but now that she is traveling to uncertainty and possible danger, everything around her reverberates with threat. And at every insufferable stop to pick up and leave off travelers, there are soldiers who come aboard. Norah's heart beats fast each time the soldiers walk down the aisle, for she hopes to see Edward. These soldiers getting on the train are going back to New York City. They have been the lucky ones, she thinks, but none of their faces reveal this. They are returning to New York City, but only briefly. They will be called to duty yet again and maybe not make it home the second time around.

At a stop in Syracuse, a few soldiers get on carrying haversacks looking as if they have just come from battle. She looks into each face thinking it will be Edward. It doesn't make sense; anyway, for why would Edward travel through Syracuse? The soldiers are thin, disheveled, and have a stench of death about them, and not a single man smiles, but one, who takes her attentive peering into his face as a sign to sit next to her. Norah nods to him, removes her book from the seat, and turns away.

"My buddies and I were fraternizing with some graybacks and we all said we could have settled this war in thirty minutes if it had been left to us," the man said.

Norah turns to him, "If it could have been settled, it would have been. I don't think Mr. Lincoln knew what was to come."

"My name's James McClure. You can call me Corporal McClure...or just Jim," the soldier said. Norah spies a glimmer of handsomeness hidden beneath his hollow eyes and sickly pallor.

"I'm Norah McCabe," she said, and looks out the window again. She doesn't want to talk about the war. She doesn't want to ask about the dead and how they died, for soon enough she'll learn about it when she gets to Gettysburg. But then Norah can't help herself to keep quiet. She has to ask if maybe he knows Edward!

"New York Regiment? Irish Brigade?" she asks excitedly, facing him with expectancy on her face.

"Yep...little late going home now. Five Points is my home and never thought I'd be happy to go back there, but after Gettysburg..." Jim clears his throat, coughs, and looks past her and out the window. He has a look of despair.

"There was an order for everyone in the New York regiments to go back to New York to help put down the damn riots, but some of us had to stay to bury the dead and things like that…And what the hell. I didn't want to go home right away and thought I'd do some train traveling first."

Jim itched his scalp and then pinched a bug between his forefinger and thumb.

"Nasty little bastards. You'd better sit closer to the window or you'll get them, too.

Norah is disgusted. It's not as if she doesn't know about the cockroaches in tenement apartments and lice on children's heads at the House of Industry, but she doesn't have any way to get rid of them here, nor can she get away. She shudders, foreboding feelings coming over her. She'll soon be traveling with a man she hardly knows in a small carriage for miles and miles. *How will I keep myself clean? What about my privacy? How will I relieve myself and what about my female matters?* "Oh, Mother of God," she hears her mother's voice in her head, "Did ye not think through this properly?" No, she thinks, she hasn't thought this through, for if she had thought it through properly, she wouldn't be here now!

"Did you enter service in New York?" she asks the soldier.

"Aye, marched out with the Fifteenth New York Light Battery B of the Irish Brigade with all kinds of cheering, but I'll be honest, some of the true Americans didn't like meeting up with us. It didn't matter if we were born in this country because if we were in the Irish Brigade, they thought we was born in Ireland. One sergeant told us that there were enough Americans to put down the trouble and they didn't need any of us red faced foreigners."

"What about all the other foreigners? What about the Italians, Germans, and Hungarians who left New York City to go to war? I saw their flags. Most of them weren't born in America, either."

"It don't matter. The Irish are as bad as the nigger in their eyes."

Norah cringes. She doesn't want to remember the riots and how enraged the Irish were against the Negro. She loves her people, but she has also come to love the Negro because of Elizabeth Jennings. And then it dawns on Norah that the soldier said he had marched out with the Irish Brigade!

"Tell me again, Jim, what regiment did you march with?"

"Fifteenth New York Independent Light Battery B of the Irish Brigade, Ma'am."

Norah's hands shake while she opens her purse to look at a letter from Edward. And there on the letter, is Edward's handwriting - Fifteenth Light Battery B! She stuffs the letter back in her purse and faces Jim with tears in her eyes. *I don't want to know, really, do I?* She turns away and rubs away her tears. And then she pulls the letter back out of her purse and quickly places it in Jim's hands.

"Did ye know this lad in the same regiment as you?"

Jim reads it over a long time before he lifts his head and looks at Norah.

"Aye, he's a hero, that one. A real hero. On July 2nd, our battery was heavily engaged in the Peach Orchard area, pushing back three rebel infantry assaults. There was so much heavy fighting and we was forced to withdraw to replenish our ammo, but then, by God, we returned right back into the thick of things."

Jim put his head down and shook it, as if to repel the memories.

"We couldn't force back the deluge of the rebel advance! Your Lieutenant Knox knew our guns would be captured and he ordered us to lie down and play dead. A wise one, he was, for the dumb rebs ran right over us, stepping on our hands and backs, but no matter how it hurt, we played dead."

Jim rubs his right hand, remembering the day.

"Those rebs were surprised after they run right past us and right into a charge made by the 72nd New York Infantry that halted them in their tracks and then they skedaddled right out of there. They walked by us and over us again, and left us with our guns. We was dead to them and they didn't care beans about the guns right then."

"Lieutenant Knox ordered us to our feet and we pulled back to Union lines, but the Lieutenant, he took a ball or two. He was badly wounded and taken off the field."

Jim tells the story looking straight ahead, as if he is there again. There is some trembling in his voice and after finishing his tale; he lifts his chin and sniffs, still looking straight before him.

189

Hope rises in Norah. *If this soldier has ended up on this particular train, at this time, sitting next to me, surely...surely now, this is a good omen. Edward has to be alive.*

"He's probably in a hospital right now, even as we speak, then."

"Aye, probably so. I know only he was badly injured, but he's a brave man. I stayed on to bury some of the dead, but I never heard what happened to him." Norah stifles a sob and he says, "No worry, Miss, I'd known if I'd buried my own Lieutenant."

"Excuse me," Jim said, standing up, "I'm desperate for a smoke."

By the time he returns, Norah has imagined Edward's leg is injured and he will soon be on crutches and hobbling along until he heals. In fact, she has seen many soldiers return from a battle injured, on crutches, and doing fine. Edward is a young man, strong in constitution, and he has an incessant will to live, she thinks, willing herself to believe this.

"Thank you, Jim. Thank you for being so brave and fighting for your country."

Jim nods and wipes his nose with the back of his hand. Norah turns back to the window. The rolling hills are piquant and effusive with splashes of color from the wildflowers and tall grasses dancing in the wind. The hills and flowers are at the height of their season for flourishing and they know nothing of human strife and war. "Your country," Norah had said to Jim.

"Thanks be to God for you, Jim, for fighting for *my* country."

Chapter Twenty-Two

Harrigan and Timothy O'Sullivan meet Norah at the train station and O'Sullivan tells Norah it is impossible to travel with such encumbrances as her trunk and hatbox.

"My photographic equipment is going to take up most of the room," he explains, a nervous twitch at the corner of his mouth.

"But I must…"

"Norah can leave some things with me. There's no problem," Harrigan interjects.

Harrigan immediately goes shopping for a carpetbag for Norah. Timothy O'Sullivan and Norah are awkward with one another as they wait for Harrigan to return. They stand next to the canvas-covered wagon that is parked near the train station. And then O'Sullivan pulls out a fold-up chair for Norah to sit in. People walk by and stare and this increases Norah's anxiety over her clumsy state. In addition, her thoughts are now preoccupied with the news of Edward and it occurs to her that she should send word to Mr. Knox and his family about what she has learned about Edward. But there is no time because Harrigan returns with a carpetbag smaller than her mid-sized trunk and she is unsure she can fit everything in.

In the end, she wears her bonnet and packs her hairnets, boots, a dress and underclothes into the carpetbag, as well as a few black lead pencils and a sketch pad. She reluctantly leaves her other items with Harrigan and after a big hug and good-bye; she is soon inside Timothy O'Sullivan's makeshift dark room on wheels clip clopping out of New York City. O'Sullivan suggests Norah not sit up front with him as it would be too dusty and uncomfortable. She agrees, for although she is cramped inside the carriage, she doesn't want to talk to him. She falls asleep on a pile of blankets that reek of a barnyard. Shortly after, she wakes and remembers she forgot to tell Harrigan to inform Mr. Knox about the news of Edward. She falls back to sleep thinking it might be best if she finds Edward before his father does, for this will reveal her earnest devotion to his son.

Each night for the entire journey, Norah sleeps inside the wagon and Timothy O'Sullivan sleeps on the ground next to the campfire. They never travel alone on the road, for there are other travelers in stagecoaches, on horseback, and even on foot. There is a rabble of drunken gangs stumbling down the road nearly every night. This frightens Norah, but O'Sullivan tells her it's normal. She wants to ask him about encountering Indians, for she is more curious than frightened. She has listened to stories about Indians since arriving in America as a young girl, but they have seemed fantastical to her and akin to the myths and lore of old Ireland. Da told her many Indians had been massacred or pushed off their land and sent to reservations. He said it reminded him of the way the British have treated the Irish in a similar fashion. Will Indians attack them while they sleep? She asks Timothy and he laughs and says that the poor buggers are either in the Confederate Army or the Union Army and the rest of them know better than to come around.

At the end of each day, Norah is so tired from the novelties of traveling in a wagon with the young photographer, she falls asleep unconcerned about Indians or anything. And she thinks that surely Mr. O'Sullivan is experienced enough with traveling and he'll know how to protect them. He keeps his rifle by his side and has a pistol that is inside the wagon. He asks Norah if she knows how to use a pistol and she tells him she doesn't but is willing to learn. He laughs and shakes his head in agitation, telling her there is no time to be teaching her properly. *What can be so difficult? You point and pull the trigger.*

Norah asks O'Sullivan about wild animals and whether they will have to shoot any. He laughs at her again and she feels utterly silly, perhaps as silly as she felt when he saw how many clothes she originally planned on taking with them. She doesn't want him to think she is a fainting lady of leisure who thinks more about her clothing and appearance than she does of anything else. *Certainly it must be a revelation to him that I possess fortitude as a newspaperwoman, so unusual for our times. I do much more than sip tea and dine at Delmonico's in my finest attire where he first met me!*

One evening after finishing their supper at the campfire, she swats at gnats and mosquitoes, whimpers about the heat, and complains that the bugs are thicker than molasses. Timothy, as he has asked her to call him, becomes impatient with her.

"Did ye think this trip was going to be easy? Harrigan assured me you were up for this."

He hands her a tin mug of coffee and Norah takes a sip, but it's bitter and she spits it onto the ground.

"My God, Norah, you should have brought tea then."

Norah feels nauseous from the fatty pork mixed in with a can of beans they've eaten for supper.

"How can a person live without a cup of tea!" she exclaims, jumping up to go to the wagon for bed.

"You, an Irish girleen, must know how to make good Irish bread. You should have brought a loaf for the trip. And you could have brought the tea, as well. Surely, it would have been a good way to keep this man happy," Timothy points to himself and laughs.

Norah looks back at Timothy angrily, "Ye should have learned how to make your own bread by now and to be knowing how to keep your own self happy. Tis not the way of the new American woman to be thinking only of her man's happiness, Mr. Timothy O'Sullivan."

"I'm your man now, Miss McCabe?" He is gleeful over this exchange and wants to continue it, "Oh, I see now," he said, "ye are one of those suffering suffragettes!"

"I am and I'm not!" Norah said, climbing into the wagon and pulling the canvas so hard after her that it tears slightly.

"Well, if ye are a suffragette and equal to me tonight, then you can get the needle and thread and sew the canvas you've torn!"

Norah ignores Timothy and lies down on the smelly blankets. She is weary of all this nonsense and thinks she should have never agreed to travel with Timothy O'Sullivan. Her hair is a dirty mass of frizzy curls. She has tried washing it in the river, but an eel came up alongside her and she screamed and gave up. She is overcome with homesickness for Katie and even the thought of finding Edward does not console her. Her courage dissipates when Timothy tells her war stories and she sees injured soldiers traveling on the road. The discomfort of the journey and the sudden longing for Katie has pulled apart her purpose for the venture as quickly as the canvas has ripped. She thinks that Mr. Timothy O'Sullivan is at times warm and understanding, but at other times quite impatient and surly. He never flirts with her or makes unseemly remarks, but he is preoccupied with his reputation as a photographer and claims he needs to catch up with the Army of the Potomac and be there when the last battle ends this godforsaken war.

And to make matters even worse, he told her yesterday that he has altered his plans and is going to leave her off in Gettysburg at an inn or somewhere she'd be safe. He told her that she could do her own investigating, sketching, and reporting and when she felt she had enough material for the *Rousing Clarion*, she'd have to take a train back to New York. He said he couldn't stay in Gettysburg, for he had already taken photos after the battle. Norah was stunned over this news and quite anxious, for the purpose of traveling with Timothy was to be safe, but also to learn something about photography. He tried to allay her fears and said she'd be fine traveling on the train and that other women traveled and she'd be sure to meet up with some. She had held back her tears, but now as she lies on the blankets and listens to Timothy whistle before the fire as if life is ordinary, they flow silently. The blanket becomes wet and cold and she is shivering, but soon she is asleep dreaming of the farm in Corning.

194

As they near Gettysburg, a wagon passes them on the road too closely. This causes Timothy's horses to become agitated and they rear up on their hind legs and snort loudly. Norah is sitting next to Timothy as he pulls on the reins and gets the horses under control, but a few items fly out of the back of the wagon and they have to pull over. The wagon that passed them goes up the road apiece and pulls to the side. The driver jumps down and runs to help Timothy pick up his canisters and his equipment. Timothy is furious at the driver and scolds him, complaining that if his equipment is ruined, he will pay dearly for it. The driver shrugs and walks away to help the passengers in his wagon climb out for a rest. Norah suggests they should rest, too, for they have been traveling for a few hours. Timothy sets up a couple of camp chairs for them to sit on, but Norah is restless and walks alongside the road in the direction of the other wagon.

The wagon that had nearly caused them to have an accident was full of women who are now milling about the side of the road. Norah wants to reach them before they climb back into the wagon and leave her bereft of their companionship. When she is a short distance away, all but one of the five women wave and smile at her.

"We're engaged in a mission of mercy," one woman says, and the others nod, as Norah draws near them.

"We must not tarry, girls! We have to get to Gettysburg. There's news of many dead, but there are many wounded who need our help. Time is running out. Get back into the wagon," a woman with a serious demeanor commands.

"Please, Mrs. Dix, it's stifling in the wagon. Might we go under the shade of the tree for a few moments?" a woman with buckteeth and sad eyes, pleads.

"Only briefly!" Mrs. Dix reluctantly gives permission.

The women climb a grassy bank to reach the leafed-out expansive maple tree that stands invitingly. Norah walks with them and a woman with sunny blue eyes and the prettiest and youngest of the others, walks beside her.

"I see that your husband prefers to sit in the sun."

"He's not my husband..."

The women walking ahead of Norah and her companion turn to her with interest. Mrs. Dix gives Norah a stern look and continues climbing.

The women get into step with Norah as they make their way to the tree. They're quiet and wait for Norah to tell them a titillating tale to alleviate the apprehension they feel as they travel to Gettysburg.

"We're nurses," the pretty one said, "or we're going to try and become nurses, anyway."

"Are you a nurse, too, then?" another woman asks Norah.

"No, I'm a milliner...well, not now, but I was in New York and now I'm a journalist."

"Is the gentleman back yonder a journalist too?" the woman asks.

"No, he's a photographer."

When they reach the tree, they flop down onto the grass. The driver follows them up the bank with two canisters of water that they all share as they wipe the sweat off their faces and fan themselves with their bonnets.

"I never met a woman journalist," the pretty woman says to Norah, "By the way, my name is Cornelia Hancock and I'm from New Jersey. We all met up at the Baltimore station with Mrs. Dix here, who is the superintendent of the Union Army nurses. She chose some of us to be nurses for the Union army."

"Well, Miss Hancock, I didn't choose you, but you stubbornly came along!" Mrs. Dix states, and the rest of the women stifle giggles.

"This is a serious affair! There's news of carnage at Gettysburg and the Army took off with most of their doctors. Out of 650 doctors, there's only a hundred left to treat thousands of wounded... Confederate and Union," Mrs. Dix said loudly as she stands to her feet and urges the women to do likewise.

"I hope we can just treat the Union soldiers. Our own soldiers," a woman says sadly.

Norah suddenly doesn't want to be a journalist traveling with the

Irish braggart, tough-guy photographer, Mr. Timothy O'Sullivan. Maybe she, too, could become a nurse. It will be more beneficial to the war cause to nurse the injured. And maybe she'll find Edward this way, for the soldier on the train said he had been injured and was in the hospital.

"Is there room for me to travel with you?" she asks Mrs. Dix.

"Why for, young lady? You've got your own work to do, I see," she said, looking towards Timothy who is frantically waving at Norah to come back to the wagon.

"I'd like to be a nurse," Norah says, feeling fickle.

"We could use another nurse, Mrs. Dix. I'm certain she'd learn fast, for she's a journalist," Cornelia said, her warmth enveloping Norah who is desperate for female friendship right about now.

Mrs. Dix looks Norah up and down, her countenance rigid and serious.

"I have strict standards for my nurses. You must be mature in years. You're too young, I'm afraid, and you're endowed with personal attractiveness that just won't do working with young soldiers."

Norah looks at Cornelia, who has to be as young as Norah. And she is a lovely lass, as well.

"I appreciate the flattery, but indeed I've much experience in hardship and I don't see how I'm any more attractive than Cornelia here."

By this time, Timothy climbs the bank and is out of breath. He holds his hat and fans himself. The women shyly look at him. He has a shocking mob of wavy hair and his moustache makes him all the more mischievous-looking and adventurous. Even Norah sees him with new eyes. Mr. Timothy O'Sullivan is indeed a striking figure of a man, after all. She can feel the women's admiration emanating towards her and it suddenly occurs to her that she doesn't really want to be stuffed in a carriage with a bunch of homely spinsters, except for Cornelia.

"Ye all look like a big bouquet of flowers up on this hill!" Timothy exclaims. The women titter and fan themselves from more than just the heat of the day.

"No more talk and silliness. Let's get on our way, ladies. I'm obligated as head of the Union Army nurses to get you to our soldiers at once!"

"No, wait. Please, wait. It won't take long a'tall. I work for the newspapers and magazines. I'm a photographer covering the war, but what bright hope it would be to have a photograph of lovely nurses standing underneath this verdant tree. Juxtapose this photograph with the pictures of the ugliness of war and it will bring courage and bravery to many!"

"They're not lovely girls, Sir! They're my nurses who are on duty at this moment!" Mrs. Dix turns and runs down the hill to the carriage. When she gets there, she motions for the girls to come down, but they stand stock still smiling at Timothy.

"Do you want me to help you with the photograph? Norah asks.

"Yes, yes, Norah...let's get this done immediately, before the old battle axe starts a bloody battle right here!"

Timothy eventually cajoles Mrs. Dix by giving her a small sum of money as a donation to the Union Army Nurses' Association. "For bandages and medicine," he says, as he hurriedly returns to his wagon to drive it and his equipment closer to the bank where the tree and nurses are. Alas, he realizes that as he had looked at the ladies from afar, they appeared as a mirage of beauty, but up close, they are mostly dreadful to look at. However, he photographs them at a distance and is assured that they will bring some cheer and relief.

After Norah assists Timothy in the puzzling operation of photography, she feels she made the right choice, after all. Traveling in a wagon with a good-looking gentleman to record the war is much better than being crammed inside a sweaty wagon with plain-looking nurses. Besides, she has never been good at caring for little Katie when the child falls down and needs bandaging. She cringes and nearly weeps at the sight of her darling's bloodied nose or scraped knees. She says goodbye to the wilting nurses-to-be and climbs back into the wagon with Timothy, feeling confident of her choice.

Chapter Twenty-Three

By the time Norah and her family had been forced to abandon their small cottage in Ireland and embark on their journey to America, Norah had seen enough suffering to last a lifetime. She watched her neighbors slowly starve and disappear in death. She had been only a child, but she will never forget their demise. She remembers some of the dead had grass-stained mouths, round and shriveled O's. It was as if they had been caught in surprise, swallowing death instead of bread or the potatoes they had both loved and hated. She gazed in horror at so many rotting potatoes and then rotting flesh that when she and her family were fleeing from it all, she had to close her eyes as they bounced along in their open wagon to the harbor. The constant performance of death had left an imprint on her mind. Maybe, she thought at the time, if she shut her eyes the images wouldn't fall from her mind into her heart, for she had felt the danger of dying herself just watching it. Norah thought her death would be a different kind of death, sort of like the wandering ghost-like mother, Mrs. Bailey, who had lived down the road in her village. Mam said that all of Mrs. Bailey's children, as well as her husband, had died from hunger, one by one and day by day. It had been a week's worth of dying, Mam said.

It hadn't only been Norah's eyes that had recorded death, but all of her senses had been stamped with the tragedy of the Famine. She had stuffed her ears with cloth when she lay down to sleep, for the wailing of the dying sounded like incessant and anguished prayers. Norah had wondered at the sins of her people and if she, too, would be next. When she tried to say her prayers, nothing would come out, but she had been tired from a lack of food, too, and somehow she felt God understood. But if she thought too much about the penance of her neighbors, she would become angry at God. But then again she thought it might be better for them to escape their sin-ridden bodies and go to Him in heaven. Why had He not listened? Had He, too, stuffed His ears?

Norah hadn't tasted death, except in the rotting potatoes when there had been nothing else to eat. But the stench, the aroma, of death had lingered long after the memories of the Famine had been shuffled into the back of her mind, and yes, into her heart. The living cannot continue to live without an organized arrangement of the memories of sorrow and tragedy. Without breath, there is no life, and Norah had inhaled deeply in order to keep living and in doing so, she had also breathed in the cloying, vile odor of dying flesh that had no soul left in it. And when Norah arrived in Gettysburg with Timothy O'Sullivan, the first sense to come rushing from her memory was this same scent of death.

There are makeshift hospitals everywhere and when Timothy and Norah pass by one of them, a chorus of moaning and weeping strike Norah's ears with familiarity. All her senses come alive in remembrance. But there is a sight her memory of the Famine had never recorded and it is even worse than the smell of death. Her eyes, in the darkening day, behold not the whole, yet diminished, person in death, but parts of the person, as if each one had been factory made and then pulled apart at the end of their lives. Norah looks upon entire limbs piled up high next to the hospital tent.

And suddenly, to her horror struck mind and senses, the limbs topple in front of their wagon. Norah feels the storehouse of memories collapse with the weight of her childhood sorrow, her near death at sea and loss of her husband, her recent encounter with the murdering of Negroes in New York, and now these limbs that have been pulled apart. The seams of her life and the world have unraveled. She faints onto Timothy's lap when he stops before the pile of men's bloodied arms, hands, feet, and legs.

Norah wakes early the next morning lying in a small, but comfortable feather bed. She is cold beneath a quilt, although the morning is heating up. She hears movement in the room and sits up quickly to figure out where she is. There are four other beds in the tastefully decorated, but austere, bedroom with walls made of large fieldstones. Young girls wearing nightcaps sleep in the other beds that are crammed into the room. She looks beneath the quilt and sees that she wears only her under clothing. She vaguely recalls a kindly older woman with rosy cheeks who smelled of onions helping her undress and into bed. She had been utterly exhausted as she traveled in the wagon with Timothy. She had wanted to tell him that she needed to climb inside the wagon and sleep because she felt feverish and was becoming ill by the minute. But he told her to quit complaining because they were soon going to be at their destination of Gettysburg. *Am I in Gettysburg now?* She spreads her hands over the quilt, pondering its unique pattern that brings to mind Elizabeth Jennings and the Underground Railroad. *What happened to the slaves I gave my hats to? Did they make it safely to Canada?* Her mind pours over all the activities in New York she had been engaged in before the Draft Riots. Elizabeth Jennings had taught her all the symbols of the quilts and this one she recognizes as the Shoo-Fly Block pattern. It means that a friendly guide to help the runaways is nearby. She is at once excited to think that this very quilt has been used to help the escaping slaves. Maybe the runaway slaves she met and helped had seen this very quilt that would have been hung out a window of this house or on a clothesline to send them off on their journey! It gives her strength to think of the slaves she has met, their faces contorted with worry and scars, but radiant with hope and bravery. *They are survivors.*

Norah takes in a deep breath and the sickening stench of her arrival in Gettysburg returns. The smell has lingered, either in her nostrils or else it has wafted into this room. She lies back down and closes her eyes and sees the images of human limbs that had fallen before the wagon. They looked like giant puppet or doll parts. She remembers she had fainted and Timothy carried her from the wagon into this large home whose lawn was littered with dead animals and the residue of battle.

Norah does not weep, but silently prays to live and to help. How to help, she does not know, but she would like to put the limbs back together and sew them on. Like what she does with old hats to make them new again. She opens her eyes and looks towards the window. The sun is streaming onto her bed and the quilt is a reminder of the fleeing slave women and to be with courage. She sits up again and stretches towards the sunbeams, feeling momentarily emboldened. She, too, is a survivor. To survive is to remain, perhaps like the debris that is left over from a vicious storm. Scraps that are left over and gathered together to make something new from threads that have to be strong. This war is real, Norah thinks, more real than she had known. And there is something happening in this war she can't define. Mankind's ideals are tainted with pride and selfishness, and even hatred, but then there is something that happens in spite of them. These thoughts swirl in her head now. *What is at stake is freedom and we don't fully grasp its meaning.* Her country, her new country, is at war with itself for freedom, not just for the slaves, but also for all of them. Norah lies back down and sleeps until the woman who helped her undress the night before awakens her.

"Miss, ye should be getting' up, for there's much to be done downstairs. We let you sleep long enough and your Mr. O'Sullivan has already gone on to follow the Army. He left you your personals and they're underneath the bed. He told me to give you this," she said, handing Norah a crumpled envelope.

Norah opens it and a few paper notes fall out. Timothy has left her money to take the train back to New York, but she already has paper money Harrigan gave her. There is a note written in scrawled handwriting, *You're quite the Irish gal for all your bellyaching and it's been a pleasure even if you can't make soda bread. Hope you can figure out how to write about this slaughter for your newspaper. The spirits do linger and the soil is now the color of blood. Use the money for the train. Yours, Timothy O'Sullivan.*

Mary, who works at the inn that Norah learns was built just before the American Revolution, helps her dress and explains that the inn is being used as a temporary hospital for both Union and Confederate soldiers, and a number of dying ones are still left and are in terrible shape downstairs.

"The ones who had a fighting chance to live and could be moved were sent over to the General Hospital on the York Pike. It's a mile east of town and there's a real surgeon, Dr. Henry James, running it, not like here without any doctor. We have two women come to be nurses, as well as the owners' young girls, but most don't know nothing about medicine. There's much to do and if you're well enough, you can help us. The innkeepers aren't taking in boarders unless they can care for the soldiers and help with the clean-up all around us. Ye have to have a cast iron stomach and be strong yourself, for it ain't a pretty sight I tell you, it aint' pretty a'tall!" Mary turns from Norah and wipes her eyes on her apron.

"I know nothing about nursing, but I'm willing to learn and I'm strong. I'll do what I can. But tell me, please, tell me about this quilt I slept under."

Norah picks up the edge of it and fingers the material.

Mary hesitates before speaking, "Not much to tell you, really. I'm not certain if I should say anything about it right now, for the war's not over yet and…"

"It's for the runaway slaves, isn't it?" Norah asks, excitedly.

"Only me and the Misuss knows the meaning of this quilt and we're not to be telling any stranger about it."

"I'm a milliner and I made hats for some of the African women who made it to New York and were on their way to Canada. I met some of them in a church in Brooklyn. Those poor women wore terribly worn out clothing and were sparsely clothed. The slave catchers could easily spot them in a crowd and know they were runaways. That's why we got them properly dressed and I made them some of my finest hats…"

"Come along, then, and I'll introduce you to the Mrs. You can tell her about this hat making business of yours for the African runaways, but right now, we've got some pretty sick soldiers who need your help more than the Africans."

Sunlight from a hall window meets Norah as she walks down the stairs. The rays wrap around her and temporarily blind her when she stands at the bottom of the stairs. The scent of death is still present, but it mingles with the smells of ordinary life, such as the burning wood in the kitchen fireplace and a hearty beef stew cooking over it. These homey aromas overtake the nefarious odor that still remains and will remain for months to come. Norah understands that life will go on with a natural cadence in which common tasks, such as cooking, will become welcomed blessings. She tries to look around, but all she can see are filmy cloud-like apparitions wavering before her. Is it smoke, she wonders? She shields her eyes from the sunlight, but when she lets go of the railing at the bottom of the stairs, she stumbles from dizziness. She grasps the railing with both hands and feels someone to her left grasp her arm and then someone else is taking her right arm. She moves her head out of the sunlight and looks to her left, but there is no one there.

"I'm here, Miss, right here. You're dizzy! That sun is blinding and it's heating up in here. We pulled all the curtains down from the windows to make bandages for the soldiers and now there's no keeping the heat out. Come and sit in the kitchen for the moment and I'll bring the Missus to you. We can't be waiting on you, but you would need some tea and bread, at least."

"Who pulled my arm, Mary?"

"There's no one else here, but me. You're confused is all from your traveling and the heat and shock."

"I don't want to be a burden and I want to help, but I need to ask about a certain soldier…"

Mary laughs, "Oh, Miss, there's too many soldiers here now and the only certain ones are the dead ones and the ones who left to continue this fight. The rest have become all one to us – bleeding and dying."

Norah tucks away her fear for Edward again, but then she pictures Katie at the farm in Corning and there's a compulsion to leave quickly to take a train back to her daughter and family. Once she is out of the sunlight, she can see the interior of the house that is filled with hand carved woodwork over the stone walls. It is quite warm, but there are ripples of cool air floating over her as she follows Mary down a long hallway. She can hear people murmuring in conversation, a woman reading aloud, and the groaning of a man who keeps crying out, "Blessed God, take me now!" She shudders and wraps her shawl around her neck and is determined to leave this house and Gettysburg as soon as she can figure out how to get to the train station.

Later, no one speaks to Norah as she eats some porridge and drinks tea in the kitchen that is sweltering from the late morning sun. She thinks it odd that she is still cold although it is so warm. There are a couple of older women and young girls coming and going out the back and down the hallway. Norah sees determination and sadness etched in their faces and some of them are as young as ten. A couple of the younger ones look her way and give her a quick nod, the corners of their mouths quivering. They want to smile, but are unable to do so, Norah thinks, and she feels awkward and in the way. She is the only one sitting and eating while everyone else busies themselves with the work of caring for the soldiers. She can only take a few mouthfuls and has difficulty swallowing. She gulps down her tea that is cold and then stands up, wiping her hands on her dress. Mary has left her in the kitchen, presumably to find the owner of the inn and Norah doesn't know what to do. She thinks she might go upstairs to the room she woke up in to retrieve her belongings and then walk to the train station. She'll ask someone for directions to get there and leave quickly. Norah walks down the hallway, but then feels a strong tug at her shoulder. She turns around to face an older woman who hands her a pail of sudsy water.

"Here, Miss, go to the keeping room and clean up the floor. Careful not to get in the way of the nurses tending to the soldiers," the woman says, pointing to the room off the kitchen.

Dazed, with her heart going into a gallop, Norah walks into the keeping room. Before she sees the six or so cots lined up side by side with soldiers on them and the two women tending to them, she is again overcome with the putrid scent of death. And then she slips and falls on the floor where blood has pooled and has not yet dried. She drops the pail and the water spills over her and onto the floor. Without thinking, Norah gets on her knees as if to pray, but instead she mops up the floor so she will not have to look up and see where the blood has come from.

Chapter Twenty-Four

Norah cleans up the blood that has mingled with the spilled water, squeezing out the bright pink rags again and again. And then she carries the pail out the back door to empty it. She walks to the pump and fills the pail with clean water and gives it to the women who are boiling water on an open fire near the pump. The women are sweating, their faces red, and they grimace while they work. None of them speak to her and the silence is pervasive, except for birdsong and the fire crackling. They empty her pail into a large cauldron over the fire and hand her another pail of warm water and a block of soap. She returns to the keeping room and continues mopping and squeezing and mopping and squeezing out the spilled life of the soldiers. She makes her way back and forth through the open door that is filled with sunlight. It is so bright she can't see anyone to the right or left of her and she is glad for it. She's numb, but is imbued with resilience that has been stored away and is now surfacing. Norah makes ten trips to and from the outside pump and fireplace and then back inside the keeping room. On her hands and knees, she moves around the floor by the legs of the nurses and the legs of the cots, but they are all the same to her. A man's dangling arm strokes the top of her head and she knows that he, like her, has strength and will live. And then she takes a large cleaning brush and scrubs until she is certain there is no trace of blood and gore. The sound of the scrub brush overcomes the sounds of moaning and only when she is satisfied that the floor is clean and no more blood has dripped from the cots (for most of the blood that spilled had been the blood of men who have already left the keeping room for the general hospital or the grave), does she stand up and look at the men who lie upon the cots. To her astonishment she sees that they all wear the remnants of the gray uniform of the Confederate soldier.

The one who had stroked her head beckons her to him, but she is unsteady and overcome with the humidity of the day. She begins to slip to the clean floor, but one of the nurses catches her and leads her to an empty cot and gets water for her. Norah takes a few sips and looks at her hands that are a bright pink. She panics and looks around the room that is fading in and out of her vision.

"I'm stained with the blood of the rebels!" she cries out before she vomits onto the floor she has scoured for what seemed like hours.

Norah is ill and the nurses move her cot as far as possible from the soldiers' cots. A couple of strapping young boys working on the grounds move a large dresser from the parlor to place in front of Norah's cot. There are no curtains to assemble around her for privacy and the dresser will suffice until she is strong enough to walk upstairs. The nurses are already taxed with caring for the soldiers and insist they are unable to care for Norah, too. It is Mary who takes charge of Norah, this task being added to all her other duties.

Mary hasn't been to her own home in days. Her young daughter, Betsy, has come to stay at the inn to help, but Mary is remiss having her only child see such terrible suffering. Mary's husband, John, is with the Army of the Potomac and although he survived the battle, she worries he'll not come home again. He already has had a few near misses on Little Round Top during the battle, but survived to tell about it. Mary, herself, was in her kitchen when a bullet came through the living room window during the battle right here in her own town. Soon after this incident, she heard that Mary Wade had taken a bullet in her own kitchen and died when she was making bread for the Union soldiers. She was the only civilian to die from the battle, they said, but still, Mary knew her neighbor well and was saddened. It could have been her, too. How did God choose one and not the other, she had thought with heaviness of heart. Mary pleaded with her husband, John, to stay and hide in their barn until the war was over. She begged him to not go, protesting that he had already served enough for his country and to look around and see what was needed right in their own community that was devastated. She tried to convince him that as a blacksmith, he needed to get back in business for the poor farmers who have lost so much. But he would not be dissuaded from going. Their small farmhouse had just a few bullet holes and it wasn't occupied like so many others. John told Mary that since their cow had been killed, as well as their chickens, she should work at the inn while he is gone. Mary has been a part-time housekeeper for many years for the McNairs who own the inn. John and Mary White have had a fairly comfortable life and make enough money for their daughter, Betsy, to take piano lessons and have some fancy things. They have protected her as much as possible, being that they are Mennonites and there is no need for the ways of the world to interfere with their way of life. But now her Betsy has grown up just in a matter of days and the innocence of their lives in rural Pennsylvania has been killed off, as had their cow and chickens.

Mary removes Norah's clothing and bathes her as best as she can, but is worried she'll herself get the fever, as well as everyone in the entire inn. After all the care they have been giving and then to have the lot of them just up and die, she thinks wearily, her faith in God dissolving little by little throughout the war-torn days and nights. She puts a clean nightgown on Norah and tells her that her daughter, Betsy, will attend to her later.

Later in the evening, Betsy's face is wan and ghost-like as she carries a candle into the keeping room. The child is merely twelve years of age and has eyes as blue as cornflowers, round orbs brimming with distress and shyness.

Norah's nightgown is drenched with sweat when she wakes

from a deep sleep and sees Betsy standing in front of a large dresser.

"Kate, did you hide Miss Maggie in the dresser so Meg won't be sellin' me pet at the fair?"

Betsy doesn't know what to say. She saw her Aunt Jane and old Mrs. Miller from her church sick in bed with fever, but she hadn't been the one to nurse them and only stood in the doorways of their bedrooms knowing they were going to die. As she looks at this woman who is beautiful in a strange sort of way to her inexperienced eyes, she feels the same thing is going to happen and she, Betsy, is much too close to it. In fact, in the last two weeks, she has been trying to stand back from death she encounters around every corner of her life.

"I'm not Kate...I'm Betsy," she said.

"Is Maggie Hen in my dresser?" Norah tries to sit up, but is too weak and lies back onto the cot.

"There be no hen in the dresser, Miss."

"I'm cold, Kate. Can ye bring me another blanket?"

Betsy decides she might as well be Kate for this poor woman who is suffering. She went to the corner of the room where a few blankets have been washed and folded. It is so muggy and warm that most of the sick men don't want a blanket over them. Betsy gets two of the blankets and places them tenderly over Norah, tucking them underneath her feet. She pours water from the pitcher into a tin that is setting on the dresser. When she gives it to Norah, she sees that her charge has fallen asleep. She turns to leave, but Norah cries out for her to come back.

"Kate, we've a house now and feather beds and there are cakes and tarts. And we have the music and dancing here in America, too. Not the same, but it's lively. Will ye come to live with us now?"

The strange rhythm to the woman's song-like speech intrigues Betsy and she wants to stay and listen to her talk more, for there is something hopeful in the tone. She hasn't heard the sounds of hope for a long time, even before the battle, for there had been much harshness between her mother and father over the fear of war.

Betsy doesn't fear she'll get the woman's fever now that the woman is talking so cheerfully and strong. Not like the others who couldn't put a sentence together before they died. Maybe the woman is going to live after all and if so, she'd like to know her better. But who is this Kate, she wonders.

"I don't know how to dance, but I'd like to learn," Betsy said.

"It's not the fancy waltzing. It's the kind of dancing the fiddle and a warm hearth make you do. My feet are like puppets attached to Da's fiddle strings. I never want to be far from his fiddle playing."

Betsy stays with Norah as Norah sleeps again. She thinks that the woman would make a perfect older sister, for her own died a few years ago.

Later, when Norah wakes, her fever and chills have lessened. She sits up and looks at Betsy.

"Who are you?"

"I'm Betsy and my mother is Mary, the woman who has helped you since you come here."

"I'm Norah McCabe."

Norah lies back down and cries quietly. She would have preferred to stay in her feverish dream and have Kate alive again.

Betsy doesn't know what to say and hesitates whether to leave or stay, but then a soldier calls out to her. There has been loud snoring in the room since Betsy has been there and she had thought the soldiers were sleeping deeply because of their wounds.

"Come here, Miss, and give me some water. And I'd like you to give the Irish girl something from me."

Betsy attends to the soldier and returns to Norah. She places a candle and a small box on the dresser.

"The soldier wants to give you this box," she says to Norah, who sits up on the cot.

Norah looks at the box and knows at once what it is. Her hands tremble when she opens it to find the four-leaf clover she had given to Edward before he went off with the Irish Brigade. It is the charm that Sarah, the runaway slave, gave her in the basement of the church in Brooklyn. Norah slowly gets to her feet and takes the candle off the dresser to go to the soldier, ignoring her weakness.

When she reaches him, she puts the candle near his face, clutching the box with the charm in her other hand. The soldier, his face full of freckles with brown eyes full of questioning, looks into her face and sings softly.

> *The Minstrel Boy will return we pray*
> *When we hear the news we all will cheer it,*
> *The minstrel boy will return one day,*
> *Torn perhaps in body, not in spirit.*
> *Then may he play on his harp in peace,*
> *In a world such as heaven intended,*
> *For all the bitterness of man must cease,*
> *And ev'ry battle must be ended.*

"I heard the Irish in your voice, Miss, and knew you to be from the same land as me."

Norah carefully sets the candle on the floor and kneels down next to the Confederate soldier. She sees that he is missing one of his legs. A stump is covered with a bulky bandage that is darkened at the end with dried blood.

"Are ye in pain?"

"A dull ache now 'tis, but not so long ago I thought I'd die from the pain."

Norah leans over him with the box in her trembling hands.

"Mother of God, where did you find this?" she asks.

"There's always stories going around the camps while we wait to engage the enemy. Fancy tales, but we sure as hell want to believe them. Bullets going through hats, sleeves of coats, and even through shoes, and the poor buggers saved from dying. Two estranged brothers meet face-to-face at Bull Run, one a Yank and the other a Confederate. They didn't kill one another, neither! Both run off from the fighting and no one knows where they are. That's a right miracle in my estimation."

"But what about this box?" Norah asks again, sighing with impatience.

"I've a hard time remembering, Miss. I want to give it to you cause I heard your voice and knew you to be from the ole country, like myself."

Norah stands up slowly, realizing now that this Confederate soldier could only have gotten this charm from Edward, who had promised to keep it with him in remembrance of her. She had insisted it was a holy thing and he'd be protected in battle. But now she knows that if this soldier, the enemy, has possession of it, it can only be that he has gotten it from Edward. And she wants the stark truth from him.

"Did you kill Edward M. Knox, 2nd Lt. in the Battery of The Irish Brigade and take this box from his person?" she asks, her entire body weak and shaking.

"Tell me!" she screams.

Before, Norah and the soldier had been speaking in whispers. After she screams, the other soldiers wake and cry out with curses. Mary, who was nearby, hears and comes rushing into the room. Betsy is sitting on Norah's cot watching and listening.

"What in tarnation is going on here, Betsy?" Mary asks. Mary points over at Norah and the soldier.

"That soldier killed someone she knows."

There is no solace for Norah as Mary makes her return to her cot. She weeps loudly and the soldiers in the room are angry, for they have wakened and are in pain. The soldier who gave her the box is trying to speak, but with the other soldiers yelling out, Norah's weeping, and Mary complaining, no one hears him. He nearly forgets he is missing a leg and starts to get out of bed, but soon realizes he is unable to walk.

"You shouldn't have come here to add to our burden!" Mary says to Norah in frustration.

"Mother, she came to help and she did clean up all the blood," Betsy replies, defending Norah, for she has developed a liking to her.

"We'll have to move her cot out of this room. It's troublesome having a woman here with these soldiers. Help me, Betsy. I'll get

213

her up and you push the cot into the parlor."

Norah allows Mary to help her to her feet and she leans into her as they walk out of the keeping room. Her temperature rises again and she is vexed that she is a burden to Mary and the household. She only wants to sleep and not think, especially since she is certain that Edward is dead.

Chapter Twenty-Five

Norah is in a fever for a few days. The inn's well runs dry and water has to be retrieved from the springs nearby, but because of thunderstorms and the runoff carrying the effluvia of decomposing bodies of horses and men, the water becomes tainted. They boil it, but it is still noxious and affects everyone in varying degrees. All over Gettysburg, there is a shortage of water. Norah lies unwashed and in a stupor in the parlor and is given sips of boiled water to drink. The inn is busy with caring for the soldiers and the coming and going of those who have come to help Gettysburg regain order. Friends and relatives come to the inn to minister to the wounded, but only to the few Union soldiers who are recovering in rooms around the inn. No one comes to help the soldiers in the keeping room. If it wasn't for the nurses and Mary and Betsy, all the men in tattered grey in the keeping room would have perished. Many of them did, for the Confederates had left only their most seriously injured men behind after the battle.

Norah is eventually restored to health and becomes acquainted with this community ravished by war and heartbreak. Her first sense of Gettysburg is that the landscape had once been serene and idyllic, but now is shattered and broken. She is learning more about the history of Gettysburg than the history of New York! She thinks she and Elizabeth could have easily walked the streets here without being pelted with stones. It had been a small bucolic agricultural community boasting flourishing industries and two educational institutions. It was settled by Scots-Irish families in the north and by German families in the south, and by 1860 the population was 2,400 that included 200 Negro citizens. Of course, there were the Indians, too, but they were not counted by the townspeople and lived mostly hidden away. How pleased Norah is to learn that the Underground Railroad runs through McAllister's Mill on the Baltimore Pike and that many of the free Negroes from this community have been active in the liberation of slaves. A Slaves' Refuge Society had been formed and there were two thriving black churches before the war. She writes Elizabeth Jennings to tell her how her people are so brave and that fugitive slaves had come from Maryland and Virginia and had found jobs and spiritual strength in Gettysburg before the battle. Norah tells Elizabeth that education was provided for all blacks by Pennsylvania's Free School and there had been thirty-three black children in school before the war.

What is most astonishing, Norah writes, *is that there has been harmony between the white and colored community. Oh, don't get me wrong, Beth. There was still inequality. And guess what? I've a new friendship with Lydia Smith, a colored woman who aids the soldiers, Confederate and Union alike.*

From Lydia Smith, Norah will learn that although hatred and injustice still existed for the Negro, there had been a slow metamorphosis that developed in Gettysburg. This transformation resulted in the Negro community in Gettysburg emerging with new wings of freedom. Many of the people owned farms and a young Negro, Daniel Payne, had become the first black student who graduated from the Lutheran Theological Seminary. *Like you, Elizabeth,* Norah wrote, *he opened a Sunday school for colored children.* Lydia explained to Norah how a dark cloud had hovered over their community as the war escalated. Gettysburg was a mere six miles north of the Mason-Dixon Line and the Negro families had lived in constant fear of slave kidnappers, but by mid-June of 1863, it had become worse. Confederate officers had been coming into Gettysburg and the surrounds to seize the Negroes to take them to slavery in the south. Lydia told Norah that by June, Negro families from Gettysburg and from south Central Pennsylvania had fled northward, carrying their feather ticks and few belongings. In fact, there had been thousands of freed Negroes who left Cumberland Valley, and only a few stayed in Gettysburg to hide in cellars and conceal themselves in wheat fields during the battle. Lydia told Norah she had sequestered herself in a hiding place until the battle was over.

"Most white people here felt sorry for us and some of us stayed in their employ to work for them, for they promised to keep us safe," Lydia told Norah.

Although Norah will turn back the pages of history to see through the chaos, the beauty and treasure of this community, Gettysburg, is now in terrible ruins. The rolling hills and farms are desolate from the sickness of war, and although some Negroes return, everyone knows it will never be the same for them. They are free, but the horror of war has clipped their new found wings. And there are 20,000 wounded and dying soldiers occupying homes and makeshift hospitals everywhere.

Union soldiers who had died in Gettysburg were embalmed and sent to their homes and others were buried in Evergreen Cemetery. The dead Confederate soldiers were buried in mass graves or where they had fallen in battle. Northern states with units in the battle sent agents to Gettysburg to take care of their dead and wounded soldiers. For weeks after, people came not only to help, but to gawk and pick through the debris for souvenirs. Just a few days after the battle, hundreds of people had arrived by wagon to view the carnage while picnicking on Little Round Top amid the shallow graves and rotting bodies of horses. Weeping mothers, wives, and sweethearts meandered through the fields and in and out of homes, churches, and inns looking for their loved ones.

McNair's Inn, where Norah is staying, is an inn that had

previously boasted of the best, steamed puddings in the north. There are very few doctors in Gettysburg and most of them have been tirelessly amputating and caring for the soldiers in the general hospitals. Many are new physicians without proper training who carry around a copy of a military surgery manual they refer to while treating patients. Disease is rampant and life is one huge, filthy mess, and Norah McCabe is in the midst of it. Eventually, a doctor comes for an entire day to care for the soldiers at the inn. Many of the soldiers in Gettysburg are worsening with the devastating symptoms of what the doctors called the eruptive fevers. While the doctor is attending to the soldiers, Mary asks him to check on Norah, for she has been recovering too slowly and her fever still persists. Mary sent Betsy home, for she fears her child will become ill from the contact with Norah and the soldiers. Mary, the nurses, and the McNairs keep feeling their own foreheads while they work, fearing they have become infected and will soon be in the grave.

"She's got the ague, as I see it," said the doctor to Mary. "She'll come through, I suspect, unlike some of the soldiers here. You've done a mighty fine job trying to clean up the place, but the poor fellows were already weakened from camp disease before this battle. The hospitals are full of soldiers with camp fever, the shakes, smallpox and you name it. They lived through their limbs being hacked off, but now they're dying like flies. And speaking of flies, I've never seen so many in one place, but here, that is. Whatever you're doing, keep it up. Give the boys and this woman plenty of beef tea and milk-punch if you have any. That's all that can be done. I've got to go to Camp Letterman now. There are some 400 hundred tents and more soldiers being transferred."

The old doctor is clearly fatigued himself and shortly after, Mary sees him to the door and watches him limp to his wagon. Then Betsy comes running up the drive and into the inn sobbing.

"I found my horse, Ma! Merry's dead and swelled up twice her size. I walked to the field behind our house and saw her there. Some men are digging graves on our land and I can't bear stepping over it all. I fear I stepped on a man's arm. It moved and maybe he's buried alive!"

Mary clutches her daughter to her bosom, squeezing her so tightly that Betsy cries out that she can't breathe. Mrs. McNair sees them and leads them into the kitchen, the only place for comfort, for there are no soldiers convalescing there.

Chapter Twenty-Six

Norah dreams of Sean, not Edward, and when she wakes, he is leaning over her, his thickly freckled face smiling down at her.

"Tis you, Sean! You've come back!" she said, but then the lad stands up and moves away from her and she realizes her mistake. It isn't Sean, but the Confederate soldier who has killed Edward. He totters as he tries to balance on his crutch and one leg.

"I've been praying to the Blessed Mother you'd wake and be well before I left."

"Go away from me!" Norah said feebly.

"I didn't kill your man. I found the box on the field after I was struck down. I lay on my stomach feeling nothing on my right side thinking I was going to die. And then I spied the box and grabbed it and kept it clutched in my hand. I knew it was a good sign. After I heard your voice, I had to give it to you."

The soldier turns and hobbles out of the room and Norah says loudly, "May God and His angels keep you safe from all harm, and the luck that wasn't on us today be upon us tomorrow."

And surely the luck of the charm continues to work its power, for this Confederate soldier lived and Norah learned he made it home to his family in Virginia. And that very day, Norah rose from her bed and was stronger than she'd been since before she had left for Gettysburg. She keeps the box in her apron pocket as she works at the inn and is certain she will eventually find Edward M. Knox. But because she dreamed of Sean, she thinks she sees him in nearly every soldier and wonders where he might have taken himself.

Betsy becomes Norah's constant companion and Mary instructs her to assist Norah in darning socks, salvaging the inn's gardens, and caring for the soldiers, but Betsy also teaches her about country life. Norah had forgotten the rhythms of the earth and the feel of soil in her hands since living in New York City. To Norah's delight, Betsy reveals to Norah where the cupboard is that the Underground Railroad used. This inn is on the first stop of the Railroad's network and the door into the cupboard is camouflaged on the wall going up the stairway. When Norah climbs in and has Betsy close the door, she is reminded of her dresser, her own place of hiding from the evils of the Famine in Ireland and then on the ship coming to America. It is also a place of dreams and often when everyone is asleep at night, Norah climbs into this place and prays to St. Brighid. At times, new designs for hats come to her and she sketches them.

New life in the midst of tragedy and death are emerging everywhere. There are no further thoughts about leaving and she writes to Katie every couple of days. Mary encourages Norah to go with Betsy and herself when they visit their home, as well as to walk into town, but Norah refuses. She has seen enough death right here at this inn and at the moment can't endure seeing anymore in Gettysburg. Just as she experienced hope in the dresser when she was a child, she is finding it in the cupboard. For now, this is what she has to do.

"But don't you want to find your sweetheart?" Betsy asks, wide-eyed with excitement. She is on the verge of womanhood and is living vicariously through Norah's dramatic life. Norah hasn't shared everything about herself, for the poor child doesn't need many more tales of sorrow. But Norah's stories of adventure, New York City restaurants, writing for the newspaper, making hats, and her love of a soldier intrigues the young girl and makes her want to someday be just like Norah McCabe.

"I have the box, remember, Betsy, and sure my Edward will be found."

Norah also writes to Nellie and Harrigan, and considers asking them to visit Edward's father for any news of Edward, but she doesn't. Better for the mysteries of life to be at hand, she tells herself, and no need to always have the stark, raving truth in one's own face. How this made any sense to Betsy and to her mother, Mary, was for them to wonder, and even Harrigan and Nellie are surprised that Norah never mentions Edward in her letter to them. They let it go, thinking it's a shock just for Norah to be in Gettysburg and although Norah promises two articles to be written within the month, Harrigan is mostly concerned for Norah's well-being. She doesn't sound like the Norah he has known.

And then the day arrives when the enigmatic and dignified Lydia Smith comes to the door asking for anything the inn might spare in food or clothing for the hospitals in Gettysburg and the surrounding area. Betsy and Norah open the door to a colored woman with skin of light-gold tint and a determined air.

"I've seen the sun rise and set on both the rebel soldier and the Union, Miss, and God's justice is that both receive comfort and help. The hospitals are in need of food, clothing, but even flowers I'd be pleased to bring them."

"I can ask Mrs. McNair, the owner of this inn, if there be anything we can give you. We have soldiers convalescing here, too, and I don't know that we would have anything extra. Would you like to come in from the heat and have some refreshment?" Norah asks.

Betsy takes Lydia into the kitchen and Norah seeks out Mrs. McNair. Mrs. McNair is a quiet woman who doesn't like to be in charge of the inn and relinquishes all duties to her staff, especially to Mary. In the afternoons, she often retreats to her own rooms for rest and no one ever faults her for it, for the first week after the battle, she had worked tirelessly without sleep. It has weakened her and now that the worst is over, she feels the need to measure out her labors. She and Mr. McNair are in their sixties and her husband, too, has become frail since the war, but continues to oversee the inn with as much vigor as he can muster. Norah knocks tentatively on the McNair's bedroom door and when the door opens, Mrs. McNair smiles at Norah and asks her what her need is. After Norah tells her about Lydia Smith, Mrs. McNair is quiet for a few moments and then motions for Norah to come into her rooms. Norah walks in and although not extravagant, the rooms are more lavish than the rest of the rooms in the house. Mrs. McNair opens a drawer with a key and pulls out a jewelry box. She hands it to Norah.

"I've already sorted through my heirlooms and kept what is most precious to me. Please take this to an appraiser who can find someone to purchase the items for a good price. And then you and Lydia Smith can buy food, clothing, and whatever necessities are needed for the soldiers. I don't know Lydia Smith, except to hear she's a strong woman who raised two sons alone and she's a friend of our abolitionist friend, Thaddeus Stevens. As a Quaker, I am ardently against slavery. I have come to trust you, Norah, and I know this to be the right thing."

"I'm pleased to help here at the inn, Mrs. McNair, but I must return to New York and to my work and family..."

"You will return home soon, but perhaps this help you give to Lydia Smith will also help you before you leave."

Norah takes the jewelry box from her and before Mrs. McNair closes the door, she gives Norah a peck on her cheek. Norah is surprised, but warmed by this gesture. What did Mrs. McNair think she needed help with?

Later, Norah and Lydia Smith climb into Lydia's wagon and head into town. Betsy had begged to go, but Mary insisted she needed her to stay and assist her at the inn. Before they left, Betsy came running out the door with pots of flowers she had picked to give to the soldiers. At Norah's suggestion, a few days before, they had picked flowers for the soldiers at the inn. It had brightened them immensely at the very sight of the colorful wildflowers, for the soldiers were unable to move from their cots.

At the end of the drive, Norah looks at the fields across the road as the sun is preparing to meet the earth at the end of the day. There are well-dressed women meandering with parasols, men carrying pick axes over their shoulders, and soft mounds dotting the landscape. Over some of the mounds, Norah can see crude crosses had been made out of branches and stuck in many of them. Someone is dragging a wagon wheel from the field and another man's horse pulls a wagon piled up with battle accoutrements left behind by soldiers who had fled for their lives. As Lydia and Norah silently travel down the road, Norah doesn't see any piles of men's body parts and is relieved. When Norah had asked Mary about the amputations, Mary told her most of the amputations had stopped, but the burying of the limbs sometimes was forgotten. Norah didn't want to see any unburied limbs! She holds onto the jewelry box tightly and dares to look around her. *Is Edward under one of those mounds or are they all Confederates buried so haphazardly?* She breathes in and out slowly and feels that the peace of a sunset is upon her to give her strength and if this Lydia Smith can be brave, she, too, can be so.

Long days are spent visiting farms in the surrounding area of Gettysburg and beyond, persuading the farmers to give what they can to help the suffering soldiers who fill the makeshift hospitals that are too numerous to count. Lydia and Norah spend hours together and eventually share confidences as if they have known one another for years. Norah has never met a woman as exotic, affectionate, and as reticent as Lydia. Although there is candid conversation between them, there is an unspoken sorrow Lydia carries and perhaps Norah knows it well because she, too, carries it. If certain heartaches are talked about too vigorously, they possess you and ruin you, she mentions one afternoon to Lydia.

"I know it to be true, Norah. I don't talk about my eldest boy who died in 1860. William. Sweet William, as the flower, he was. And now my banjo playing barber son, Isaac, he went and joined the Colored Troops just a while ago. He's alright. He writes his mama regular."

"What about the boys' father?" Norah dares to ask.

"He and I separated a long time ago. If you're born a Negro here, you already got a burden to carry, but if you add too much anger to that burden, you are weighed down to the ground so bad that you can't see the road ahead of you. That was my husband, Jacob."

"Being Irish is sort of like that and I've seen the Irishman pile on hate to the hate already heaped on him. Does no good."

"My Daddy was Irish and my Mama had other blood in her besides the Negro blood. But it don't matter if you only have a pinch of Negro blood, it's all the same to the bloodhound slavers. Or even the kindly white folk in the north who can sniff out the little bit of Negro blood and keep you at a distance."

"I was born in a country knowing nothing about that kind of skin hate, Lydia. But we right well knew the hate of the British who reigned over us."

Like Elizabeth Jennings, Lydia Smith had pride and belief in her worth. She told Norah about buying her house in Lancaster, the same year her son, William, had died. She said she was also the housekeeper and confidant of Thaddeus Stevens, an abolitionist and Congressman. She told Norah they traveled to Washington together and she had bought the house next to his in Lancaster.

"He had a hard upbringing and so we share similar stories, as well as our opposition to slavery. He treats me with utmost respect, Norah, and that for any woman, especially a woman of color, is more precious than gold."

Norah wanted to ask Lydia if she and this Thaddeus were more than friends, but at once understood there was a secret bond between the two people and it was not to be shared. Norah is learning from Lydia there are many women, Negro and immigrant, who are living with a boldness and freedom cultivated from hardship. Norah excitedly tells Lydia about the women she made hats for traveling in the Underground Railroad network and Lydia smiles knowingly. By the end of their travels together and before Norah leaves to return to New York, Lydia holds Norah close to her and tells her she'd miss the Irish girl and they should keep in touch with letter writing.

"I declare, Norah McCabe, it's as if I've known you all my life. And other than Thaddeus Stevens, you have become a treasured friend."

Chapter Twenty-Seven

When Norah and Lydia arrive at the makeshift hospitals with their wagon heaped with clothing, food, as well as niceties, Norah doesn't go inside the buildings or tents. Men come to unload the goods and Norah helps, but she will not accompany Lydia inside for a short visit with the soldiers. At each hospital, she thinks of Edward, but she doesn't look for him. It is superstitious of her, she knows, but more than that, it's about protecting herself. Lydia knows about Norah's lost soldier and does not fault her for staying with the wagon. However, at each hospital, she quietly inquires if there is a soldier named Edward Knox. And although nothing is spoken between them about this, Norah knows Lydia does this.

One sweltering day after they have unloaded blankets and bandages, as well as baskets of lemons, oranges, jellies, and sweet cakes, Norah watches Lydia walk out of a ruined church being used as a hospital. Next to her is an older gentleman with a familiar dignified gait who wears his famous hat. Mr. Charles Knox greets Norah with an embrace and holds her for what seems to Norah, a long time. She doesn't know whether it is her heart beating or his as he holds her close to him. When he pulls back from her, his face is flushed but less stern than she last remembered. His eyes are tired and his face is creased with lines that are new.

"Come inside to see Edward, my dear, for I have only recently found him. He has been asking for you."

Perhaps it is the heat of the day and the shock of knowing Edward lives that causes Norah to nearly faint and have to be taken under a tree for shade. When she revives, she walks with Lydia on one side and Mr. Knox on the other as they climb the steps to go inside the church to see Edward. As they enter, Mr. Knox warns her that Edward is in much pain and that he might never walk again.

Norah is surprised to see Saint Francis Xavier Catholic Church filled with bustling nuns and a priest scurrying here and there tending to the wounded soldiers. The poor sufferers are stretched out on boards laid across the high-backed pews. Norah follows Mr. Knox down an aisle, peering into very white faces drawn with pain. Anguish and dread fills her, as she steadies herself clutching Lydia's arm. And then there is a pull on her arm and a cheerful voice rings out.

"Tis the journalist who was traveling with the photographer! I see you've come to be a nurse after all!" exclaims the woman.

Norah turns to see Cornelia, the only pretty, young nurse amongst a gaggle of homely ones that she had met on the road to Gettysburg.

"I'm here to see a friend..."

Cornelia hugs Norah, "Go to him, then, but please stay on, if only to read to the poor men. Your voice and sweet face would bring much solace."

Lydia and Norah follow Mr. Knox to the back of the church and the sour smell of blood and men's sweat fills Norah's nose and throat. There is a chilly dampness that wraps around her and she shivers, even in the humidity. There are few windows and as they approach pews that have been moved away from the others, Norah sees Edward. His handsome face is moon pale in the dimness of the church and when he turns his head to her, he smiles, feebly, but his smile is just for her. Lydia and Mr. Knox leave Norah and she kneels down beside Edward who is lying not on a board, but up against the back of a pew. Blankets cover him from his waist down. He lifts his arms to her and she leans lightly onto his chest and feels the rhythm of his heart against hers. She wants to believe their hearts are beating in cadence, but her beats strike after his own and at a much faster pace, two beats to his one. When she lifts herself from him, he wearily drops his arms to his sides and she grasps one of his hands and holds it with both her hands. He is cold, even on this summer day and she rubs his hand between her own to bring warmth back. She takes his other hand and does the same. She will revive him and she is at once filled with hope and longing for him.

"Are you well, Norah?" Edward asks in a raspy whisper.

"I am well, especially now that I've found you."

"How long have you been in Gettysburg?"

"Too long, it seems. I'm not sure. I've lost track of the days, and lost track of you as well, my darling. I came with a photographer to write about this battle for the paper, but I really came to find you. I was ill for a time and have been cared for at an inn here in town. I have been helping with cleanup and…Oh, Edward, it's hideous, this war! I've never seen so much suffering and pain!"

Norah lays her head on Edward's chest. She is tired of being strong. Edward unties her hair from its loosely coiled bun and strokes her head gently.

"I'm paralyzed, Norah. My men were saved, but my legs were not, I'm afraid. I am of no use to a vibrant, lovely woman as you. No use to you, Norah. You must go back to New York and live your life as God would direct you. I'll not burden you. We will always love each other, but go home now, Norah. When, or if I can make peace with this infirmity, we'll be friends. Please go home and care for Katie and yourself."

Norah sits up and looks at Edward and his eyes are distant, as if he is remembering another time. She knows at once that he is no longer able to love her. It should be her who has to grapple with love altered because of his injury, but it isn't. She is ready to love him into eternity no matter how crippled he is. But Edward has already made his decision about her way before she arrived.

Before she leaves Edward, she kisses him full on the mouth and remembers their passion and is sorry she did not allow him to become one with her in lovemaking. Perhaps she'd be with child now and he would have to marry her, for he would only do right by her. But as sensuous as his lips feel, there is no heat in them as before. The warmth comes from her lips only and when she says goodbye, tears fill his eyes but she knows they are not because she is leaving. They are tears of pity he has for himself, but that is to be expected, she thinks, and soon, enough time will heal and they'll be together as they had been. Norah leaves Edward hopeful for their love. What would it matter if he can't father another child! She has Katie and this war will soon be over for all of them.

Charles Knox saw so many graves and dying men in Gettysburg that he knew if he didn't take his son away from the ruins, his son would perish, too. The nurses said Edward was in no state to travel, but Mr. Knox knew differently. He remembered how he himself had come from Ireland against all odds with every hindrance known to man and had survived. He had more than survived and now his son, with the same courage, would live and not die, even without the use of his legs. He had a carriage come to the church in the morning and father and son left before sending news to Norah that they were leaving. When Norah arrives later that morning with a large basket full of freshly picked cherries and warm Sally Lunn buns, her hope and love are strong. But when she walks to the back of the church and doesn't see Edward, she drops the basket onto an empty pew and visits each soldier in the building. She walks up and down the aisles methodically peering into each face and when she has gone throughout the entire building and doesn't find Edward, she starts walking up and down the aisles again. Halfway through the building for the second time, Cornelia catches up with her and touches her arm.

"You'll not be finding him here, I'm afraid. His father insisted on removing him. They are right now on a train to New York and I hope the dear man survives the trip."

"Did they not leave word for me?" Norah asks.

"I'm sorry, but there was no message."

Norah turns to leave, but Cornelia catches her arm again.

"Will you be so kind as to share your basket of goods with some of the soldiers, then? Maybe it will help…"

"I've no strength for it!" she replies.

Norah walks to the back of the church and finds a pew that is empty. It's probably the pew Edward had laid upon, she thinks wearily. She sits down and tears spill out of her eyes as she weeps quietly. She reaches into her apron pocket for a handkerchief and pulls out the box with the four-leaf clover. She dries her eyes and puts the box back into her apron. She'll carry it with her now to pass the luck onto the soldiers that need care that she will try to give to them.

"Earth has no sorrows that heaven cannot heal," Norah says quietly. It is an adage her Mam had often repeated throughout her childhood. Norah finds Cornelia and together they bring comfort as they feed the soldiers warm bread and cherries.

Norah stays in Gettysburg and helps at the McNair's Inn and at Saint Francis Xavier Catholic Church reading to the wounded and bringing small comforts to them. Sometimes religious services are held for the men and although many of the soldiers aren't Catholic, they make the sign of the cross and close their eyes in prayer. She participates, too. Every little thing, including prayer, helps. She is thankful Edward is alive and Katie is well and writes to her each week, sending pictures she has drawn. She thinks of writing to Edward, but she's too busy caring for the soldiers and keeping up with her letter writing to Katie, Harrigan, and Nellie. She sketches hat designs on butcher paper each evening before she goes to bed and writes out plans for setting up a shop when she and Katie move back to New York City. Each night, exhaustion seeps into her and she sleeps deeply, without dreaming. And because she is coming to know the soldiers, they tell her stories about their lives prior to the war. She asked them if she might write their stories for her newspaper in New York and they were cheered by her interest that their lives mattered enough to be written about. Some of the soldiers know they are going to die and to freely share confidences with this empathetic woman meant that their lives had not been lived in vain. Each week, Norah sends a soldier's story to Harrigan to print in *The Rousing Clarion*. She titles her column, *A Soldier's Life*.

Betsy accompanies Norah to the church and is much better at changing wound dressings and assisting the nurses with the soldiers' physical needs than Norah is. Some of the soldiers suffer violently from general toxemia before dying. Their skin sloughs off in great patches, their teeth and tongues blacken, and they bleed from internal hemorrhaging. There are times in the midst of their great anguish and pain that they clutch Norah's arm and beg her to stay with them until they die. Sometimes the priest is there and gives last rites, assuming the soldiers are Catholic. Norah feels the priest sometimes interferes in a soldier's progression into a certain peace with death; the soldiers long for tenderness and the touch of another human being without preaching or prayers. Norah sings to some of the soldiers and finds that her voice has a sweet timbre unknown to her before. Songs from around the hearth in Ireland return to her in the Irish language and she sings them unrestrained and free. Oftentimes, a hush comes over the church as Norah sings to a dying soldier. These times, she does not remember the meaning of the words and only trusts they had come from heaven. And then there are soldiers who are dying with so much anger that they punch the air and shout curses. Norah stands back from them and prays silently. Sometimes she will grab their arms and hold them down, telling them to finish being angry and then let love come. She does not know who she has become during this time at Saint Francis Xavier Church, but there is no time to figure it out. She wonders if someone else might be visiting her body while she cares for the soldiers. And if ever she had the time to wonder about it, she feels this visitor a better person than herself. And she quietly hopes that this person abiding within her will stay after the war is over and when she returns home.

It seemed to Norah and everyone in Gettysburg that the battle was the end of the war, even the end of the world, to the people there who suffered and who cared for the injured and brought daily restoration. These were ones who didn't ask about the Army of the Potomac and how the war was fairing. They dared not know, for every breath and thought was for the moment in that time and place that was becoming sacred ground to them. There had been over fifty thousand Union and Confederate casualties and thirty thousand missing or captured soldiers, and three thousand horses and mules dead. Some corpses were not buried for over a month and the swelling of the bodies of both horses and men brought flies and disease. Norah McCabe's life was imprinted now with an American tragedy and not only an Irish one. Still, she felt a holiness in the landscape and this grace and reverence honored the dead and the living in Gettysburg, although no-one spoke of it until much later.

It would be nearly two years before General Robert E. Lee surrendered his Confederate Army to General Ulysses S. Grant on April 9th in 1865 at the village of Appomattox Court House in Virginia. Victory would be bittersweet and it seemed there would be no end to tragedy when the war weary president, Abraham Lincoln, was shot in April of 1865. In May, the remaining Confederate forces would surrender and America would be reunited as the Civil War ended. Over 620,000 Americans would die in the war, with disease killing twice as many as those who would die in battle. There would be 50,000 survivors who returned home as amputees and one in particular who lost both legs in the battle of Gettysburg but would find his heart in Norah McCabe.

Chapter Twenty-Eight

James McKee heard Norah singing in the Irish language ten days after he had his legs chopped off by an army surgeon. Before he was struck down and passed out on the battlefield his brother went down right next to him, his eyes wide open. A couple of days after, James lay in a stupor with maggots crawling around his bleeding stumps in a tent underneath a willow tree. And then he had a letter from his mother in Virginia. His father had dropped dead from a heart attack and she was returning to Ireland. James was moved from the tent to Saint Francis Xavier's Church when the doctors believed he was no longer in danger of gangrene and death. The church was the place for survivors. The Sanitary Commission and medical representatives from the Christian Commission were helping Gettysburg and this church was one of the first hospitals enforcing the new sanitary conditions. Saint Francis wasn't free from disease and the shortage of potable water, but this church and a few other makeshift hospitals were functioning as long-term convalescent facilities and had altered from giving crisis surgery to bedside care. This is not to say that some soldiers didn't die from gangrene and disease at Saint Francis, but the worst was over for most of the soldiers once they arrived at the church. But now it was their hearts and minds that were in dire crisis and James McKee seemed to have lost both, the nuns believed. He cursed at God and wanted to die, not unlike many who cried out to be free from their pain. But most men would not dare curse God, believing to be so near death. James McKee was one angry man. And it wasn't until he heard his native language being sung by Norah that some of that anger dissipated as he felt a hand cover his heart and massage it back to a form he hadn't known since childhood.

"My legs are still with me, Norah, and there's cramps and pain in my feet and ankles."

"Ghost pains, James. Your brain doesn't know that most of your legs are gone. Ye must become acquainted with them as they are. It will take time," Norah replied.

Corneilia told her this about the amputees when Norah began to assist her with the care of the soldiers. She herself knew well about ghost pains. She would always feel hungry even when she was full.

"I was a strapping young lad you'd not be able to resist, Norah, when I had me legs."

James would often repeat this during the first week Norah met him. The night she met James, she had been singing to a sixteen year old boy who was dying a week after his right arm had been amputated. He had blood poisoning and pneumonia that slowly brought his life to an end and Norah sang him into eternity. It was late in the evening and the church was still, except for the crack of thunder, the rain pelting the roof, and the sobbing of some of the men. The young boy had been taken out of the church after his death. Most of the soldiers were going to recuperate and their pain was bearable, but not so their psychic pain. And so it was for James McKee, for he was getting better, but only wished to die. Then the young boy died and Norah and a doctor carried his cot out of the church for burial. Norah was glad Betsy had gone home and didn't have to see a young man just a few years older than herself die without his family surrounding him. Norah would list his name tomorrow and get the news to his family in Maryland. He was a Confederate and his amputation had come too late, for the Union soldiers were first in line for surgery. It was the rules of war. But after his surgery, he had been lovingly cared for by everyone at the church, including Norah. And so had James McKee been treated with the utmost care.

"Ye are from the same cursed land as me and yet you sing like a bird let free from her cage," James McKee said as Norah walked by him on her way back into the church after helping the doctor with the dead boy. She stopped and looked at him. Corneilia said he was the one who tried to bite her hand when she was trying to wash his face after his surgery.

"He's a demon, Norah. Or he has a demon. I'd stay clear from him. Only the doctors are attending to him now."

But Norah couldn't resist the sorrow in his voice.

"I'm only new at the singing, lad, and 'tis for this place only."

James raised himself up from his cot and looked into her face imploringly. Norah held her candle up to his face and saw eyes the color of the sea, a mix of blue and green that blazed at her. There was a familiarity in his eyes.

"Only when you sang to the boy did I listen and only then, for just a wee moment, did I not wish to die. Might you sing to me now...'tis like an angel singing."

Norah's voice was not so much angelic, but earnest and sweet, and it was the spirit of it that took over and had power. She knew not the scope of this, but she also didn't believe her voice was like Jenny Lind's. It was for this time here in Gettysburg only, she believed, and perhaps it would be no more after she left.

James McKee lay back down, closed his eyes and wept. Even in the dimness of the evening she could see his tears streaming down his face. She sat herself down where his legs should have been and sang to him until the storm and his tears stopped. And then she kissed his cheek, worrying not about him biting her, and left for the evening. Thereafter, James McKee began to heal from the inside out and Norah McCabe sang to him each evening before she returned to the inn.

The day before Norah left Gettysburg, she and James had a picnic under the same willow tree James had once wished to die under. He felt more alive than he had ever been in his life and he was preparing to ask Norah McCabe if she would spend the rest of her life with him. He had never cared about living in Virginia, anyway, and he was willing to live in New York if she would marry him. He himself was not a slaver and he had convinced Norah that he had only gone to war for his father. In fact, he told Norah, he had been in love with one of the Negro kitchen girls when he was a young boy first come from Ireland. He was confident of Norah's love, for she had sung to him every night before he fell to sleep. And once she had allowed him to kiss her when it was late and the nuns and priests had left and the rest of the soldiers were sleeping. He felt he was stronger and it was only when Norah had to help him move about that he remembered he no longer had legs.

"I'm betrothed to another soldier, James. He's recuperating in New York," she said to James, looking away from him. She had not written to Edward M. Knox since he had left Gettysburg and he had not written to her. Nor had she mentioned him to James.

"Ye are not!" James responded with incredulity.

"I am. He was wounded here in Gettysburg."

"But why would you carry on so with me, Norah, especially since I'm a Reb!"

Norah had no answer to give James. She should feel guilty, but she didn't. She felt free as a bird when she sang and this made her feel all the more in touch with her senses. And her sense of touch and her need to be touched had become all the more heightened. James McKee possessed the finest features in a man and his full lips were sweet and gratifying to kiss. She had come to know James quite easily; for she had washed him and helped him dress and she had not been embarrassed. It was as natural to her as the rain and sunshine and she did it all while singing. And she was so at ease with this Irish lad! James possessed poetry that tumbled out of him like a waterfall and he was ever so in awe of her.

"Will ye break it off with the fellow and marry me, then, Norah McCabe?

"I love you like the brother I never had, Mr. James McKee..."

"Mother of God, what kind of brother would ye be kissing?"

Norah blushed and turned away from James. It was true. At first he had been like a brother, but she had never had one so how would she know, anyway. But then she couldn't resist the man, legless and all, but in the last few days he had become like a brother again. She had been thinking a good deal about Edward and had written to him that she was coming home to the city after first retrieving Katie in Corning.

"Ah, Norah darling, you and me...we should be together. And how could ye resist taking me home with you when you know my old mudder has left me here alone in Amerikay," James said, laughing.

"You really don't have anyone?"

"My father's family, but they're not my own. My real Da died in Ireland before we left for America. Mam caught the eye of a planter from Virginia after we first arrived. She was a domestic at his sister's home and when he was visiting, they met. Our lives went from feeling like slaves to becoming slavers, it seems, although he had a small farm compared to others on the James River and in Charles City. He was a kind man to me and my brother and even to the few slaves he owned. He grew tobacco and rice, but when the war came, everything came to an end. My brother died. I lost my legs. The Yankees burned down our house. My father died and there's nothing left, but my mother, and she's going home. She wants me to go with her, but there'll be nothing but hardship coming her way back in Ireland..."

James looked away, overcome with sorrow.

"How old were you when you left Ireland?" Norah asked.

"A wee boy of twelve, so I remember Ireland, its hardships, and the British lording it over us, but remember well the beauty. An Irishman's heart is always wed to his country, like she was his bride."

"You know, James, you could have been the one to have injured my betrothed. I should hate you for being the enemy, but I haven't it in me."

The sun was setting and painted a glorious band of gold and

copper. James and Norah said nothing more about love, war, or Norah leaving for New York. But eventually it was time to say goodbye. She was strong and he was very thin and slight since the war began, especially without his legs. She lifted him gently into a cart and pushed him over the lawn and back into the church.

The next morning, Norah rose before everyone else at the inn and went to the large field behind the house, delicately making her way over debris and a few graves. There was an intimate presence in the landscape and one she needed to pay homage to before she said goodbye. There hadn't been enough time for the fields of Gettysburg to absorb the sorrow it had received so unexpectedly; to mingle blood and soil to create consecrated ground whose presence would be felt for generations. But already there was a reverence and spirits lingering in the many fields. And Norah felt this and wished to honor it, something she had not done before leaving Ireland.

The warming sun spread its comforting golden light over Gettysburg and Norah said goodbye to the dead and the living. And then she was soon on a train headed home to Katie and her family. On the seat next to her was a big hatbox that Mrs. McNair had given her that had been placed carefully on a pair of stumps that were covered in blue overalls. James McKee was going to go on a long visit to Corning, New York and Norah was certain Da would welcome him with open arms. When Norah had said goodnight to James in the church the night before, he had whispered to her that although he might not be able to help her father in the field, he could play fine Irish music on a melodeon and had won medals for it in Ireland. He would help her Mam in the kitchen, too, peeling the spuds and making bread. How could Norah deny him a place in her family, for she had already made a place for him in her heart?

Chapter Twenty-Nine

Da welcomes James McKee into his home as if he is a long, lost son. He carries James into the kitchen and offers him his Sleepy Hollow armchair to sit in. Mam gives James the chore of peeling potatoes and he cradles a large bowl in his lap while sitting in Da's chair. It becomes James McKee's special chair and Da never sits in it again. And who helps James McKee to his bed each night and carts him around the farm? Da! At first, Mam isn't pleased having another mouth to feed, but she warms to James after he sings *The Banks of Claudy* and other Riley ballads that bring her to tears.

"Faith and *begorrah*, 'tis the strong onions making me weep so!"

Norah's hard-shelled mother softens a bit because the likes of a poor Irish lad with no legs helps her remember Ireland again. Da has been trying to keep Ireland alive in Mam for years, but hasn't succeeded like James McKee. James settles into the McCabe family as he settles into Da's chair, comfortable and natural as if he has always been with them. Even Meg and her family like James McKee, for he makes Meg laugh and that is something she doesn't do easily. Katie adores him and calls him 'Uncle Jim' in a week's time. And then they have a Hooley and all the neighbors come to play music and dance. No one knows James McKee has been a *Johnny Reb* from Virginia, for he has never lost his Irish accent and begs the McCabes not to speak of how he had to shoot at their own Union boys. He claims he killed no one, as far as he can remember, being that his only real battle had been Gettysburg and that battle ended his soldiering days.

"Tis bad enough they know I was born in Ireland, but if they've taken a liking to the McCabes, sure now, they'll forgive me for it," he says to Da and Norah one evening when James and Da are playing music in the kitchen.

Norah waits for the right time to tell Da and James that she is leaving to settle back into New York City. No one asks if she is going back and for the last few weeks, she has been sketching patterns and designing a hat, as well as sending Harrigan a few articles about Gettysburg.

"Katie and I are leaving for New York in a few days. Nellie is expecting us, and she's adopted a little girl Katie's age. Polly was a baby when her mother left her on our doorstep years ago, but the mother had taken her back. It's a long story, but a good one."

"There'll be no good story if ye all have to live in that small apartment, then," Da said.

"There'll be room enough, Da, and I want to get back to selling my hats and working for Harrigan..."

"And seeing the lad you're going to marry," James said.

Norah has not told her family that she is betrothed. And she has not heard from Edward M. Knox, either, but is certain he is busy getting well, for Nellie has written that she visited the father at his store and he claims Edward has a long, hard road to become healthy again.

"Why Norah, how would ye have kept such a thing from all of us?" Da says, stamping out his pipe in the ashtray a little too hard.

"But again, I'm not surprised!" he continues. "Ye have been quite the girleen for surprises your entire life!"

"I'm sorry for spilling the beans, then," James says, putting his head down.

"Has she told you how she ran off with an Irish rebel to go and fight for Ireland?" Da asks James.

"Please Da. I haven't told James about that time."

"Who is the fellow you're marrying, Norah? Is he taking you off to Ireland? Why is it you are determined to live on the edge of life, like sitting on the bank of a river on a hot summer day and never jumping in!"

Norah stands up, confused why her father is angry at her. He has always supported her, unlike her mother who often criticizes her.

"I jumped in so deep into life, Da, I nearly drowned. Maybe you don't remember? But I've learned to swim and not because the man I want to marry has taught me! I've taught myself. Life has taught me! And I thought you understood you have also taught me!"

Norah leaves the room and goes to bed, but is unable to sleep. If there is no peace with her father, there is little peace in her. But she has to go her way without his blessing, for she is a grown woman with a child of her own and she is resolved in her convictions. James McKee has been devious; for he knows her family didn't know about Edward. And although she adores James, she told him they are like brother and sister now that he has moved in with the McCabes. He laughed at her, pulling her down to kiss her cheek, confident that Norah would, in time, fall sway to his caresses again.

Katie cries inconsolably when they say goodbye to her *Maimeo* and *Daidoe*. She is displeased her child is more attached to her grandparents than to her and she has regrets having left Katie for the length of time she did in Gettysburg. Gettysburg is an ache forever in her heart, but it's a sweet one. Although Norah has determination, she has become malleable and not only has her Mam's edges been softened, so has Norah's. She found her voice in Gettysburg, this battlefield a sacred place that has married Norah's Irish suffering to an American one. And when James asked her to sing at the Hooley, she did so with the same sweetness and enchantment. The Irish lyrics were recalled, but this time Da told her what they meant. After Gettysburg, how can she doubt that life has meaning in the midst of suffering and that she will sing, not only dance, during hard times.

But now for the romance in her life, she must face the truth and not dally with mystery any longer. She is full to the brim with love for mere life these days and perhaps it is enough. Edward seems so far away from her and at times, it feels as if he has died in battle. When she has time to consider him, she feels love, but is perplexed. But soon she will learn the truth about Edward and whether he has healed enough in his mind and body, and perhaps heart, to marry her.

In the meantime, Norah is going to open her own millinery store and not wait for a big department store to sell her hats. Harrigan wrote that he has a gob of back pay due her and hopes she still has her account at the Emigrant Savings Bank. Well, he is probably exaggerating, she thinks, but Da assuaged the rift between them by placing an envelope with bank notes in her hand before she left Corning. It isn't so much the money, although she needs it, but that he said he believes her millinery store will become a thriving success.

Norah comes home just in time to see Barnum's notice in the New York Times, *'Three Giants, Two Dwarfs, Indian Warriors, French Automatons, & Dramatic Entertainments Morning, Afternoon, and Evening.'* Yes, she surely is back in New York City with the confusion, din, and opportunity! Nellie and her adopted daughter, Polly, meet Katie and Norah at the train station when they arrive early in November. Nellie directs the carriage driver to take them to Orchard Street and Norah wonders why they aren't going to Chatham Square. They stop in front of a small, wooden clapboard house. Nellie is beaming with happiness.

"It's our house, Norah! For the four of us! That is, if you agree to purchase it with me. The bank will give us a wonderful deal! Our children need more room and there's a small room for your hat making…"

"Yes, Nellie, yes! When do we sign?"

Norah is surprised that she has said yes and that Nellie has made this arrangement knowing she is going to marry Edward. Has Nellie forgotten she is going to marry Edward? Norah says nothing about Edward, for first things must come first and she can't pass up the chance for better living conditions for Katie and herself. And it might be a long time before Edward is well enough to marry, anyway. The sun sets as they stand in front of the house they'll soon move into, its rays casting a warm, golden glow of cheer over the house as a benediction. It is a humble abode and not as large and beautiful as the McCabe farmhouse in Corning, but it will be her own home and for right now, it is perfect.

A week later, Norah walks to the Knox department store at the bequest of Mr. Charles Knox. She recalls the time not so long ago when she had been full of trepidation while carrying her bag of dreams and hats, hoping to convince Mr. Knox and other department store owners to let her set up a shop in their stores. She had been certain they wouldn't be able to resist her. She feels some embarrassment now for how cheeky and over confident she'd been, a faltering confidence, she knows now. But this day, she is sure of herself as a milliner, whether or not anyone else is. She laughs, remembering how perplexed she had been after Mr. Knox turned her down. The only one who couldn't resist her had been Edward and it wasn't her hats he couldn't resist. And now she is going to see the father, not Edward, for Mr. Knox has sent a letter inviting her to meet him at the store to talk about Edward. She is trying to allay her fears that Mr. Knox is going to tell her that Edward has gotten worse. After arriving in the city, she had tried to see Edward, but was told it was too soon. She has been waiting and then this invitation arrived. She thinks that he must be worse. *What else can it be? Why would Edward not write to her himself?*

Norah takes a short cut down a side street and suddenly a man with ginger hair wearing a tattered cap comes out of an alleyway and saunters down the street towards her. He has the same familiar hair and the same built and cocky walk! Norah picks up her skirts and rushes to meet him, her heart thumping loudly in her ears.

"Sean!"

But just as she is about to fling herself upon him, he takes off his cap and Norah sees it isn't Sean. The man possesses a remarkable resemblance, but his eyes are of a different color and shape, and his mouth is thin and not full like Sean's. He gives her a half-smile, bemused by this woman ready to throw herself at him.

Later, Norah leaves the Knox department store and steps into a carriage that Mr. Knox hired to take her to Chatham Square. She's eager to go home and help Nellie pack up the house, for they are moving in a few days and there's much to do. She sits in the carriage and closes her eyes, overcome with sorrow for Edward, for all the soldiers she has known and cared for, and for the mothers, wives, sweethearts, and sisters who feel the loss of love. But she doesn't feel sorrow for herself. How can she? She has lived with an abundance of love in her young life and this love far outweighs the sorrow. But her darling Edward has only ever sipped a teaspoon of hardship here and there in his young years and this war has nearly drowned him in sorrow. How would she have responded to suffering if she had lost the use of her legs? Would she still be resilient? She thinks back to her conversation with dear old Mr. Knox.

"My dear, here is a letter Edward asked me to give to you. He desired me to speak to you first and assure you that by no means has he left the country to abandon you, but to learn how to walk again. Going overseas to Geneva is the only hope for him to receive the surgery necessary to correct his injuries."

All Norah could say was, "Oh!"

Mr. Knox continued, "He didn't want you to see him in such a weakened state. He is injured considerably, but his morale and enthusiasm for life is not what it once was, I'm afraid..."

Mr. Knox had turned away from her and gazed at the photos on the wall, one of Ireland and one of his family.

"I could have helped him. I wouldn't have been demanding. I'm acquainted with suffering. I would know what to say and how to conduct myself. I fear he no longer loves me."

It had been Norah's turn to look away and out the window, tilting her head upward to bolster her confidence and keep her tears from spilling out of her eyes.

"Edward loves you, Norah McCabe, so much that he doesn't wish to burden you with further hardship in your life. This journey might take a few years and none of us are getting younger. He wishes you to be happy and live a full life. You have your millinery and newspaper work. He doesn't want you to be burdened with an invalid."

There had been nothing more to be said. So he loved her so much he didn't want to burden her, but what if in letting her go, he brought more heartache into her life? If only Edward could have met the enemy, James McKee, without a leg to stand on! And if only she could be with Edward now that she had found her voice. She could have sung him back to health in his mind and heart, just as she had done with James McKee. But she had felt heavy laden with immense despair at that moment and to try and convince Mr. Knox what she had done for other soldiers and what she could do for Edward had felt just too burdensome.

"Norah McCabe of Ireland as I am of Ireland, please don't hesitate to visit me again and if there is anything I can help you with, call on me. I think for now it's best to let some time pass, but in the future, let us always be friends."

Edward's letter had been succinct in an attempt to persuade Norah of his undying love, and it was altruistic in stating that he must let her go because he loved her. She read between the lines that he was too injured in body and spirit to love anyone, and yes, perhaps he was too young and inexperienced in the ways of romantic love. She didn't question his love for her. But he needed time and the more she thought about it, she also needed time.

A week later, Norah is sitting in the office of the *Rousing Clarion* and reading the remarks made by some of the Gettysburg natives who had attended the dedication of the Soldiers' National Cemetery on November 19, 1863.

"*Mighty good speech for old Abe!*"
"*It was a fine speech!*"

"My tears started flowing as soon as he started speaking!"

"Too short. We all wanted more 'cause what we heard gave us spine tingles!"

She is preparing to write an article about the dedication, but she hasn't yet read the speech. First, she wanted to read the reactions of the press and people who attended the event. Harrigan had left to go to an eatery to buy them lunch, for they were going to be working late into the evening to get the next issue out. Norah continues to read the responses to Lincoln's speech.

> **The Chicago Times:** *The cheeks of every American must tingle with shame as he reads the silly, flat, and dishwatery utterances.*
>
> **The Springfield Republican:** *His little speech is a perfect gem; deep in feeling, compact in thought and expression, and tasteful and elegant in every word and comma.*
>
> **The Chicago Tribune:** *The dedicatory remarks by President Lincoln will live among the annals of man.*
>
> **Horace Greeley:** *I doubt that our national literature contains a finer gem than that little speech at the Gettysburg celebration.*
>
> **Harrisburg Patriot and Union:** *We pass over the silly remarks of the President; for the credit of the Nation we are willing that the veil of oblivion shall be dropped over them and that they shall no more be repeated or thought of.*

Finally, Norah reads Abraham Lincoln's two-minute address that was given after the nearly two hour main address by the Honorable Edward Everett, a leading orator from Boston.

> *Fourscore and seven years ago our fathers brought forth, on this continent, a new nation, conceived in liberty, and dedicated to the proposition that all men are created equal. Now we are engaged in a great civil war, testing whether that nation, or any nation so*

conceived, and so dedicated, can long endure. We are met on a great battlefield of that war. We have come to dedicate a portion of that field, as a final resting-place for those who here gave their lives, that that nation might live. It is altogether fitting and proper that we should do this. But, in a larger sense, we cannot dedicate, we cannot consecrate—we cannot hallow—this ground. The brave men, living and dead, who struggled here, have consecrated it far above our poor power to add or detract. The world will little note, nor long remember what we say here, but it can never forget what they did here. It is for us the living, rather, to be dedicated here to the unfinished work, which they who fought here have thus far so nobly advanced. It is rather for us to be here dedicated to the great task remaining before us—that from these honored dead we take increased devotion to that cause for which they here gave the last full measure of devotion—that we here highly resolve that these dead shall not have died in vain—that this nation, under God, shall have a new birth of freedom, and that government of the people, by the people, for the people, shall not perish from the earth.

What a heartfelt and moving speech, Norah thinks. She is disappointed that most of the newspapers reported President Lincoln was haggard, dour, and ghastly pale when he gave his address. *It's a wonder*, Norah thought, *that this feeling man can go on.* She remembers the tears in his eyes at the House of Industry when he looked solemnly at the poor children. Surely, he looked out upon the fields of Gettysburg and was overcome with grief. *Had he seen any of the limbs of soldiers lying about, as she had? After such a battle and this war, will there be a new birth of freedom for Elizabeth Jennings and her people and for her own people and other immigrants making America their home?*

Chapter Thirty

For nearly a year, Norah searched for a store to lease for her millinery business, but never found one. But during this time, some of her former Five Points' customers are softened by the horrors of the war and forget that one of Norah's best friends is a colored woman. Norah is selling hats to them and to her neighbors, and word is getting around that Norah McCabe can make you look like a million bucks in a specially designed hat. She uses a corner of her bedroom as her sewing room and is teaching Katie how to stitch some of the Parisian flowers onto her hats. She takes money out of her savings to buy frames and material for the hats and is certain she will eventually double her money in sales. And she is right, for eventually she not only doubles, but triples, the money she spends on materials!

Nellie and Elizabeth help her when they can, for there is a surge of customers in the spring and summer of 1864. Norah's fortune has changed and she keeps her four-leaf clover with her all the time, but then one day she can't find it. She is frantic as she looks throughout the house and in the pockets of her clothing. It's silly, she thinks, but believes it has brought her luck in the millinery business. And now it's gone! As she searches for it, she hears a little voice singing sweetly from her dresser. Her Irish dresser sits in the corner of the bedroom she shares with Katie and of late, Katie has been climbing into it to take naps. Norah opens the cupboard and there is Katie Marion holding the box with the four-leaf clover in it.

"Come out of there and give your Mam her charm and I'll tell you a magical story about it."

So begins Norah's storytelling adventures with Katie Marion. She has heretofore been reluctant to share her past with her daughter, for she feared it would only frighten her. She wanted to ensure Katie would have a life free from the tragedies she herself had lived through, but now, with some sadness, she knows she can't protect Katie from hardship. But she can share her own stories about the faithfulness of life and how love can come in the most unexpected and thrilling ways. Love, with all its complexities and unimagined depths. Can she explain to her daughter that love is strong, but is as fleeting and hard to capture as the fireflies she puts in a jar in summer? Love of city, of country, of friends, even love for a sister who can't show her love? And what of the love for a wartime enemy who might have killed her lover? She can tell Katie that the backdrop of darkness is sometimes the only way to experience the brilliance of love's light; that they can't see the glow of fireflies without the dark night. Norah sings to Katie some of the stories of her past. She sings about a ship that sailed across the sea with a little girl hiding in a dresser and she sings to her of the slaves hiding in the basement of a church. She sings to Katie of rotting potatoes and of flowers in the field that grew alongside them.

One day, Kathleen Hartnett, the successful milliner from Boston, comes to visit.

"I secured a patent for a hat design, Norah. It's not a trifling matter going through the process, but it's worth it. You can do the same. You and I, dear, won't be tied up in apron strings in the kitchen, will we now? We Irish gals have to work hard at convincing the aristocratic codfish of our worth, but we're more than able for it."

So Norah takes Miss Hartnet's advice and talks to Harrigan about getting a patent for a favorite hat she sketched while she was at McNair's Inn. She tells him that she had picked up a number of hat frames, bodies, and materials in Philadelphia after leaving Gettysburg before returning to Corning. While there, she said, she found the office for Godey's Lady's Book, but became too timid and didn't knock on the door. "I did leave a note instead and told them of my work as a milliner and a newspaper journalist."

Norah explains that in a week's time at her family's farm, she made a spoon bonnet, oval shaped, typical of the most popular bonnets of the era. While shopping in Philadelphia, she found splendid cream lace and flowers and feathers of every hue of the color purple. Violet and lavender, her favorite colors, and so rare to find this color in nature, she said with great enthusiasm. Harrigan, of course, enjoyed her descriptions and listened attentively.

"I sewed on just a few sprigs of flowers on the inside of the brim, but covered the back with ribbons, flowers, and purple feathers. Most of the well-favored spoon bonnets are designed with the flowers placed inside the brim to circle the face of the wearer. Oh Harrigan, I think a woman's face should resemble a flower and not compete with the flowers for attention. So I arranged a profuse bundle around the back of the bonnet instead. It isn't necessarily an original bonnet in that the shape and materials are extraordinary, but it's the design of the material, the purple flowers placed just so around the outside of the hat."

"And then the wholesaler gave me such compliments!" Norah changed her voice to sound like the merchant,

"You've an eye for such bold beauty, my dear, and I assure you that a purple hat will bring you much good fortune! You'll be surprised at the attention you'll receive from these colors! Purple, the blend of passionate red and the calming effect of blue; a marriage of perfect color, indeed!"

Later that week, Harrigan surprised her with an ad in the *Rousing Clarion* for her *Bee in Your Bonnet* millinery business. He also spoke to a lawyer who works in a law firm that specializes in patent law. It takes a few months and a lot of paperwork, but soon Norah has a patent for her elegant spoon bonnet design that she names, the *Hope Bonnet*. *The Rousing Clarion* advertises the *Hope Bonnet* with a full-page ad that includes a sketch Harrigan and Norah work on together. Harrigan surreptitiously sends it out to be advertised in newspapers in New York, Chicago, and Philadelphia.

One day a few weeks later, Mrs. Sarah Hale of *Godey's Lady Book* calls in at the office of *The Rousing Clarion*. Harrigan is so astonished that he trips over Norah's Victorian spats when Sarah Hale presents herself. Norah had left them in front of the door. Her feet are bare, for she has taken off her stockings and boots while working. She quickly picks them up to put them on, but Mrs. Hale laughs and says she might join Norah in escaping from her hot boots. Harrigan makes some tea and they sit together for a few minutes before Mrs. Hale speaks about the reason for her visit.

"We've seen your spoon bonnet you've advertised in some of the newspapers. It's feminine and elegant, and we'd like to show off your hat in *Godey's*. The sketch, of course, will be hand colored by our employees, all of whom are women. I'd also like to include an article about your business, *A Bee In Your Bonnet.*"

After Mrs. Hale leaves, Norah dances a jig around the office. *Godey's* is a magazine for the upper classes of women and to think Mrs. Sarah Hale herself has come calling on Norah McCabe because of her *Hope Bonnet*! The times are changing so quickly, she thinks, and I'm getting in step with them. *After mourning, comes joy! And hats and hats...and dancing!* Mrs. Hale is in her seventies, but such a handsome and robust woman. This woman who has come from humble beginnings, suffered the loss of family members, her husband, and two children intrigues Norah. *And the woman has written novels, poetry, and became the first woman editor of a popular woman's magazine!* She's a hero, of sorts, to Norah, because she has been a champion for not only women, but also the poor.

Norah watches fashion changing and women's skirts being elevated to reveal a fancy petticoat or underskirt and French inspired flirtation ribbons, or kissing strings, stream alluringly from bonnets. Women grace the streets of New York with color and beauty while the war rages on. She reads *Godey's Lady's Magazine* that highlights the novel styles with their elegance and charm. The magazine does not address the vicissitudes of war in their editorials, nor is there mention of Gettysburg or other battles. Norah understands that Godey's is a reprieve and a place to go for solace and order in the midst of the upheaval and heartache of war. And yet the magazine isn't merely a frivolous escape into fashion, for it addresses social conditions and offers suggestions for women to find work and gives examples of European women who are painting and creating handiwork to support their families. And then the *Hope Bonnet* appears in color alongside an article about her. She reads about herself, and it's as if she is reading about someone other than herself. *Norah McCabe, who hails from Ireland and Five Points, has created, A Bee in Your Bonnet business...* And then there are more requests for her specially designed bonnets.

It's November and New Yorkers are weary of the war. Many people doubt Abraham Lincoln is capable of bringing about its end and peace to the country. But then in spite of much criticism, Lincoln is re-elected. Norah is preparing to secure a lease for a shop on Orchard Street. Nellie is busy at the mission and Elizabeth Jennings has started a kindergarten school for colored children. Neither friend is able to assist Norah in keeping up with her hat orders, so Norah has been interviewing young women. She will have to train them and they want high pay. The nerve! But Norah is happy and she will do what she has to do to meet the demands for her hats. She is so busy that she has to take time off from working at *The Rousing Clarion*. And then one evening before she delivers the signed lease to the landlord for her new shop, New Yorkers again take to the streets in panic and riotous fear.

Norah, Nellie, Polly, and Katie have been in a gleeful mood and decide to go to Barnum's, for Norah has never taken Katie to the museum. She recently told Katie the story about her visit to Barnum's as a young girl and meeting the poet, Walt Whitman. The three walk hand in hand into the museum on a brisk late November afternoon.

Norah immediately senses dread while an onslaught of noise emanates from the surfeit of exhibits and activities. They meander from room to room to view dioramas, panoramas, and shows. In one room, they watch a learned seal named Ned as he performs. Katie adores him and begs to stay, but is distressed when she sees Feejee the Mermaid who looks like a monkey with a fish tail. Norah picks Katie up and she cries as they move through a crowd of people. Katie is over stimulated and both Nellie and Norah decide they have all seen too many freakish and outlandish exhibits. Even the beluga whale in an aquarium seems out of place, for although it's a fascinating sight, the creature's eyes are melancholy. Barnum's has giants, midgets, Siamese twins, and even Grizzly Adams's trained bears, but after seeing the strange mermaid, Feejee, they are ready to quit the museum and go home. As they try to make their way through the crowd, there's sudden screaming and yelling that there's a fire. People become alarmed and push and shove one another in an attempt to get out. Norah holds Katie tightly, as Katie clings to her neck and cries, "Sing Mama, sing!" Nellie picks up Polly and reaches back to hold Norah's skirts and yells "I'm going to lead us out of here... follow me!" Nellie pulls Norah and Katie through the crowd as Norah sings in her Irish tongue she knows not what, but it seems to open a way through the crowd to get out of the building. As they make their way out, they smell smoke and see a fire has been set in a stairwell. When they are on the street heading towards home, they encounter mobs of people yelling that the dirty Rebs are burning down New York. By the time they arrive on Orchard Street, they are a tangle of nerves and fear. All they can do is clean up the best they can and go to bed without dinner or even a cup of tea. They all climb into Nellie's feather bed, for none of them want to be alone. Although at first they can't sleep listening to the sounds of a city undergoing turbulence, they're so weary that sleep finally comes. But before Norah falls asleep, she makes a decision that she can no longer live in a city where her daughter's life is in danger. Katie has lived through a near abduction, the Draft Riots, and now some kind of siege. Her *Bee in a Bonnet* business is finally flourishing, but little does it matter to Norah if Katie's life is so vulnerable.

The next day, the newspapers write that the diabolical plot was schemed by Confederate agents come to infiltrate northern cities, including New York, to commit widespread acts of arson and death. The insurgents had planned on occupying federal buildings, seizing weapons, and then placing a Confederate flag over City Hall to declare that New York had aligned itself with Richmond. These plans had been originally concocted to disrupt the election, but Lincoln had sent thousands of federal troops to ensure the election would be peaceful. This ridiculous and ambitious plot had been thwarted, but the Confederates decided to exact revenge and set fire to as many hotels as possible. The fires did not spread in any of the hotels, nor Barnum's Museum, and no one was seriously injured. It wasn't like the Draft Riots, but Norah McCabe has made up her mind to leave and now she has to figure out the best way to do so.

Chapter Thirty-One

Norah and Katie don't move out of New York City and within the next few months, many women in Five Points and the surrounds are wearing Norah's Hope Bonnet. Norah's fingers are red and sore from sewing, although she has the help of a young woman she hired as a trimmer. She doesn't open a shop, but conducts her business from her new home on Orchard Street. Except for war weariness and the vigilance she exercises over Katie's well being, Norah is fulfilled. She occasionally writes small articles for *Godey's Lady's Magazine* and for the *Rousing Clarion*, but she is happiest designing and creating bonnets. Mostly, Norah is at home with herself and who she has become and also who she has not become in her life.

And then the war is over and jubilation rushes sorrow onto the dance floor and whirls it away in celebration. "Union, Victory, Peace!" The New York Times announces the surrender of General Robert E. Lee and his whole army to Ulysses S. Grant on April 9, 1865. America's grueling tribulation with democracy has reverberated throughout the world and repercussions have been keenly felt. Even in Cuba, slaves had been crying out, "Onward, Lincoln, Onward! You are our Hope!" All over America, people gather in crowds displaying celebration. Bells ring, guns fire, and there are parades throughout the streets. Nellie and O'Leary (for they are still sweethearts), Norah, Katie, Polly, Elizabeth and her husband, Charles, celebrate with sparkling wine and dinner on Orchard Street. No one throws stones or yells out obscenities at Elizabeth or Charles when they stride up to Nellie and Norah's house. It isn't that prejudiced hearts have changed that quickly, but the joy of victory has overruled hate. Happiness, like a quick dip in a cool spring on a hot summer day, comes to them as they eat and drink together. It isn't until they are sitting eating apple pie and drinking tea, does Norah feel sorrow. There had been another celebration not that long ago, although it seems ages ago. It was the time they had gone to the Emancipation Jubilee at Cooper Union on January 1st in 1863 and Sean had declared that her involvement in helping escaped slaves to freedom was too dangerous. He had expressed his love to her publicly, but in an unseemly way that had derided the triumph of Lincoln's declaration for slaves to be freed in the Confederate states. He had slammed the door on her and they had been shut out from one another ever since. She has no idea if he is dead or alive.

There is elation, however, that the war is over and it seems real that President Lincoln cares about someone like Elizabeth Jennings and the African race. Norah's hats are becoming prized possessions and she is at ease and joyful. Her dance card is full and she has no fear of stumbling on the floor of this grand ballroom of life! But as she looks into each endearing face of her friends, she wonders whether there is room for one more name on her proverbial dance card. Edward is convalescing and she knows where he is. But Sean Connolly without the "O" is missing from her life.

And then tragedy diabolically strikes the nation, but to Norah and Elizabeth Jennings, it feels so personal they can barely function, let alone dance. Abraham Lincoln is dead and the nation mourns and wears not just one layer of mourning clothing, but two. Victory for the north is shrouded in the dark veils of the aftermath of war and now President Lincoln has been murdered and the nation knows that they have lost a president who has dug deeper into the meaning of America's freedom than any other president ever has.

Norah walks through the streets of New York in a trance, wearing a black shawl and a black bonnet with black netting over her face. It is the day after Lincoln's assassination and she left Katie with Polly and Nellie in the late afternoon to go to Elizabeth and Charles' home. She passes by a storefront and sees Mr. Garritt, the merchant, weeping next to his wife, who has laid her head on his shoulder. There are no sounds of children playing and fighting on the streets as usual. Flags around the city are flown half-mast and are trimmed in black. People walk by her wearing somber faces and black and white badges. The streets are covered in black crepe and Norah feels the entire city is at a funeral. When she reaches the street where Charles and Elizabeth live, she hears keening not so unlike the keening imprinted on her memory as a child.

As if sensing Norah is nearby, Elizabeth comes rushing out the door and down the stairs to meet her friend, tears streaming down her face. Norah and Elizabeth hug one another for a moment before Elizabeth takes her hand and leads her inside. When Norah walks into her friends' home, it is filled with people sitting and lounging on furniture and on the floor.

"Our Father Abraham has been crucified!" cries out one woman who rocks back and forth on a chair weeping.

Elizabeth leads Norah into the kitchen and makes her a cup of tea.

"Since the news yesterday, we have come together to mourn. We shudder to think of our future. Do you know what the papers are saying, Norah?"

Norah sips her tea and is quiet. She doesn't want to tell her friend what she read in the newspapers at the *Rousing Clarion* office yesterday. But her friend will want to know and Norah has brought copies of the papers with her that Harrigan gave her.

"We want to know! We'll be finding out one way or 'nother."

Norah pulls out the papers and hands them to Elizabeth. Elizabeth takes them and scans them quickly.

"You'll be doing us all a favor to address this now, Norah, and read from the papers. Most of them here have no reading skills."

"Please read what it says in the papers. I can read them, but I'm too overcome," Elizabeth said.

Elizabeth gives the newspapers back to Norah and leads her into the living room filled with Elizabeth's Negro friends. Norah doesn't want to read aloud the words that have stung her heart that now will come forth like curses from her own mouth, but these people deserve to hear the truth and know what they're up against once again. When Elizabeth hushes everyone, she motions for Norah to speak. Norah drops the newspapers on the floor, but one, and opens it slowly. All the while her head feels separate from the rest of her body and she hears the sound of rushing wind filling it. The room is still and when she dares to look up, she sees the most weariest and sorrowful of faces. Craggy old Mr. Lincoln had carried the same countenance. Her neighbors in Ireland had had the same. She reads solemnly and then it is quiet for a few long moments.

Abraham Lincoln died on Good Friday, a Christ-like savior to them all sitting in this room. How does she tell them that the world has few saviors left for them? The Democrats are eager to celebrate his death and their newspapers call him, "A Yankee Son of a Bitch." The Chattanooga Daily Rebel said, "Old Abe has gone to answer before the bar of God for the innocent blood which he has permitted to be shed, and his efforts to enslave a few people."

"People are slaves to their own hate. Ain't nothing going to change the hearts of those people. No emancipation laws going to change them!"

Norah leaves Elizabeth and Charles' house later that evening, knowing well she won't see the people gathered there ever again. She and Elizabeth embrace one another like a last goodbye. Although it seems the wrong time to tell her friend that she is moving out of the city, she must. There is no use hiding anything from anyone, for whatever reasons. She is not only leaving behind a city besought with struggle and violence, she is leaving behind the differences between Elizabeth and herself. They have become friends in an impossible environment, one that was infertile to growth between an Irish woman and a Negro woman. How many times has Norah said to Elizabeth on their walks in the city together, "Look at those flowers growing alone in such a miserable place. That's like you and me, Elizabeth Jennings!" Right now, Elizabeth has to be with her people and help them in this complex time, for although freedom has come, it won't be as real as they dreamed. They can't help but look into Norah's face and see the oppressor. At least now, she thinks, and well she can understand.

After Lincoln's untimely death, Andrew Johnson, Vice-President, becomes President of the disunited states and like Lincoln, he wants to be lenient with the Southern states, but for different reasons. He dislikes the Southern aristocracy, all right, but possesses no benevolence for the Negroes and it is said that deep inside his Southern soul, he despises the African race. Lincoln had wanted reconstruction that would heal the rift between the North and the South and to treat the South like brothers. Johnson soon grants amnesty to former Confederate rebels and allows them to elect new governments. These governments enact new laws that are measures designed to control and repress the freed slave population. Johnson opposes civil and voting rights for ex-slaves and vetoes the Civil Rights Act of 1866 and the Freedman's Bureau bill aimed at protecting Negroes. Eventually, he is impeached and the 13th and 14th Amendments are passed granting citizenship to the African American. But for four grueling years, he is no president the country needs. It is a solemn time for America. The Southern states pass the "Black Codes" and bar interracial marriage, with death as punishment. There is violent opposition to the Reconstruction Act and whites everywhere go on a rampage killing, beating, burning and destroying any Negro they can find.

It is yet another time of great uncertainty in the nation and in Norah's life. It is a time to be sequestered with family and so Norah gives up her profitable millinery business and newspaper writing. On the night of her going away party Harrigan arranged, she hugs his neck, inhaling the scent of his cologne that mingles with his own scent she has grown to know and like. Harrigan has become as comfortable a friend as a pair of well-worn boots. Indeed, her Victorian spats and Harrigan have much in common! But it is time to leave him and New York City. He insists that he'll visit her three times a year, but Norah knows he'll probably always be too busy and will never go to Corning, New York. They will stay in touch with letter writing, for Harrigan must always be a part of her life. When it is time to say goodbye to Nellie and Polly, she knows it is only temporary and they will visit one another. In fact, the timing couldn't have been better for Norah to move, for Nellie has finally said yes when Leary, or O'Leary, asked for her hand in marriage. And Katie has no tears at all in saying goodbye to her New York City friends and life. She is elated to be going home to the farm to *Maimeo* and *Daidoe* and all the chickens, especially one named Miss Maggie, just like her Mam once had in Ireland.

Norah doesn't take much with her, except her gowns and hats, a few pieces of china, the earrings and heart necklace Harrigan has given her. "For you to always love and remember me and New York City, Norah dear." And, of course, there is her Irish dresser that has to make the journey from the city to the country. Da pays a dear price to have it shipped on the train with them to Corning. For the party, Harrigan hired a bakery to make a large cake in the shape of the *Hope Bonnet. The Rousing Clarion*, where the party is held, is packed full of well-wishers. And who comes to say farewell that really surprises her? Many of the neighborhood women of Five Points arrive at the party wearing the bonnets Norah has designed for them. But most of all, she is pleased when Elizabeth and Charles walk through the door and are not only greeted by Katie and herself, but welcomed by some of the very women in Five Points who had once scorned Norah and Elizabeth's friendship.

Chapter Thirty-Two

Corning, New York, November 1870

Norah pedals her velocipede down the unpaved streets of Market and Walnut. She has closed up her shop for the day and desires to move her limbs and be outside before going to Washington Hall to attend a lecture. It is nearing winter, but it has been an unusually warm day and she wants to keep riding her bike for as long as she can before the snow arrives. Earlier, she walked to St. Mary's Academy to pick up Katie from school to leave her off at her friend, Dora's. Katie loves school and has made many friends in Corning. Nellie, Leary, and Polly visit often and have invited Katie to stay with them in the city, but Katie is a country girl now and doesn't want to go back to New York City. Norah knows she'll change her mind when she is older. She herself misses New York City, especially Harrigan, the eateries, working for the newspaper, and strolling down Fifth Avenue in fine fashion.

It isn't easy for Norah to ride her bike in her skirts, but she has learned how to do it with a creative flair. She gathers her skirts to one side and ties the bottom with a big pink ribbon, careful to keep her legs properly covered. It still looks odd having her skirts hiked up, but she always wears her Victorian spats that go clear up to her knees. She adores wearing her fancy duds and elaborately made bonnets, but when she rides her bike and takes long walks along the Chemung River, she removes the crinoline, bustle, and padded bust and makes her clothing simple. She is the only woman in town who rides a bicycle and she is proud of it. She isn't immune, however, from the sting of teasing comments made by young men and the *tsk-tsk* of fuddy duddy old ladies shaking their heads as she rides by, but the stares and disapproval have lessened. She's had her bicycle for a year already, a gift from her Da shortly before he died from scarlet fever. Norah thought she'd never recover from her father's death, but he made her promise to ride the bike with style and a smile. She is grateful for the four good years she had with him after moving to Corning.

These days, Norah is concerned for her mother who is frail and vehemently declares she'll wear her mourning clothes until she dies. "I'll soon be wearing a wedding dress, Norah, the likes I never had in me life. I'll be wearing it when I reunite with your Da in heaven." Norah thinks now how incredible and miraculous it is that her Da and Mam lived and loved through a famine, new country and its prejudices, as well as a war. And so had she! But how hard it is for Mam now! It is Katie and Meg's children that keep her going, as well as Da having made Mam promise to finish her days on earth with hope before joining him.

Southern boy, James, even without his legs, found love in a widow on the farm next to the McCabes. The couple help Mam on the farm (James does most of the cooking and cleaning up in the kitchen), along with Meg and her family, who have moved permanently to Corning.

It is all as it should be, Norah thinks, as she rides her bike, except for the ones who have gone from her life. But Norah doesn't pummel her prayers with questions so much anymore, but offers gratitude and acceptance. She can sometimes feel Da's presence when she rides her bike, mostly on summer eves during the gloaming. It is her favorite time of day because it is the celebration of light and darkness coming together in a display of gentle beauty. To Norah, it is a melding of the beginning and the end, the flourishing and the quiet, the joy and the sorrow. This is what this time of day means to her and she tries not to miss it, even in winter.

A Bee In Your Bonnet, on Market Street, is thriving and the wives of the workers at Hoare & Daily and the Corning Flint Glass Works buy at least two hats a year. Her *Hope Bonnet* was re-designed as fashion changed, but it is still the *Hope Bonnet* and each one is custom designed and priced accordingly. After all, it is to give women hope, no matter rich or poor!

Norah has met a few of the colored women who live in their own enclave in Corning, as do the Germans, and her own Irish people who live on Irish Hill on the Southside. She'll often have tea with Mrs. McCrae and Mrs. O'Donnell who live there, and Norah delights in the gathering of the Irish Catholic women who are proud to be from Ireland. My, how things have changed, Norah often says aloud, as if she has lived sixty years rather than nearly thirty. Corning has a large Irish community and although the editor of the Corning Journal is an abolitionist and speaks against slavery, he sometimes complains about the Fenians in town. But after meeting Norah McCabe, he changed his mind about his sentiments against the Irish. She convinced him he was being a right hypocrite if he was for freedom and education of blacks, but despised the Irish. Their priest, Father Colgan, is well respected and although some of the Protestants complain of the religious elements of his school, many send their children there to receive a fine education.

Yes, Irish people are mostly Democrats, and there is another paper that represents them. Bigots, the lot of them, Norah thinks at times, but when there's a community event, funeral, or national holiday, everyone in Corning comes together in peace and celebration. The railroads have brought prosperity and although in the last two years, there has been some financial duress, there are bakeries, taverns, factories that make candy, shirts, and carriages, as well as boat builders, mills, and even jewelry makers. It's the glass industry that gives Corning an original shine and makes it a gem set in the hills of the Finger Lakes of New York. Norah loves the glass made at the Works!

Corning Flint and Glass Works provides ample employment and Meg's husband, Teddy, is employed there, as well as many of Norah's friends. There has been progress, Norah thinks, and a lot of it. There is prosperity and a demand for luxury that dominates the times, and Corning with its share of potential and resources, is on that train bound for glory, despite the floods of the river, rampant diseases, and recessions. And Norah is bound for glory, too, as she rides her velocipede throughout Corning.

Corning is now home to Norah McCabe and she knows it to be so because she has come home to herself first. Yes, there are nights she wakes with a start and her heart beats rapidly, for she misses her husband foremost, as well as the two men who have permanently left her life. Edward and Sean. How she had been the flirtatious girl with both of them, thinking they would always be in her life. The war has changed them all.

But what is still most egregious to Norah is the continued hatred of the Negro. Elizabeth often writes to her about how difficult it is in New York City for her friends and family to find work, get an education, and good places to live. "Norah, there are only a few streets we can walk proudly down wearing those beautiful hats you made us. And those streets, I'll tell you ain't paved with gold. Fifth Avenue is a long way off for us, my friend." Norah writes to Elizabeth about the fine Negroes living in Corning and that she should move here to be with them and herself. She wrote a letter begging her and Charles to move to Corning:

> *Colonel William Murrell, a Negro citizen of Corning, was born a slave in Georgia, but escaped and joined the 138th U.S. Colored Infantry. He suffered wounds, but he's honored here in Corning, Elizabeth! And there's Marcus F. Lucas, who was a free Negro when he became head of the part of the Corning Underground Railroad. I've met him and he's a polished speaker, a beautiful soul, and is respected here. Your people work in the mills and*

in businesses here. You have to know that many residents here supported the cause of abolitionism and the editor of the Corning Journal, Mr. Pratt, has been one of the most active abolitionists in this part of New York State. It's not all equal as it should be, Elizabeth, nor is it so for women, but Corning has a spirit and heart to it that I couldn't get a hold of in New York. For now, I need to be here and I miss you so and would love to have you here, too. There are also many baseball games and they make for a time of frivolity and easy times, I think. During a game, everything is forgotten but the game itself. And, Elizabeth, I have a velocipede I ride around on, even in my skirts. It's great fun and you can ride it when you come to visit. There are railroad excursions to Rochester, the Finger Lakes, the Thousand Islands, and even to Washington, D.C. When you come, you must stay long enough for us to take a trip together dressed in new hats I'll make for both of us!

Elizabeth wrote back that the Lord's calling for her is to be in New York City, at her church, her school, and with her husband and community. But she promises to come and visit and Norah waits two years before Elizabeth makes her way there, alone without Charles, for he is too busy at his job to come. Norah proudly introduces her friend to some of the people in Corning, and although she is received kindly enough, Elizabeth doesn't feel at home as Norah hoped. And it happened that while she was visiting, a small Ku Klux Klan group visited the Methodist Church and stirred up some furor. The members tried to say it was just a rally for all things American and to preserve justice, but most of the people in Corning knew otherwise. And mostly, the people of Corning had been very disturbed by this incident.

Norah knows right well that Elizabeth has a reason for concern. There has been outright rage and terror being conducted throughout the South in response to a Republican-led government and the Fifteenth Amendment giving the vote to Negroes in every state of the union. Ulysses S. Grant won the office of the president and the Republicans won a majority in Congress. But during the elections in the South, there had been brutal violence at the voting booths. The Republican voters in Kansas, Georgia, and Louisiana experienced the most heinous assaults and after the end of the election, nearly 5,000 people had been murdered or beaten. Elizabeth and Norah continue their correspondence about these matters, but not only to one another, but to legislators in Washington. And finally, Congress passes the Enforcement Acts, which makes it a crime to interfere with registration and voting.

Norah thinks a good deal about change. There is fashion change with large elaborate chignon hairdos and hats tilted forward and bonnets set farther back. She has to go with the times, but still keep her hats fresh and individual. It isn't easy. There's change in manufacturing and now there's beautiful cut glass being made. There is change from canal shipping to railroad shipping. But change in government and change in people is the most difficult. For Norah life has become a whirlwind of change and she keeps up with it all by reading newspapers and attending a few lectures. *But why can't hearts be changed about Negroes and women as quickly as the businessman, Erastus Corning, making millions in railroads, iron works, and banks!*

One evening, Norah rides her fancy new bicycle to Washington Hall to hear Susan B. Anthony lecture on women's rights and suffrage. She is laughing as she stops in front of the hall.

"The saints be praised! I've become a right women's righter!"

There once was a time she walked out of a women's rights meeting and had felt sorely out of place. But here she is feeling right at home going to one of these meetings. She leaves her bike by the flaming maple trees standing as sentinels to the lecture hall and walks inside. An organ is playing and Norah sits down in the third row and nods in greeting to a few of the women and men she knows. There is Editor Pratt himself, all spiffed up as a peacock and looking right important. He smiles at her and gives a nod. She thinks about asking him if she might write for his newspaper, but she's not certain she can put up with the man's hubris. And he might not be able to trust her, being that she is one of those Fenians! She takes in a deep breath, letting it out slowly, and smiles at all the craziness of life. Editor Pratt smiles at her again, this time showing his teeth and blushing. Isn't the man married? But then she sees that he's looking at the woman behind her and not her. My, she's getting old and doesn't turn heads as she once did.

Most of the men she's met who show interest in her would want her in the kitchen all day! She could never abide that a woman's place is only in the home and not having the right to vote and make her own money. Out of necessity, as well as passion, she has defied the belief that women who work outside the home are vulgar. And now she wants more than success as a milliner. She wants the right to vote, as does Elizabeth Jennings, as does her mother, Nellie, and all the women in her country. Yes, *her* country!

Norah looks around and notices the lecture is sparsely attended. She's disappointed at first, but not when she listens to the passionate pleas of Susan B. Anthony ring out to the eighty or so people in Washington Hall.

Thus may all married women, wives, and widows, by the laws of the several States, be technically included in the Fifteenth Amendment's specification of "condition of servitude," present or previous. And not only married women, but I will also prove to you that by all the great fundamental principles of our free government, the entire womanhood of the nation is in a "condition of servitude" as surely as were our revolutionary fathers, when they rebelled against old King George. Women are taxed without representation, governed without their consent, tried, convicted and punished without a jury of their peers. And is all this tyranny and less humiliating and degrading to women under our democratic-republican government today than it was to men under their aristocratic, monarchial government one hundred years ago?

Everyone attending the lecture stands and claps for the woman who has not only stood against slavery, but against the tyranny of women. There is cheerfulness and anticipation in the room as people leave. Norah says goodbye to her neighbors and walks down the steps. Suddenly, she feels a tug on her arm and before she turns, she knows who it is. It is the scent of him that has been recorded in her memory and yes, perhaps her heart, since she was a young girl.

"Wee one! Tis you! And what would you be doin' now going to a meeting with a bunch of cackling and crowing suffragists?"

Sean, who once left her as a boy to become a ship's mate and then left her as a man to resist a war and find solace, has come home to himself, as Norah has come home to herself. And because they both hailed from Ireland, it is a sure thing that their Celtic hearts had found a home in one another far across the sea before either of them had ever crossed it to come to America.

Author's Note

The adage, "Truth is stranger than fiction..." by Mark Twain holds true for my story about Norah McCabe. From the beginning, I knew Norah McCabe must have lived, for she seemed so real to me. But it wasn't until after my first two books about Norah were published that I learned there had been a real Norah McCabe who came from Ireland to New York City in 1847. Someone once asked what sort of work I did and I answered lightheartedly, "I work with the dead." We laughed and I had to explain that I wrote historical fiction, but honestly, I believe those who have lived in times past visit me. I never intended to write historical fiction. It was when I was dancing in an Irish pub peering at a poster of an Irish dresser did I imagine a young Norah hiding in the cupboard dreaming of a better life in Ireland during the Great Hunger. The journey with Norah McCabe has been unimaginably transforming as I dug through journals and books to learn about her times. And when I chose the name, The Star, for the ship Norah McCabe traveled on to come to America, I didn't know there was a real ship that carried hundreds of Irish immigrant families from an estate in County Wicklow to North America. And on The Star, there had been a family with the name, Neale, and a little girl the same age as my Norah. I was encouraged to not give up, for my ancestors were whispering in my ears to tell their story.

As I dreamed of Norah McCabe as a milliner in New York City during the Civil War and sketched out her story, I learned about fascinating people of the times. It's true that an author can become so enamored with research that he or she desires every historical gem to be used in the story. Aware of this, I cautiously chose only the people and details that lingered in my mind long after I learned about them. One such character is Elizabeth Jennings, an African-American teacher who insisted on riding a streetcar and was forcibly removed. She sued and won. Norah and Elizabeth become best friends during these times of distrust and racial tension. Norah McCabe also meets Charles Knox and his son, Edward M. Knox. Charles Knox and his sister traveled from Ireland and their ship went off course. They walked from Delaware to New York. Charles became an errand boy, and opened Knox Hatters and later expanded from a modest shop to a larger one. He eventually sold hats all over America and to 23 presidents, including the famous top hat Abraham Lincoln wore. His son, Edward M. Knox, drew a mustache on his seventeen-year-old face to appear old enough to join the Union Army. He was injured in the Battle of Gettysburg and received a Medal of Honor. It was just natural and magic for Norah to meet Edward and Elizabeth Jennings! There are other real life characters and events in this novel, but Elizabeth Jennings and Edward M. Knox are most significant in Norah McCabe's life in *The Irish Milliner.*

We need to haunt the house of history and listen anew to the ancestors' wisdom. ~Maya Angelou

About the Author

Cynthia G. Neale is a native of the Finger Lakes region of New York and now resides in New Hampshire. She has long possessed a deep interest in the tragedies and triumphs of the Irish during the Great Hunger. Ms. Neale also writes plays, short stories, and essays, and holds a B.A. in Writing and Literature from Vermont College.

Author's website: www.cynthianeale.com

Author's blog: cynthianeale.wordpress.com

Other books by Cynthia Neale

Norah

The Irish Dresser:
A Story of Hope during The Great Hunger
(An Gorta Mor, 1845–1850)

Hope in New York City:
The Continuing Story of The Irish Dresser

NORAH
by Cynthia Neale

*Norah is an evocative, compelling
story of survival, intrigue, and love*

"You don't have to be Irish to appreciate Norah McCabe. Hers is an American story of self-creation through sheer grit and imagination. This historical novel paints an authentic and compelling picture of what it means to be young, poor, and female longing for a better life in 1850s New York City...You'll root for Norah as {she} embarks on a dramatic journey to achieve a hard-won identity as a self-sufficient Irish-American woman in a turbulent time."

~ **Nancy Kelley, author of This Whispering Rod**

Other Titles by Fireship Press

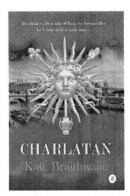

CHARLATAN

by Kate Braithwaite

How do you keep the love of the King of France?

1676. In a hovel in the centre of Paris, the fortune-teller La Voisin holds a black mass, summoning the devil to help an unnamed client keep the love of the King of France, Louis XIV.

Three years later, Athénaïs, Madame de Montespan, the King's glamorous mistress, is nearly forty. She has borne Louis seven children but now seethes with rage as he falls for eighteen-year-old, Angélique de Fontanges. Athénaïs must do something to keep the King's love and secure her children's future, but how? And at what length is she willing to go?

At the same time, police chief La Reynie and his young assistant Bezons have uncovered a network of fortune-tellers and poisoners operating in the city. Athénaïs does not know it, but she is about to named as a favoured client of the infamous La Voisin.

Breakout from Sugar Island
by Seamus Beirne

When Michael Redferne pulls the body of twenty year old Maureen Kelly from a frozen Irish lake, something tells him he should leave well enough alone. But fear conquers instinct and he hides the frozen corpse in the ice house on Lord Preston's estate. Unaware that sinister forces in the persons of Lady Preston and her lover are conspiring against him, he walks into a trap and is shipped in chains to Barbados, known as Sugar Island. Once there, Redferne joins thousands of African and Irish laborers who are forced to work in the cane fields from dawn to dusk under the cowhide whips of brutal overseers. The rising and setting sun becomes a doomsday clock, ticking off Redferne's slow march to the grave. He must escape if he hopes to redeem his past and save his future.

Paint 'n Spurs
by Barbara Marriott

The Men Who Founded the Cowboy Artists of America

George Phippen
The family man who fought his shyness and blazed the pathway for Southwest cowboy art with his original and authentic works.

Charlie Dye
A tough nut that grew up in the cowboy world, earned national recognition as an illustrator and gave it up to pay tribute to the cowboy way of western life with his brilliant action driven art.

Joe Beeler
Everyone's friend; his cheerful personality and mischievousness covered an exceptional young talent that hit the national scene with canvas and bronze that showed the old west of cowboys and Indians in a new exiting way.

John Hampton
The charmer from Brooklyn New York turned out to be more cowboy that most western cowpokes. Using his incredible talent and charm he got the attention of lovers of the Old West and won plenty of new fans and friends.

Fred Harman
A man of many talents with a phenomenal memory. A patriot who served his country as a spy, but mostly known for his alter-ego the comic character Red Ryder and Little Beaver…you betchum.

Barbara Marriott had the words jumping off the page at me. Couldn't put the book down. —**Cheraux Hampton**

For the Finest in Nautical and Historical Fiction and Non-Fiction
www.FireshipPress.com

Interesting • Informative • Authoritative

All Fireship Press books are available through
leading bookstores and wholesalers worldwide.

CPSIA information can be obtained
at www.ICGtesting.com
Printed in the USA
FFOW03n1922171117
43527650-42255FF

9 781611 793802